北京市高等教育精品教材立项项目

总主编 胡壮麟

U0141032

英语综合教程

第 1 册

（教师用书）

主　编　关慧兰

副主编　何建芬　程幼强

编　者　王世庆　李四清　李正鸿　魏　巍
　　　　孙　元　何建芬　程幼强

北京大学出版社
PEKING UNIVERSITY PRESS

图书在版编目(CIP)数据

英语综合教程. 第 1 册(教师用书)/ 关慧兰主编. —北京:北京大学出版社,
2008.11

(21 世纪英语专业系列教材)

ISBN 978-7-301-12959-3

Ⅰ.英… Ⅱ.关… Ⅲ.英语–高等学校–教学参考资料 Ⅳ.H31

中国版本图书馆 CIP 数据核字(2007)第 169857 号

书　　　名:英语综合教程. 第 1 册(教师用书)

著作责任者:关慧兰　主编

总　策　划:张　冰

责 任 编 辑:刘　爽

标 准 书 号:ISBN 978-7-301-12959-3/H·1870

出 版 发 行:北京大学出版社

地　　　址:北京市海淀区成府路 205 号　　100871

网　　　址:http://www.pup.cn

电　　　话:邮购部 62752015　发行部 62750672　编辑部 62767315　出版部 62754962

电 子 邮 箱:zbing@pup.pku.edu.cn

印　刷　者:河北滦县鑫华书刊印刷厂

经　销　者:新华书店

　　　　　　787 毫米×1092 毫米　16 开本　20.25 印张　478 千字

　　　　　　2008 年 11 月第 1 版　2008 年 11 月第 1 次印刷

定　　　价:38.00 元

未经许可,不得以任何方式复制或抄袭本书之部分或全部内容。

版权所有,侵权必究　举报电话:010–62752024

电子邮箱:fd@pup.pku.edu.cn

《21 世纪英语专业系列教材》编写委员会

(以姓氏笔画排序)

王守仁　王克非　申　丹

刘意青　李　力　胡壮麟

桂诗春　梅德明　程朝翔

总　序

北京大学出版社自 2005 年以来已出版《语言与应用语言学知识系列读本》多种，为了配合第十一个五年计划，现又策划陆续出版《21 世纪英语专业系列教材》。这个重大举措势必受到英语专业广大教师和学生的欢迎。

作为英语教师，最让人揪心的莫过于听人说英语不是一个专业，只是一个工具。说这些话的领导和教师的用心是好的，为英语专业的毕业生将来找工作着想，因此要为英语专业的学生多多开设诸如新闻、法律、国际商务、经济、旅游等其他专业的课程。但事与愿违，英语专业的教师们很快发现，学生投入英语学习的时间少了，掌握英语专业课程知识甚微，即使对四个技能的掌握也并不比大学英语学生高明多少，而那个所谓的第二专业在有关专家的眼中只是学到些皮毛而已。

英语专业的路在何方？有没有其他路可走？这是需要我们英语专业教师思索的问题。中央领导关于创新是一个民族的灵魂和要培养创新人才等的指示精神，让我们在层层迷雾中找到了航向。显然，培养学生具有自主学习能力和能进行创造性思维是我们更为重要的战略目标，使英语专业的人才更能适应 21 世纪的需要，迎接 21 世纪的挑战。

如今，北京大学出版社外语部的领导和编辑同志们，也从教材出版的视角探索英语专业的教材问题，从而为贯彻英语专业教学大纲做些有益的工作，为教师们开设大纲中所规定的必修、选修课程提供各种教材。《21 世纪英语专业系列教材》是普通高等教育"十一五"国家级规划教材和国家"十一五"重点出版规划项目《面向新世纪的立体化网络化英语学科建设丛书》的重要组成部分。这套系列教材要体现新世纪英语教学的自主化、协作化、模块化和超文本化，结合外语教材的具体情况，既要解决语言、教学内容、教学方法和教育技术的时代化，也要坚持弘扬以爱国主义为核心的民族精神。因此，今天北京大学出版社在大力提倡专业英语教学改革的基础上，编辑出版各种英语专业技能、英语专业知识和相关专业知识课程的教材，以培养具有创新性思维的和具有实际工作能力的学生，充分体现了时代精神。

北京大学出版社的远见卓识，也反映了英语专业广大师生盼望已久的心愿。由北京大学等全国几十所院校具体组织力量，积极编写相关教材。这就是说，这套教材是由一些高等院校有水平有经验的第一线教师们制定编写大纲，反复讨论，特别是考虑到在不同层次、不同背景学校之间取得平衡，避免了先前的教材或偏难或偏易的弊病。与此同时，一批知名专家教授参与策划和教材审定工作，保证了教材质量。

当然，这套系列教材出版只是初步实现了出版社和编者们的预期目标。为了获得更大效果，希望使用本系列教材的教师和同学不吝指教，及时将意见反馈给我们，使教材更加完善。

航道已经开通，我们有决心乘风破浪，奋勇前进！

胡壮麟
北京大学蓝旗营

前　言

　　《英语综合教程》是根据《高等学校英语专业英语教学大纲》编写,致力于培养学生具有扎实的语言基本功、宽广的知识面、一定的相关专业知识、较强的能力和较高的人文素质。本套教材为基础英语课程教材,共四册,可供高等院校英语专业一二年级学生使用。本册为第一册,适用于一年级第一学期。

　　本册教材共分 15 个单元,每个单元由 Text A 和 Text B 两篇课文、辅学资料及相关的练习构成。全书 30 篇课文均选自英语原文文本,根据学生现阶段的语言能力和水平,编者仅对其中语言难度过大的部分进行了必要的删改。

　　本册教材的选题旨在帮助学生树立正直的人生态度。注意由浅入深、难易结合。全书 30 篇课文分别涉及家庭亲情、生活准则、道德伦常、民生关爱、文化教育、国际政治、哲学宗教、古典艺术等多个主题,在夯实学生语言基本功,拓展其知识面的同时,提高英语专业学生的人文素养,健康、向上,具有代表性。课文收录了有关悉达多·乔达摩、苏格拉底和米开朗基罗等历史巨人的生平,旨在为学生树立高尚、坚韧的人生楷模;有关非洲贫困问题的报道分析、前德国总理施罗德就二战期间德国纳粹对犹太人所犯罪行的诚挚致歉以及乔姆斯基对美国政府尖锐的抨击,则有助于唤起学生对正义、良知的深入思索。

　　本册教材的每一单元由 Unit Goals,Before Reading,Text A,Better Know More,Check Your Understanding,A Sip of Phonetics,You'd Like to Be,Text B,Comprehension Questions,Writing Practice,Further Study 共十一个部分组成:

☞ 每个单元以 Unit Goals 开篇, 明确指出该单元的学习重点和难点,让教与学均做到目的清晰,增强学生的学习意识。

☞ 每个单元设有特色的预热练习, 引导学生进入单元学习。Hands-on Activities and Brainstorming 以文化补充为目的使学生在学习本单元前对背景知识等有一个初步了解, 并培养学生的动手能力和表达能力。A Glimpse at Words and Expressions 展示 Text A 课文中的部分重点词语,让学生在学习课文之前能够了解课文的语言特色,并培养学生的语感。

☞ Better Know More 就 Text A 涉及的人物、文化背景和专有名词进行必要的解释和说明。

☞ Check Your Understanding 以口头形式考查学生对 Text A 内容的理解。这一部分练习旨在鼓励学生开口,强化其语用能力和对语法的感知能力。

☞ A Sip of Phonetics 分阶段向学生介绍语音知识,训练学生正确发音。

☞ You'd Like to Be 为 Text A 的练习,共分六个部分,着重操练课文中的语言点,培养学生在语篇和语境中学习语言的能力。其中 A Strong Bridge Builder, A Smart Word Player 和 A Skilled Text Weaver 侧重词汇练习;A Sharp Interpreter 检验学生对课文关键句和难句的理解;A Solid Sentence Constructor 训练学生对课文中重点句型和新词语的运用能力;A Superb Bilingualist 是汉译英的练习。练习的标题一气呵成,正是培养英语专业学生的目的所在。

☞ Comprehension Questions 鼓励学生对课文深入思考并展开讨论。

☞ Writing Practice 围绕 Text B 以撰写课文梗概的方式,训练学生的短文写作能力。这一部分在不同的单元,设计有所不同。1—5 单元的练习较简单,先向学生提供一系列有关课文内容的引导性问题,同时提供关键词,然后要求学生将问题答案连接起来,稍作处理即成为 Text B 的梗概。在 6—10 单元,编者有意取消了关键词,仅保留引导性问题,要求学生通过熟读课文独立找到答案,进而形成课文梗概。在 11—15 单元,编者要求学生就 Text B 的内容自主提问,然后自行回答,并独立形成撰写课文梗概的思路。该写作练习由易到难,逐步培养学生的阅读能力和逻辑思维能力。

☞ Further Study 对学有余力的学生进行宽泛知识的推介,例如相关电影及网站,使学生可以深入学习。

本教材由天津外国语学院和南开大学共同编写。程幼强负责教材的设计和创意,并与李正鸿、王世庆、魏巍、李四清和何建芬分担各个单元的选材和编写。在编写过程中,总主编胡壮麟教授给予了专业指导,提出了很多宝贵的建议。在此全体编者向胡壮麟教授表示衷心的感谢! 外籍专家 Michael DeRabo, Joshua Parker 审读了本书稿,我们也一并在此表示谢意。

本教材同时配有教师用书,为教师提供讲解教材所需的教学思路、必要的补充材料和练习参考答案。本册教材如有疏漏和不完善之处,恳请广大读者批评指正。

编者
2007 年 3 月

Contents

目 录

1

Positive Attitude

Unit Goals

After studying this unit, students should be able to:

☞ **understand the importance of attitude in everyday life;**

Attitude is the way we reflect on events and respond to people's behaviors under certain circumstances. In daily life, how do we maintain a positive attitude? First of all, we should be able to understand the saying that "attitude is everything," frequently quoted by Velibor Bora Milutinović, the former head coach of Chinese national soccer team. Attitude, whether positive or negative, shows itself in our daily lives, and it is, in a sense, more important than experience or education.

Secondly, we should be responsible for our attitudes as well as actions. A sense of responsibility motivates us to remain positive in whatever we do and in responding to events and people.

Thirdly, we should understand that our attitude works on our future. A positive attitude is the centerpiece that helps us create our future. In this sense, a right attitude is critical to our success in career and to our happiness in family life.

☞ **know how to pronounce /ɑː/, /ɒ/, /ɔː/, /ʊ/ and /uː/, and how to utilize the words and structures that contribute significantly to the texts;**

In this section, the instructor should explain to the students how to pronounce these vowels and demonstrate the correct pronunciations of each. He or she should also contrast some wrong pronunciations with the correct ones, and offer analysis to those errors in order to avoid making repeated mistakes.

It is strongly suggested that the instructor encourage students to read aloud tongue twisters and refer to the tips provided in the section.

☞ **understand and know how to cope with a positive attitude.**

To share with Jerry's insight in life that keeps him positive even when he is put in a dilemma of life and death, the instructor should help the students go deeper into the meaning of the statement "It's your choice how you live life." The instructor should set the students on the right track that leads to an understanding that a positive attitude in life suggests an active power to stay optimistic and be one's own savior in time of extreme difficulty.

Before Reading

📖 Hands-on Activities and Brainstorming

The instructor should allow 15 to 20 minutes for the students to do presentation either on the statement of "Attitude is everything" or "Your attitude is Your Window to the World."

📖 A Glimpse at Words and Expressions

这部分是学习课文前的预习,其目的是为了让学生在开始学习课文之前,了解文中纯正英语的表达方式,以培养学生的语感,提高学生运用英语表达思想的能力。学生需要在阅读课文前试着理解下面的句子,尤其是划线部分的含义。划线部分的词或短语可能是学生在以前学习中遇到过的,但在此文中,这些词或短语的意义则有所不同。建议教师在处理这部分时尽量采用启发方式,引导学生做出正确的判断。

教师要求学生在阅读课文之前完成这些练习。在没有查阅字典和通读全文的情况会遇到一些困难,教师可以根据学生的水平,让他们在第一次完成练习后,参阅课文单词表重新做该练习。教师在讲解课文后,可以再次让学生对下列句子做整句释义,以考查学生的理解能力并强化他们的语言综合能力。

A. To help the students work out the meaning of the expression "get" in the text, the instructor should resort to the basic meaning of it by offering such an example as "Where did you get those figures?" To approach the appropriate meaning of "get" in the sentence, the instructor is obliged to highlight the pronoun "it" that follows "get." "It" stands for the fact that Jerry is able to hold a positive attitude all the time. "I don't get it" means "I don't understand it." The expression "get" is used informally here, meaning "understand." More examples:

1) She didn't get the joke.

2) I don't get it—why would she do a thing like that?

B. To understand the expression "bottom line," the instructor should get the students to relate "bottom line" to the meaning of the sentence right after the colon. If the instructor is able to ensure that the students agree on the idea implied in the sentence that "it is up to you to decide how to live life," the students will come to figure out the interpretation of "bottom line," which means "the most important point or the essential point." For example: The bottom line is that we have to make a decision today.

C. The key to understand the phrase "lose touch" in this sentence is "lost" and "thought about him." These expressions suggest that they are no longer working together. They lost contact. The instructor should drop some hint that enables the students to be aware of the meaning of "lose touch," which means "do not contact each other afterward." For example: I have lost touch with all my old friends in that city.

D. The instructor should draw students' attention to the context that contributes to the meaning of the phrase "hold up" and the factors that lead to the robbery. The instructor is also responsible for picking up expressions such as "gunpoint" and "armed robbers" to build up the meaning of "hold up," which can be understood as "to rob a bank, store or a shop by violence." For example:

1) The thief held up four employees at gunpoint and forced them to open the safe.

2) He was held up at the point of a gun just as he left the bank.

E. The instructor should be clear that the key word to throw light on the whole sentence is the transition "but" and the emphatic "did," the former of which suggests the negative meaning of the predicate verb "decline," but the latter, a positive one. This might direct the students towards an understanding of "decline," which means "to refuse politely to accept or to do sth." For example: I offered to give them a lift, but they declined.

F. Based on such examples as "to read a book," the instructor should arouse the students' interest in respond to the meaning of "read a person" and "read from one's eyes," the interpretation of which is to "understand in a particular way." For example:

1) How do you read the present situation?

2) Silence must not always be read as consent.

G. A better way to approach the meaning of "release" is to put it together with "from the hospital." "Release from the hospital" suggests that "Jerry is no longer hospitalized." Then the students are able to explain the expression as "be allowed to leave a place." For example: She is expected to be released from hospital today.

Keys

A-6   B-1   C-7   D-2   E-4   F-3   G-5

Text A

Introduction of the Text

The significance of learning the text lies in its power to awaken the students to the fact that attitude plays an important role in life. Does it mean that "we do not need anything else?" Many people wonder, "What should I do with my life?" Well, the bottom line is that we choose to be free and happy. However, we do not realize how much it involves in maintaining a positive and optimistic mood in life. A person definitely has the competence to choose his own attitude, but he or she may not be able to control everything happening around him or her. Nevertheless, people are able to adopt either a positive or negative attitude in response to events, but it is instructive to stay positive and everyone is able to do so if he or she strives to achieve a goal in life.

📖 Suggested Explanations on Text A

1. Jerry was the kind of guy you love to hate.

   Meaning: Jerry was the kind of person that people admire for his character trait to keep himself in an enthusiastic mood that he annoys those who are incapable of.

2. He was always <u>in a good mood</u> and always had something positive to say.

   Meaning: He is able to keep himself friendly and happy and manages to see the good aspect in life.

   ▶ in a mood: in a state of mind or feeling at a particular time

   eg. 1) My wife is in a good mood today.

   2) I'm just not in the mood for party tonight.

3. "If I were any better, I would be twins!"

   Meaning: I consider myself so happy that only when I became two of myself would I be able to contain all the happiness available to me.

4. He was <u>recognized</u> as a special manager because he had several waiters who had followed him around from restaurant to restaurant.

   Meaning: The fact that several waiters became so clung to Jerry that they were ready to support him whichever restaurant he was working distinguished him as a manager with unusual personality.

   ▶ recognize (v.): to accept or approve of sb./sth. officially (usually used in collocations as "to recognize sb./sth. as sb./sth.," or "to recognize sb./sth. to be...")

   eg. 1) I recognized the handwriting as that of my father.

   2) John is recognized to be their natural leader.

   3) His claims were recognized as justified.

   4) Acid rain is recognized as one of the most serious global environmental problems.

5. Seeing this style really made me <u>curious</u>, so one day I went up to Jerry and asked him, "I don't get it! You can't be a positive person all of the time. How do you do it?"

Meaning: The way Jerry was coping with life and business was appealing to me, for which I went to Jerry for guidance. "I don't understand how you managed to do so. It is impossible to have a positive attitude all the time. How do you work to achieve it?"

▶ curious (*adj.*): having a strong desire to know about sth.

eg. 1) We were very curious about the people who lived upstairs.

    2) Everyone was curious as to why Mark was leaving.

6. Each time something bad happens, I can choose to be a <u>victim</u> or I can choose to learn from it.

Meaning: Whenever something negative occurs, it's up to me to decide whether to accept the situation as it is or to stay active and confident to work out the positive aspect of the happening.

▶ victim (*n.*): a person who has been attacked, injured or killed as the result of a crime, a disease, an accident, etc.

eg. 1) The president seemed to be the victim of his own foolishness.

    2) Mother asked us to take the victims of the storm into our house for the night.

    3) Thousands of animals have been victims of this strange new disease.

7. Every time someone comes to me complaining, I can choose to accept their complaining or I can <u>point out</u> the positive side of life.

▶ to point out: to mention sth. that one thinks is important and / or the reason why a particular situation exists

eg. 1) The instructor pointed out the dangers of driving alone.

    2) Rebecca tried in vain to point out to him the unfairness in his actions.

    3) He pointed out that there was little chance for success.

8. You choose how you <u>react to</u> situations.

▶ react (*v.*): to change or behave in a particular way as a result of or in response to sth.

eg. 1) The villagers reacted violently to the new policy.

    2) Children react to prompt encouragement by becoming more self-confident.

▲ reaction (*n.*): an action or a state resulting from, in response to sth.

eg. 1) What is his reaction to your proposal?

    2) Do you believe that there is a healthy reaction after a cold bath?

9. "Life is all about choices. When you <u>cut away</u> all the junk, every situation is a choice."

Meaning: Life is hardly anything but a challenge to one's judgment and decision-making. What remains is to choose how to live after discarding the unimportant factors.

▶ to cut away: to remove sth. from sth. by cutting (usually used in passive form)

eg. 1) The front of the coat should be cut away so as to show the colors.

    2) The working model was cut away to show the inside of the building.

    3) He cut away the material which he didn't need.

▲ to cut away: to leave; to run away in a hurry

eg. As soon as he saw the policeman, he cut away.

10. I reflected on what Jerry said.

▶ to reflect on/upon: to think carefully and deeply about sth.

eg. 1) Kate was left to reflect on the implications of her decision.

    2) The likely reactions of the market would need to be reflected on before we acted.

▲ reflection (*n.*): careful thought about sth., sometimes over a long period of time

eg. 1) A seven-day holiday would give him enough time for reflection.

    2) Mrs. Wendy decided on reflection to accept the stranger's offer.

11. ... he left the back door open one morning and was held up at gunpoint by three armed robbers.

▶ armed (*adj.*): carrying a weapon

eg. 1) The robber is armed and dangerous.

    2) Police outside the castle were heavily armed.

▲ to arm oneself/sb. with sth.: to provide weapon for oneself/sb. in order to fight a battle or a war; to provide someone with the means to gain sth. (figurative use)

eg. 1) Armed with only a spear, he drove off five of his attackers.

    2) The government was armed with many facts and figures.

12. While trying to open the safe, his hand, shaking from nervousness, slipped off the combination lock.

Meaning: Jerry was unable to stay calm while working on the codes of numbers and letters to open the safe that his hand was trembling and consequently slid unintentionally and fell off from the combination lock of the safe.

▶ to slip off: to slide away; to fall off by sliding unintentionally

eg. I thought I was safe on the branch, until my foot slipped off and I fell off the ground.

▲ to slip off: to depart or get away quietly, or so as to escape observation

eg. Francie devoutedly hoped he might soon get tired, and slip off to bed.

13. The robbers got scared and shot him.

▶ scared (*adj.*): being frightened of sth. or afraid that sth. bad may happen

eg. 1) My teenage daughter is scared of going out alone.

2) Local people are scared to take buses at night.

3) The thieves got scared and ran away.

14. After 18 hours of operation and weeks of <u>intensive care</u>, Jerry was released from the hospital with <u>fragments</u> of the bullets still in his body.

▶ intensive care: 重病特别护理

eg. It costs the patient $1,000 a week to keep in intensive care.

▶ fragment (*n.*): a small part of sth. that has broken off or come from sth. larger

eg. 1) The detective found fragments of glass near the stove.

2) Mary read everything, digesting every fragment of news.

▲ fragmentary (*adj.*): made of small parts that are disconnected or incomplete

eg. 1) There exists only fragmentary evidence to support this new theory.

2) There is a fragmentary report of the event in the local newspaper.

15. I <u>declined</u> to see his wounds, but did ask him what had <u>gone through</u> his mind as the robbery took place.

Meaning: I refused to see his scare, but in a polite way. What I was interested to know was what he was really thinking during the crisis of robbery.

▶ decline (*v.*): to refuse politely to accept or to do sth.

eg. 1) The White House spokesman declined to comment on the sudden change of policy.

2) It was very strange that we offered Miss Smith a lift in the rain but she declined.

▶ to go through: to experience or suffer sth.

eg. 1) She's been going through a bad patch recently.

2) He's amazingly cheerful, considering all he's had to go through.

3) He has already gone through unutterable agonies.

▲ to go through: to look at or examine sth. carefully, especially in order to find sth.

eg. 1) Bob always starts the day by going through his e-mail.

2) The inspector went through the account of the firm, looking for evidence of fraud.

3) It would take far too long to go through all the propositions.

16. "Weren't you scared? Did you <u>lose consciousness</u>?" I asked.

▶ to lose consciousness: to lose the ability to use senses or metal power

eg. I just don't remember it—I must have lost consciousness.

▲ to regain consciousness: to get consciousness again

eg. Cindy did not regain consciousness and died the following day.

17. Jerry continued, "The <u>nursing</u> staff was great."

▶ nursing (*n.*): the job or skill of caring for people who are sick or injured eg. 1) a nursing mother

    2) the nursing profession

    3) a career in nursing

    4) nursing care

▲ nurse (*v.*): to care for sb. who is ill/sick or injured

eg. 1) Her current boss worked in a hospital for three years nursing cancer patients.

    2) The baby-sitter nursed her daughter back to health.

18. But when they <u>wheeled</u> me into the emergency room and I saw the <u>expressions</u> on the faces of the doctors and nurses...

  ▶ wheel (*v.*): to move sb./sth. that is in or on sth. that has wheels

eg. 1) The nurse wheeled the old lady along the hospital corridor.

    2) Her niece wheeled her tricycle across the street.

  ▶ expression (*n.*): a look on a person's face that shows his thoughts and feelings

eg. 1) Her face wore an expression of disapproval.

    2) Mike's expression changed from bewilderment to one of enchantment.

19. "She asked if I was <u>allergic to</u> anything."

  ▶ allergic to:　having a medical condition that causes one to react badly when he/she eats or touches a particular substance (Allergic usually goes with "to" followed by an object.)

eg. 1) His wife likes cats but unfortunately she is allergic to them.

    2) My doctor told me that it is allergic reaction.

20. Jerry lived <u>thanks to</u> the skill of his doctors, but also because of his <u>amazing</u> attitude.

Meaning: It was not only his doctor's medical skill but also Jerry's positive attitude that surprised most people and enabled Jerry to have survived the operation.

  ▶ thanks to: sth. has happened because of sb. or sth.

eg. 1) It was a great success—thanks to the hard work of every member in the institution.

    2) I was flunked, all thanks to professor Smith.

    3) Thanks to his strong constitution, Jack was able to pull through his recent serious illness.

  ▶ amazing (*adj.*): very surprising esp. in a way that makes one feel pleasure or admiration

eg. 1) It's amazing how quickly people adapt to computer technology.

    2) Penicillin is an amazing discovery in medicine.

Better Know More

　　这部分是课文的注释,有利于学生对整篇课文的透彻理解。教师讲解的时候,可以适当向学生介绍更多的相关信息或者推荐相关的文献供学生课下阅读,以增加学生的信息量,提高学习兴趣。

　　文化知识的讲解是语言教学的一个重要组成部分。广博的文化知识是学好一门语言的基础,也是运用语言进行交流的必备利器。只有深入了解英语国家的文化、吸收和秉承本民族文化之精髓,语言作为交流工具的作用才能凸现出来。

Check Your Understanding

　　这部分是考查学生对课文内容的理解。教师可以在讲课当中使用这里的问题提问学生,也可以在课文全部学完之后,用来检查学生对课文的理解情况。如果教师感觉有些问题适合小组讨论,还可以组织相应的课堂活动来完成这部分练习。

Translate the following sentences into Chinese.　Please make sure that your language flows smoothly.

1. She asked if I was allergic to anything.
   她问我是否对什么药物过敏。

2. The bottom line: It's your choice how you live life.
   最重要的是:怎么生活是你自己的选择。

3. Jerry lived thanks to the skill of his doctors, but also because of his amazing attitude.
   杰瑞活下来了,救他命的不仅仅是医生们精湛的医术,也是他自己令人难以置信的乐观态度。

4. I declined to see his wounds, but did ask him what had gone through his mind as the robbery took place.
   我没有看他的伤口,但是我的确问他:抢劫发生的瞬间他脑子里想的是什么。

5. He was always in a good mood and always had something positive to say.
   他总是心境极佳,总能说出一些积极向上的话来。

6. I learned from him that every day we have the choice to live fully.
   从他身上我懂得我们每天都可以对如何活得充实做出选择。

Answer the following questions based on the text you have just learned.

1. What kind of person was Jerry?

   Jerry was the kind of guy you love to hate.   He was always in a good mood and always had something positive to say.   When someone would ask him how he was doing,   he would reply, "If I were any better, I would be twins! "

2. What did he mean when he said, "If I were any better, I wound be twins!"?

   He meant to say that he was so happy that only when he became two of himself would he be able to contain all the happiness available to him.

3. Why did several waiters follow him from restaurant to restaurant?

   The reason the waiters followed Jerry was because of his attitude.   He was naturally good at encouraging everyone round him. If an employee was having a bad day, Jerry was there telling the employee how to look on the positive side of the situation.

4. What did the narrator seem to feel about Jerry's attitude?

   It is easy to recognize that some people are optimistic in the usual sense. But Jerry was different because he was a positive person all of the time.

5. What happened to Jerry one morning when he left the restaurant back door open?

   He was held up at gunpoint by three armed robbers.

6. Why were the robbers scared? And what did they do then?

   When he was trying to open the safe as ordered by the robbers, his hand slipped off the combination lock as a result of nervousness.   The robbers were scared of the accident and shot him.

7. How did Jerry make doctors and nurses laugh in the emergency room?

   When the nurse asked if he was allergic to anything,   he said "yes."   He took a deep breath and yelled, "Bullets! " Everyone there burst into laughter.

8. Why did people love to hate Jerry?

   Judging by his career and background, Jerry was really an ordinary person. So people had a difficult time trying to figure out why he was always in a good mood and always had something positive to say while others found it impossible to keep such a balance in life.   They were even annoyed that it was beyond them to find an answer to Jerry's ability to remain optimistic whatever happened to him.

A Sip of Phonetics

Know Their Faces

When teaching this group of back vowels /ɑː/, /ɒ/, /ɔː/, /ʊ/ and /uː/, the instructor should draw students' attention to the differences in pronunciation between these vowels and the corresponding Chinese Pinyin. It is important to note that the five back vowels find no direct equivalent in Chinese Pinyin even though they share similarities.

/ɑː/ in English is pronounced in a different way from the corresponding Chinese /ɑ/, which is pronounced with the tongue positioned not as far back as /ɑː/. The students are supposed to open their mouths wide enough with the back of the tongue raised just high enough for the doctor to examine the throat.

The pair /ɒ/ and /ɔː/ discussed here are not pronounced the same as the Chinese final /o/, which is pronounced with the mouth rounded, but with a slight movement of the lips, whereas there is no movement in the mouth when /ɒ/ and /ɔː/ are being pronounced. Chinese students of English are liable to make such mistakes.

Similarly, though /ʊ/ and /uː/ share with the Chinese final /u/, they differ in pronunciation in that there is neither friction nor movement of the lips while fiction exists when /ʊ/ is pronounced.

Train Your Tongue

1. A tutor /who tooted the flute/tried to tutor /two tooters to toot./Said the two/ to the tutor,/ "Is it tougher to toot or to tutor /two tooters to toot?"
2. Cheerful Charles/ chose cherry chocolates for Cheri.
3. How many cuckoos /could a good cook cook/if a cook could cook cuckoos.
4. Mr. See had a saw/and Mr. Soar owned a seesaw.
5. How much dough /would Bob Dole dole/if Bob Dole could dole dough?
6. Sam's shop /stocks short spotted socks.

You'd Like to Be

这部分是 Text A 的练习,共有六个部分组成。每部分都是按照大纲要求掌握的各项基本功精心编写的。教师应该指导学生在熟读和理解课文的基础上,认真做每一项练习,严格训练学生的基本知识和基本的语言能力。

该练习部分摒弃传统的模式,潜心打造每个练习的主题,旨在与学生形成互动,鼓励他们提高各项技能,从而成为一名优秀的语言学习者。

A Strong Bridge Builder

这部分的练习旨在训练学生正确运用介词、副词和连词的能力。学生应在熟读课文的基础上，注意这些介词、副词和连词的用法，尤其是一些固定的词组搭配，以便今后能够正确地使用这些用法。

Fill in the blanks with the given words to complete the following sentences. Please note that some can be used more than once.

in	of	to	down	on	from
after	at	toward	for	near	with

1. Very luckily, the victim was found near the back door <u>of</u> the barn some 14 hours <u>after</u> the disaster and rushed <u>to</u> the local hospital. After 10 hours of operation and weeks of intensive care, she was released <u>from</u> the hospital <u>with</u> fragments of the bombs still <u>in</u> her legs. "I am not afraid <u>of</u> anything now <u>after</u> my first death." She said she when interviewed <u>on</u> TV the other day.

2. Mr. Cord arrived <u>at</u> his personal goal thanks <u>to</u> his dedication <u>to</u> painting, but also because <u>of</u> his amazing attitude <u>toward</u> his ambition. We could learn <u>from</u> him that nothing is impossible <u>to</u> a willing heart.

3. I stay healthy <u>for</u> the past decade, and my wife just takes it <u>for</u> granted. Consequently, she was surprised when I told her that I suffered <u>from</u> serious allergy these days. "How come? Allergic <u>to</u> what, my dear?" she asked <u>with</u> a worried expression <u>on</u> her face. "Nothing serious, really. I ...I just fell allergic <u>to</u> the housework you assigned me."

4. After the presentation I reflected <u>on</u> what Dr. Nord said. Yes, it is far <u>from</u> enough for a student to just remember what the professor and the textbooks are saying. <u>In</u> terms <u>of</u> memory we are definitely no better than modern computers. But we do have our strength: the creativity. Not only are we expected to acquire the knowledge passed <u>down</u> <u>from</u> older generations, but also we are supposed to create new knowledge of our own. This is why we are always asked to write something original in our term papers.

A Smart Word Player

这部分是另外一种完形填空的练习。学生要根据括号中提供的词，变化其形式，填写到段落或句子当中去。这些词都是课文里出现的。这部分练习的目的是拓展学生的词汇量，能够利用派生词和同源词来学习并运用更多的词汇。这项练习训练学生的阅读能力和语用能力。如果学生有理解上的困难，教师应该予以适当的解释和指导。

Fill in the blanks with the proper words that need to be transformed from the ones provided in the brackets.

1. To be a real researcher, one is expected to possess a number of qualities including open mindedness, <u>creativity</u> (create), <u>curiosity</u> (curious), honesty, and a continual interest in <u>reflection</u> (reflect).

2. Each group applying for the award must consist of members from at least three countries. Such a rule was set up to <u>encourage</u> (encouraging) young scientists to <u>intensify</u> (intensive) international collaboration(协作).

3. There are many <u>complaints</u> (complain) about the inefficiency of that company. But I made an order earlier today and was <u>amazed</u> (amazing) at how quickly the delivery boy came.

A Skilled Text Weaver

　　这部分是完形填空练习。要求学生用课文中出现的词(以生词为主,不排除以往学过的词)进行填空,故而可以达到温故而知新的目的。填空多用小段落的形式,充分培养学生的阅读能力和语用能力。

Fill in the blanks with the words you have learned in this text. One word is for each blank. Here is a piece of advice: You must be really familiar with the text to accomplish the following tasks.

1. I have a lot to say about the fiction *The Bridge of Madison County*—the theme, the language, the suspense and so on, but the <u>bottom</u> <u>line</u> is quite simple: it is so far the best love story that gives respect for family.

2. Five years after the 9·11 attack, New York has witnessed a(n) <u>amazing</u> recovery. While people give much of their sympathy to the <u>victims</u> of the disaster, many people start to <u>reflect</u> <u>on</u> where this country has been, where it is going next and how it may get there.

3. It was the first time that Mary <u>declined</u> to come to my birthday party. I was really <u>curious</u> about what had <u>gone</u> <u>through</u> her mind, because we had been friends for years.

4. He had a bad day yesterday. He was <u>supposed</u> to attend an important meeting at 9, but he got up late. When he got off the bus, it was 8:55. In a hurry, one of his shoes <u>slipped</u> <u>off</u> before the bus door closed. He had to stop by a shoe store before hurrying for the meeting. Guess what? When he arrived at the company, it was 10:30.

〰️ A Sharp Interpreter

　　这部分为句子释义练习，目的是为了让学生了解地道的英文的表达方式，并在理解的基础上，重新组织语言以表达同样的思想内容。这部分练习不仅可以提高学生的阅读理解能力，还能提高学生对词汇、语法的运用能力，是训练他们娴熟口头表达能力和写作能力的重要途径。

Please paraphrase the following sentences. Change the sentence structure if necessary.

1. Jerry was the kind of guy you love to hate.

　◈ *Paraphrasing:*

　Jerry was the kind of person whom people admire so much that he annoys those who are incapable of becoming one like him.

2. "If I were any better, I would be twins!"

　◈ *Paraphrasing:*

　I consider myself so happy that only when I became two of myself would I be able to contain all the happiness I have.

3. He was recognized as a special manager because he had several waiters who had followed him around from restaurant to restaurant.

　◈ *Paraphrasing:*

　He was acknowledged as a special manager as he had the charm that attracted several waiters who were determined to work for him only,　no matter which restaurant hired him.

4. I reflected on what Jerry said.

　◈ *Paraphrasing:*

　I thought very carefully about what Jerry said.

5. We lost touch, but I often thought about him when I made a choice about life instead of reacting to it.

　◈ *Paraphrasing:*

　Although we lost contact with each other,　my mind often went to him in the first place when I made a decision as to how to live life before dealing with it.

〰️ A Solid Sentence Constructer

　　这部分为造句练习，目的是加强学生语言的运用能力。教师应提示学生先找出课文中使用这些词组的原句，以它们为例句模仿造句。教师在讲解课文的时候，应注意提示在使用这些词或词组时应该注意的问题。

Please make a sentence with each word or expression listed below.

1. in a good mood
   ✥ *Original sentence in the text:*
   He was always in a good mood and always had something positive to say.
   ✥ **Suggested sentence:**
   She seemed to be in a good mood thanks to her quick recovery.

2. to be recognized as
   ✥ *Original sentence in the text:*
   He was recognized as a special manager because he had several waiters who had followed him around from restaurant to restaurant.
   ✥ **Suggested sentence:**
   Grace is recognized as one of the best sales agents.

3. to react to
   ✥ *Original sentence in the text:*
   We lost touch, but I often thought about him when I made a choice about life instead of reacting to it.
   ✥ **Suggested sentence:**
   You can handle the material more safely if you know how it will react to changes in temperature.

4. the bottom line
   ✥ *Original sentence in the text:*
   The bottom line: It's your choice how you live life.
   ✥ **Suggested sentence:**
   The bottom line in the debate is the increasing number of motorcycle accidents and fatalities.

5. to go through one's mind
   ✥ *Original sentence in the text:*
   I declined to see his wounds, but did ask him what had gone through his mind as the robbery took place.
   ✥ **Suggested sentence:**
   What had gone through your mind when you first read the news?

6. to be allergic to
   ✥ *Original sentence in the text:*
   "She asked if I was allergic to anything."
   ✥ **Suggested sentence:**
   Never tell me that you are allergic to housework. Every one in the family must have a share of it.

7. thanks to

✶ ***Original sentence in the text:***

Jerry lived thanks to the skill of his doctors, but also because of his amazing attitude.

✶ **Suggested sentence:**

A large number of ski resorts opened early last year thanks to an early-October snowstorm.

📖 A Superb Bilingualist

这部分是汉译英的练习，目的是让学生进一步加深对课文中出现的词和词组的印象。教师要引导学生尽量模仿课文中词和词组的用法，或者文中的句型结构。教师还要鼓励学生使用不同的方式去做翻译，不要只拘泥于参考答案。

Please translate the following sentences into English with the prompts provided in the brackets.

1. 尽管我们失去联系多年了，我还是会时常想起她。(lose touch, think about)

Though we lost touch for years, I think about her from time to time.

2. 比尔·盖茨是那种让人又爱又恨的人，他居然能在别人的一个简单的理念上营造起自己的经济帝国。(love to hate)

Bill Gates, who is able to build up his economic empire based on a borrowed idea, is the kind of person people love to hate.

3. 两个星期的假期把我从工作中暂时解放出来。(release)

I was released from my work temporarily by a two-week holiday.

4. 我们应该思考一下我们能从这次失败中学到什么。(reflect on, learn from)

We should reflect on what we can learn from the failure.

5. 人生充满了选择。我们理应做出正确的选择，可有时我们却做不到。(all about, be supposed to)

Life is all about choices. We are supposed to make right ones, but we are sometimes unable to.

6. 幸亏他对香蕉过敏，才躲过了这场由香蕉引起的食物中毒。(thanks to, be allergic to, food poisoning)

Thanks to the fact that he was allergic to banana, he escaped the food poisoning caused by banana.

7. 我从他的脸上看出来他今天的心情很不错。(read, in a good mood)

In his face, I read he is in a good mood today.

Text B

Introduction of the Text

Research suggests that a good laugh—or even the anticipation of laughter—does good to your health and sometimes turns out to be very effective. Scientists have found that exposure to humor has healthy effects because it tends to lower the level of stress hormones. Some claim that laughter functions in a similar way like physical exercise. Laughter has a positive effect on the cardiovascular system. Your blood pressure is lowered overall and heart rate decreases. What's more, your immune system appears to be tuned up by your hearty laughter.

This text tells us how humor or laughter functions as a therapy to bring about an unexpected effect to patients sick with fatal diseases. On the one hand, humor and laughter are of an inseparable means traced to a positive attitude toward life as discussed in Text A. On the other hand, studies witness the significance of humor and laughter in difficult situations, especially with people suffering from heart disease.

Comprehension Questions

After reading Text B, please answer the following questions with the words and expressions given in the brackets.

1. What did best-seller author Norman Cousins say in his book? (genuine belly laughter)
   (Paragraph 2—3) Cousins wrote in his book: "I made the joyous discovery that ten minutes of genuine belly laughter had an anesthetic effect and would give me at least two hours of pain-free sleep." Gradually the pain went away, he became more mobile and he did what doctors didn't expect: He got better.

2. According to the researchers at the University of Texas, what might be the function of laughter? (a much lower risk of)
   (Paragraph 5) Researchers at the University of Texas found that subjects who scored high on a happiness questionnaire had a much lower risk of stroke than others. The happier folks were, the more protective the effect seemed to be.

3. What did Japanese researchers announce? (diabetes)
   (Paragraph 6) The Japanese researchers announced that a little laughter around the dinner table might help people with Type II diabetes, the most common form of the disease.

4. What research findings did the doctors of the University of Maryland Medical Centre present? (buffer)

(Paragraph 7)Their findings at the University of Maryland Medical Centre suggested that laughter may be a buffer against heart attacks.

5. What did Zeltzer's team find? (less pain)

(Paragraph 14—15) The Zeltzer's team found that healthy children were able to keep their arms in ice water longer while watching funny videos. The kids also reported less pain and had lower levels of stress hormones.

6. What can we conclude about laughter? (the best medicine)

(Paragraph 16) Although there is not yet a final say about the real function of laughter, it is widely believed that a sense of humor and the ability to laugh over whatever is laughable to you is still the best medicine for a better day.

Writing Practice

Put your answers to the above questions together and form a summary about the text and share with your classmates the summary you have completed.

Cousins wrote in his book: "I made the joyous discovery that ten minutes of genuine belly laughter had an anesthetic effect and would give me at least two hours of pain-free sleep." Gradually the pain went away, he became more mobile and he did what doctors didn't expect: He got better. Researchers at the University of Texas found that subjects who scored high on a happiness questionnaire had a much lower risk of stroke than others. The happier folks were, the more protective the effect seemed to be. The Japanese researchers announced that a little laughter around the dinner table might help people with Type II diabetes, the most common form of the disease. Their findings at the University of Maryland Medical Centre suggest that laughter may be a buffer against heart attacks. The Zeltzer's team found that healthy children were able to keep their arms in ice water longer while watching funny videos. The kids also reported less pain and had lower levels of stress hormones. Although there is not yet a final say about the real function of laughter, it is widely believed that a sense of humor and the ability to laugh over whatever is laughable to you is still the best medicine for a better day.

2

Happy Childhood

Unit Goals

After studying this unit, students should be able to:

☞ **understand the historical background of racial discrimination and the Great Depression;**

      Text A narrates Bill Clinton's childhood with his grandparents. The narration focuses on the influence of racial issue and the Great Depression on American families, particularly those living in the South at that time. In teaching this text, the instructor should also help the students understand that the childhood experience and the power of his grandparents to treat the colored people as equal have contributed significantly to Bill Clinton's interpretation of life, and helped in shaping his political viewpoint.

☞ **know how to pronounce /i:/, /i/, /e/ and /æ/, and how to utilize the words and structures that contribute significantly to the texts;**

      In this section, students are to learn how to pronounce /i:/, /i/, /e/ and /æ/ correctly, and more importantly to discern between /i:/ and /i/, and /e/ and /æ/. It is strongly suggested that the instructor encourage students to read aloud tongue twisters before and after class. The instructor may refer to the advice provided in the section **A Sip of Phonetics**. Most useful words and structures of **Text A** can be found in **You'd like to Be**. This is where students practice what they have learned from **Text A.**

☞ **learn to appreciate the virtue of family members.**

      The authors of both **Text A** and **B** share with us their childhood experience with benevolent grandfather, whose magnetic and powerful personality gave them profound influence. As a matter of fact, many of our family members have the virtues that are indispensable in shaping what we are. The unfortunate thing is we tend to ignore their existence. The reward for learning this unit is that the students will be able to discover and appreciate the virtue of family members.

Before Reading

Hands-on Activities and Brainstorming

The instructor should allow 15—20 minutes for students to do presentation either on Bill Clinton or on his grandfather.

A Glimpse at Words and Expressions

A. The key word to be worked out is "unaware," which is formed by a negative prefix "un" and the adjective "aware." Here is the formation of "unaware":

un (not) + aware (know) = not knowing → not knowing or realizing that sth. is happening

"Un" is usually added before an adjective or a verb without changing its part of speech, other examples being "able—unable," "friendly—unfriendly," "to fasten—to unfasten." To clarify the meaning of the word "unaware," the instructor may refer to another example: Although he was unaware of the alarming number of child workers, he is aware of the consequence.

B. The part of speech of "adored" indicates that students will have to select the answer from No. 5, No. 6 and No. 7 under Column B, each containing the explanation of verb. Obviously neither No. 5 nor 6 serves as a good answer. Therefore, try No. 7!

C. Students must have been exposed to "run for (usually an important position)" before. Therefore, they will have to rely on the prior knowledge to make a good choice. The following example might also be helpful: It was only last February that he announced he would run for president. In this sense, "to run for attorney general" and "to run for president" mean "to take part as a candidate in an election."

D. The context in the sentence lies in the contrast between the action "looking for" that is lasting for hours and the negative result suggested in the phrase "to no avail." When the instructor succeeds in getting the students to this point, they will be able to figure out and understand the phrase as "with little or no success." It will be more helpful for the instructor to offer an example with a context: They tried to pull the trunk out of the river but to no avail.

E. The instructor should first point out that the relationship between "fat" and "self-conscious" in this sentence is between cause and effect. In this sense, being "self-conscious" is not being comfortable. It is also natural for a "fat" boy who hates being "fat" to be very sensitive to those around him. He is very careful about how others comment on him. In this way the instructor is able to build up the students' understanding of the expression "self-conscious," which means "nervous or embarrassed about one's appearance or what other people think of him." The following example offers a better context for understanding this expression: He's always been self-conscious about being so short.

F. It should be noted that No. 2 is the only one among all listed under Column B that carries a noun form correspondence. However, the instructor should let students know that "kind of interesting business" is not an explanation of "sort of adventure," but serves linguistically as a replacement of it.

G. The phrase "on credit" is new to the students. To make it easier, the instructor might start by asking the students if they know about "credit card." Some might be able to contribute to the interpretation of "credit card." Students know if you pay by credit card, they do not have to pay cash until the bill comes. Similarly, to sell something "on credit" is to allow somebody to take what he/she buys without full payment being demanded at the time of the purchase, with the rest of payment cleared off at their convenience.

Keys

A-5   B-7   C-6   D-1   E-4   F-2   G-3

Text A

Bill Clinton

Clinton was born on August 19, 1946, in Hope, Arkansas, three months after his father died in a traffic accident. When Bill was four, his mother married Roger Clinton. After graduation from Georgetown University (1968), he won a Rhodes Scholarship to Oxford University. He received a law degree from Yale University (1973). Clinton returned to his home state, where he was a lawyer and law professor. In 1976, he was elected Attorney General of Arkansas, and won the governorship in 1978.

Bill Clinton was president of the United States for two terms, from 1993 to 2001. He was the first Democratic president since Franklin D. Roosevelt to have won a second term. During his administration, the United States enjoyed more economic well-being than at any time in history with the lowest unemployment rate in modern times, the lowest inflation in 30 years, the highest home ownership in the country's history, dropping crime rates in many places, and reduced welfare rolls. He drew huge crowds when he traveled through South America, Europe, Russia, Africa, and China.

My Life is a 2004 autobiography written by Bill Clinton, who left office on January 20, 2001. The book was published by the Knopf Publishing Group at Random House on June 22, 2004, and set a worldwide record for single day non-fiction book sales according to the publisher; the book sold in excess of 400,000 copies.

⌇ Suggested Explanations on Text A

1. While mother was in New Orleans, I was in the care of my grandparents.

   ▶ in the care of: taken care of

   eg. 1) Around 20% deaths occurred while the infant was in the care of a non-parental caregiver.

       2) From that time, he was in the care of his younger son David until his death in 1982.

2. They loved me very much; sadly, much better than they were able to love each other or, in my grandmother's case, to love my mother.

   Meaning: They loved me very much, though grandfather and grandmother always had frictions between themselves, and it seemed that my grandmother did not like my mother.

3. ...I came to realize how fortunate I had been.

   ▶ to come to be/do: be brought in the course of time to become, do, etc.

   Note: "Come to be/do" refers to a state, which can be considered a stative verbal phrase, to express emotion, knowledge or belief. Generally speaking, stative verbs describe a state of affairs that do not occur in the progressive form.

   eg. 1) During the process, I've come to realize the value and significance of the issues.

       2) All of us, from the very youngest children to the oldest members of our cultures should come to realize our own potential as teachers.

       3) You may come to be ashamed of what you've done today.

       4) I hope we shall be friends and come to understand one another.

4. Most children will make it if they have just one person who makes them feel that way. I had three.

   Meaning: Most children will be successful in life if they have just one person who makes them feel that they are important. Luckily, I had three people within my family, all thinking I was the most important person to them.

   Note: The understatement of this sentence can be: Since there were more people in my family who thought I was the most important person to them, I became more successful in life than most other people.

   ▶ to make it: (informal) succeed, be able to do, be successful in life

   eg. 1) He became very bitter when he realized that he would never make it.

       2) It's hard to make it to the top in show business.

Note: In the phrase "make it," "it" can be considered as a function word that does not refer to anything specific in the sentence even though it functions as an object of "make." It is hard to clarify what exactly "it" refers to without a context.

According to Jack Richards' *Longman Dictionary of Language Teaching & Applied Linguistics*, words can be divided into two classes: content words and function words. Content words refer to a thing, quality, state, or action, which have lexical meaning when used alone. Function words have little meaning, but show grammatical relationships in and between sentences (carrying the grammatical meaning).

5. My grandfather was an incredibly kind and generous man.

▶ incredibly (*adv.*): unbelievably, extremely

eg. 1) It was incredibly hot outside.

　　2) Their mother was incredibly good-looking.

▲ incredible (*adj.*): hard to believe, amazing

eg. 1) It seemed incredible that people would still want to play football during war time.

　　2) Computer programs are incredible inventions. They allow us to play video games, create spreadsheets (制作表格), and send emails.

6. He grew up to be a distinguished, successful lawyer.

Meaning: He grew up and became an outstanding and successful lawyer.

▶ distinguished (*adj.*): characterized by excellence or high standing

eg. 1) Each year the university invites distinguished professionals to make presentations on topics of current interest.

　　2) Rorty was awarded the Thomas Jefferson Medal for distinguished achievement in the arts, humanities or social sciences from the American Philosophical Society.

▲ distinguish (*v.*): to recognize as being different or distinct.

eg. 1) It is difficult to distinguish clearly between fact and fiction in this book.

　　2) Speech distinguishes man from the animals.

▲ distinction (*n.*): a clear difference or contrast especially between people or things that are similar or related

eg. 1) Please do not blur the distinction between Trojan(特洛伊木马)and Worm(蠕虫)virus.

　　2) One of the aims of the current administration is to reduce the distinction between town and country.

7. Forty years later, he told me he still never walked by that stretch of sidewalk without trying to spot that dime.

Meaning: Forty years later, he told me whenever he walked by that section of the sidewalk, he would try to locate that dime.

▶ spot (*v.*): to notice or find

eg. 1) No matter how hard I tried, I failed to spot any error in my essay.

2) She had spotted a man with a shotgun taking aim.

3) On a shelf beneath he spotted a photo album.

▲ spot (*n.*): a particular area or place

eg. 1) There are a lot of spots to visit in the old city.

2) She stood rooted to the spot with fear. 她呆立在原地，吓傻了。

▲ on the spot: without delay; at once; at the scene of action

eg. 1) The president made the decision on the spot.

2) When Tom ruined the expensive machine, his boss fired him on the spot.

▲ to put sb. on the spot: to make sb. feel embarrassed by asking tough questions

eg. 1) The reporter's tricky questions put him on the spot.

2) They all dumped troubles on him. No one cares that he was put on the spot.

8. It's hard to <u>convey</u> to young people today the <u>impact</u> the Depression had <u>on</u> my parents'
and grandparents' generation.

Meaning: It is difficult nowadays to have the young people understand how the Depression affected my parents' and grandparents' generation.

▶ convey (*v.*): to make ideas, feelings, etc. known to sb.

eg. 1) It is amazing that Dr. Smith conveys the idea clearly in six languages.

2) This picture will convey to you the idea of beauty (美的理念).

▲ convey (*v.*): to take or carry from one place to another; transport

eg. 1) The company has a fleet of trucks for conveying produce (农产品)to the wholesale
market.

2) Pipe conveys hot water from this boiler to every part of the building.

▶ impact on: the powerful effect that sth. has on sb. or sth.

eg. 1) The presence or absence of clouds can have an important impact on heat transfer.

2) The railways made a direct physical impact on the landscape.

3) The mission of this organization is to reduce human impact on the Earth.

9. ...when my grandfather came home from work and <u>broke down</u> ...

▶ to break down: to lose control of oneself

eg. 1) One night as they stayed in a small village inn, homeless and afraid, his wife broke
down and cried in despair.

2) At the gate of the police station, the mother broke down and became hysterical(歇
斯底里). Without even thinking, I zoomed wide and included her in the shot.

▲ to break down: to stop working; suffer an illness of some time

eg. 1) The air-conditioner worked for about half an hour and then broke down, after
which I never saw it work again.

2) The elevator broke down suddenly and consequently three of us were trapped in it.

3) Tom broke down and was unable to work.

10. ...but my mother had been faithful to her father's Easter ritual.

Meaning: ...but my mother simply wouldn't make any change to my grandfather's Easter
tradition.

▶ be faithful to: not changing anything

eg. 1) Our obligation is not so much to be faithful to the speaker's words, but to convey
his message for the sake of communication.

2) We have to stay faithful to facts.

▲ to be faithful to: not having sexual relationship with anybody other than spouse

eg. 1) Mary had been faithful to her husband throughout those difficult years.

2) He was almost killed by the idea that his wife might not have been faithful to him.

11. ...and he supplemented his income by working as a night watchman at a sawmill.

▶ supplement (*v.*): to add sth. to sth. else in order to improve it or make it more complete

eg. 1) To supplement its advertising effort, the company used a variety of sales-promotion
techniques.

2) Clearly people choosing to supplement their diets with herbals, vitamins, minerals,
or other substances want to know more about the products.

▲ supplement (*n.*): a thing added to sth. else to either improve or complete it or make up
for a deficiency

eg. 1) Research indicates that several dietary supplements can be useful for lowering and
controlling insulin and blood sugar levels.

2) The encyclopedia has a supplement covering recent events.

12. It got him out of the house and reminded him of the mill work he'd done as a young man
around the time of my mother's birth.

▶ to remind sb. of sth.: to cause sb. to remember sth.

eg. 1) The building reminded me strongly of my old school.

2) She kept looking at her watch to remind him of the time.

▲ to remind sb. that: Note: "Remind" can also take a noun clause that functions as an object.

eg. 1) She gently reminded him that the baby was getting cold and should be taken indoors.

2) An event like this serves to remind us that we do not have control over nature.

13. Except for the time grandfather closed the car door on my fingers in the dark, those nights were perfect adventures.

Meaning: Those were the most enjoyable nights with exciting experiences excluding the accident that grandfather shut my finger in the car door.

▶ except for (also except): apart from

eg. 1) The purse was empty except for some coppers.

2) She was quite alone in the world except for an invalid aunt in the South.

Note: 赵振才教授在《英语常见问题解答大词典》一书中根据钱哥川先生的《英语疑难详解》总结了 except 与 except for 用法上的区别。根据钱哥川先生的讲解，前后有相称的同类语时就用 except, 否则用 except for。例如："I looked everywhere except in the bathroom." 句中 everywhere 与 in the bathroom 为相称的同类语。在 "The dress is ready except for the buttons." 句中 ready 与 the buttons 不相称，为非同类语。

但是 "Soon everyone was gone except for Miss Penrose." 又似乎推翻了钱哥川先生的论述。应该指出，钱哥川先生的论述符合传统语法家们的观点。F.T. Wood 对于 except 与 except for 也做过类似的区分："except 是从一组……中排除其特殊的一个或几个；except for 则是以保留的方式对整个句子内容进行修正，也就是说，两部分所用的词或词组所表示的并非一类事，而它们之间有所属关系，句子后半部分对前半部分所说的基本情况在细节上加以修正，就要用 except for。" 然而目前人们使用 except 与 except for 时，表现出了极大的灵活性。R.A. Close 和 LDCE 的编者们认为 except 与 except for 在许多情况下已不存在上面的区别。教师在讲授该语言点时，抓住 except 和 except for 的基本用法。尽管在使用中有其灵活性，但是还要强调掌握使用原则。

14. Second, grown-ups I didn't know came in to buy groceries, for the first time exposing me to adults who weren't relatives.

Meaning: The fact that the adult customers came for groceries started my direct contact with the adults outside my family.

▶ expose (*v.*): to allow to be subjected to an action or an influence

eg. 1) A wise mother never exposes her children to the slightest possibility of danger.

2) These units exposed children to many viewpoints of the issue of gun control.

15. Though the South was completely segregated back then, some level of racial interaction was inevitable in small towns ...

Meaning: Though the south was totally separated along racial lines(以种族为界)at that time, a certain degree of communication between the black and white was simply taking place naturally, especially in small towns.

▶ interaction (*n.*): communication between people

eg. 1) The interaction between human and robot is amazing.

2) The complex interaction between animals and environment has been observed in terms of their life pattern.

▲ to interact with: to mix with other people; act together with; have effect on

eg. 1) Timmy interacts very well with other children.

2) These two chemicals interact with each other at a certain temperature to produce a substance which could cause an explosion.

▶ inevitable (*adj.*): that cannot be avoided or prevented

eg. 1) The scandal made her resignation inevitable.

2) They came to see defeat as inevitable.

16. However, it was rare to find an uneducated rural southerner without a racist bone in his body.

Meaning: Racial prejudice was popular among uneducated people in the rural area in the South, but my grandfather, though uneducated, was an exception, who was always fair to the black people.

17. <u>Occasionally</u>, black kids would come into the store and we would play.

▶ occasionally (*adv.*): sometimes but not often

eg. 1) Like humans, dogs do occasionally suffer from depression.

2) The sports official acknowledged Monday that some winners may occasionally use drugs.

▲ occasion (*n.*): an important event, ceremony, or celebration

eg. 1) The queen's coach is only used for state occasions.

2) There was a party to mark the occasion of their daughter's graduation.

18. It took me years to learn about segregation and prejudice and the meaning of poverty, years to learn that most white people weren't like my grandfather and grandmother, whose views on race were among the few things she had <u>in common</u> with her husband.

Meaning: My grandparents treated the black people as their equal that they did not do anything that suggested the existence of racial difference in the world. That's why I had a hard time getting to know about segregation and racial discrimination themselves and even poverty. Later I came to realize that my grandparents distinguished from most other white people in their attitude toward the black. Grandmother seldom agreed with grandfather, but she did share the same view with grandfather on the issue of race.

▶ in common: sharing the same interests or experiences

eg. 1) He had very little in common with his sister.

2) Britain, in common with many other industrialized countries, has experienced

major changes over the last 100 years.

19. After I became President, I got <u>another firsthand account of</u> my grandfather's store.

    <u>Meaning</u>: After I became President, I got another comment on my grandfather's store from a former customer's daughter, who experienced in person my grandfather's generosity and kindness.

    ▶ account (*n.*): written or spoken description of sth. that has happened

    eg. 1) She received a glowing account of her son's progress.

        2) Dr. Richards describes this very vividly in his account of the events.

    ▲ account (*n.*): an arrangement that one has with a bank to keep money there or take some out

    eg. 1) I deposited the check into my savings account.

        2) Can you tell me the balance of my bank account?

    ▲ account (*n.*): an arrangement with a store to pay bills for goods

    eg. 1) Put it on my account, please.

        2) Charge this to my account, please.

20. ...about her grandfather buying groceries from mine "<u>on account</u>" and bringing her with him to the store.

    ▶ on account: if sb. buys sth. or pays on account, he pays nothing or only a small amount immediately and the rest later

    eg. 1) Could you give me a loaf of bread on account?

        2) As a general policy, the company does not sell merchandise on account.

    ▲ on account of: due to; because of

    eg. 1) I've come to see you on account of my daughter. She is very sick.

        2) I was thinking of going down to Richmond for a fortnight, on account of my health.

    ▲ to account for: to give a satisfactory record of; to explain

    eg. 1) He could not account for his foolish mistake.

        2) The suspect couldn't account for his time that night.

Better Know More

The Great Depression in the United States

    The Great Depression in the United States lasted from the end of 1929 to the early 1940s, which was the worst and longest economic disaster in the history of the modern industrial world. The depression started in the United States, and then spread to most of the world's industrial countries. The Great Depression caused rapid decline in production and an abrupt drop in goods sales with a sudden rise of unemployment rate. Consequently, people lost their jobs, houses, and savings, and many of them could only survive on charity.

The Great Depression had a direct and extensive impact on the lives of American people. Many people were suffering from insufficient supply of food, shelter, and clothing. Psychological impact was equally damaging. The unemployment brought about by the depression was a devastating blow. People fell into difficult circumstances with self-blame and self-doubt even though they understood that it was a social problem rather than personal failure that set them in distress. To make things worse, the effects of the depression on children were often different from the impact on their parents' generation. Many children took on greater responsibilities at an earlier age than later generations would. Sometimes children had to console their hopeless parents.

The impact was more damaging for the non-white Americans. About 50 percent of the nation's black workers were unemployed by 1932. The blacks were frequently forced to give their jobs to the unemployed whites. The hardships they had experienced affected people's attitudes toward life, work, and society in general.

Check Your Understanding

Translate the following sentences into Chinese. Please make sure that your language flows smoothly.

1. While Mother was in New Orleans, I was in the care of my grandparents.
当母亲在新奥尔良时,我便由外祖父母来照看。

2. My grandfather loved working there, too. It got him out of the house and reminded him of the mill work he'd done as a young man around the time of my mother's birth.
外祖父也喜欢在那儿干活。这样他便可以从家里躲出来,去回忆他年轻力壮时做的木匠活,那时我的母亲刚刚出生。

3. Occasionally, black kids would come into the store and we would play.
有时候,黑人孩子会到店里来,我们便在一起玩。

4. It took me years to learn about segregation and prejudice and the meaning of poverty, years to learn that most white people weren't like my grandfather and grandmother, whose views on race were among the few things she had in common with her husband.
我多年以后才搞懂到底什么是种族歧视、偏见以及贫穷的含义;终于闹明白原来大多数白人和我的外祖父母很是不同。多数情况下,我的外祖母总是和丈夫观点相悖,可他们在种族问题上的态度却是少有的一致。

5. One of the most memorable stories of my childhood was my mother's tale of a Depression Good Friday when my grandfather came home from work and broke down and cried as he told her he just couldn't afford the dollar or so it would cost to buy her a new Easter dress.

令人难忘的童年故事之一是母亲给我讲的一件事。故事发生在大萧条时期的一个复活节,外祖父(神情)沮丧地下班回家,哭着告诉我母亲,他没能给她买条在复活节穿的裙子,其实那裙子只要一块来钱。

6. She recalled that he had told her that good people who were doing the best they could deserved to be able to feed their families, and no matter how strapped he was, he never denied them groceries on credit.

她(母亲)回忆外祖父曾告诉她,那些尽全力工作的好人理应做到让家人填饱肚子,所以不管他自己有多窘迫,他都会给那些人赊账。

7. In 1997, an African-American woman, Ernestine Campbell, did an interview for her hometown paper in Toledo, Ohio, about her grandfather buying groceries from mine "on account" and bringing her with him to the store.

1997 年,一位叫欧内斯廷·坎贝尔的黑人妇女,在俄亥俄州的托莱多接受当地报纸采访时谈到我的祖父曾经赊账给她的祖父,而且她的祖父还曾把她带到店里来。

Answer the following questions based on the text you have just learned.

1. Why did Bill Clinton feel himself fortunate years later?
   Because his grandparents and his mother always made him feel he was the most important person in the world to them.

2. What kind of old man was his grandfather?
   His grandfather was an incredibly kind and generous man.

3. How did Bill's grandfather influence him?
   Bill's grandfather took the responsibility to take care of his family and was also kind to his neighbors. And more importantly, he had no prejudice against the black.

4. What did John Wilson ask Bill Clinton's grandfather to do with his quarter when he was a boy? Why?
   He asked him to give him two dimes and a nickel instead of a quarter so that he could feel he had more money.

5. Why did Bill Clinton feel that the grocery store was a different sort of adventure?
   There are three reasons: First, there was a huge jar of cookies on the counter. Second, it was a place where he was exposed to adults who weren't relatives. Third, a lot of his grandfather's customers were black.

6. How were the blacks treated by the white when Bill was a kid?
   Though the South was completely segregated back then, some level of racial interaction was inevitable in small towns. It was rare to find an uneducated rural southerner

without a racist bone in his body.

7. Why did Bill's grandfather let the blacks shop on account?

Because he believed that good people who were doing the best they could deserved to be able to feed their families.

8. How does Bill feel about his childhood?

He feels he has a very happy childhood. He thinks he is lucky to have such a great grandfather and the best childhood his mother and grandparents could give to him.

A Sip of Phonetics

Know Their Faces

本课涉及的四个元音 /i:/, /i/, /e/ 和 /æ/ 是前元音。教师应该提醒学生注意区别 /i:/ 和 /i/ 的发音程度。教师还可以带领学生练习以下的词，体会 /i:/ 和 /i/ 发音的区别，避免出现错误。

1. peach	pitch	4. sheet	shit
2. beat	bit	5. teen	tin
3. seat	sit	6. seen	sin

学生另一个容易读错的音是 /æ/，例如，学生常常错误地把 bag/bæg/ 发成 beg/beg/。发 /æ/ 音时舌尖抵下齿，舌前部稍微抬高，舌位比发 /e/ 时低，而口腔开度比 /e/ 大。教师应该特别提示这一点并做正确发音的示范。

Train Your Tongue

1. How / can a clam cram / in a clean cream can?

2. Denise sees the fleece, / Denise sees the fleas. / At least / Denise could sneeze and feed / and freeze the fleas.

3. I slit the sheet, / the sheet I slit, / and on the slit sheet / I sit.

4. Six sick hicks / nick six slick bricks / with picks and sticks.

5. Peter Piper /picked / a peck of pickled peppers.

You'd Like to Be

A Strong Bridge Builder

Fill in the blanks with the given words to complete the following sentences. Please note that some can be used more than once.

about	before	in	of	into	until	to
with	without	or	on	for	after	

1. I have no money and am homeless. I was in the care of the local authority until my 16th birthday. What help is available to me?
2. It was a challenge to talk with students about building the foundation of their business systematically.
3. Before going into a discussion of China's impact on the Internet, it's important to understand the current situation there.
4. After the two World Wars, Copenhagen's reconstruction was gradual but faithful to the city's traditions.
5. People have different views on what happiness is. Some believe that being wealthy means being happy. Others consider happiness as warmth in their home and health of their family.
6. The search for truth, meaning and purpose is something that all students have in common. They often ask some questions like, "Should excellence be without/with a soul?"
7. He found that in his case, those options were either too complex to plan or too limiting for users.

A Smart Word Player

Fill in the blanks with the proper words that need to be transformed from the ones provided in the brackets.

1. On an occasion of this kind, words are a poor (poverty) vehicle to express the sadness (sadly) we feel at the passing of Dr. Dickson, who was incredible (incredibly) to all of us. What he usually said to each of us is still clear, "I am very proud (pride) of you. You should have faith (faithful) in yourself too."
2. Japan's population is aging (age) more rapidly than any nation on earth. It is reported that

the retirement of a large number of people between 2007 and 2010 will give a great impact on Japan's economy. Unfortunately (fortunate), this problem has extended to the developing (development) countries too. The number of Chinese citizens aged (age) over 60 presently stands at 134 million, which is nearly half of all the people over 60 in Asia. The Chinese Government is now focusing on improving its insurance systems and trying to provide supplementary (supplement) fund to solve this problem.

A Skilled Text Weaver

Fill in the blanks with the words you have learned in this text. One word is for each blank. Here is a piece of advice: You must be really familiar with the text to accomplish the following tasks.

1. George found his wallet gone when he came back home. He walked back along the sidewalk, searched every corner, tried to spot his wallet, but the result went to no avail.
2. At work, he is a successful attorney general; at home, he is a kind and generous father.
3. He understands the meaning of poverty because his family couldn't even afford a good meal on the New Year's Eve when he was a child.
4. He dressed the same as other classmates—light-colored long-sleeved shirt and black pants. But the view on him was quite different only because he belonged to a different race.
5. The money he makes is far from enough to feed the family, not to mention to cover those unpaid bills.

A Sharp Interpreter

Please paraphrase the following sentences. Change the sentence structure if necessary.

1. My grandparents and my mother always made me feel I was the most important person in the world to them. Most children will make it if they have just one person who makes them feel that way. I had three.
   ❖ *Paraphrasing:*
   My grandparents and my mother always made me feel I was the most important person in the world to them. Most children will be successful in life if they have just one person who makes them feel that they are important. Luckily, I had three people within my family, all thinking I was the most important person to them.
2. During the Depression, when nobody had any money, he would invite boys to ride the ice truck with him just to get them off the street.

✤ *Paraphrasing:*

During the economic hard time, nobody had any money. But he would invite those boys to ride the ice truck for him. He did it for the purpose to keep the boys busy doing something.

3. Forty years later, he told me he still never walked by that stretch of sidewalk without trying to spot that dime.

   ✤ *Paraphrasing:*

   Forty years later, he told me whenever he walked by that section of the sidewalk, where his dime got lost, he would try to find that dime.

4. It's hard to convey to young people today the impact the Depression had on my parents' and grandparents' generation, but I grew up feeling it.

   ✤ *Paraphrasing:*

   It's hard to let today's young people understand the impact the Depression had on my parents' and grandparents' generation, but I did feel it while I was growing up.

5. It hurt, but my mother had been faithful to her father's Easter ritual.

   ✤ *Paraphrasing:*

   It hurt, but my mother would never make a change to her father's Easter ritual, which means that she insisted that I wear new clothes on Easter.

6. Though the South was completely segregated back then, some level of racial interaction was inevitable in small towns, just as it had always been in the rural South.

   ✤ *Paraphrasing:*

   Though the South was totally separated along racial lines at that time, a certain degree of communication between races was simply taking place naturally, especially in small towns.

7. However, it was rare to find an uneducated rural southerner without a racist bone in his body.

   ✤ *Paraphrasing:*

   Most uneducated rural southerners had racial prejudice against the black people.

📖 A Solid Sentence Constructer

Please make a sentence with each word or expression listed below.

1. in the care of

   ✤ **Original sentence in the text:**

   While Mother was in New Orleans, I was in the care of my grandparents.

   ✤ **Suggested sentence:**

   The stolen laptop was <u>in the care of</u> the police station.

2. on account

⊕ *Original sentence in the text:*

... *about her grandfather buying groceries from mine "on account"*...

⊕ **Suggested sentence:**

No food or drink will be served <u>on account</u> in restaurant.

3. occasionally

⊕ *Original sentence in the text:*

Occasionally, black kids would come into the store and we would play.

⊕ **Suggested sentence:**

Most stock analysts work overtime. He said he <u>occasionally</u> gets to leave work "early" —at 8 p.m.

4. segregation

⊕ *Original sentence in the text:*

It took me years to learn about segregation and prejudice and the meaning of poverty...

⊕ **Suggested sentence:**

The gap between the rich and the poor will finally lead to segregation.

5. to break down

⊕ *Original sentence in the text:*

... *when my grandfather came home from work and broke down and cried*...

⊕ **Suggested sentence:**

Twice he <u>broke down</u>, in hot but silent tears.

6. in common

⊕ *Original sentence in the text:*

...*whose views on race were among the few things she had in common with her husband.*

⊕ **Suggested sentence:**

In that respect, at least, China and India have something <u>in common</u>.

7. to deserve

⊕ *Original sentence in the text:*

She recalled that he had told her that good people who were doing the best they could deserved to be able to feed their families...

⊕ **Suggested sentence:**

Paralympic athletes <u>deserve</u> as much respect as the able-bodied.

8. to remind ... of ...

⊕ *Original sentence in the text:*

It got him out of the house and reminded him of the mill work he'd done as a young man around the time of my mother's birth.

⊕ **Suggested sentence:**

She refused to see the movie *Holocaust*, as she was so much afraid that it would remind her of the nightmare she had gone through when she was merely a teenager.

A Superb Bilingualist

Please translate the following sentences into English with the prompts provided in the brackets.

1. 父亲不仅白天在工厂做工,晚上还去史密斯先生的杂货店值夜班。他尽力给我和弟弟提供最好的生活条件。我为有这样的父亲而感到骄傲。(feel pride that ...)
   ⊕ *Suggested translation:*
   Father was not only working in the factory at daytime, but also serving as a watchman in Mr. Smith's grocery store at night, trying to offer the best to my brother and me. I felt pride that I had such a father.

2. 她很难说清楚童年对她今后的生活产生了怎样的影响。但她觉得她之所以要努力成为一名优秀的教师,是因为在她的同龄人中很少有人在小时候受到过系统的教育。(convey, impact, distinguished, rare)
   ⊕ *Suggested translation:*
   It's hard for her to convey how much impact her childhood had on her future life. She thinks that the reason she tries to be a distinguished teacher is that it is rare that people of her age received systematic education when they were young.

3. 不管我多么努力,都不能改变约翰对我的偏见。(no matter how, prejudice)
   ⊕ *Suggested translation:*
   No matter how hard I have tried, I cannot change John's prejudice against me.

4. 你要相信自己,不能被一次失败打垮。(believe in, break down)
   ⊕ *Suggested translation:*
   You should believe in yourself. You cannot break down just because of one-time failure.

5. 他在接受采访的时候说,他的成功有赖于老师的帮助和父母的关爱,他觉得自己非常幸运。(interview, fortunate)
   ⊕ *Suggested translation:*
   He said in an interview that he owed his success to his teachers' help and parents' love and care. He felt that he was fortunate.

Text B

Introduction to "Chicken Soup for the Soul"

"Chicken Soup for the Soul" is a series of books, featuring a collection of short, inspirational stories and motivational essays. The name "Chicken Soup" was chosen for this series because of the use of chicken soup as a home remedy for the sick. The 101 stories in the first book of the series were compiled by motivational speakers Jack Canfield and Mark Victor Hansen.

There have been numerous volumes of Chicken Soup issued. The first book sold over 2 million copies and launched the series. There are now over 100 million copies in print and in 54 languages world-wide. "The Chicken Soup for the Teenage Soul" series is one of the first series of non-fiction books which are still popular among the teens in many countries. The official website of Chicken Soup can be found at: http://www.chickensoup.com/.

What is "freeze tag"?

Tag is an informal playground game that usually involves three or more players attempting to "tag" other players by touching them with hand. At the beginning of the game, one player is designated "it." After "it" is chosen, the other players scatter. "It" must chase them down and tag them, usually by tapping them on the body. A tagged player becomes "it," and the former "it" joins the others in trying to avoid being tagged. This process repeats until the game ends.

Freeze tag (or frozen tag) varies from normal tag in that once a player is tagged, he does not become "it"; rather, he is "frozen" and must stand in place without moving while "it" continues to tag and "freeze" the other players. Whoever is the last to be tagged is the winner. Another variation is that "it" wins only if he or she is able to tag all the other players.

Comprehension Questions

After reading Text B, please answer the following questions with the words and expressions given in the brackets.

1. How often did grandfather come to our house every year? And when did he come to us? (once a year, the first frost)

   He came to our house once a year in autumn when the frost first played freeze tag with the grass.

2. What did grandfather do when he came to our house? (coal shovel, ice chest, backyard, dig)

   Grandfather would bring an old battered coal shovel and an old-fashioned ice chest with him. He hustled all six of us kids out to the backyard. Then, he started digging.

3. According to grandfather, what is the importance of the magic snow bank? (a good snowy winter, give, earth, seeds)

   He told us that if you wanted a good snowy winter, you always had to save a little snow from the winter before and put it into the magic snow bank. The snow balls in the ice chest were our seeds given to the earth.

4. What is the procedure of the digging? (dig, old ice chest, snowballs, hole, plant, seeds, bury)

   After we dug, we took snowballs from the old ice chest and put them into the hole. We would plant the seeds into the earth by burying our snowballs.

5. Can kids hold the snowballs for long or throw them? Why or why not? (hold ...for long, melt, selfish, offer)

   No. If we held it for a long time, it would melt, which meant we were selfish, having nothing to offer to the earth.

6. What is the magic of these snowballs? (unite, secret, contribute, harmonious relationships)

   The magic of grandfather's snowballs was to unite us closely with a secret that we had worked together to help the snow fall once again. The shared childhood secret contributes significantly to our further harmonious relationships.

Writing Practice

Put your answers to the above questions together and form a summary about Text B and share with your classmates the summary you have completed.

My grandfather came to our house once a year in autumn when the frost first played freeze tag with the grass. As he came to our house, he would bring an old battered coal shovel and an old-fashioned ice chest with him. He hustled all six of us kids out to the backyard. Then, he started digging. We dug the hole in turn as well. He told us that if you wanted a good snowy winter, you always had to save a little snow from the winter before and put it into the magic snow bank. The snowballs in the ice chest were our seeds given to the earth. After we dug, we took snowballs from the old ice chest and put them into the hole. We couldn't hold the snowball for long, because it would melt the snow, which meant we were selfish having nothing to offer to the earth. Every year when the first snow falls, it reminds me of my grandfather. The magic of grandfather's snowballs united us closely with a secret that we had worked together to help the snow fall once again. The shared childhood secret contributes significantly to our further harmonious relationships.

3

The Eyes of Tex

Unit Goals

After studying this unit, students should be able to:

☞ **learn to appreciate the support and love between animals;**

     Text A tells a story of love between two dogs. One was newly adopted Heinz, and the other was Tex who was progressively turning blind. While their owners were worrying that the adoption of Heinz might worsen the situation of Tex, a new partnership between the two dogs began to come into shape, with Heinz serving as a seeing-eye dog for Tex. The story is all about the support and love between animals, but it leaves much room for human contemplation.

☞ **know how to pronounce /ʌ/, /ɜː/ and /ə/, and how to utilize the words and structures that contribute significantly to the texts;**

     In this section, the instructor should explain to the students how to pronounce /ʌ/, /ɜː/ and /ə/. Instructors should be aware that the last two vowels can be rather confusing to many Chinese students, especially to those who decide to learn the American accent. It is strongly suggested that the instructor encourage students to read aloud tongue twisters before class and follow the advice provided in the section **Before Learning**.

☞ **accept the respect for life and compassion for all living things as a basic value.**

     Both **Text A** and **B** tell us that life deserves respect and compassion. It's easy to fall in love with an adorable puppy or kitten. But raising a pet means a commitment that could last up to 20 years! Pets require your time and money, and more importantly, your efforts in taking a good care of them. Raising a pet is a lot of responsibility, but also very rewarding. Learning to provide a pet with good caring may help you become a better person.

Before Reading

Hands-on Activities and Brainstorming

The instructor should allow 15—20 minutes for students to have a discussion on their experience with pets.

A Glimpse at Words and Expressions

A. To help the students make the right choice, the instructor should teach them to follow the clues: first, the article "a" indicates that "purebred" must be a noun; second, "pure" implies that it should be something that is not mixed. Then it won't be difficult to observe that Item No. 3 best meets those requirements among all the seven items listed under Column B.

B. This one is far from tough as most of the students know the meaning of "sense" as a noun. Noting that here "sense" is used as a verb can be very helpful to students. Here is another example: *He sensed that this might be his final opportunity to justify himself.*

C. Matching correctly for this sentence is not difficult, because No. 4 listed under Column B looks very similar to Sentence C. However, figuring out that "he" is the agent(施动者) for both "stayed ..." and "traveling..." is critical for students to fully comprehend what Sentence C means.

D. Students should know that the meaning of "make an appointment" goes beyond "making a formal arrangement." It means "to go to see a doctor."

E. "Dump" might be a new word, yet, it does not mean we are brought to a dead end without knowing the meaning of it. Here are some clues: first, "the little mixed-breed female" must refer to a dog, or cat perhaps; second, if a little puppy or kitten appears at the front gate of a family, it might be thrown away, or in another word discarded by somebody else.

F. This is an easy one, but knowing how to use "running full speed" is more important.

G. "Course" refers to direction, therefore, "to keep sb. on course" means "to make the dog be on the route or path." Without knowing what "course" means, the students will have to rely on the two clues "keep" and "besides," as well as combing the matches provided under Column B to get to the meaning of "course." Here is another example: *The faster you move, the more attention must be given to keep on course, for a slight deviation can lead to disaster.*

Keys

A-3   B-5   C-4   D-6   E-7   F-1   G-2

Text A

Suggested Explanations on Text A

1. ... the little mixed-breed female had been <u>dumped</u> at the Seals' front gate.

   ▶ dump (*v.*): to get rid of sth. that one does not want

   eg. 1) It is not right for her to keep dumping troubles on me.

   　　2) Automobiles dump too much poisonous gas into the air.

   ▲ dump (*v.*): (business) to get rid of goods by selling them at a very low price, often in another country

   eg. The goods arrived late, and could not catch the selling season. The owner of the goods had to dump (倾销) them.

2. It's hard to tell. From her color <u>markings (花纹)</u> and the way she holds her ears in a half lop, I'd say she's part German shepherd.

   ▶ marking (*n.*) (usually *pl.*): a pattern of colors on animals

   eg. 1) That violin was soon recognized by its unique color markings.

   　　2) He was amazed at Chihuahua's (吉娃娃) tri-color markings.

3. We can't just <u>turn her away</u>.

   ▶ to turn sb. away: to refuse sb.

   eg. 1) People came to me with confidence that they were coming to somebody who could help them. So I couldn't turn anyone away.

   　　2) The stadium was full, and many funs were turned away.

   　　3) I tried to adopt a kitten from the RSPCA (the Royal Society for the Prevention of Cruelty to Animals) but was turned away because I have a full time job and live on a main road.

4. Standing between them, the puppy seemed to <u>sense</u> that her fate was being decided.

   ▶ sense (*v.*): to become aware

   eg. 1) Sometimes you may not be able to tell what has happened—you sense it.

   　　2) It is said that wild animals have the ability to sense the impending tidal wave and run for higher ground before the waves strike.

   ▲ sense (*n.*): an understanding about sth.; an ability to judge sth.

   eg. 1) Tianjin is a city in which you easily lose your sense of direction.

   　　2) It will never be boring when talking to a person with a sense of humor.

△ senseless (*adj.*) (antonym): having no meaning or purpose

eg. It's senseless to recall the good old days. One's mind should be directed to what can be done in the future.

5. "Okay, if you want to <u>fool with her</u>, go ahead."

▶ to fool with sb.: to deceive or annoy sb. for one's own amusement

eg. 1) He often made promises, but usually he was only fooling with us.

2) He invented the car accident to fool with us.

6. Let's <u>get one thing straight</u>: We don't need a <u>Heinz-57</u> mongrel.

Meaning: We should make it clear that we do not need a mixed-breed dog that has blood from many breeds.

▶ to get sth. straight: to make sth. clear

eg. 1) I'm still trying to get everything straight in my head so that I can feel more confident coming to you guys with a proposal.

2) Reporters must get facts straight before writing reports.

▶ Heinz-57: of many kinds, varieties (Also see Note 1 in **Better Know More** in student's book)

7. We don't want Tex <u>exposed</u> to anything.

▶ exposed (*adj.*): not protected from attack

eg. Children cannot be sheltered all the time. At some point, they may be exposed to things that parents don't want them exposed to. If a parent has done a great job of sheltering a child, then that child, when exposed to the material, may react in a negative manner.

8. He has all the troubles he can <u>handle</u>.

Meaning: He won't be able to handle more troubles than he is having now.

(It is suggested that the instructor explain to students the implied negative meaning in this sentence, which is conveyed by the combined use of adjective "all" and modal verb "can." It means that the subject "he" has encountered all the troubles he is able to deal with, and therefore he won't be able to face more troubles.)

▶ handle (*v.*): to deal with or to cope with

eg. 1) The oil price is on the rise. It is not easy to handle the crisis within a short period of time.

2) To everybody's surprise, the giant panda soon learned how to handle feeding her twin babies at the same time.

△ handle (*n.*): the part of an object, such as a cup, a bag, or a tool that you use to hold it

eg. Hold the handle tight, and let go slowly the string of the kite.

9. But when they brought Tex to a specialist in Dallas, he <u>determined</u> that the dog's poor eye-sight was only partially due to cataracts.

Meaning: But when they brought Tex to a specialist in Dallas, he discovered that cataracts were not the only factor that led to the dog's loss of vision.

▶ determine (*v.*): to discover the facts about sth.; to calculate sth. exactly

eg. 1) Soon the detective determined that the criminal had killed the victims with the poison.

    2) Based on the weather forecasts, it was determined that it would be safer to set out a little earlier that day.

▲ determined (*adj.*): if one is determined to do sth., he has made a firm decision to do it and he will not let anyone prevent him

eg. 1) Apple was determined to integrate as much of its own technology into the new model as possible.

    2) The young man was determined to join either the military or the new moded police.

10. They explained that no medical or surgical <u>procedure</u> could have stopped or delayed Tex's <u>progressive</u> loss of <u>vision</u>.

▶ procedure (*n.*): a medical operation

eg. Abortion is not just a simple medical procedure. For many women, it is a life changing event with significant physical, emotional, and spiritual consequences.

▲ procedure (*n.*): a series of actions conducted in a certain order

eg. 1) The goal of having this policy is to ensure that faculty, staff, and students know what to do if harassment(骚扰) occurs, and will be able to follow the procedures outlined when a problem arises.

    2) I gave up the test drive(试驾) as I did not want to go through such a complicated application procedure.

▶ progressive (*adj.*): developing steadily

eg. 1) The aim of the team is to achieve the best quality of care for patients with progressive illness who require special psychological care.

    2) This chart clearly demonstrates the progressive demand for independent third-party auditing (独立第三方审计).

▶ vision (uncountable *n.*): the ability to see

eg. After operation, the old lady gained her vision again.

▲ vision (uncountable *n.*): the ability to think about or plan the future with great imagination and intelligence

eg. Paul is a leader of vision and a superb technologist.

11. As they talked on their way home, the Seals realized that over the last few months, they had watched Tex <u>cope with</u> his blindness.

Meaning: Only in the talk on their way home, did the Seals come to realize that they were actually seeing Tex struggling in his blindness during the past few months. / The Seals had actually already seen how Tex struggled in his blindness, but they did not know it until they found it out in the talk on their way home.

    这句话貌似平淡,但有两处需要特别注意:"realized"和"had watched";"realized"表示"意识到",意识到的内容则是"that they had watched...";既然是在几个月后意识到以前曾经看到过……,其中便有了"突然意识到"或"恍然大悟"的味道。

Translation: 在回家的路上,希尔斯夫妇谈着谈着(突然)意识到,原来泰克斯在过去的几个月里始终在黑暗中挣扎(和失明进行着抗争)。

▶ to cope with: to deal successfully with sth. difficult

eg. 1) The "Heartfelt Laughing Club," set up by the university's psychological consultancy center, helps students cope with the stresses and strains of everyday life.

    2) Everyone in the department has to cope with this incompetent boss.

12. If he <u>wandered off</u>, he <u>quartered</u> back and forth until he was on the gravel again.

▶ to wander off: to move away from the place where one ought to be

eg. 1) Police are searching for a 3-year-old who wandered off from his home yesterday.

    2) In 1990s, seven travelers lost their way between these oases (绿洲) and wandered off into the desert, never to return.

▶ quarter (v.): to cover an area of ground by ranging over it from side to side

eg. 1) He quartered around the tree and picked up on the scent of the running deer and trailed it nearly 80 yards back into the forest.

    2) He quartered in the old abbey (修道院), wondering how monks of the old days willingly shut themselves within the walls.

13. Without any training or <u>coaching</u>, Heinz had become Tex's "seeing eye" dog.

▶ coaching (n.): the process of teaching sb. in a particular subject

eg. 1) Peer coaching is a process during which two teachers attend each other's courses and later discuss what they saw and help each other solve problems.

    2) Reading quickly and with ease is a very important ability that requires a lot of coaching and practice.

14. Each evening when the dogs <u>settled in</u> for the night, Heinz gently took Tex's nose in her mouth and led him into his house.

▶ to settle in: to move into a home, job, etc. and start to feel comfortable there

eg. 1) Her mother accompanied her to be sure that she was properly settled in the apartment of a quiet family.

2) Later in September, the family settled in a small village in central France south of Paris that consisted largely of French farmers and refugees.

15. In the morning, she got him up and <u>guided him out of</u> the house again.

▶ to guide sb. out of sth.: to direct or influence sb. from sth.

eg. 1) Stuck in the fire, Sinclair had no clue where to go or what to do, until he heard a man yell: "If you can hear me, head toward my voice." "He kept saying that over and over," Sinclair said. "And that is what guided us out of the smoke and fire."

2) Reading this book is like finding a tool to guide you out of isolation and into rich, rewarding lives.

16. Heinz <u>placed</u> herself between Tex and the wire.

▶ place (*v.*): to put sth. in a particular area, especially when doing so carefully or deliberately

eg. 1) Of course I would place my family in the first place.

2) Do not place leftovers into plastic storage containers until they have cooled.

17. "On sunny days, Tex sleeps <u>stretched out</u> on the driveway asphalt," says Jeffrey.

▶ to stretch out: to put one's arms or legs out straight and tighten the muscles

eg. 1) Google Earth has been accused of violating privacy rights as it places the pictures on the Internet of people lying stretched out on their roofs, sunbathing.

2) Every time I go through the TV room, he's in there, stretched out across the couch, watching whatever is on.

▲ to stretch out: to lie down, usually in order to relax or sleep

eg. 1) He stretched out comfortably to the fullest and dozed away.

2) She stretched out on the picnic blanket and closed her eyes.

▲ to stretch out: to put out an arm or a leg in order to reach sth.

eg. 1) He stretched out his arm to silence the people cheering below.

2) He stretched out his arms to give her a hug.

18. Any number of times we've seen Heinz <u>push</u> Tex <u>aside</u> to get him out of the horses' way.

▶ to push sb./sth. aside: to move sb./sth. quickly away

eg. 1) The man pushed her aside and made his way inside.

2) He returned to the window and pushed the curtain aside.

▲ to push sth. aside: to avoid thinking about sth.

eg. 1) Months went by and I pushed the idea aside.

2) In my view, they have just pushed the issue aside all of these years. Problems remain unattended.

19. The Seals were <u>awed</u>.

▶ awe (*v.*): to fill sb. with the feelings of respect

eg. 1) We made our way towards the Great Wall and were awed by the beauty of the greens-covered mountains around us.

    2) The audience were awed by Heifetz's breathtaking musical ability. (Heifetz: 1901—1987, renowned Lithuanian born American violinist.)

▲ awe (*n.*): feelings of respect and slight fear; feelings of being very impressed by sth./sb.

eg. 1) People speak of Beethoven with awe.

    2) While she was in awe of her grandfather, she adores her grandmother.

▲ awesome (*adj.*): [AmE, Informal] very good, enjoyable

eg. 1) The program is awesome in terms of its user—friendly interface and multiple purposes, but the server is obviously too slow to run the program smoothly.

    2) The awesome beauty of the painting *The Birth of Venus* always has the audience ignore that the love goddess has an improbably long neck, and her left shoulder slopes at an impossible angle. (*The Birth of Venus*, oil painting by Italian painter Sandro Botticelli: 1444—1510)

20. Without any training, the young dog had <u>devised</u> whatever means were necessary to help, guide and protect her blind companion.

Meaning: Without any training, the young dog had invented all possible ways that were necessary to help, guide and protect her blind friend.

Without ..., the young dog had devised <u>whatever</u> <u>means</u> <u>were</u> <u>necessary</u> to help, guide and...

关系代词 从句主语 系词 从句表语　　从句状语

状语　　主语　　谓语　　　　　宾语从句

▶ devise (*v.*): to invent a new way of doing sth.

eg. 1) "Nothing has been devised yet that is fully reliable," said John Thompson, general manager of Automobile Designing Company.

    2) The team devised an effective low-cost data-gathering technique.

Better Know More

Dog stories were originally written primarily for children, but in the last 200 years, dog literature has developed for adults, captivating readers with its portrayal of the dog's unique features. Courage, fidelity, love, and devotion are the hallmarks of 20th-century dog literature. Jack London wrote vivid accounts of the courageous endeavors of dogs. If one didn't know

Buck in Jack London's *Call of the Wild* was a dog, his heroic action would have made him human. At the end, even a dog can forgive and forget. This is more than some humans can do, or try to do. Capping his career as the most profound of social commentators, the novelist John Steinbeck, in *Travels with Charley*, circumnavigated(环游) the continental United States, accompanied by his dog and confidant(密友). "Of course his horizons are limited," said Steinbeck, "but how wide are mine?"

Check Your Understanding

Translate the following sentences into Chinese. Please make sure that your language flows smoothly.

1. "We can't just turn her away," Jeffrey pleaded.
   杰弗瑞恳求地说："我们不能置之不理呀。"

2. Okay, if you want to fool with her, go ahead.
   好吧，如果你非要摆弄她，随便吧。

3. We don't want Tex exposed to anything.
   我们不想让泰克斯受到任何伤害。

4. Not long before Heinz showed up, the Seals had noticed that Tex appeared to be losing his eyesight.
   海因茨没来之前，希尔斯一家已经注意到泰克斯的视力好像越来越差了。

5. As they talked on their way home, the Seals realized that over the last few months, they had watched Tex cope with his blindness.
   在回家的路上，希尔斯夫妇谈着谈着（突然）意识到，原来泰克斯在过去的几个月里始终在黑暗中挣扎。

6. And why he usually stayed on the gravel walkways travelling to and from the house.
   这就是为什么泰克斯从家里进进出出时，总是要走那条鹅卵石子铺的路。

7. Each evening when the dogs settled in for the night, Heinz gently took Tex's nose in her mouth and led him into his house.
   每天晚上要回窝睡觉时，海因茨（总是）轻轻地用嘴叼着泰克斯的鼻子，领它回窝。

8. In the morning, she got him up and guided him out of the house again.
   早晨，海因茨叫起泰克斯，然后把它领出窝。

9. Without any training, the young dog had devised whatever means were necessary to help, guide and protect her blind companion.
   没有经过任何训练，这只小狗想出了种种办法，帮助、引导、保护自己失明的同伴。

Answer the following questions based on the text you have just learned.

1. What were the reasons that Eric Seal didn't want to have another dog?

   He didn't think they were in need of another dog. Even if they needed one, they should get a purebred instead of a mixed-breed.

2. What attitudes did Tex hold to the new comer—Heinz?

   Tex was very friendly to the new comer. Although he already shared his doghouse with a yellow cat, Tex happily moved over and made room for Heinz.

3. How did the Seals realize that Tex had been blind?

   The Seals had noticed that Tex appeared to be losing his eyesight. He sometimes missed a gate opening or bumped his nose on the chain link fence. And he usually stayed on the gravel walkways traveling to and from the house. If he wandered off, he quartered back and forth until he was on the gravel again.

4. Why did the Seals build another doghouse?

   Because it was soon obvious that the little German shepherd crossbreed would be a large dog—too large to continue sharing a doghouse with Tex and the yellow cat.

5. What was the purpose of Heinz's pushing and dragging at Tex while they were playing?

   The purpose of Heinz's pushing and dragging at Tex was to give him guidance since Tex had lost his vision.

6. In what way did Heinz guide Tex into his house?

   Heinz gently took Tex's nose in her mouth and led him into his house.

7. Give your reasons to explain why the Seals were awed by the dog.

   Without any training, the young dog had devised whatever means were necessary to help, guide and protect her blind companion. It was clear that Heinz shared more than her eyes with Tex; she shared her heart.

8. What does the story teach us?

   This is an open question.

A Sip of Phonetics

本课涉及三个中元音 /ʌ/, /ɜː/, /ə/。/ɔ/ 为中元音、短元音。教师应注意学生发 /ɔ/ 音时，不要与 /ɑː/ 混淆。/ʌ/ 的口型没有 /ɑː/ 的大，也没它发音时间长。教师还可以带领学生练习下列发音，以便对比两个音的区别。

cut   cart   hut   hard   bucket   basket

/ə/ 为中元音、短元音。发音时牙床开得比发 /əː/ 时稍大。/ɜ/ 是英语元音中舌高点活动范围最大的一个。/əː/ 经常出现在非重读音节。教师还可以带领学生练习下列发音，以便对比两个音的区别。

better   international   other   river   poverty   power

/ɜː/ 为中元音、长元音。发音时牙床开得较窄，唇形扁平。/ɜː/ 不仅要拉长 /ə/ 的音，而且开口要大于 /ə/ 的音。美式英语在 /ɜː/ 后加 /r/ 音，即 /ɜr/。/ə/ 经常出现在重读音节。教师还可以带领学生练习下列发音：

dirty　　alert　　person　　over　　beer　　merge　　term

在教授这部分内容时，教师应该要求学生准确掌握中元音的发音音位，除了做到正确发音外，应教会学生识别这些字母或字母组合的发音规律，强化学生学习词汇的能力。教师应在课堂上领读示范，并及时纠正学生的一些错误发音。

同时，教师还可以利用这些绕口令，强化这三个元音的练习。教师应指导学生如何换气和断句、领悟句意，以便达到读得又快又准的效果。

Train Your Tongue

1. A skunk sat on a stump/ and thunk the stump stunk/, but the stump thunk the skunk stunk.
2. Elizabeth's birthday/ is on the third Thursday of this month.
3. Tommy Tucker tried to tie/ Tammy's Turtles tie.

You'd Like to Be

A Strong Bridge Builder

Fill in the blanks with the given words to complete the following sentences.   Please note that some can be used more than once.

off　　with　　away　　aside　　to　　up

This winter has been strange; the temperature rises and falls dramatically. It is hard to cope with.   Mother Nature in this sense makes the anticipation of the actual springtime even that much more difficult.   And then there are snows that are not quite storms but enough to make travel difficult. It is expected that someone clean the snow up.

It was on one of those snowy days that I had to go out shopping, because there was nothing to eat. Some people showed up on the street, walking cautiously. It looked as though I was walking with a white sheet wrapped around me.   I was mentally guiding myself to the supermarket. Snow was completely covering any sign of a road. I wandered off the road for quite a while. I had to take a bus rather than walk/drive there, but I was turned away by four passing buses which were full of passengers. Afraid of being pushed aside, I made my way to the front of the group of men who were also waiting for the fifth bus.

A Smart Word Player

Fill in the blanks with the proper words that need to be transformed from the ones provided in the brackets.

Yesterday, 13-year-old Sara had once again run away from home. She went to see Miss Smith, the head-teacher, to seek <u>comfort</u> (comfortable). Sara had cataracts that had to be <u>surgically</u> (surgery) removed as soon as possible. After a few minutes' talk, Miss Smith sensed that her student was <u>progressively</u> (progressive) becoming detached from her parents due to possible family violence. Sara was very <u>cautious</u> (cautiously) about being around with her parents. Meanwhile, Miss Smith felt that she simply could not turn her away and have the girl <u>handle</u> (handling) all the troubles herself. She decided to talk to the social security people concerning Sara's case.

A Skilled Text Weaver

Fill in the blanks with the words you have learned in this text. One word is for each blank. Here is a piece of advice: You must be really familiar with the text to accomplish the following tasks.

1. Some years ago, mixed <u>breed</u> puppies were advertised by owners as "free to a good home." Then when the public became more aware of proper <u>veterinary</u> procedures for dogs, ads offered those puppies for $50 or so, which would supposedly cover the cost of a pup's first shots and vet check. But now, you'll find similar ad offerings for $100—200, with owners seeking to make a profit. Some people are now deliberately <u>mixing</u> breeds and selling them at even higher prices as new "breeds." Purebred lovers tell us this with a laugh, and sometimes with a helpless <u>shrug</u>.

2. Helen's <u>fate</u> was decided <u>due</u> <u>to</u> the <u>delay</u> of treatment, all because her husband <u>missed</u> the phone call she <u>devised</u> to make when she was still clear.

A Sharp Interpreter

Please paraphrase the following sentences. Change the sentence structure if necessary.

1. We don't need a Heinz-57 mongrel.
   ✜ *Paraphrasing:*
   We don't want to have a mixed breed dog.

2. Tex, the six-year-old cattle dog the Seals had raised from a puppy, was unusually friendly for a blue-heeler, a breed established by ranchers in Australia.

✣ *Paraphrasing:*

The six-year-old herding dog Tex had been raised by the Seals since very young. Tex was particularly mild, and that is uncommon among other blue-heelers, a breed created by Australian farmers.

3. So, although he already shared his doghouse with a yellow cat, soon Tex happily moved over and made room for the new puppy the Seals called Heinz.

✣ *Paraphrasing:*

Tex happily moved over to allow the new comer, a young dog named by the Seals as Heinz, to come to live in the doghouse, which he had already shared with a yellow cat.

4. They explained that no medical or surgical procedure could have stopped or delayed Tex's progressive loss of vision.

✣ *Paraphrasing:*

The doctors told the Seals that Tex's eyesight kept worsening, and no medicine or operation could prevent that.

5. If he wandered off, he quartered back and forth until he was on the gravel again.

✣ *Paraphrasing:*

When Tex moved away from the gravel walkways, he would try hard to measure the path back and forth until he returned to it.

6. It was soon obvious that the little German shepherd crossbreed would be a large dog—too large to continue sharing a doghouse with Tex and the yellow cat.

✣ *Paraphrasing:*

Not long after, the Seals found Heinz, the mix-breed German shepherd, would be a very large dog. The doghouse shared by Heinz, Tex and the yellow cat would be too small for them to live together.

7. It was then they recognized that what they had believed was puppy playfulness—Heinz's pushing and dragging at Tex while playing with him—actually had a purpose.

✣ *Paraphrasing:*

At that moment they came to realize that they had misunderstood Heinz's pushing and dragging at Tex as puppy playfulness. In fact, Heinz had a good purpose to do that.

8. When the two dogs approached a gate, Heinz used her shoulder to guide Tex through.

✣ *Paraphrasing:*

When Heinz and Tex came to the gate, Heinz would use her shoulder to lead Tex to go through the gate.

A Solid Sentence Constructer

Please make a sentence with each word or expression listed below.

1. to turn sb. away

   ✤ *Original sentence in the text:*

   "We can't just turn her away," Jeffrey pleaded.

   ✤ **Suggested sentence:**

   The high price of a house turned away many prospective buyers.

2. to fool with

   ✤ *Original sentence in the text:*

   "Okay, if you want to fool with her, go ahead. But let's get one thing straight: We don't need a Heinz-57 mongrel. "

   ✤ **Suggested sentence:**

   It was found later that these video recordings were faked to fool with UFO fans.

3. exposed to

   ✤ *Original sentence in the text:*

   "Let's wait a few days to put her in the pen with Tex. We don't want Tex exposed to anything. He has all the troubles he can handle."

   ✤ **Suggested sentence:**

   As a conductor, he wants his students to be exposed to as much classical music as possible.

4. to show up

   ✤ *Original sentence in the text:*

   Not long before Heinz showed up, the Seals had noticed that Tex appeared to be losing his eyesight.

   ✤ **Suggested sentence:**

   Rain bow will show up after heavy rain.

5. to cope with

   ✤ *Original sentence in the text:*

   As they talked on their way home, the Seals realized that over the last few months, they had watched Tex cope with his blindness.

   ✤ **Suggested sentence:**

   Parents should help children cope with difficulties and crises.

6. to and from

   ✤ *Original sentence in the text:*

   And why he usually stayed on the gravel walkways traveling to and from the house.

✧ **Suggested sentence:**

Trains are an efficient, environmentally friendly way of travelling to and from Tibet.

7. to settle in

✧ *Original sentence in the text:*

Each evening when the dogs settled in for the night, Heinz gently took Tex's nose in her mouth and led him into his house.

✧ **Suggested sentence:**

The film had already started before we settled in.

8. companion

✧ *Original sentence in the text:*

Without any training, the young dog had devised whatever means were necessary to help, guide and protect her blind companion.

✧ **Suggested sentence:**

Bluetooth is a good companion to this laptop.

9. to guide sb. out of ...

✧ *Original sentence in the text:*

In the morning, she got him up and guided him out of the house again.

✧ **Suggested sentence:**

The ranger guided us out of danger when we lost ourselves in Tasmania.

📖 A Superb Bilingualist

Please translate the following sentences into English with the prompts provided in the brackets.

1. 说不清我们面对的是现实还是梦境。(hard to tell)

✧ *Suggested translation:*

It's hard to tell what we confronted with was a reality or a dream.

2. 我决定用音乐来表现他是如何自力更生克服困难的。(decide, handle trouble)

✧ *Suggested translation:*

I decided to tell the story by music, about how he handled all the troubles on his own.

3. 我们得把这事弄明白,你当时到底知不知道他在哪儿? (get ... straight)

✧ *Suggested translation:*

Let's get this straight—Did you know or not where he was at that time?

4. 人们常常看见,早上妻子挽着盲人丈夫的手臂,带他穿过繁忙的街道。在人们的眼里,夫妻二人是同甘共苦的好典型。(blind, guide, share)

✧ *Suggested translation:*

Quite often in the morning, people saw the wife take her blind husband's arm and guide him across the busy road. They were regarded as a model couple who share roses and thorns.

5. 别问我这匹马是什么品种, 它简直就是个大杂烩。(a Heinz-57)

　◈ *Suggested translation:*

Don't ask me the breed of the horse. It/he/she is simply a Heinz-57.

Text B

Introduction of the Text

Text B tells us to be aware of dog bites.　It is reported that in the United States some 4.7 million people were bitten by dogs in one year,　and in most cases,　they were bitten by their own dogs. We don't deny that dogs are our friends, but some caution should be taken against the possible threat they pose to us.

Tips on Treating a Dog Bite

Minor bites can be treated at home. To stop wound bleeding, press a clean, dry cloth or sterile gauze against the wound. Determine how serious the wound is. Wash the wound clean with the mild soap and running water beforehand. Remove bits of dirt or other foreign matter. Wash the wound for several minutes, pat the wound dry with a clean cloth and apply antibiotic ointment.　If you haven't had a tetanus　(破伤风)shot in the past five years,　you need to get one, as quickly as possible. During the first 24 to 48 hours after the bite, watch the wound persistently. If it gets worse, you should visit the emergency immediately.

Comprehension Questions

After reading Text B,　please answer the following questions with the words and expressions given in the brackets.

1. What information was released in the 1994 survey conducted by CDC? (medical treatment, bites)

According to a 1994 survey conducted by CDC in Atlanta, some 4.7 million people were bitten by dogs.　About 800,000 required medical treatment.　Many bites are to children, and most are from family pets or familiar dogs, not strays.

2. How much did the Insurance Information Institute and Homeowner-liability pay for dog-bite-related medical treatment respectively? (claim, cost)

The Insurance Information Institute says that dog-bite-related medical treatment costs $1 billion a year. Homeowner-liability claims paid about $250 million of that in 1996.

3. Why did the author suggest you choose mixed breeds? (one-person or one-family dog, loyal-to-one-person dog, biter)

The purebred puppy will grow up to be an aloof, one-person or one-family dog. It's the way the dog is supposed to be. So if you want a dog every one could love, don't choose a loyal-to-one-person dog; he could become a biter. You are recommended to adopt a mixed breed because it often gets the best of both parents.

4. What is the next important step after a family has adopted a dog? (commitment to, under control)

The next step is to provide the dog with a continuing commitment to training from the start. This means finding time for walks, play and obedience classes, and keeping faithfully to the owner.

5. Why is it necessary for people to have pet dogs exposed to new people? (aggressive behavior, protect territory)

If dogs lack socialization, they behave aggressively and may bite from fear or from an instinct to protect their territory when exposed to new people.

6. According to Dr. Sinclair, who often ends up getting bitten? (forget, precautions, stunts, blow)

According to Dr. Sinclair, people who think they are "good with dogs" often end up getting bitten. That's because they forget to take the proper precautions with dogs they don't know.

7. What are the unacceptable behaviors for dogs? (growling, biting, refusing, snapping, aggression)

It's not all right to let a dog get away with growling over food or possessions, biting out of fear, refusing to be controlled around other dogs, snapping. These behaviors are unacceptable for dogs who are family pets.

Writing Practice

Put your answers to the above questions together and form a summary about the text and share with your classmates the summary you have completed.

According to a 1994 survey conducted by CDC in Atlanta, some 4.7 million people were bitten by dogs. Many bites are to children, and most are from family pets or familiar dogs. The Insurance Information Institute says that dog-bite-related medical treatment costs $1 billion a year. So if you want a dog every one could love, don't choose a loyal-to-one-person dog which could become a biter. You are recommended to adopt a mixed breed because it often gets the best of both parents. After the adoption, the next step is to provide the dog with a continuing commitment to training from the start and make sure the dog has sufficient socialization. If dogs lack socialization, they behave aggressively and may bite from fear or from an instinct to protect their territory when exposed to new people. Growling over food or possessions, biting out of fear, refusing to be controlled around other dogs, snapping are unacceptable for dogs who are family pets.

Unit 4

Ancient Myths

Unit Goals

After studying this unit, students should be able to:

☞ **understand the interpretation of the origin of humans from western perspectives;**

The Greek Myths offers us a window into the distant past, a view of a world that existed in the hearts of the humble and long suffering natives of ancient Greece. In **Text A**, students will be exposed to the Greek interpretation of the origin of humans, while **Text B** provides us with a biblical one. Before moving into the texts, the instructor should walk the students through **A Glimpse at Words and Expressions**, which will help warm up the students. Students' preview of both **Text A** and **Text B** should be strongly encouraged.

☞ **know how to pronounce /eɪ/, /əʊ/, /aɪ/, /aʊ/ and /ɔɪ/, and how to utilize the words and structures that contribute significantly to the text;**

In this section, the instructor should explain to the students how to pronounce /eɪ/, /əʊ/, /aɪ/, /aʊ/ and /ɔɪ/, some of which can be very confusing to Chinese students, such as /eɪ/ and /aɪ/, and /əʊ/ and /aʊ/. Contrasts and comparisons will be especially effective in teaching. The instructor may refer to the advice provided in the section **A Sip of Phonetics**. Most useful words and structures of **Text A** can be found in **You'd Like to Be**. This is where students practice what they have learned from **Text A**.

☞ **be familiar with some important figures in Greek Mythology and the story of Adam and Eve in the *Bible*.**

Prometheus is famous for a couple of stories: the gift of fire to mankind and the chaining to a rock where an eagle ate his liver daily. **Text A** explains to us why Prometheus was called the benefactor of mankind. By learning **Text A**, students should also become familiar with the figures such as Zeus, Pandora, Aphrodite, and Athena. Each of them has their own unique legends that form an indispensable component of Greek Mythology.

Adam and Eve give us a different story in **Text B**. That can be a good start for students to learn about the *Bible*, a portal to the understanding of western culture. It is strongly suggested that the instructor should organize the students to either perform the play "Prometheus and Pandora" or develop the story of Adam and Eve into a drama, and then perform it.

Before Reading

Hands-on Activities and Brainstorming

The instructor should allow 15—20 minutes for students to do presentation on Greek Mythology.

A Glimpse at Words and Expressions

A. The instructor should help students notice the use of "only to." Usually, the meaning of the things appearing before and after "only to" should be in opposition. In another word, "only to do sth." indicates a surprise ending. Here is another example: He spent ages negotiating for a pay increase, only to resign from his job soon after he'd received it.

B. To help students understand a word in a sentence, the instructor should teach them how to figure out the clue in the sentence that may lead to the meaning. In this sentence "the unfortunate result" indicates that it must be something bad, which is exactly the case that "all living creatures on earth had been destroyed."

C. The case of "fashion" is different from the above two cases. Students can be familiar with the word "fashion," standing for the prevailing style, for example, the garment style, but in Text A it adopts a wholly different meaning, in form of transitive verb, which means "to make sth. by using your hands." For example: He fashioned a hat for himself from/out of newspaper.

D. "Restore" means "to establish sth. again or to bring back into sth. that has been absent for a period of time." For example: Some people are in favor of restoring capital punishment for murderers.

restore = re (again) + store (to establish, or to erect) = reestablish

E. Careful students may find that the idiom "not only...but also..." offers a clue, implying that the two things (or characteristics) appearing respectively after "not only" and "but also" should be of the same nature, with the latter one being even stronger than the former one. Therefore, the fire on one hand brings mankind warmth, and on the other the safety.

F. The instructor should help students understand that "displease" is a verb and it is opposite in meaning of "please." It means "to cause someone to be annoyed or unhappy." For example: I wouldn't want to do anything to displease him.

G. "Enchant" means "to charm or please someone greatly." For example: The audience was clearly enchanted by her performance.

Keys

A-6   B-4   C-1   D-7   E-2   F-5   G-3

Text A

Introduction of Greek Mythology

Greek Mythology is a set of mythological stories created by the ancient Greeks, concerning the origins of the world and the lives and adventures of a large number of gods, goddesses, heroes, heroines, and other mythological creatures.

Greek Mythology has exerted extensive influence on the development of Western culture, the arts and the literature and remains part of Western heritage and language. Poets and artists from ancient times to the present have derived inspiration from Greek Mythology and they keep discovering the contemporary significance and relevance in classical mythological themes.

Suggested Explanations on Text A

1. Titan brothers Prometheus and Epimetheus remained loyal to Zeus, who chose to reward them by having them repopulate the earth.

   ► loyal (*adj.*): faithful to person or cause

   eg. 1) Jack has been a loyal worker in this company for almost 50 years.

   2) When all her other friends deserted her, Steve remained loyal.

   ▲ loyalty (*n.*): the quality of being loyal

   eg. Her loyalty to the cause is impressive.

   ► reward (*v.*): to give sth. to sb. because they have done sth. good

   eg. 1) The company rewarded him for his years of service with a grand farewell party and several presents.

   2) All his hard work was rewarded when he saw his book in print.

   ▲ rewarding (*adj.*): giving a reward, especially by making sb. feel satisfied that he has done sth. important or useful, or done sth. well eg. 1) Is this a rewarding job?

    2) This is a rewarding business venture.

▶ repopulate (*v.*): to provide with inhabitants

eg. 1) The government has promised to repopulate the whole island, however there is still no news when the new houses are going to be reconstructed.

    2) The government decided to repopulate the island with political dissidents.

2. Prometheus took great care in <u>fashioning</u> the <u>mortals</u>, <u>longing</u> to give them comfort and <u>sustenance</u>.

Meaning: Prometheus carefully created humans by hand and wanted to provide them with comfort and food.

▶ fashion (*v.*): to make/shape sth. with one's hands or only a few tools

eg. 1) He fashioned a hat for himself from/out of newspaper.

    2) The boy fashioned a box from a few old pieces of wood.

▶ mortal (*n.*): a human being, especially an ordinary person with little power or influence

eg. 1) Prometheus stole fire from Zeus and gave it to the primitive mortals on the earth.

    2) We are mortals and have beginnings and ends.

▲ mortal (*adj.*): that cannot live for ever and must die

eg. 1) We are all mortal.

    2) Despite his great wisdom, he is still mortal.

▶ long (*v.*): to want to do sth.

eg. 1) We all long to see him again.

    2) I am longing for news of her.

▶ sustenance (*n.*): the food and drink that people, animals and plants need to live and stay healthy

eg. 1) During this freezing weather, the food put out by householders is the only form of sustenance that the birds have.

    2) The children were thin and badly in need of sustenance.

▲ sustain (*n.*): to make it possible for someone to stay strong or hopeful

eg. 1) A good breakfast will sustain you all morning.

    2) They were sustained by the knowledge that help would come soon.

3. After cheating Zeus, Prometheus was sentenced to continued punishment, <u>only to</u> be <u>rescued</u> by Heracles...

▶ only to: to indicate a surprise ending

eg. 1) I went all the way to his home only to find him out at a meeting.

    2) He lifted the stone only to drop it on his own feet.

▶ rescue (*v.*): to help sb. or sth. out of a dangerous, harmful or unpleasant situation

eg. 1) The lifeboat rescued the sailors from the sinking boat.

2) The government has refused to rescue the company from bankruptcy.

4. <u>Woven</u> into this story is that of Pandora...

▶ weave (*v.*): to make sth. by twisting pieces of sth. together

eg. 1) The biography is woven from many people's accounts of her life story.

2) Fir branches were woven together to make garlands.

5. In this story, Pandora brings along a jug, refusing to <u>heed</u> Zeus's warning to leave it closed.

Meaning: In this story, Pandora brings with her a jug and refuses to listen to Zeus's warning that she should keep the jug closed and not open it.

▶ heed (*v.*): (formal) to pay attention to sth., especially advice or a warning

eg. 1) If only she had heeded my warnings, none of this would have happened.

2) The airline has been criticized for failing to heed advice/warnings about lack of safety routines.

▲ heed (formal *n.*): close attention, notice

eg. 1) The company took no heed of public opposition to the plans.

2) Tom paid no heed to his father's warning.

▲ heedless (*adj.*): not giving attention to sth.

eg. 1) Heedless destruction of the rainforests is contributing to global warming.

2) They walked deep into the forest heedless of the coming danger.

6. During the <u>medieval</u> period, the jug was translated as a box...

▶ medieval (*adj.*): connected with the Middle Ages (the period in European history between antiquity and the Renaissance, often dated from A.D. 476 to 1453)

7. The gods kept starting wars, with the unfortunate result that all living creatures on Earth had <u>perished</u>.

▶ perish (*v.*): to die, especially in an accident or by being killed, or to be destroyed

eg. 1) Three hundred people perished in the earthquake.

2) He believes that the European countries must form closer ties within themselves, or Europe will perish.

8. Zeus decided <u>it was time to restore</u> earth to its former <u>splendor</u>.

Meaning: Zeus decided it was time to bring back earth to its original magnificence.

▶ it is time to do sth. (sentence pattern): used when sb. should do sth., or when sth. is expected to happen eg. 1) Come on kids, it's time to go home.

2) It's time to make preparations before guests arrive.

▲ it's time sb. did sth. / was doing sth. (sentence pattern): used in saying that sth. should be done very soon, in fact it should have happened earlier

eg. 1) It is about 11 now, well past the time when you usually go to bed at 9. It is time you went to bed.

2) It's time you sold that old car.

► restore (v.): to bring back to or put back into a former or original state

eg. 1) The badly neglected paintings have all been carefully restored.

2) After a week in bed, she was fully restored to health.

3) The government is trying to restore public confidence in its management of the economy.

▲ restoration (n.): an act of restoring

eg. 1) The first task following the disaster was the restoration of clean water supplies.

2) Restoration work on the old building is now complete.

► splendor (n.): great beauty which attracts admiration and attention

eg. 1) They bought an old garden and restored it to its original splendor.

2) The tourists are greatly impressed by the splendor of the Cathedral.

▲ splendid (adj.): very impressive, beautiful

eg. 1) The building stands in splendid isolation, surrounded by a large piece of grassland.

2) She delivered a splendid lecture at Peking University.

9. As you work, you can give each creature gifts to make it swift, strong, or whatever you see fit to bestow.

Meaning: When you create humans and animals, you can give each of them special talents to make them move quickly, have strong bodies or give them whatever talent you consider appropriate.

► see/think fit: to consider an action or decision to be correct for the situation

eg. 1) Spend the money as you see fit.

2) You are encouraged to try whatever means you see fit.

3) Just do whatever you think fit—I'm sure you'll make the right decision.

10. The brothers journeyed to earth and began to create many creatures.

► journey (literary v.): to travel especially a long distance

eg. 1) As we journeyed north, the landscape became drier and rockier.

2) They journeyed for seven long months.

▲ journey (n.): an act of traveling from one place to another, especially when they are far apart eg. 1) The Russian space station was the most visited place in space with more than 70 astronauts from many countries making the jouney from earth to orbit (轨道).

2) *Journey to the West* is a historic Chinese novel that is considered one of the four classics from the Ming Dynasty.

11. Prometheus was so slow that Epimetheus <u>used up</u> all the good gifts on the animals he created.

▶ use up: to finish a supply of sth.

eg. 1) Don't use up all the milk; we need some for breakfast.

2) The earth's resources are being used up at an alarming rate.

12. Prometheus <u>sneaked</u> up to Olympus, stole an <u>ember</u> from the fire there, and gave it to man, warning them to never let it <u>die out</u>.

▶ sneak (*v.*): to go somewhere secretly

eg. 1) I managed to sneak in through the back door while she wasn't looking.

2) I thought I'd sneak up on him and give him a surprise.

▶ ember (*n.*): a piece of wood or coal that is not burning but is still red and hot after a fire has died

eg. We sat by the glowing/dying embers of the fire.

▶ die out: to become less common and finally stop existing

eg. 1) Dinosaurs died out millions of years ago.

2) It's a custom which is beginning to die out.

13. The fire not only kept mankind warm, but also <u>kept the beasts at bay</u>.

Meaning: The fire not only kept mankind warm, but also kept animals away from harming mankind.

▶ keep ... at bay: to prevent sb. or sth. unpleasant from harming you

eg. 1) Exercise can keep cold at bay.

2) Mary bit her lip to keep the tears at bay.

14. The smell of roasting meat drifted to the heavens, <u>alerting</u> Zeus to Prometheus's <u>betrayal</u>.

Meaning: The smell of roasting meat moved slowly to the heavens, making Zeus aware of the fact that Prometheus had betrayed him.

▶ alert (*v.*): to warn sb. about a dangerous or urgent situation

eg. 1) The rest of students quickly alerted the police after they heard the shooting.

2) The web master was alerted to the server problem last night when a new user emailed to say that he couldn't register.

▲ alert (*adj.*): able to think quickly, quick to notice things

eg. 1) I'm not feeling very alert today—not enough sleep last night!

2) Parents should be alert to sudden changes in children's behavior.

► betrayal (*n.*): the act of being disloyal to sb./sth. or the fact of being betrayed

eg. 1) I saw her actions as a betrayal of my trust.

2) I felt a sense of betrayal when my friends refused to support me.

▲ betray (*v.*): to be disloyal

eg. 1) He was accused of betraying his country during the war.

2) She felt betrayed by her mother's lack of support.

15. He <u>summoned</u> Prometheus to his court.

► summon (*v.*): to order sb. to come to or be present at a particular place, or to officially arrange a meeting of people

eg. 1) The general summoned reinforcements to help resist the attack.

2) On July 20th, the council was summoned to hear an emergency report on the outbreak of war.

16. Put the fine meat in one sack with the <u>entrails</u> on top.

► entrails (*n.* always plural): the organs inside the body of a person or an animal, especially their intestines

eg. 1) My family do not eat animal entrails.

2) The effects of eating entrails where the poison is concentrated remain unknown.

17. Don't <u>defy</u> me.

► defy (*v.*): to refuse to obey or show respect for sb. in authority, a law, a rule etc.

eg. 1) A few workers have defied the majority decision and gone into work despite the strike.

2) A forest fire raging in the north of the country is defying all attempts to control it.

▲ defiant (*adj.*): proudly refusing to obey authority

eg. 1) Adolescents often hold a defiant attitude toward their parents.

2) The terrorists sent a defiant message to the government.

▲ defiance (*n.*): bold resistance to an opposing force or authority

eg. 1) The workers went on strike in defiance of union policy.

2) The demonstration is a pointless act of defiance against the government.

18. Epimetheus was immediately <u>enchanted</u> with Pandora's beauty and skills.

Meaning: Immediately Epimetheus was greatly attracted by Pandora's beauty and skills.

► enchant (*v.*): to charm or please someone greatly

eg. 1) The audience was clearly enchanted by her performance.

2) The football fans were enchanted by / with the wonderful goal.

▲ enchanting (*adj.*): attractive and pleasing

eg. It's described in the guide book as an enchanting medieval city.

▲ enchantment (*formal n.*): a feeling of great pleasure

eg. She said, in her visit to Beijing last year, she was touched by the enchantment of the metropolitan of Beijing.

19. ...but Epimetheus could only <u>gaze</u> on Pandora in wonder.

Meaning: ... but Epimetheus could do nothing but fix his eyes on Pandora and admire her astounding beauty.

▶ gaze (*v.*): to fix the eyes in a steady look often with eagerness or studious attention

eg. 1) The little girl gazed admiringly at his father as he spoke.

2) He spends hours gazing out of the window when he should be working.

20. Before Epimetheus could stop her, Pandora broke the <u>seal</u> on the jar and lifted the lid.

▶ seal (*n.*): sth. fixed around the edge of an opening to prevent liquid or gas from flowing through it

eg. 1) Clean the seal on/around the fridge door regularly so that it remains airtight.

2) Earlier this year, they signed an exclusive contract to record for RCA Red Seal Classics. (这一年的早些时候，他们和 RCA 红印经典系列签订了独家录制合同。RCA 为美国广播唱片公司，全称为 Radio Corporation of America，成立于 1901 年，总部设在纽约)

▲ seal (*v.*): to close with or as if with a seal

eg. 1) He sealed (down) the envelope and put a stamp on it.

2) Seal the package (up) with sticky tape.

21. Out flew all the blessings of the world, returning quickly to the <u>heavens</u>.

这里的"heavens"是指天空、天界。传说宙斯住在奥林帕斯山的绝顶，并非《圣经》中所指的天堂。古人认为天空是分很多层的，即便是在中国文化中也有"九重天"的说法，因此使用 "the heavens" 来表示天上或天界。若是指基督教中的天堂，则必须用 "Heaven"，而且必须用单数形式。

22. The mortals began to suffer these miseries immediately, while Zeus observed in <u>disgust</u> (宙斯恶狠狠地望着这一切).

Meaning: The humans immediately began to suffer these disasters and misfortunes and Zeus was watching this with anger and distaste.

▶ disgust (*n.*): strong feeling of disapproval and dislike at a situation or person's behavior, etc.

eg. 1) She looked at him angrily and walked out in disgust.

2) He was lost in the rumors about him in disgust.

▲ disgust (*v.*): to make sb. feel shocked and almost ill because it is so unpleasant

eg. 1) The violence in the film really disgusted me.

　　2) The worms disgusted all of us.

▲ disgusted (*adj.*): feeling or showing disgust

eg. 1) I was disgusted at/by the thought that he had cheated in exam.

　　2) He was disgusted to see that the professors were actually living in ghettos.

▲ disgusting (*adj.*): extremely unpleasant or unacceptable

eg. 1) It's disgusting that there are no schools or hospitals for these people.

　　2) Passengers were kept for hours in a disgusting waiting room.

23. That is why today all of mankind has only hope to <u>counter</u> all the challenges they face from birth to death.

▶ counter (*v.*): to react to sth. with an opposing opinion or action

eg. 1) Extra police have been moved into the area to counter the risk of violence.

　　2) It is said that bird's nest soup can be very effective to counter insomnia.

24. Known for being the strongest man in the world, he then <u>tore apart</u> the chains.

▶ tear apart: to pull sth. so violently that it breaks into two or more pieces

eg. 1) A dog can tear a rabbit apart in seconds.

　　2) She tore apart the letter in disgust.

Better Know More

1. Greek and Roman Mythology

　　In learning Greek Mythology, students should be aware of its twin brother—Roman Mythology, which is closely related to and associated with Greek Mythology. Many of the famous Roman myths were copied or borrowed from the Greek Mythology, but they reflect a slight change. Many of the gods' names were changed and characters were slightly reshaped based on traditional Roman values. For example, Zeus, the king of heaven and Earth and of all the Olympian gods, was called Jupiter by the Romans; the courageous and strong man Heracles appeared in Roman Mythology as Hercules. Yet many names remained the same in both two mythologies, such as Apollo, Atlas, Europa, etc. It is also worth noting that as time passed, more myths from other cultures began to find their way into Roman Mythology as well.

2. Latins (拉丁人) and Romans

　　The Latins were an ancient Italic people who migrated to central Italy, in the second millennium B.C., maybe from the Adriatic East Coast(亚得里亚海东岸)and Balkanic Area(巴尔干地区). As one of the main groups of Italic peoples, the Latins developed an organized society, which was the main source of the people who settled in Rome as well as other cities in today's Italy. Although they lived in independent city-states, the Latins had a common language, which is Latin, common religious beliefs and a close sense of kinship. Rome's territorial ambitions led to the union of all the Latins who rebelled against it in 341 BC, but the final victory was on Rome's side in 338 BC. Consequently some of the Latin states were incorporated within the Roman state, and their inhabitants were given full Roman citizenship(罗马公民权). Others became Roman allies(盟友) and enjoyed certain privileges.

In modern times the term "Latin" is most commonly applied as an adjective to people of Italy, France, Portugal, Romania and Spain because their languages descend from Latin. People also use "Latin America" to refer to those territories in the Americas where Spanish or Portuguese prevail: Mexico, most of Central and South America, plus Cuba, Puerto Rico and the Dominican Republic in the Caribbean. This is a term usually contrasted to Anglo America, referring mainly to North America, a place to host the European heritage.

3. Prometheus

Prometheus is considered the great benefactor of mankind. His name means "forethought" and he was able to foretell the future. Prometheus created mankind out of clay and water. When Zeus mistreated man, Prometheus stole fire from the gods, gave it to man, and taught him many useful arts and sciences. Compared with his brother, Epimetheus was foolish and impatient. His name means "afterthought" and he was always busy thinking yesterday, or last year, or a hundred years ago, that he had no care at all for what might come to pass after a while.

Check Your Understanding

Translate the following sentences into Chinese. Please make sure that your language flows smoothly.

1. After cheating Zeus, Prometheus was sentenced to continued punishment, only to be rescued by Heracles, known to the Latins as Hercules.
因为欺骗了宙斯，普罗米修斯被判接受永无休止的惩罚，直到后来意外获得大力神赫拉克勒斯，也就是罗马神话中的赫丘利的解救才得以脱身。
2. As you work, you can give each creature gifts to make it swift, strong, or whatever you see fit to bestow.

在缔造生灵的时候,你们可以赋予每一种生灵一些天赋,让他们行动敏捷,身体强壮,另外,你们还可以给予他们一些你们认为合适的才能。

3. He sent for Prometheus and his brother Epimetheus, both Titans, powerful giants who lived on earth.

他派人找来普罗米修斯和他的兄弟埃庇米修斯,他们都是提坦,居住在地球上的力大无穷的巨人。

4. Prometheus sneaked up to Olympus, stole an ember from the fire there, and gave it to man, warning them to never let it die out.

普罗米修斯悄悄地攀上奥林匹斯山,从火中偷了一把余火送给人类,并警告说永远不要让它熄灭。

5. The mortals began to suffer these miseries immediately, while Zeus observed in disgust.

顷刻间,人类便开始遭受到诸般苦难,而(天上的)宙斯正满心厌恶地怒视着这一切。

6. Known for being the strongest man in the world, he then tore apart the chains.

这个举世闻名的强汉一把扯断了铁链。

Answer the following questions based on the text you have just learned.

1. What had happened on earth before Zeus decided to restore it to its former splendor?

   There were once wars between Titans and the Olympian gods and as a result, all living creatures on earth had perished.

2. Why did Zeus send for Prometheus and Epimetheus to complete the task of creating mortals?

   Prometheus and Epimetheus were loyal to Zeus so Zeus decided to reward them by giving them the task to fashion new men and beasts.

3. How would Prometheus and Epimetheus produce creatures when they got to earth, according to Zeus?

   They would go to the river and use the clay on the bands to create mortals, both human and animal. When they work they should also bestow some gifts on each of them.

4. Did they create mortals in the same way? How did they do their job respectively?

   No. Prometheus created man in the image of god very carefully, while Epimetheus created animals as quickly as he could.

5. Why did Zeus refuse to share fire with the mortals on earth?

   He said that fire was for gods, not for mortals.

6. When Zeus found Prometheus had taken Gods' fire to the earth, what proposal did Zeus have for Prometheus?

   He proposed if men could share whatever delicious meats with him, he would allow them to keep the fire and part of the meat for themselves.

7. What instructions did Prometheus give to the mortals in regard to preparing the meat for Zeus to choose from?

   He asked them to kill an ox and divide the meat into two equal parts and then put the fine meat in one sack with the entrails on top and the bones in the other sack with the fat on top.

8. When Zeus called Epimetheus to his throne, what did he say to Epimetheus?

   Zeus said that he would give Epimetheus a woman as his helpmate on earth and a gift of a clay jug, which could not be opened without his permission.

9. What happened when Pandora opened the clay jar?

   When Pandora opened the jar, all the blessings of the world except hope flew back to the heavens. Following the blessings came the plagues of the world that brought miseries to the mortals immediately.

10. What do you think that humans would be like now if Pandora had not opened the jar?

   This is an open question.

A Sip of Phonetics

本课介绍五个双元音 /eɪ/, /əʊ/, /aɪ/, /aʊ/, /ɑɪ/。

📖 Know Their Faces

1. 双元音 /eɪ/: 先发 /e/ 音, 然后滑到发 /ɪ/ 音。/e/ 发音重且长而清晰,/ɪ/ 发音轻且短而含糊。教学中教师要特别注意学生不要将 /eɪ/ 读作 /e/。请比较以下两组单词:

/eɪ/	/e/
late	let
sail	sell
paper	pepper
trade	tread
rake	wreck
fail	fell

   请带领学生朗读以下单词:say/ name/ shape/ race/ fate/ wait/ lake/

2. 双元音 /əʊ/: 由中元音 /ə/ 滑到后元音 /ʊ/, 舌位由半低到高, 口形由半开到小。在发第二部分 /ʊ/ 时, 嘴唇收得比较圆。请比较以下两组单词:

/əʊ/	/ɔː/
so	saw
low	law
snow	snore
boat	bought

close claws
coke cork

3. 双元音 /aɪ/:这个双元音的第一部分要发得长且重而清晰。它得开口很大,发音时舌尖抵住下齿的齿龈区。完成第一部分发音后,舌位紧接着向第二部分滑动。发音时注意和 /e/、/æ/ 以及中文中的"爱"音相比较,体会双元音发音从第一元音到第二元音的滑动过程。

/aɪ/	/e/	/aɪ/	/æ/
light	let	kite	cat
price	press	bike	back
night	net	fine	fan
bride	bread	height	hat
tide	Ted	mine	man

请带领学生朗读以下单词:my/ cry/ dry/ like/ rice/ shine/ fight

4. 双元音 /aʊ/:/aʊ/ 的第一个音素 /a/ 同上面 /aɪ/ 中的 /a/ 开口一样大,但发音位置更为靠后。完成第一个音素立即向第二个音素 /ʊ/ 滑动,同时注意有一个从扁唇向圆唇的变化。
请朗读以下单词:now/ loud/ doubt/ mouse/ shout/ power/ town

5. 双元音 /ɔɪ/:发音时双唇从圆到扁,口形从开到合,发好这个音的关键是首先把后元音 /ɔ/ 发足,然后滑到 /ɪ/ 音。教师教学中要注意强调双元音的滑动过程,并让学生练习体会,以便把这个音发得饱满。
请朗读以下单词:boy/ toy/ noise/ oil/ voice/ joint/ hoist/ annoy/

Train Your Tongue

1. My dame/ has a lame/ tame crane. My dame/ has a crane/ that is lame.

2. Nine/ nice night nurses/ nursing/ nicely.

3. A tidy tiger/ tied a tie/ tighter/ to tidy/ her tiny tail.

4. A laurel-crowned/ clown!

5. A flea and a fly/ flew up in a flue/. Said the flea/, "Let us fly/!" Said the fly/, "Let us flee/!" So they flew/ through a flaw/ in the flue.

6. A noisy noise/ annoys/ an oyster.

7. The old school scold/ sold/ the school coal boat/; if the old school scold/ sold/ the school coal boat/, the school/ would scold/ and drove/ the old school scold.

You'd Like to Be

A Strong Bridge Builder

Fill in the blanks with the given words to complete the following sentences. Please note that some can be used more than once.

| about | to | by | out | in | along | of | up | with |

1. When you come to the party <u>with</u> presents, don't forget to bring <u>along</u> your smiles. You can also make more sincere friends and get more happiness <u>out</u> of life.
2. Every day, <u>up</u> to 100 species of animals become extinct, and each year this number grows. Scientists feel that more than forty thousand species of animals may die <u>out</u> each year.
3. All people should have the ability to invest <u>in</u> their health and education and to shape their own lives <u>by</u> being able <u>to</u> participate <u>in</u> the opportunities provided <u>by</u> economic growth and have their voices heard <u>about</u> decisions that affect their lives. Access <u>to</u> essential public services, such as health, education and safe water, is critical and should be provided equitably.

A Smart Word Player

Fill in the blanks with the proper words that need to be transformed from the ones provided in the brackets.

He further maintains that the church and kingdom <u>sustain</u> (sustenance) some sort of a relation, and an unfailing <u>loyalty</u> (loyal) with which people make <u>splendid</u> (splendor) achievement <u>sacredly</u> (sacred) instead of <u>shivering</u> (shiver) in the dark <u>bound</u> (bind) and gagged by <u>misfortune</u> (fortunate)...

A Skilled Text Weaver

Fill in the blanks with the words you have learned in this text. One word is for each blank. Here is a piece of advice: You must be really familiar with the text to accomplish the following tasks.

1. It was dark at night. They finally reached the valley. Looking up to the sky, they were <u>en</u>

chanted by the beautiful moon.   They decided to build a campfire and dance in the moon-light.   They wanted to pray and do whatever they saw fit to thank God,   for God had be-stowed life and happiness on them.

2. He resigned from the committee in disgust at the corruption. Two years later, he was reelected by the people to be president of this small country.   Since he has restored his power,   he is resolved to take effective measures to keep corruption at bay.

3. It was said that someone had sneaked into the building and put a bomb in it. The security guards heeded the warning and immediately evacuated all the people in it.   The police ar-rived and removed the bomb just before it tore the building apart.

A Sharp Interpreter

Please paraphrase the following sentences. Change the sentence structure if necessary.

1. Prometheus took great care in fashioning the mortals, longing to give them comfort and sustenance.

✦ *Paraphrasing:*

Prometheus carefully created humans by hand and wanted to provide them with comfort and food.

2. Pandora brings along a jug, refusing to heed Zeus's warning to leave it closed.

✦ *Paraphrasing:*

Pandora brings with her a jug and refuses to listen to Zeus's warning that she should keep it closed.

3. You can give each creature gifts to make it swift, strong, or whatever you see fit to bestow.

✦ *Paraphrasing:*

When you create humans and animals,   you can give each of them special talents to make them move quickly and have strong bodies;   you can also give them whatever tal-ent you consider appropriate.

4. My people are carefully crafted.

✦ *Paraphrasing:*

My people are carefully created by hand.

5. The fire not only kept mankind warm but also kept the beasts at bay.

✦ *Paraphrasing:*

The fire not only kept mankind warm, but also protected them from animal attacks.

6. The smell of roasting meat drifted to the heavens, alerting Zeus to Prometheus's betrayal.

✦ *Paraphrasing:*

The smell of roasting meat moved slowly to the heavens,   making Zeus aware of the fact that Prometheus had acted against him.

7. Surely a little peek won't hurt anything.

✧ *Paraphrasing:*

I'm sure a quick look at it won't cause any trouble.

A Solid Sentence Constructer

Please make a sentence with each word or expression listed below.

1. only to

✧ *Original sentence in the text:*

After cheating Zeus, Prometheus was sentenced to continued punishment, only to be rescued by Heracles, known to the Latins as Hercules.

✧ **Suggested sentence:**

He spent ages negotiating for a pay increase,   only to resign from his job soon after he'd received it.

2. to take great care in doing...

✧ *Original sentence in the text:*

Prometheus took great care in fashioning the mortals, longing to give them comfort and sustenance.

✧ **Suggested sentence:**

Credit card companies should take great care in protecting customers' information.

3. to see fit

✧ *Original sentence in the text:*

As you work, you can give each creature gifts to make it swift, strong, or whatever you see fit to bestow.

✧ **Suggested sentence:**

You are encouraged to try whatever means you see fit.

4. to send for

✧ *Original sentence in the text:*

He sent for Prometheus and his brother Epimetheus,   both Titans,   powerful giants who lived on earth.

✧ **Suggested sentence:**

A traveller sent for an ambulance immediately after the fatal road accident had occurred.

5. to die out

✧ *Original sentence in the text:*

Prometheus sneaked up to Olympus, stole an ember from the fire there, and gave it to man, warning them to never let it die out.

✦ Suggested sentence:

Some rare species of fish in the river have died out.

6. to keep ... at bay

✦ *Original sentence in the text:*

    The fire not only kept mankind warm, but also kept the beasts at bay.

✦ Suggested sentence:

    Exercise can help keep fat at bay.

7. in disgust

✦ *Original sentence in the text:*

    The mortals began to suffer these miseries immediately, while Zeus observed in disgust.

✦ Suggested sentence:

    She looked at him angrily and walked out in disgust.

8. to tear apart

✦ *Original sentence in the text:*

    Known for being the strongest man in the world, he then tore apart the chains.

✦ Suggested sentence:

    A dog can tear a rabbit apart in seconds.

📖 A Superb Bilingualist

Please translate the following sentences into English with the prompts provided in the brackets.

1. 我做实验的时候，你要乖乖地做功课，不许偷看，等我完事，我会奖励你。(peek, a reward)

✦ *Suggested translation:*

Do your homework carefully while I am doing experiments. Don't peek at me. When I am done, I'll give you a reward / reward you.

2. 赛车急速转弯穿越车道，观众们看入了迷。(swift, enchant)

✦ *Suggested translation:*

The spectators were enchanted by the swift turns of the racing cars down the lanes.

3. 随着社会的发展，很多旧的风俗正在逐渐消失。(die out)

✦ *Suggested translation:*

Along with the development of society, many old customs are gradually dying out.

4. 兄弟俩听从了父母的劝告，又恢复了以往的亲密关系。(heed, restore to)

✦ *Suggested translation:*

The two brothers heeded their parents' advice and restored to their close relations.

5. 她对朋友很忠诚，可当她发现朋友们一直都在欺骗她时便愤然离去。(loyal, in disgust)

   ✡ *Suggested translation:*

   She was loyal to her friends, but when she found that they had been cheating her, she left in disgust.

6. 我们感谢大自然对我们的慷慨恩赐。(bestow on/upon)

   ✡ *Suggested translation:*

   We are grateful for the benefits nature has so generously bestowed upon us.

7. 绿茶有助于预防心脏病和癌症。(keep ... at bay)

   ✡ *Suggested translation:*

   Green tea may help keep heart disease and cancer at bay.

8. 我建议你认为怎么合适就怎么做。(propose, see fit)

   ✡ *Suggested translation:*

   I propose that you just do whatever you see fit.

9. 朋友的背叛使他感到非常痛苦。(betrayal, torment)

   ✡ *Suggested translation:*

   He was tormented by his friend's betrayal.

Text B

Introduction to the Fall of Mankind

The Book of *Genesis* (《圣经》中的《创世纪》)tells that God created Adam by breathing life into "the dust of the ground." Later, God created Eve from Adam's rib. God placed Adam and Eve in the Garden of Eden(伊甸园), telling them that they could eat the fruit of all the trees in the garden except the fruit of the tree of knowledge of good and evil. They lived happily until the serpent (Satan) tempted Eve to eat the forbidden fruit. She ate, and gave the fruit to Adam, who also ate; they immediately became aware and ashamed of their nakedness. Because of Adam and Eve's disobedience, God drove them from the garden into the world outside, where Eve would suffer in childbirth and Adam would have to earn his livelihood by the sweat of his brow. The direst consequence of Adam and Eve's disobedience was death: "Dust thou art," said God, "and unto dust shalt thou return." After their expulsion(驱逐), Eve gave birth to sons, first Cain and Abel and then Seth, and thus Adam and Eve became the parents of humankind. Adam and Eve's sin and their consequent loss of God's grace and the enjoyment of paradise are referred to as the Fall of Man or simply "the Fall."

Comprehension Questions

After reading Text B, please answer the following questions with the words and expressions given in the brackets.

1. What can be found in the middle of the garden and what are the differences between them? (enable ... to live forever, bring life to an end)

   In the middle of the garden there were two trees. One was called the tree of life, fruit of which could enable someone to live forever; the other was called the tree of knowledge of good and evil, whose fruit could bring life to an end.

2. Who would like to challenge God and how? (through a serpent, tempt)

   Lucifer wanted to challenge God. Through a serpent, he tempted Adam's wife to eat the fruit of the tree of knowledge of good and evil successfully. Later Adam took some of the fruit from his wife.

3. What happened after Adam and his wife took the fruit of the forbidden tree? (a robe of light, naked, fig leaves, hide themselves from God)

   They ate them, and soon found the robe of light that had covered them was gone and they were naked. They used fig leaves to cover their body and hid themselves from God.

4. How did God punish them when he learned the fact? (crawl upon his belly, give birth to children, work hard to live from the land)

   When God learned what had happened, he decided to punish them. As a result, the serpent could only crawl upon his belly and eat the dust of the earth; the woman was told that there would be dislike between her descendants and the descendants of the serpent and that she would suffer much pain giving birth to children; and Adam would have to work hard to live from the land.

5. How does the story end? (out of the garden, without the fruit of the tree of life)

   Adam and Eve were sent out of the garden. Without the fruit of the tree of life, they could not live forever.

Writing Practice

Put your answers to the above questions together and form a summary about the text and share with your classmates the summary you have completed.

In the middle of the garden there were two trees. One was called the tree of life, fruit of which could enable someone to live forever; the other was called the tree of knowledge of good and evil, whose fruit could bring life to an end. One day Lucifer wanted to challenge God. Through a serpent, he successfully tempted Adam's wife to eat the fruit of the tree of knowledge of good and evil. Later Adam took some of the fruit from his wife. Soon after that, both Adam and his wife Eve found the robe of light that had covered them was gone and they were naked. They used fig leaves to make clothes for themselves and were hiding themselves when God came to talk to them. Soon God learned what had happened, and he decided to punish them. As a result of God's punishment, the serpent could only crawl upon his belly and eat the dust of the earth. The woman was told that there would be dislike between her descendants and those of the serpent, and the woman would suffer much pain giving birth to children. And Adam would have to work hard to live from the land. At last Adam and Eve were sent out of the garden. Without the fruit of the tree of life, they could not live forever.

5

Happiness

Unit Goals

After studying this unit, students should be able to:

☞ **understand the importance of "living right here and now";**

Text A is an insightful discussion about the attitude we are expected to hold toward what we are in possession of. As implied in the quote "living right here and now," to be grateful for and appreciative of what we have achieved fills our heart with the joyful feeling and allows us to fully appreciate everything around us and offer access to experiencing the full wonder of "here and now." The point is how we may learn to cultivate gratitude and appreciate the interior abundance that life offers to everyone. When you are complaining about life, you are not realizing the abundance life potentially offers to you and to everyone about you. Hopefully, after learning this text, students may rethink about their life experiences and come up with a positive attitude towards their future development.

☞ **know how to pronounce /ɪə/, /eə/ and /ʊə/, and how to utilize some useful words and structures that contribute significantly to the texts;**

In this section, the instructor should start by contrasting simple vowels and diphthongs to emphasize that a simple vowel is pronounced without movement of the mouth, but a diphthong is done with a glide from one sound to the next, as is the case with the above /ɪə/, /eə/and /ʊə/. The principal difference between a single vowel and a diphthong plays a key role that enables the students to capture the essence in pronouncing correctly the three diphthongs above.

☞ **understand and appreciate the "interior abundance" that life offers to everyone.**

To be grateful for what you have already got hold of in life is the ability to appreciate what life has brought to you. Just as the text suggests, it is important to keep your consciousness awakened all the time to your daily blessings. You will feel much blessed with a feeling of "interior abundance" rather than "interior scarcity" if you value the space in your consciousness for appreciation. A sense of "interior abundance" is built on an active power to remain appreciative of what you have. This sort of feeling is closely related to material abundance. However, you might be able to materialize your craving for wealth, but you will lose your power to enjoy the material success because of the inner emptiness.

Before Reading

Hands-on Activities and Brainstorming

The instructor should allow 15 to 20 minutes for the students to do presentation either on the relationship between gratitude and happiness regarding the title of the text "'There' is No Better than 'Here.'"

A Glimpse at Words and Expressions

A. It is suggested that the instructor use a simple expression such as "to arrive at Beijing Airport" to contribute to the students' understanding of "to arrive at ... goal," which can be defined as to "to succeed in having achieved what one has been aiming at." For example: *Luckily the dissertation arrived at the conclusion he had expected.*

B. It might be a good idea for the instructor to pick up the synonym "to heighten" for "to enhance" for brainstorming to set the students on the track for a better understanding of the expression based on the context in the sentence.
"Be enhanced by" here means "be improved by." For example: *Your life would be significantly enhanced by your interest in music.*

C. The difficulty here in interpreting the word "to cultivate" is that there is less context in the sentence. Therefore, a synonym such as "to grow better," serves as a means to understand "to cultivate," which means "to develop in a person the quality of..." For example: *The most important job for all teachers is to help students cultivate a positive attitude toward life.*

D. To figure out the meaning of "to amass," the instructor should focus on the context of the sentence. The logic in the sentence is that years of hard-work leads to material success. In this sense, "to amass" can be understood as "acquire in large quantity." For example: *Her family amassed a large fortune in copper mining.*

E. To approach the meaning of "to crash" in the sentence, the instructor might first focus on the meaning of its noun form in expressions such as "car crash," "air crash," which make it possible for the students to track down the meaning by following the clue offered. Hence, "The stock market crashed" means "to experience financial crisis and disaster." For example: *Can you imagine that century-old bank crashed just overnight?*

F. The instructor should be aware that the key word in the phrase is "to land," which the student is familiar with. It means "to bring an airplane to earth." The instructor can offer a similar phrase such as "to stand on one's feet," to help the student define "to land on their feet" with the help of the context, which can be interpreted as "to achieve a complete recovery and come back to reality." For example: *After all these years of misfortune and suffering, she landed on her feet.*

G. The difficulty in understanding the phrase "take stock (of)" is that the individual words lost their basic meanings, especially the verb "take." However, we can still work on the noun "stock," which means "a store of goods ready for sale or distribution." The meaning of "to take stock of" in the sentence is supposed to be based on its first interpretation: "to make an inventory of stock on hand." For example: *The grocery store took stock every week on Friday mornings.* Following the explanation, the students might find it easier to define the meaning of the phrase in the text. "To take stock (of)" can be interpreted as "stop and think carefully about the way in which a particular situation is developing in order to decide what to do next." For example: *Jim decided to sell all his company shares after he had taken stock of the recent happenings.*

H. The instructor should first draw the students' attention to the root of "to signify." "Sign," as the root, means "indication or clue" as a noun and "to indicate or express" as a verb. There are some expressions derived from the root: "signal," "signature," "significance" etc. besides "signify." The explanation seems to lead the students to an understanding of "to signify," which is explained as "be the indication of." For example: *The publication of this article signifies a radical change in educational research.*

Keys

| A-4 | B-3 | C-1 | D-7 | E-2 | F-8 | G-5 | H-6 |

Text A

📖 Introduction of the Text

By learning Text A, students will come to know the importance of living in the present. It is understandable that young people are ambitious and have dreams about their future. But one thing we must remind them is that the future starts from "here" and that your attitude toward "now" will have a great impact upon your future. This text focuses on the attitude we are expected to hold toward the present. It tells us, on top of everything else, that we should be grateful for and appreciative of what we have gained in life. As you strive to keep your focus on the present moment, you can experience the full wonder of "here."

It also tells us how we learn to cultivate gratitude. Before discussing the text with your students, get your students to interpret "gratitude." Their attitude toward life shows whether they feel grateful to their parents, friends, teachers and classmates and whether they are thankful to what the country has offered to them. These questions may serve as the starting point for class discussion.

Suggested Explanation on Text A

1. Many people believe that they will be happy once they arrive at some specific goal they set for themselves.

   Meaning: According to many people, happiness derives from the attainment of their particular objectives they expect themselves to achieve in life.

2. However, more often than not, once you arrive "there" you will still feel dissatisfied, and move your "there" vision to yet another point in the future.

   Meaning: Nevertheless, it usually happens rather than otherwise that you are not as satisfied as you have expected yourself to be after having achieved a certain goal, while you change your idea and strive to go further ahead to obtain more than you are in possession of in the future.

   ► more often than not: very often; usually

   eg. 1) More often than not, married women bring home a second check.

   2) It was strongly held in Chinese culture that people need to have an offspring to take care of themselves when they grow old. But in modern Chinese families, more often than not, the elderly are taking care of their working children.

   ► vision (*n.*): an idea or a picture in your imagination

   eg. 1) She was with such an elusive vision many years ago.

   2) He had a vision of Britain as a prosperous country leading the world.

   ▲ vision (*vis+ion*): vis as a prefix, meaning to see, other derivations being visible, invisible, invisibility, visual, visualize, visit, etc.

   eg. 1) Converging or diverging lens can be used to correct common defects of vision resulting from an incorrect relation between the parts of the optical system of the eye.

   2) We need a man of vision as president.

   3) In the fog, the visibility is very poor.

   4) Though he described the place carefully, I couldn't visualize it because it was so different from anything I'd known.

5) This animal's visual organs are different from ours.

6) Germs are invisible to the naked eye.

3. By always chasing after another "there," you are never really appreciating what you already have right "here."

Meaning: If you are in a rush to go after one goal after another without stopping when you reach a certain goal, you are hardly able to enjoy what you have obtained so far.

► to chase (after): to run, drive sth./sb. in order to catch; to go after, pursue

eg. 1) On the average, some 12 candidates are chasing an alluring position.

2) Our women's national hockey team is chasing its first Asian title.

3) The policeman chased after the burglar but could not catch him.

► appreciate (v.): to recognize the good qualities of sth. or sb.

eg. 1) Very soon you'll appreciate the beauty and elegance of the minority language.

2) My father often told me to appreciate family tradition.

▲ appreciate (v.): to be grateful

eg. 1) We sincerely appreciate your hospitality and timely help.

2) He didn't seem to appreciate my offer to take him home in my car.

4. It is important for human beings to keep sober-minded about the age-old drive to look beyond the place where you now stand.

Meaning: It is important for human beings to be clear-headed about the long existing desire and dream to constitute even greater achievements in the future than you have accomplished now.

► drive (n.): a strong desire or need in people

eg. 1) You can never deny there is a compelling drive for something better.

2) Motivation is defined in various ways, but the basic implication is a kind of inner drive.

▲ drive (n.): a journey in a car

eg. 1) Shall we go for a drive in the mountains this weekend?

2) It's about half-an-hour drive to the nearest town.

▲ drive (v.): to force sb. to act in a particular way

eg. 1) Take it easy please. Don't drive yourself too hard.

2) Intensive hatred drove her to act violently.

► to look beyond: to direct one's eyes past (sth.); to consider, know, imagine sth. further or greater than sth. (oft. in the future)

eg. 1) If you look beyond the trees, you can just see the village in the distance.

2) We have to look beyond these early difficulties to the hope of future success.

5. On the other hand, these drives can pull you farther and farther from your enjoyment of your life right now.

Meaning: On the other hand, these desires rush you to move further ahead, making you overlook your current fulfillment, and thus loose the interest to appreciate your present life.

6. By learning the lessons of gratitude and abundance, you can bring yourself closer to fulfilling the challenge of living in the present.

Meaning: If you are able to understand the principle that you should be grateful for the enormous amount of wealth you have obtained enough for you to enjoy a good life, you will be ready to meet the demands of your present life so that you will never fail to see the significance of the life you are living now.

▶ gratitude (*n.*): the feeling of being grateful and wanting to express your thanks

eg. 1) At the grand ceremony, the chairman expressed her gratitude to all the employees in the firm for their dedication and creative work.

2) His grandma left the hospital with a very deep sense of gratitude.

▲ gratitude: grat is the root, meaning pleasing, the expressions derived from the root being *grateful, gratify, gratification, congratulation, gratitude etc.*

eg. 1) I am grateful to the friends who have helped me.

2) Your parents will be gratified to learn that you have passed the entrance examination to the university.

3) The gratification of every wish of every person is not possible.

4) I can hardly express my gratitude to you for your timely help.

5) I send you my warmest congratulations on your success.

▶ abundance (*n.*): (formal) a large quantity that is more than enough

eg. 1) Apples and grapes grow in abundance on the hills.

2) Thailand boasts an abundance of clean and safe beaches.

▲ abundant (*adj.*): (formal) existing in large quantities

eg. 1) Tropical fish are abundant along this particular zone of ocean.

2) The police have collected abundant evidence to prove that she is guilty.

▶ fulfill (*v.*): to do or achieve what was hoped for or expected

eg. 1) Here is the right position where you can fulfill your ambition soon.

2) She quit her good-paying job to return to the village to fulfill her obligation as a daughter.

7. To be grateful means you are thankful for and appreciative of what you have and where you are on your path right now.

▶ grateful to sb. for sth.: feeling or showing thanks to sb. who has done sth. kind for you or has done as you asked

eg. 1) She is grateful both to all the professors for their kindest help in accomplishing the dissertation and to her students for their sincere cooperation in the experiment.

2) I am very grateful to you for having taken so much trouble.

3) The dean hinted to me that I should be grateful to have a position in his department.

4) Jerry was grateful that the boss let him off this time.

▶ appreciative of: feeling or showing that you are grateful for sth.

eg. 1) The university was very appreciative of her efforts in promoting the relations between the two institutions.

2) He was rather appreciative of failure.

3) Finally I saw appreciative smile on the president's face.

8. Gratitude <u>fills</u> your heart with the <u>joyful</u> feeling and allows you to fully appreciate everything that arises on your path.

Meaning: Being grateful for what you have accomplished and enjoying life with all your heart lead you to developing the ability to treat everything that comes up in your life with a feeling of thankfulness.

▶ fill (v.): to make sth. full of sth.

eg. 1) Eager listeners filled the auditorium half an hour before the presentation began.

2) They are filled with admiration for my proficiency in four foreign languages.

▶ joyful (adj.): (used in written context) very happy

eg. 1) On new year's eve Chinese families would have a joyful reunion.

2) It was full of joyful feelings at the get-together.

9. As you <u>strive</u> to keep your focus on the present moment, you can <u>experience</u> the full <u>wonder</u> of "here."

▶ strive (v.): (formal) to try very hard to achieve sth.

eg. 1) We encourage our students to strive for native-like fluency in oral presentation.

2) We have striven to the full to convince him, but our efforts went no avail.

▶ experience (v.): to have and be aware of a particular emotion or physical feeling

eg. 1) All the passengers experienced a moment of panic when they got on the bus and saw the conductor.

2) The city has experienced water shortage for as long as 10 years.

▶ wonder (n.): sth. or a quality of sth. that fills you with surprise and admiration. The adjective form is "wonderful."

eg. 1) The Three Gorges along the Yangtze River are natural wonders of the world.

2) Computer must be regarded as a wonder of modern technology.

10. Imagine what your life would be like if you lost all that you had. This will most surely <u>remind</u> you of how much you should appreciate life.

   ▶ remind (*v.*): to help sb. remember sth. that they must do

   eg. 1) Travelers are reminded that inoculation against yellow fever is advisable.

   2) Remind your father to buy some drinks on his way back home.

   3) It was fortunate that you reminded me of the meeting with Jones.

11. Make a list each day of all that you are grateful for, so that you can <u>stay conscious daily of</u> your blessings.

   Meaning: To ensure that you are able to realize the good and advantage right in your everyday life, it is helpful for you to number all the things you are thankful to.

   ▶ stay (*v.*): (used as a link *v.*) to continue to be in a particular state or situation

   eg. 1) Many strive to stay healthy after retirement, but for some it is a bit late.

   2) A few days before the festival, the supermarket stayed open until 11 P.M.

   ▶ conscious of /that: aware of sth.; noticing sth.

   eg. 1) More and more graduates become conscious of the challenge to find a satisfying job.

   2) Though she did not actually see anything, she was somewhat conscious that she was followed.

   3) Singaporeans are very much language conscious.

12. Spend time offering assistance to those who are less fortunate than you, so that you may gain <u>insight</u> into life.

   Meaning: You are supposed to devote your time helping those people who are not as blessed and successful as you are before you are able to have a better under-standing of life.

   ▶ insight (*n.*): the ability to see and understand the truth about people or situations

   eg. 1) Rod Ellis is a researcher of great insight.

   2) The film gives us fascinating insights into life in the Netherlands.

   3) By now we all have gained some insights into the difficulties confronting us.

13. However you choose to learn gratitude is <u>irrelevant</u>.

   Meaning: It doesn't matter how you choose to learn gratitude.

   ▶ irrelevant (*adj.*): off the point, foreign, the opposite of "relevant." Please see the definition of "relevant" in the following.

   eg. 1) Her lawyer claimed that the witness' evidence was irrelevant to the case.

   2) Politics is not irrelevant to you. As a matter of fact, it is connected with every aspect of your life.

▲ irrelevant (*adj.*): ir is one of the five prefixes (*in, im, il, ig, ir*) in the group that is added to the start of adjectives, nouns and adverbs to make them negative. IN is mostly added to words ended with Latin suffix such as ate, ent, ant, ite, ible. IM goes with those starting with letters p, b, m for the sake of convenience of pronunciation, IL with those staring with letter l, and IG with letter n. Look at the following examples:

prefix	examples				
IN	inability	inadequate	inaccessible	inclement	inarticulate
IM	immoral	immature	imbalance	implacable	imperfect
IL	illegal	illusion	illicit	illiterate	
IR	irrelevant	irreverent	irresistible	irreproachable	
IG	ignore	ignoble	ignominy		

▲ relevant (*adj.*): closely connected with the subject you are discussing or the situation you are thinking about

eg. 1) It's an interesting question. But I'm afraid it isn't relevant to our discussion.

2) A relevant point for your reference is how you are going to measure poverty in different countries.

14. One of the most common human fears is scarcity.

Meaning: It is common for many people to be afraid of not having enough of what they need or want.

► scarcity (*n.*): shortage of sth.

eg. 1) My parents were born in 1930s, a time of scarcity.

2) We must make our children aware of the fact that our country suffers from a scarcity of natural resources.

▲ scarce (*adj.*): not enough of sth.

eg. It is not a pleasant community to live where mutual trust is scarce.

15. They both worked very hard for years, amassing a small fortune, so they could move from their two-bedroom home to a spacious seven-bedroom home in a high-class neighborhood.

► spacious (*adj.*): large and with plenty of space for people to move around

eg. The university boasts a very spacious music hall.

▲ spacious (*adj.*): ous as a suffix means "having," "full of," "characterized by," which is usually added to a noun and turns into an adjective

eg. 1) dangerous, courageous, mountainous, various

► neighborhood (*n.*): a district or an area of a town

eg. 1) She was born in the poorest neighborhood in the town.

2) I have made up my mind to move to a quiet neighborhood.

▲ neighborhood (*n.*): hood as a suffix means "state" or "quality," which is added to adjectives and nouns

eg. falsehood, manhood, bachelorhood, childhood, priesthood, nationhood

16. They focused their energies on accumulating all the things that they believed signified abundance: <u>membership</u> in the local <u>exclusive</u> country club, <u>luxury</u> cars, <u>designer</u> clothing, and high-class society friends.

Meaning: They extended great efforts to hoard a large quantity of wealth to show that they are well-off, which includes the qualifications of being a member in the local privileged club, driving the most expensive cars, wearing clothes by a famous designer with a fashionable brand name, and being in contact with friends from upper circles.

▶ membership (*n.*): the state of being a member of a group, club, organization etc.

eg. 1) Can students apply for the membership of the association?

2) At the entrance you need to produce your membership card.

▲ membership (*n.*): ship, a suffix added to nouns, denoting quality, state, rank, skill; all persons of

eg. 1) presidentship 总统(会长)的职位

2) scholarship 学识,学问;奖学金

3) fellowship 情谊,同伴关系

4) authorship 著者身份

5) readership 读者身份

6) marksmanship 射术

▶ exclusive (*adj.*): (of a group, society, etc.) not very willing to allow new people to become members, especially if they are from a lower social class

eg. 1) He moves in exclusive social circles and belongs to the most exclusive clubs.

2) This school is exclusive, only very bright children can go to it.

▲ exclusive (*adj.*): of a high quality and expensive and therefore not often bought or used by most people

eg. 1) exclusive hotel

2) an exclusive designer shop

▲ exclusive (*adj.*) ⟶ exclusion (*n.*) ⟶ exclude (*v.*) ⟶ excluding (*prep.*)

eg. 1) Memories of the past filled her mind to the exclusion of all else.

他满脑子都是对过去的回忆。

2) The cost of borrowing has been excluded from the inflation figures.

膨胀数字不包括借款成本。

3) Lunch cost $10 per person, excluding drinks.

午餐每人 10 美元,酒水除外。

▶ luxury (*n.*): expensive and having a famous brand name. "Luxury" here is used as an attribute modifying another noun.

eg. 1) Do you think luxury cars are a symbol for social status?

2) She's living in luxury all her life.

⛰ luxury (*pl. ies*)

eg. 1) Sleeping in a warm bed was a luxury for the poor man.

2) If prices arise higher, we shall have to do without our few remaining luxuries.

▶ designer (*adj.*): (used only before noun) made by a famous designer; expensive and having a famous brand name

eg. 1) You may imagine how wealthy she is from her designer jewelry.

2) Young girls are crazy about designer jeans.

17. They were unable to <u>erase</u> the deep fear of scarcity both had <u>acquired</u> in childhood.

Meaning: They were unable to get rid of the deep fear that they would never have got enough wealth, a fear both of them developed in their childhood.

▶ erase (*v.*): to remove sth. completely

eg. 1) I tried to erase the memory of that horrible morning, but I just couldn't.

2) All her doubts were erased when she watched the feature report on CNN.

▶ acquire (*v.*): to gain sth. by one's own in-built or gifted ability, efforts or behavior

eg. 1) It was approximately one year after I arrived in America that I had acquired a taste for cheese.

2) It is still not clear how precisely children acquire their mother tongue.

⛰ acquisition (*n.*): the act of getting sth. especially knowledge, skill etc.

eg. 1) Second language acquisition research has enjoyed a great progress in the last two decades.

2) He devoted his time to the acquisition of knowledge.

18. A strange but <u>costly</u> lawsuit <u>depleted</u> another huge part of their savings.

Meaning: The unusual and expensive lawsuit they were involved in consumed a considerable sum of their savings.

▶ costly (*adj.*): costing a lot of money, especially more than you want to pay

eg. 1) New houses are unduly costly in this city for wage-earners these days.

2) I am sorry to tell you, Mr. Bush, you have made a costly mistake.

▶ deplete (*v.*): to reduce sth. by a large amount so that there is not enough left

eg. 1) In 1942 when London was heavily bombed, food supplies were seriously depleted.

2) His energy was severely depleted in the project.

▲ to deplete of : to empty or almost empty (sth.) of (sth. it contained)

eg. Mankind must take care not to deplete the earth of its natural resources.

▲ depletion (*n.*): exhaustion, consumption

eg. 1) energy depletion 能源枯竭

    2) to cause a depletion of coal deposits 耗尽煤藏

19. Only now, as they <u>assess</u> what they have left —a <u>solid</u>, loving marriage, their health, a dependable income, and good friends—do they realize that true abundance comes not from amassing, but rather from appreciating.

Meaning: Only when they make an account of what they have in their possession—a stable, loving marriage, their good health, a reliable income, and good friends—do they come to understand that real wealth is not obtained by hoarding, but by being grateful for and appreciating what you have already achieved.

▶ assess (*v.*): to make a judgment about the nature or quality of sb./sth.

eg. 1) It is still early to assess the effects of the reform campaign in the country.

    2) She was assessed as a dangerous driver.

▶ solid (*adj.*): that you can rely on; having a strong basis

eg. 1) Their achievement in the initial stage lays a solid foundation for future development.

    2) Will you make your suggestion more solid and practical next time?

20. Scarcity consciousness arises as a result of the "hole-in-the-soul" <u>syndrome</u>.

Meaning: The spiritual emptiness and a sense of material insufficiency result in a feeling of fear that drives them to fill the gap in their inner lives by getting hold of more from the outside world to ensure a sense of fullness, but they will never succeed.

▶ syndrome (*n.*): a set of physical conditions showing that a person has a particular disease or medical problem

eg. 1) This syndrome is perhaps a result of chronic headache.

    2) Acquired Immune Deficiency Syndrome (Aids or AIDS) 艾滋病

▲ syndrome (*n.*): a way of behaving that is typical of a type of person, attitude, or social problem

eg. 1) With this team of students, be careful with their "I see" syndrome.

    2) In our society we should guard against the widespread "nothing is comparable to foreign countries" syndrome.

21. We already have enough, so we should <u>revel</u> in our own <u>interior</u> abundance.

Meaning: We already have enough, so we should take delight in the wealth of our inner lives.

▶ revel (*v.*): to spend time in a noisy, enthusiastic way

eg. 1) The TV star was obviously reveling in the attention she had attracted.

　　2) Pay attention to your kids when you notice that they seem to revel in causing pains to others.

▶ interior (*adj.*):connected with the inside part of sth.

eg. 1) The interior decoration of our new country house is under way.

　　2) Grace, a Harvard graduate, specializes in interior design.

▲ interior (*n.*): the central part of a country that is a long way from the coast

eg. She is from the interior of the country.

Better Know More

📖 Notes

The Relationship between "Here" and "There"

　　"Here" involves what you have in your present life, mostly focusing on material gains. Those who are not satisfied with "here" tend to believe that they should have attained more than they have now. Hence, "there" becomes an objective to accomplish. It is good that they set certain goals and strive to improve their present life. However, if they have too strong a desire for material success, which they think, is the only purpose in life, they turn to be narrow-minded and insatiable for more wealth and luxuries. Consequently, they are constantly driven by the desire to move from "there" to another "there" without a stop to enjoy "here."

Check Your Understanding

　　Translate the following sentences into Chinese. Please make sure that your language flows smoothly.

1. To be grateful means you are thankful for and appreciative of what you have and where you are on your path right now.

　　感恩指的是你对现在拥有的一切和当前的境况很知足,怀有感激之情。

2. Make a list each day of all that you are grateful for, so that you can stay conscious daily of your blessings.

　　你可以每天列一个单子,把你怀有感激之情的事情都写在上面,这样就能每天都意识到自己的收获和所得。

3. However you choose to learn gratitude is irrelevant.

你选择什么方式学习感恩并没有关系。

4. Many people are afraid of not having enough of what they need or want, and so they are always striving to get to a point when they would finally have enough.

许多人担心自己的所获比自己真正需要和想要得到的要少，所以他们总是不停地奋斗拼争，以期有朝一日会最终心满意足。

5. It took several years and much hard work for Alan and Linda to land on their feet, and though they now live a life far from luxurious, they have taken stock of their lives and feel quite blessed.

阿兰和琳达经过好几年的努力才重新获得稳定的生活。尽管他们现在的生活远没有达到奢侈的水平，但他们认真反思生活后，对目前的状况感到非常知足。

6. We already have enough, so we should revel in our own interior abundance.

我们的所得已经足够丰厚，因此我们应该为内心的充实感到快乐。

Answer the following questions based on the text you have just learned.

1. How do most people think of happiness?

   Many people believe that they will be happy once they arrive at some specific goal they set for themselves.

2. What does the author remind us regarding the age-old drive to look beyond the place where you now stand?

   The author reminds us that it is important for human beings to keep sober-minded about the age-old drive to look beyond the place where you now stand. On one hand, your life is enhanced by your dreams and ideals. On the other hand, these drives can pull you farther and farther from your enjoyment of your life right now.

3. How can you bring yourself closer to fulfilling the challenge of living in the present?

   By learning the lessons of gratitude and abundance, you can bring yourself closer to fulfilling the challenge of living in the present.

4. What should be done to make the feeling of gratitude an integral part of life?

   It does not matter how you choose to learn gratitude. The most important thing is that you create a space in your consciousness for appreciation for all you have right now, so that you may live more joyously in your present moment.

5. What is the cause that drives a person to keep working toward "there"?

   One of the most common causes is human fear about scarcity. Many people are afraid of not having enough of what they need or want, so they are always striving to get to a point when they would finally have enough.

6. Why do you think that Alan and Linda feel very blessed even though they are by no means living a life as luxurious as before?

Because they have taken stock of their lives and feel quite blessed. Only now, as they assess what they have left—a solid, loving marriage, their health, a dependable income, and good friends—do they realize that true abundance comes not from amassing, but rather from appreciating.

7. Can you guess how they understood happiness before?

Most probably, they used to view membership in the exclusive club, luxury cars, designer clothing, and high-class society friends as their main source of happiness.

8. What is the origin of the "hole-in-the-soul" syndrome?

It originates from the scarcity consciousness when we attempt to fill the gaps in our inner lives with things from the outside world.

A Sip of Phonetics

Know Their Faces

What characterizes English diphthongs in pronunciation is the glide from one vowel to another. Among the eight English diphthongs in three groups that end in phonemes /ɪ/, /ʊ/ and /ə/, this group with three diphthongs, ends in /ə/.

When teaching the three diphthongs, /ɪə/, /eə/ and /ʊə/, the instructor should draw the students' attention to the key point that though there is a glide from one phoneme to the other in each of the diphthongs, each is pronounced as on syllable without distinct pause in between and with a natural transition from one simple vowel to the other.

Train Your Tongue

1. How many berries /could a b<u>a</u>re berry carry/ if a b<u>a</u>re berry /could carry berries?
2. Well they can't carry berries/ which could make you very w<u>a</u>ry, but a b<u>a</u>re berry carried/ is more sc<u>a</u>ry!
3. N<u>ea</u>r an <u>ea</u>r, a n<u>ea</u>rer <u>ea</u>r, a n<u>ea</u>rly <u>ee</u>rie <u>ea</u>r.
4. A big black bug/ bit a big black b<u>ea</u>r /and made the big black b<u>ea</u>r /bleed blood.
5. The soldier's shoulder/ s<u>ure</u>ly hurts!
6. If Stu chews shoes,/ should Stu choose the shoes/ he chews?

You'd Like to Be

A Strong Bridge Builder

Fill in the blanks with the given words to complete the following sentences. Please note that some can be used more than once.

of	on	into	about	beyond	by
for	over	to	with	from	without

1. I was never satisfied with what I had gained before I met Jane. Her words changed me. "Just look beyond today for blessings," she said, "There's happiness ahead for you." I learned to be happy with what I've achieved so far. And I gradually become more and more conscious of the need to maintain my focus on the right things.

2. When I was pulling away from the parking place yesterday, a car crashed into mine. The worse part of it was that the local witnesses were reluctant to talk to the police, which brought the investigation to a dead end.

3. Last night I taught my son a lesson about gratitude. He came over to me with a question in his exercise book. After I satisfied him with an answer, he attempted to leave without saying anything that he was expected to. I tried to remind him by asking if he had other questions. He said no. I grew a little disappointed. "Do you think you should say something to me?" I hinted. He looked at me, puzzled. Then perhaps inspired, he asked in a low voice, "Do you mean THANKS?" "Why not, my dear son?" I asked. He said "thanks" with an embarrassed smile on his face.

A Smart Word Player

Fill in the blanks with the proper words that need to be transformed from the ones provided in the brackets.

Wood fuel has been around since human's acquisition (acquire) of fire and use of wood fuel remains popular in developing countries. Wood fuel is becoming scarce (scarcity) due to the high increase in demand across the world. The problem is especially serious with the areas with human communities that depend (dependable) on wood fuel for energy. People tend to say that wood fuel is cheap, costing (costly) not a cent. This is actually not true as the forest left unburned is no longer <u>abundant</u> (abundance). <u>Reminding</u> (remind) the local people is now exceedingly important in view of the fact that over-<u>dependence</u> (dependable) on wood fuels will finally result in the <u>depletion</u> (deplete) of forest.

A Skilled Text Weaver

Fill in the blanks with the words you have learned in this text. One word is for each blank. Here is a piece of advice: You must be really familiar with the text to accomplish the following tasks.

At tonight's ceremony, I would like to give my hearty thanks to those who helped me finally <u>land</u> on my feet with the book. The ability to <u>fulfill</u> this challenge on my part would have never been possible if it were not for Dr. Eastwood's guidance and direction over the years. I cherished every piece of conversation with him, which helped strongly in <u>cultivating</u> my research ability. Dr. Eastwood once said to me: "While writing a book involves the patience in <u>amassing</u> the first-hand data and the interest in working out the <u>puzzle</u> pieces, what really matters is to <u>fit</u> in all where they <u>belong</u>." Under his instruction, I <u>strove</u> to keep my <u>focus</u> on data collection and making sure that all the first-hand data appear in the right place. His words of encouragement and support have been greatly <u>appreciated</u>. I feel quite <u>blessed</u> knowing him. If it were not for his <u>considerable</u> amount of devoted instruction and willingness to share much of his research experience, today I would remain a mediocre (平庸的) young researcher with no much <u>insight</u> in history. Finally, I'd like to give my <u>gratitude</u> to my parents for the <u>abundance</u> of love and <u>dependable</u> support they have been giving freely...

A Sharp Interpreter

Please paraphrase the following sentences. Change the sentence structure if necessary.

1. By always chasing after another "there," you are never really appreciating what you already have right "here."
   ✥ *Paraphrasing:*
   If you are always going after your one goal after another just for material abundance, you are unable to be grateful for and enjoy what you already have got at the present moment.
2. It is important for human beings to keep sober-minded about the age-old drive to look beyond the place where you now stand.
   ✥ *Paraphrasing:*
   It is important for human beings to have a clear understanding and stay sensible about

the long existing desire to achieve something more or better than what you are having now.

3. On the other hand, these drives can pull you farther and farther from your enjoyment of your life right now.

   ✧ *Paraphrasing:*

   On the other hand, these desires to achieve far more than what you have obtained so far not only kill your passion for life, but also widen the gap that makes it impossible for you to be satisfied with the life you are living now.

4. Gratitude fills your heart with the joyful feeling and allows you to fully appreciate everything that arises on your path.

   ✧ *Paraphrasing:*

   If you are able to feel thankful to what is around you, you will experience a very happy feeling from the bottom of your heart and you are able to fully enjoy everything existing in your life.

5. What really matters is that you create a space in your consciousness for appreciation for all you have right now.

   ✧ *Paraphrasing:*

   What makes a difference is that you are able to have in mind the value and significance of what you have already gained in life so that you feel grateful to things around you.

6. They were unable to erase the deep fear of scarcity both had acquired in childhood.

   ✧ *Paraphrasing:*

   They were unable to get rid of the deep fear that they would never have got enough wealth, a fear both of them developed in their childhood.

7. A strange but costly lawsuit depleted another huge part of their savings.

   ✧ *Paraphrasing:*

   The unusual and expensive lawsuit they were involved in consumed a considerable sum of their savings.

8. Scarcity consciousness arises as a result of the "hole-in-the-soul" syndrome.

   ✧ *Paraphrasing:*

   The spiritual emptiness and a sense of material insufficiency result in a feeling of fear that drives them to fill the gap in their inner lives by getting hold of more from the outside world to ensure a sense of fullness, but they will never succeed.

9. No amount of external objects, affection, love, or attention can ever fill an inner emptiness. We already have enough, so we should revel in our own interior abundance.

   ✧ *Paraphrasing:*

   We are not able to compensate for our spiritual emptiness including affection, love and attention, no matter how much external wealth we are hoarding. It is significant to think that we have enough and should be happy with it, which adds our gratitude to our inner lives.

A Solid Sentence-Constructer

Please make a sentence with each word or expression listed below.

1. to be appreciative of

   ◈ *Original sentence in the text:*

   To be grateful means you are thankful for and appreciative of what you have and where you are on your path right now.

   ◈ **Suggested sentence:**

   Even though students may be frustrated with your strictness, I am sure that some day they would be appreciative of your hard-task-master attitude towards them.

2. to stay conscious of

   ◈ *Original sentence in the text:*

   Make a list each day of all that you are grateful for, so that you can stay conscious daily of your blessings.

   ◈ **Suggested sentence:**

   Dozens of years after their divorce, she still stays conscious of her ex-husband's immense love for her.

3. to be irrelevant to

   ◈ *Original sentence in the text:*

   However you choose to learn gratitude is irrelevant.

   ◈ **Suggested sentence:**

   Do you think the last example is irrelevant to the thesis?

4. to get to a point

   ◈ *Original sentence in the text:*

   Many people are afraid of not having enough of what they need or want, and so they are always striving to get to a point when they would finally have enough.

   ◈ **Suggested sentence:**

   |Their project is getting to a point where they may have a breakthrough soon.

5. to take stock of

   ◈ *Original sentence in the text:*

   It took several years and much hard work for Alan and Linda to land on their feet, and though they now live a life far from luxurious, they have taken stock of their lives and feel quite blessed.

   ◈ **Suggested sentence:**

   Taking stock of my present life, I feel quite satisfied though I still do not have luxury cars, designer clothing or high-class society friends.

6. to revel

◈ *Original sentence in the text:*

We already have enough, so we should revel in our own interior abundance.

◈ **Suggested sentence:**

I still remember how we reveled in the first harvest.

📖 A Superb Bilingualist

Please translate the following sentences into English with the prompts provided in the brackets

1. 年轻人应该有理想、有抱负，而且对将来要制定具体的计划。只有逐一实现了具体的目标，才能不断接近最终的目标。(arrive at, bring oneself closer to)

◈ **Suggested translation:**

Young people should have their ambitions and make their concrete plans accordingly. Only when they arrive at their specific goals one after another, could they bring themselves closer to the ultimate one.

2. 这篇文章的表达非常有特点，如果你注意观察作者的选词和篇章结构，就会体会到其中的妙处。(keep one's focus on, experience the wonder of)

◈ **Suggested translation:**

The article distinguishes itself by its wording and expressions.　You may have a feeling of wonder if you keep your focus on the choice of words and the structure of the article.

3. 在学生中做一次无记名的问卷调查能够让老师深入了解学生。(gain insight into)

◈ **Suggested translation:**

An anonymous survey among students will help the teacher gain insight into his or her students.

4. 现在许多人梦想着发大财，总是担心自己赚的钱不如别人多。但是他们似乎不明白重要的并不是财富的积累，而是他们心底是否感到了充实和幸福。(dream of, be afraid of, amass)

◈ **Suggested translation:**

Many people dream of making their fortunes,　but are constantly afraid of not making as much money as others. However, it seems that they do not understand that what matters is not just amassing material wealth but whether there is interior abundance and joy in their hearts.

5. 想象一下你失明以后生活会变成什么样子，这可不是无稽之谈，因为它会提示你好好珍惜自己的眼睛。(remind... of)

◈ **Suggested translation:**

Imagine what your life would be if you lost your eyesight.　This is not utter nonsense because it reminds you of the necessity to protect your eyes.

Text B

Introduction of the Text and the Author

The Road to Happiness is another insightful discussion about happiness. Russell in this article provides us with both a theoretical perspective about happiness and the possible accesses to happiness.

Bertrand Russell was born on 18th May, 1872 at Trellech, Monmouthshire, Wales into an aristocratic family. At the age of three he was left an orphan. Then he was brought up by his grandmother. He was taught by governesses and tutors and acquired a perfect knowledge of French and German. In 1890, he went into residence at Trinity College, Cambridge, and left there in 1894.

Betrand Russell has been described as the greatest logician since Aristotle, but during his lifetime he was known equally well for his writings on social, political and educational themes. In 1903, he wrote his first greatest philosophical work, *The Principles of Mathematics.* In 1910, he was appointed lecturer at Trinity College. In 1912, he began with *The Problem of Philosiphy*, a bestseller that revealed to the public Russell's gift for writing. His large ambitious book *The Theory of Knowledge* was abandoned in 1913 due to the severe cirticisms it received from Wittgenstein, but the following year Russell published *Our Knowledge of the External World*. After the first World War broke out, he took an active part in antiwar campaigns. His college deprived him of his lectureship in 1916. He was then offered a position at Harvard University, but was denied a passport. In 1918, he was sentenced to six months' imprisonment for a pacifistic article he had written in the *Tribunal*. While in prison he wrote *Introduction of Mathematical Philosophy*. Immediately after the war, he delivered another series of public lectures on philosophy, published in 1921 as *The Analysis of Mind.* Books such as *On Education (1926), Marriage and Morals* (1929), and *The Conquest of Happiness* (1930), helped to establish Russell in the public eye as a philosopher with important things to say about the moral, political and social issues of the day.

In 1920, Russell paid a short visit to Russia to study the conditions of Bolshevism on the spot. In the autumn of the same year he went to China to lecture on philosophy at the Peking University. In 1938, he went to the United States and taught at many of the country's leading institutions.

Russell was awarded the Nobel Prize for Literature in 1950.

Comprehension Questions

After reading Text B, please answer the following questions with the words and expressions given in the brackets.

1. What are considered unwise ways in pursuit of happiness? (by means of)

   It is considered unwise to pursue happiness just by means of pursuing it and by means of drinks.

2. Why did Epicurus succeed in pursuing happiness? (congenial society, dry bread, little cheese)

   Epicurus succeeded in pursuing his happiness because he was living only in congenial society and eating only dry bread plus little cheese on feast days.

3. How do most people comment on the pursuit of happiness? (abstract, theoretical, adequate)

   For most people, the pursuit of happiness, unless supplemented in various ways, is too abstract and theoretical to be adequate as a personal rule of life.

4. What does the author think of the personal rules of life one chooses? (incompatible)

   The author believed that whatever personal rule of life you may choose, it should not, except in rare and heroic cases, be incompatible with happiness.

5. What is taken as the cause that some people remain unhappy even though they live in abundant material happiness? (fault, wrong theory, how to live)

   The cause that a great many people with all the material conditions of happiness are profoundly unhappy is that there is a fault that they hold a wrong theory as to how to live.

6. What distinguishes human beings from animals? (impulse, external conditions)

   Human beings distinguish from animals in that they do not live on impulse like animals who are happy as long as external conditions are favorable.

7. What are the satisfying external conditions for a cat to enjoy happiness? (warmth, night, tiles)

   The satisfying external conditions for a cat to enjoy happiness are food and warmth and opportunities for an occasional night on the tiles.

8. What does a businessman have to sacrifice if he aims at success and becomes rich? (health, affection)

   A businessman may be so anxious to grow rich that to this end he has to sacrifice health and private affections.

9. What ridicule can be found in the scene of rich ladies talking about fashionable new books? (boring hours, learning, new books, delight)

The ridicule is found that many rich ladies, although nature has not endowed them with any spontaneous pleasure in literature or art, decide to be thought cultured, and spend boring hours learning the right thing to say about fashionable new books that are written to give delight, not to afford opportunities for dusty snobbism.

10. What similarity do happy men and women share? (gradually build up, come into existence)

The most important thing they share is an activity which gradually builds up something that they are glad to see coming into existence. Women who take an instinctive pleasure in their children can get this kind of satisfaction out of bringing up a family. Men get happiness in this way if their work seems good to them.

11. According to Russell, what is the source for happiness? (devote weekends, unremunerated toil, gardens)

There are many humbler forms of the same kind of pleasure. Many men who spend their working life in the city devote their weekends to voluntary and unremunerated toil in their gardens, and when the spring comes, they experience all the joys of having created beauty.

Writing Practice

Put your answers to the above questions together and form a summary about the text and share with your classmates the summary you have completed.

It is considered unwise to pursue happiness just by means of pursuing it and by means of drinks. Epicurus succeeded in pursuing his happiness by living only in congenial society and eating only dry bread plus little cheese on feast days. For most people, the pursuit of happiness, unless supplemented in various ways, is too abstract and theoretical to be adequate as a personal rule of life. The author believed that whatever personal rule of life you may choose, it should not, except in rare and heroic cases, be incompatible with happiness. The cause that a great many people with all the material conditions of happiness are profoundly unhappy is that there is a fault that they hold a wrong theory as to how to live. Human beings distinguish from animals in that they do not live on impulse like animals, who are happy as long as external conditions are favorable. The satisfying external conditions for a cat to enjoy happiness are food and warmth and opportunities for an occasional night on the tiles.

   A businessman may be so anxious to grow rich that to this end he has to sacrifice health and private affections. The ridicule is found that many rich ladies, although nature has not endowed them with any spontaneous pleasure in literature or art, decide to be thought cultured, and spend boring hours learning the right thing to say about fashionable new books that are written to give delight, not to afford opportunities for dusty snobbism. The most important thing men and women share is an activity which gradually builds up something that they are glad to see coming into existence. Women who take an instinctive pleasure in their children can get this kind of satisfaction out of bringing up a family. Men get happiness in this way if their work seems good to them. Those who devoted their weekends to voluntary and unremunerated toil in their gardens, experience all the joys of having created beauty.

Unit **6**

Angel

Unit·Goals

After studying this unit, students should be able to:

☞ **understand the pains the homeless have been suffering and their aspirations for a bright future;**

      Text A tells a moving story of a homeless family of five enjoying an especially warm Christmas Day in a hospital. The family's painful and humble experience in search of a warm shelter for Christmas in the hospital provoked the nurses' compassion. They went into action to suffice the family's need and exceeded their expectations by giving them insight into the goodness of human being and the significance of future life. The Christmas party held for the family treated them not only with food, gifts, but also with a good share of humanity, happiness and love, the embodiments of the Christmas spirit. The "angels" carried out a special mission on Christmas Day to take care of the less fortunate.

☞ **know how to pronounce /p/, /b/ and /t/, and how to utilize the words and structures that contribute significantly to the texts;**

      This section focuses on the three explosives /p/, /b/ and /t/. The instructor's job is to demonstrate the correct pronunciation of each; to be sensitive to the existing problems in their pronunciation and able to correct them. To practice these explosives, the instructor should encourage students to read aloud tongue twisters before class.

☞ **be willing to share what they have with those who are in need.**

      The Christmas spirit can be interpreted as the willingness to share with those in need shown in *Working Christmas Day* and *Silent Angel*. Both **Text A** and **B** witness the Christmas spirit that inspires the nurses to offer their love and compassion for their patients, which imparted grace to their well-earned name "angels." The Christmas party held for the homeless family and the big but tender hug given to the soldier add a distinctly humanistic touch in the story.

Before Reading

Hands-on Activities and Brainstorming

The instructor should allow 15—20 minutes for students to do presentation either on the topic *Christmas Day in a hospital with a homeless family* or on *A warm and special Christmas Day in a hospital with a group of nurses.*

A Glimpse at Words and Expressions

A. Before approaching the meaning of the phrase "to sign in," the instructor should first work on the verb "to sign" with the help of the following sentences "She signed her name to the document" and "Please sign on the dotted line." The instructor should also point out that "to sign" in the former sentence is a transitive verb, but an intransitive one in the latter. Based on this, the instructor should follow up with another example "Every morning when we go swimming, we have to sign in at Health Club." The sentence suggests a context that leads the students to understand the phrase as "to note down one's name when arriving at a hotel, hospital, etc." For example: *Every girl must sign in when she comes back to the dormitory.*

B. The potential problem for the students to define the meaning of "picture" is the missing of context in the sentence itself. However, students are able to pick up a grammatically acceptable match from either number 1 or 4 in column B. In this case, students should be conscious that what is required of them is not to offer the literary meaning of the word "picture." So "image" is not a better choice than "scene." The answer "scene" interpreted as "a vivid or realistic verbal description" matches with it perfectly. For example: *In his later years at Eton the picture underwent considerable change.*

C. The context to ensure students' understanding of "checked the chart" is the latter part of the sentence. The instructor should emphasize the action "checked the chart" took place after all the family members had signed in or "registered," an expression provided in the sentence. To help the students get the meaning of the word "chart," the instructor is obliged to offer examples, such as "a grammar chart," "a chart of price changes." The phrase "to check the chart" means "to examine the registration information." For example: It is possible to automatically check the chart of accounts.

D. To help the students understand "her reflection in an ornament," the instructor might as well tell a story about a greedy dog, which saw his reflection in the water with a bone in his mouth, thinking the reflection was another dog with another bone. He lost the bone when opening his mouth to get the other bone. This story not only interprets the meaning of the word "reflection," but also offers the clue that the ornament is something bright and shining that enables people to see their own image in it. Similarly, "reflection" can be understood as "image." For example: *He saw his reflection in the shop window.*

E. The instructor should remind the students that the prefix "un" suggests negative, meaning "not." Thus, "unconvinced" equals to "be not convinced," implying that the speaker assumed a questioning attitude toward what was happening. If the students are able to identify the negative meaning of "unconvinced," they will be able to pick up the answer in column B, because there is only one answer with a negative word, that is, "not believing."

F. The instructor should draw students' attention to the negative implication suggested by the expression "to turn away" by giving examples as "Hundreds of people were turned away from the concert because all seats were sold out." and "He turned all the applicants away because none of them fitted the position." The former grants a negative context that hundreds of people were not able to get the tickets to the concert, and the latter tells that he did not take in any applicant. In addition to that, "We would see them" also implies the strong affirmative meaning of "not to turn away." "not to turn away" can be explained as "not to refuse patients who wanted to see a doctor."

Keys

A-5   B-4   C-2   D-1   E-6   F-3

Text A

Suggested Explanations on Text A

1. Working Christmas Day

   Meaning: Working on Christmas Day

   Note: Text A has two types of expressions: "having to work on Christmas Day" and "working Christmas Day," both meaning the same, in different linguistic forms though. The nominal phrase "Christmas Day" here functions as an adverbial, and therefore it should be noted that the head word (中心词) of "working Christmas Day" is "working" instead of "Christmas Day." It is interesting that some other scholars believe that "Christmas Day" may serve as the factual and functional object of the verb "work," even though it may not be taken so grammatically.

Here are two more examples:

eg. 1) When they were traveling abroad, they sometimes had to lower the cost by <u>sleeping churches</u>.

2) Mr. Robin and his colleagues keep costs down by <u>flying economy class</u> and keeping an office in Shenzhen rather than in pricy Hong Kong.

2. Quiet, <u>that is</u>, except for the nurses who were standing around the nurses' station <u>grumbling about</u> having to work on Christmas Day.

▶ that is: (a formula introducing or following an explanation of a preceding word or words, used as a parenthesis in a sentence) more accurately, in other words, that means...

eg. Arabic is written in the opposite direction to English, that is, from right to left.

Note: In written English, "that is" is usually replaced by the Latin word *ie*, the short form of *id est*. However, in spoken English "that is" rather than *id est* is preferred. *A Dictionary of Current Idiomatic English* and most other dictionaries put "that is" and "that is to say" under the same entry because the two phrases play the same role in sentences, as will be shown in the following examples.

▲ that is to say: more accurately, in other words, that means; at least

eg. 1) He was a genius, that is to say, a man who does superlatively and without obvious effort, something that most people cannot do by the uttermost exertion of their abilities.

2) He has never been to Tibet, that is to say, it is not recorded that he has.

▶ to grumble about/over: to complain bitterly and often unreasonably about

eg. 1) There is no way to please our teacher, who always grumbles about our work even when we've done our best.

2) It is no use grumbling at me about your treatment in hospital. Write to the Board of Management.

3. Just then a clerk came back and told me I <u>had five patients waiting</u> to be <u>evaluated</u>.

▶ had five patients waiting to be evaluated (structure)

Note: The instructor should draw the students' attention to the structure "to have sb. doing sth." This structure goes to two implications. First, the subject initiates the action to take place or intentionally causes a person to do something, for example "If you do not have antivirus running on your system, you could become infected with a virus." The difference between "to have sb. doing sth." and "to have sb. do sth." lies in the idea that the former puts more emphasis on the ongoing process, while the latter implies that the act is going to happen. Second, the subject is not inclined to start somebody to do something or make something happen, as is the case in the following examples.

eg. 1) If you do not set up a fence round your garden, you'll have people walking in and stealing your fruit (就会有人走进去偷你的水果).

  2) I felt sorry about Jack's failing that course, but he had it coming to him (但那是他自找的).

▶ evaluate (*v.*): to form an opinion of the amount, value or quality of sth. after thinking about it carefully

eg. 1) The scientists were still evaluating their data.

  2) The role of stay-at-home mother is more positively evaluated in working-class communities.

▲ evaluation (*n.*): the opinion formed after thinking about sth. carefully

eg. 1) Students frequently do have good grounds for mistrusting their teacher's evaluation.

  2) Evaluation is the systematic determination of merit, worth, and significance of something or someone.

4. I <u>whined</u>, "Five, how did I get five..."

  ▶ whine (*v.*): to complain in a querulous tone or in a feeble or undignified way

eg. 1) They whined about having to work extra hours.

  2) If you have time to whine and complain about something then you have the time to do something about it.

  3) Hard-working students never whine about stress in their academic study.

5. Well, there are five <u>signed in</u>.

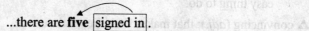

...there are **five** signed in.

Note: The instructor should call the students' attention that "signed" is not a predicate verb, rather, it is a past participle used to modify(修饰)"five" as an attribute. Students should be clear that it is a mistake to put another predicate verb following "there be" structure, such as "There are five students know it." It is a prevailing error that results from the influence of the Chinese language. To improve the structure, we should change "know" into "knowing" or "who know," either of which functions as an attribute: "There are five students knowing/who know it." Remember the rule in the following can be very helpful: A simple sentence is a sentence with only one predicate.

  ▶ to sign in: to register

eg. 1) After you sign in, you will find your Shopping Cart contains the items you have decided to purchase.

  2) You will find that Google has more to offer when you sign in to your Google Account.

6. ... a pale small woman and four little children <u>in somewhat ragged clothing</u>.

▶ in (ragged) clothing: wearing (ragged) clothes

eg. 1) She was in a new black overcoat with a velvet collar.

　　2) The kid looked out of the window to see men in dark suits coming for him and immediately fled on his skateboard (滑板).

7. "Are you all sick?" I asked <u>suspiciously</u>.

▶ suspiciously (*adv.*): in a way that shows one thinks sb. has done sth. wrong or illegal

eg. The soldiers eyed me suspiciously, hesitating if they should let me go.

▲ suspect (*v.*): to have an idea that sth. especially sth. bad, is probably true or likely to happen, but without having definite proof

eg. 1) She suspected that Sylvia had not been telling the truth.

　　2) I rather suspect they were trying to get rid of me.

8. "Okay," I replied, <u>unconvinced</u>, "who's first?"

▶ unconvinced (*adj.*): not believing

eg. 1) The economist's explanation left many consumers unconvinced.

　　2) Yet I could see in her eyes that she remained unconvinced of the importance of physical exercises.

▲ convinced (*adj.*): believing

eg. 1) She became convinced that something was wrong.

　　2) She was later convinced that breaking the "glass ceiling" of prejudice was not an easy thing to do.

▲ convincing (*adj.*): that makes sb. believe sth. is true

eg. 1) The album is wholly convincing, which assured us there was a romance between the two.

　　2) "There is no convincing evidence that taking this medicine can alleviate depression," says the doctor.

▲ convince (*v.*): to make sb. believe sth. is true

eg. 1) You need to convince them that you are the one they want.

　　2) Many were convinced that doctors get additional money for prescribing certain medications.

▲ conviction (*n.*): a strong opinion or belief

eg. 1) His theory of poetry is characterized by his conviction that "poetry should be analyzed on the basis of the text (文本)."

　　2) Lao Tze's invention of Tao as the universal law governing Nature and his conviction that soft and weak are superior to hard and strong are not only valid(合理的), but also timely for the current world.

9. When it <u>came to</u> descriptions of their presenting problems, things got a little <u>vague</u>.

Meaning: When it was time for them to give an account of what the matter was with them, they had difficulty making their explanations clear.

▶ to come to: used in many expressions to show sth. has reached a particular state

eg. 1) When it comes to mathematics, I'm completely at sea.

2) The intelligent programmer always lost his temper when it came to debugging(程序查虫).

▶ vague (*adj*.): not clearly expressed; of uncertain or ill-defined meaning or character

eg. 1) The identity of the city in the novel is deliberately left vague.

2) The law is notoriously vague on this point.

10. Two of the children had headaches, but the headaches weren't accompanied by the normal body language of holding the head or trying to keep it still or squinting or grimacing.

Meaning: Two of the children reported to have headaches, but they do not wear the usual distorted facial expressions with their eyes half shut due to pains, or have a hard time holding their heads in an undisturbed state.

11. ...ambulances had <u>brought in</u> several, more <u>critical</u> patients...

▶ to bring in: to take sb./sth. indoors

eg. 1) We want to bring in enough food before it starts snowing there.

2) Bring the washing in, it's raining.

▲ to bring in: to ask sb. to come to one's help

1) They've brought in experts to advise on the scheme.

2) We need to bring in new people who are creative, energetic and can bring spice to the company.

▲ to bring in: to introduce (an idea)

eg. Britain already has extensive rules covering broadcasters and the video industry, and now it needs to bring in new regulations for the Web.

▶ critical (*adj*.): serious, uncertain and possibly dangerous

eg. 1) The premier didn't realize the unemployment problem was all that critical here.

2) There is a critical weakness in the country's economy.

▲ critical (*adj*.): expressing disapproval of sth./sb.

eg. 1) The report is highly critical of the railway's poor safety record.

2) Many European security officials were highly critical of the U.S. for not sharing evidence crucial for investigations and trials.

12. <u>On a hunch</u>, I checked the chart after the clerk had finished registering the family.

▶ on a hunch: a feeling that sth. is true even though there is not any evidence to prove it eg. 1) Obviously, he made this decision on a hunch and not by any facts.

2) Investors should not buy stocks purely on a hunch.

13. The nurses, grumbling about working Christmas, turned to compassion for a family just trying to get warm on Christmas.

Meaning: The nurses who were complaining about having to work on Christmas Day now changed their attitude and became sympathetic about a family seeking a warm shelter on Christmas Day.

▶ to turn to: to direct one's attention or thoughts etc. from sb. or sth. towards sb. or sth. else

eg. 1) After working as an attorney, he turned to painting, moved on to sculpture and finally photography.

2) The debate on "Real Right Law" then turned to the definition of "real right."

▲ to turn to: to apply to (for advice, assistance, etc.)

eg. 1) The child felt there was no one he could turn to with his problem.

2) To look for a new home, they had to turn to the Internet. They found a traditional two-story house, but the reality was quite different from what they saw on the computer screen.

3) For centuries, people have turned to classical music for its calming and relaxing effects.

▶ compassion (*n*.): pity inclining one to help or be merciful

eg. 1) Anger, blame and prejudice can be replaced with compassion, caring, and support.

2) Hundreds of volunteer doctors from Doctors without Borders (无国界医生组织), driven by compassion and love for humanity, were sent to the area that was seriously stricken by tsunami.

▲ compassionate (*adj*.): sympathetic

eg. 1) His research success was largely due to his compassionate devotion to his patients, who confidently placed their trust in him, and to his colleagues and students.

2) Our offer to pay half of the medical fees was simply a compassionate gesture. Unfortunately, it carried a wrong message that we were the ones who were held responsible for the car accident.

14. The team went into action, much as we do when there's a medical emergency.

Meaning: All the nurses were soon on the move taking care of the family as promptly as possible, just like what we usually do when dealing with an emergency.

The team went into action, much as we do when there's a medical emergency.

主句

状语从句内的时间状语从句

从属连词　much as 引导的方式状语从句

Note: It should be noted that "much as," used to add or interject a comment relating to the statement of a fact, here functions as a subordinate conjunction（从属连词）that links together the main clause "the team went into action" with the subordinate clause "we do when there's a medical emergency."

▶ much as (*conj.*): used to make a comment or to add information about what one has just said

eg. 1) Plants need food, much as we do.

　　2) The mother fish cares for her young much as a hen cares for her chickens.

▲ much as: however much, even though, although（表让步）

eg. 1) Much as I admire his courage, I don't think he acted wisely.

　　2) Pluto（冥王星）died much as it lived. 冥王星虽名噪一时, 却终究谢世。

Note: "much as," the subordinator in the above sentences introduces a concessive clause in an inverted syntactic order. When the predicate verb is "to be," the adverb is replaced by an adjective.

eg. 1) Complex as is the path to the moon, it is possible to predict unerringly（精确地）eclipses many years in advance of their occurrence.

　　2) Significant as is the subject of high-speed flight, our book will not devote to it but to the subject of low-speed flight.

It is also worth noting that "be" comes before the subject because of the subject being too long and the sentence would be out of balance if otherwise. What is more, the instructor should draw students' attention that not only adverbs and adjectives, but also predicate verbs can be fronted too.

eg. 1) Try as he may, he never succeeds.

　　2) Change your mind as you will, you will gain no additional support.

It is also important for the instructor to point out that "though" shares the same function as "as" when used to introduce a concessive clause.

eg. 1) Much though I admire her, I cannot excuse her faults.

　　2) Modest though his needs were, he found it hard to get by on his income.

　　3) Fail though he did, I would not abandon my goal.

▶ to go into action: to start a planned operation

eg. 1) It was only a short time later when the fire trucks pulled up in front of the house and the firemen went into action.

2) Always ready to go into action at a moment's notice, our soldiers are often the first ones at the scene of disaster.

15. We were all offered a free meal in the hospital cafeteria on Christmas Day, so we <u>claimed</u> that meal and prepared a banquet for our Christmas guests.

▶ claim (v.): to demand or ask for sth. because of people's belief in their legal right to have it

eg. 1) The author of the book has the right to claim authorship.

2) Half of the people who originally overpaid for the iPhone never bothered to claim for the rebate(返款).

▲ claim (n.): a request for a sum of money that is believed one has a right to, especially from a company, the government, etc.

eg. 1) He put in a claim for compensation because he lost his luggage in the train crash.

2) Baggage Claim is the area of an airport where one claims one's baggage from the aircraft after a flight.

16. We made little <u>goodie</u> bags of candy **that** one of the doctors had brought the nurses, crayons the hospital had from a recent <u>coloring contest</u>, nurse bear buttons the hospital had given the nurses at annual training day and little fuzzy bears **that** nurses <u>clipped onto</u> their stethoscopes.

Note: The instructor should first focus on the structure of the sentence, which is well balanced with four noun clauses (attributes) qualifying the four noun phrases: goodie bags of candy, crayons, nurse bear buttons and little fuzzy bears. As is known by the students, the conjunctive pronoun "that" can always be omitted, when used as an object in a noun clause serving as an attribute. However, the two "thats" in the above sentence are retained to exert emphasis on the agent of action(强调施动者).

The instructor might as well ask the students to work out a simple sentence by leaving out the noun clauses: "We made little goodie bags of candy, crayons, nurse bear buttons and little fuzzy bears."

▶ goodie (n.): (also goody) sth. attractive or delectable, especially sth. sweet to eat

eg. The goodie bag contains free cinema tickets, video rentals and a pair of swimming goggles.

Note: The expression like "goodie" is used informally, which reads baby talk that conveys sweetness and friendliness, with an implication of "smallness, childlikeness, intimacy and affection." There are some similar examples as follows.

1) birdie—bird   2) bookie—book

3) nursie—nurse   4) doggy—dog

5) piggy—pig   6) daddy—dad

7) auntie—aunt   8) mummy—mother

9) Johnny—John   10) footy—football

▶ coloring contest: Coloring contest is a contest usually held for children to fill in a black and white drawing with colors. It is an activity that pushes the children to use their imagination and creativity in making the colors go together in terms of their arrangement, proportions and beauty, which in turn challenges their artistic and intellectual potentiality. While we may say: "Our community held a kite coloring contest under the influences of our project," the expression can also be written in "coloring-in contest" to make it more grammatically acceptable.

▲ to color in: to fill sth. such as a drawing with color

eg. 1) It's easier to color in the picture before you cut the shapes out.

    2) Decide what elements of the photo you would like to emphasize with color, and use color pencils or chalk to color in those areas.

▶ to clip onto/on: to fasten sth. on one's clothes or person with a special fastener

eg. 1) He carried a board, onto which his secretary had clipped all the documents.

    2) Would you clip these earrings on?

17. We also found a mug, a package of powdered cocoa, and a few other <u>odds and ends</u>.

▶ odds and ends: (informal) small articles of various kinds or small pieces of sth. usually of little value

eg. 1) The tailor made a suit for the boy out of the odds and ends of the cloth.

    2) He made a meal of the odds and ends that were left in the refrigerator.

    3) I only heard some odds and ends. 我只听说了一些零零碎碎的事情。

18. We <u>pulled ribbon and wrapping paper and bells off</u> the department's decorations to which we had all contributed.

Meaning: We took ribbon, wrapping paper and bells off the department's decorations brought here by each one of us.

▶ to pull...off: to remove sth. from...

eg. 1) There is a piece of thread on your skirt, let me pull it off.

    2) Help him pull off his muddy boots.

19. As seriously as we met physical needs of the patients who came to us that day, our team worked <u>to meet the needs</u>, and <u>exceed</u> the expectations, of a family who just wanted to be warm on Christmas Day.

Meaning: Just as we took great responsibility to treat whoever came to our hospital that day, we devoted ourselves not only to satisfying their minimum demand of a warm shelter on Christmas Day, but to offering more than what they had expected to receive on Christmas Day.

▶ to meet the needs: to satisfy what one desires

eg. 1) I highly recommend this book to teachers who try to reach and meet the needs of every learner in their classrooms.

2) We are planning to build a website to meet the needs of people with disabilities.

▶ exceed (*v.*): to be greater than

eg. 1) The results of the competition exceeded our expectations.

2) China's inflation rate is likely to exceed the central bank's target of three percent, a top official said Wednesday.

20. We <u>took turns</u> joining the Christmas party in the waiting room.

▶ to take turns: to play, act, etc. one after another in proper order

eg. 1) Students, class representatives and teachers take turns giving a talk or sharing their ideas with others.

2) The three sisters took turns looking after their sick mother.

3) They drove to the South of England last Friday, taking turns with the driving.

21. Each nurse took his or her lunch break with the family, choosing to spend their "<u>off duty</u>" time with these people whose laughter and delightful chatter became quite <u>catching</u>.

▶ off duty: (used as a compound word, and better in the form of off-duty) not engaged or occupied with one's normal work

eg. 1) In his off-duty time, Gary enjoys song writing.

2) A Michigan robber finally learned not to take a toy gun to a real gun fight when he attempted to rob an off-duty police officer and his girlfriend.

▲ on/off duty: engaged/ not engaged or occupied with one's normal work

eg. 1) A policeman does not wear his uniform while off duty.

2) What gave you the idea I am "off duty"?

3) When do you come off duty?

▶ catching (*adj.*): (of an emotion or mood) passing quickly from one person to another

eg. 1) A yawn is quite catching. It just takes one yawn to start off other yawns.

2) The tunes are quite catching and really stick in your head.

22. The six-year-old started the conversation. "I want to be a nurse and help people," she <u>declared</u>.

▶ declare (*v.*): to say sth. firmly and clearly

eg. 1) The President declared that the next meeting of the Council would be held on 28 March 2001 at 2:30 pm.

2) The accused man declared he was not guilty.

3) North Korea has agreed to declare and disable all its nuclear facilities by the end of the year.

Note: Please note that "declare" is mostly used in formal situations, implying one's firmness in talking. The author of the text employs "declare" here to convey a sense of humor that reveals the six-year-old's seriousness in her future plan.

△ declaration (*n.*): an official or formal statement, especially about the plans of a government or an organization

eg. 1) On December 10th, 1948, the General Assembly of the United Nations adopted (正式通过) the Universal Declaration of Human Rights (世界人权宣言).

2) Drafted by Thomas Jefferson between June 11th to 28th, 1776, the Declaration of Independence was at once the nation's most cherished symbol of liberty.

23. She smiled and said, "I just want my family to be safe, warm and content—just like they are right now."

▶ content (*adj.*): satisfied, adequately happy

eg. 1) I am not content with beautiful dreams: I want beautiful realities.

2) He's perfectly content to live in a hut and paint pictures all day.

24. The "party" lasted most of the shift, before we were able to locate a shelter that would take the family in on Christmas Day.

▶ shift (*n.*): a period of time worked by a group of workers who start work as another group finishes

eg. 1) When the men finish work in the daytime, the night shift starts to work.

2) We can keep the factory going all the time because we have two shifts—a day shift and a night shift.

▶ locate (*v.*): to find the exact position of sth./sb.

eg. 1) By putting the plumbing under pressure, we're able to locate the leak and make appropriate repairs.

2) Despite the massive hunt launched by FBI for the killer at Red Bridge, they were unable to locate him until 7 years later.

△ location (*n.*): a place or position in which a person or thing is

eg. 1) Its location being popular, the shop attracts a lot of customers.

2) The name of each Hutong in Beijing indicates its origin, location or history.

▶ to take sb. in: to allow sb. to stay in one's home

eg. 1) These homeless dogs need kind, patient people willing to take them in to help tame them.

2) The farmer took in the lost travelers for the night.

25. After the four children had shared their dreams, I looked at the Mom. She smiled and said, "I just want my family to be safe, warm and content—just like they are right now." The "party" lasted most of the shift, before we were able to locate a shelter that would take the family in on Christmas Day. The mother had asked that their charts be pulled, so these patients were not seen that day in the emergency department. But they were treated.

Note: It is worth noting that the author adopted simple past tense throughout her writing, with a few exceptions only. The students should be alerted to the jump in tense in the shaded areas that indicate those actions that happened earlier. Therefore, the sentence "The mother had asked that their charts be pulled, so these patients were not seen that day in emergency department." should be translated as: 早些时候,孩子们的母亲曾要求我们把他们的表格撤走,这样他们就不会在急诊室留下就诊纪录。

Another thing that the instructor should alert the students is the subjunctive mood employed in the shaded sentence. Generally, verbs such as "order," "propose," "insist," "demand," "suggest" and "advise" are followed by the noun clause in subjunctive mood. And the complete format of the sentence structure goes with a modal verb "should" to express the will of the agent, however, for simplification, "should" is usually omitted. Similar examples can be found in the following:

1) The husband ordered that a magnificent tomb be built for him and his wife.

2) They insisted that Peter report this to the manager himself.

3) The policemen especially advised that the Robins keep the gate locked.

4) The doctor prescribed that Tony take a double dose of Vitamin C for treatment.

► to treat sb.: to entertain sb. with sth. special

eg. 1) She treated me with homemade ice-cream.

2) Never had they been treated to such a performance before.

▲ to treat sb.: to give medical care or attention to a patient, an illness, an injury, etc.

eg. 1) The doctor successfully treated the wound.

2) His burns were treated with snake oil and tree bark.

Better Know More

The Christmas Spirit

The word "Christmas" means Christ's Mass, the Christian observance (庆祝) of the nativity (诞生) of Jesus on 25 December. According to Christianity, Jesus Christ was the Son of God and God manifest in the flesh. He was crucified and died on the cross. Speaking in Christian logic, the Christmas Spirit is all about the spirit of Christ, the one who gave His life to pay the penalty for the sins of mankind, and therefore, the essence of the spirit is "giving" instead of "getting." The tradition of giving Christmas gifts in western countries is also related to the idea of "giving."

　　The Christmas spirit is basically the spirit of love expressed in giving, the spirit of making others happy and the spirit of gratitude to the bestowed love, which is in turn expressed in good will and love to all men all over the world.

Check Your Understanding

　　Translate the following sentences into Chinese.　Please make sure that your language flows smoothly.

1. "Okay," I replied, unconvinced, "who's first?"
   "好吧，"我回答道，心里并不相信他们真的病了，"谁先看病？"

2. Two of the children had headaches, but the headaches weren't accompanied by the normal body language of holding the head or trying to keep it still or squinting or grimacing.
   通常头痛会伴有用手托头、尽量保持头部不动、眯眼睛或表情痛苦等肢体语言，可这两个说头痛的孩子并没有这些表现。

3. On a hunch, I checked the chart after the clerk had finished registering the family.
   凭着直觉，我在工作人员为这一家人登记后，查看了一下登记表。

4. The nurses, grumbling about working Christmas, turned to compassion for a family just trying to get warm on Christmas.
   那些（刚刚还在）抱怨在圣诞节还得上班的护士们转而对这一家人充满了同情，他们不过是想在圣诞节能有个暖身之处。

5. We also found a mug, a package of powdered cocoa, and a few other odds and ends.
   我们还找出一个茶缸、一袋可可粉，还有些其他零七八碎的东西。

6. We pulled ribbon and wrapping paper and bells off the department's decorations to which we had all contributed.
   我们把丝带、包装纸和铃铛从急诊部的圣诞装饰上解下来，这些饰物都是我们各自带来的。

Answer the following questions based on the text you have just learned.

1. How did it look like in the emergency room on Christmas Day?

   It was unusually quiet in the emergency room on December 25th. Quiet, that is, except for the nurses who were standing around the nurses' station grumbling about having to work Christmas Day.

2. Why did the author whine when she knew there were five patients waiting to be evaluated?

   She whined because she was just out there and no one was in the waiting room.

3. How did the author figure out that something was wrong with the picture?

   She found that two of the children had headaches, but the headaches weren't accompanied by the normal body language of holding the head or trying to keep it still or squinting or grimacing. Two children had earaches, but only one could tell her which ear was affected. The mother complained of a cough, but seemed to work to produce it. Therefore she figured out something was wrong with the picture.

4. What was the purpose of the woman and her children going to the hospital?

   The homeless family just wanted to be warm on Christmas Day. And the mother just wanted her family to be safe, warm and content.

5. How did the nurses gather the presents?

   They put together oranges and apples in a basket one of their vendors had brought them for Christmas. They made little goodie bags of candy that one of the doctors had brought the nurses, crayons the hospital had from a recent coloring contest, nurse bear buttons the hospital had given the nurses at annual training day and little fuzzy bears that nurses clipped onto their stethoscopes. They also found a mug, a package of powdered cocoa, and a few other odds and ends. They pulled ribbon and wrapping paper and bells off the department's decorations that they had all contributed to. All these were offered as Christmas presents.

6. Why did the mother ask to have their charts pulled?

   Because the mother and her brood did not come to the emergency room for medical treatment.

7. What did the four-year-old child say to the nurse?

   She whispered, "Thanks for being our angels today."

8. Why did the author say "...patients were not seen that day in the emergency department. But they were treated."?

   Although they were not medically treated as patients, they were offered something very pleasant and enjoyable by the nurses of the emergency room.

A Sip of Phonetics

Know Their Faces

本课涉及三个辅音 /p/、/b/、/t/。英语发音有一规律,叫做"清辅音浊化",指的是在 /s/ 音后,清辅音要发成对应的浊辅音。本课中的 /p/ 和 /t/ 是清辅音,在 /s/ 后要分别发成 /b/ 和 /d/ 的音。如 sport, space, start, stop。

在讲解这部分内容时,教师应该训练学生做到发音正确,识别字母或字母组合的发音规律。教师还可以利用以下这些绕口令,强化这三个辅音的练习。教师应指导学生如何换气和断句、领悟句意,以便达到读得又快又准的效果。

Train Your Tongue

1. Bring back/ my beauty blue balloon.
2. Peter Piper/ picked a peck of pickled peppers/. Did Peter Piper/ pick a peck of pickled peppers? / If Peter Piper/ picked a peck of pickled peppers/,   where's the peck of pickled peppers/ Peter Piper picked?
3. So she bought a bit of butter/, better than her bitter butter/, and she baked it/ in her batter/, and the batter was not bitter/. So it was better Betty Botter/ bought a bit of better butter.
4. If Pickford's packers packed a packet of crisps/ would the packet of crisps that Pickford's packers packed/ survive for two and a half years?

You'd Like to Be

A Strong Bridge Builder

Fill in the blanks with the given words to complete the following sentences. Please note that some can be used more than once.

in	up	at	by	on	throughout	about	away

(The following passage was based on a CCTV report.)

When the infant, Ayeblak (阿依不拉克), was brought in, Abuliz (阿布力孜) was 64 years old, his wife 59. With all their sons growing <u>up</u> one <u>by</u> one to establish their own families, the couple might at last take a breath and lead a more affluent life. And here showed <u>up</u> Ayeblak.   The old couple disagreed on whether they should adopt the newly born sick baby. <u>On</u> a hunch that her husband might keep the baby, Abuliz's wife grumbled <u>about</u> having to cook, clean <u>up</u>, herd sheep and grow grapes <u>throughout</u> her whole life.   But no matter what she said, Abuliz pointed <u>at</u> little Ayeblak, saying "I shall be her father. And you the mother, period." Actually, Abuliz's action was not surprising to his neighbors, who told the CCTV reporter that he was so benevolent(仁慈的)a man that he would never turned <u>away</u> anyone asking for help.

A Smart Word Player

Fill in the blanks with the proper words that need to be transformed from the ones provided in the brackets.

No one expected that the Children's Coloring Contest would be cancelled because of food poisoning. 26 <u>contestants</u> (contest) out of 30 were found sick before the contest was held. While most children suffered from diarrhea (腹泻) <u>accompanied</u> (accompany) by high fever, some cases became extremely critical.   When the children were sent to the hospital, doctors found it very hard to conduct patient <u>evaluation</u> (evaluate) because some children were too young to <u>describe</u> (description) their <u>presenting</u> (present) problems. Worrying parents found the organizer's explanation that the food poisoning was accidental especially <u>unconvincing</u> (unconvinced)   and they <u>suspected</u> (suspiciously)   that the organization committee had purchased low-quality food in order to reduce the cost.

A Skilled Text Weaver

Fill in the blanks with the words you have learned in this text.   One word is for each blank.   Here is a piece of advice: You must be really familiar with the text to accomplish the following tasks.

1. You are supposed to <u>evaluate</u> the patients by a set of clear criteria and produce a really definite report. Most importantly, nothing <u>vague</u> can be accepted.
2. Thomas was pretending to be sick again, but this time, it seemed that his trick did not work. The <u>squinting</u> and <u>grimacing</u> that he worked to <u>produce</u> left his supervisor <u>unconvinced</u>, as his facial color appeared to be normal.

3. You can't help turning to <u>compassion</u> for the hen which had her wings spread to <u>huddle</u> her <u>brood</u> and gave a fierce look to those who would harm it.

4. Tom thought Mom would be <u>content</u> because his final scores had far <u>exceeded</u> her low <u>expectation</u>.

5. In two minutes time, the police besieged the building and tried to establish communication with the suspect, but received no answer. They soon went into <u>action</u>, searching every corner of the building for him on a <u>hunch</u> that he still remained inside.

A Sharp Interpreter

Please paraphrase the following sentences. Change the sentence structure if necessary.

1. When it came to descriptions of their presenting problems, things got a little vague.
   ✧ *Paraphrasing:*
   When the mother and the children were asked to describe what was wrong with them, they were unable to give a clear explanation.

2. The mother complained of a cough, but seemed to work to produce it.
   ✧ *Paraphrasing:*
   The mother said she had a cough, but it seemed she pretended to cough.

3. As seriously as we met physical needs of the patients that came to us that day, our team worked to meet the needs, and exceed the expectations, of a family who just wanted to be warm on Christmas Day.
   ✧ *Paraphrasing:*
   Just as we took great responsibility to treat whoever came to our hospital that day, we devoted ourselves not only to satisfying their minimum demand of a warm shelter on Christmas Day, but to offering more than what they had expected to receive on Christmas Day.

4. The mother had asked that their charts be pulled, so these patients were not seen that day in the emergency department. But they were treated.
   ✧ *Paraphrasing:*
   The mother asked the nurses to withdraw their registration forms; therefore, there would not be records for them to see doctors. However, they were offered something very pleasant and enjoyable in the emergency room.

5. The "party" lasted most of the shift, before we were able to locate a shelter that would take the family in on Christmas Day.
   ✧ *Paraphrasing:*
   Before we were able to find an appropriate place for the family to spend their Christmas

Day，we had been accompanying and entertaining the family for most of our working time that day.

A Solid Sentence Constructer

Please make a sentence with each word or expression listed below.

1. to sign in

   ✥ *Original sentence in the text:*

   "Well, there are five signed in."

   ✥ **Suggested sentence:**

   First year students were signed in and given a number, called student ID, which allowed them various discounts at the University Center.

2. to be unconvinced

   ✥ *Original sentence in the text:*

   "Okay," I replied, unconvinced, "who's first?"

   ✥ **Suggested sentence:**

   Though Tom nodded，it seemed he was still unconvinced of the plan they were talking about.

3. body language

   ✥ *Original sentence in the text:*

   Two of the children had headaches，but the headaches weren't accompanied by the normal body language of holding the head or trying to keep it still or squinting or grimacing.

   ✥ **Suggested sentence:**

   Usually body language occurs unconsciously, which helps the speaker put emphasis on what he expresses.

4. on a hunch

   ✥ *Original sentence in the text:*

   On a hunch, I checked the chart after the clerk had finished registering the family.

   ✥ **Suggested sentence:**

   I came to the concert on a hunch, but was extremely disappointed.

5. to turn to compassion for sb./sth.

   ✥ *Original sentence in the text:*

   The nurses，grumbling about working Christmas，turned to compassion for a family just trying to get warm on Christmas.

   ✥ **Suggested sentence:**

   As we have watched these tragedies unfold, animal lovers have also turned to com-

passion for the poor cats and dogs left homeless.

6. odds and ends

✤ *Original sentence in the text:*

We also found a mug, a package of powdered cocoa, and a few other odds and ends.

✤ **Suggested sentence:**

Yesterday, Martin and I went shopping for the CD player and got some CD shelves and boxes and odds and ends that we needed.

7. to contribute to sth./doing sth.

✤ *Original sentence in the text:*

We pulled ribbon and wrapping paper and bells off the department's decorations to which we had all contributed.

✤ **Suggested sentence:**

The experience he had in early life all contributed to his later struggling for equal rights.

A Superb Bilingualist

Please translate the following sentences into English with the prompts provided in the brackets.

1. 他穿得很体面,而他的孩子却穿得破破烂烂的。(in ragged clothing)

✤ *Suggested translation:*

He dressed decently, but his son was in ragged clothing.

2. 经理压低了声音说,"轮到你了。认真些!"(lower, turn)

✤ *Suggested translation:*

The manager lowered his voice and said, "It's your turn. Take it serious."

3. 上了岁数的人,不仅要吃饱穿暖,他们更需要有家人的陪伴。(be accompanied by)

✤ *Suggested translation:*

The aged should have a shelter and warm clothes; what's more, they should also be accompanied by their family members.

4. 当医生大声呵斥病人时,我感到很不舒服。(patient, treat)

✤ *Suggested translation:*

When the doctor raised his voice in treating the patient, I felt very uncomfortable.

5. 凯瑟琳在这场比赛中取得了第二名的成绩,对此她很满足。这个成绩远远超过了她原先的料想。(be content with, exceed the expectation)

✤ *Suggested translation:*

Having won the second place in such a contest, Katherine felt very much content. It exceeded her expectation.

Text B

〰️ Introduction of the Text

Using the past indefinite to tell a story sounds simple, yet the story is easy to slip from the past into present indefinite and the reader probably does not even notice it. The narrator uses the past indefinite when he wants the reader to be a bit detached from the events—as if the light of time has made everything far from them, and he would use the present indefinite when he wants to catch the vividness of sensation. The instructor may ask the students if they are able to figure out the intention of the author of Text B to slip from past into present indefinite from time to time.

〰️ The Vietnam War

The Vietnam War refers to the conflict in Southeast Asia, primarily fought in South Vietnam between government forces aided by the United States and guerrilla forces aided by North Vietnam, and that also explains why the war is also called the American War in Vietnam. The war began soon after the Geneva Conference of 1954 provisionally (临时性地)

divided Vietnam into the Democratic Republic of Vietnam (North Vietnam) and the Republic of Vietnam (South Vietnam). It escalated (逐步升级) from a Vietnamese civil war into international conflict in which the United States was deeply involved. The war finally came to an end with the South Vietnam's collapse(崩溃) and the unification(统一) of Vietnam by the North.

The war was cruel to all parties involved. More than 47,000 Americans were killed in action, nearly 11,000 died of other causes, and more than 303,000 were wounded. The casualty (伤亡) for the Vietnamese were far less. The involvement of the United States in the war was highly controversial(有争议) both domestic and abroad.

📖 Purple Heart

The Purple Heart was established by General George Washington at Newburgh, New York, on 7 August 1782, during the Revolutionary War. The Purple Heart is a United States military decoration awarded in the name of the President to those who were wounded or killed while serving on or after 5 April 1917 in the U.S. military.

Comprehension Questions

After reading Text B, please answer the following questions based on what you have learned in Text B.

1. Where did the author spend the Christmas Day of 1967?

   He spent the Christmas Day of 1967 at the Ninety-Third Hospital near Saigon, Vietnam.

2. Why was he wounded?

   He was wounded because he was ambushed along a jungle path by a small group of guerillas. His right thumb was ripped from his body by a claymore mine blast.

3. How was he feeling on that day?

   He was feeling helpless. His spirit felt empty, and his body felt broken.

4. How did his attitude toward the Cambodian soldier change?

   As time passed, his attitude changed and hatred disappeared. They never said a word to each other, but they glanced into each other's eyes and smiled. Communication emerged. He felt compassion for him, knowing they both had lost control of their destiny. They were equals.

5. Everyone in the ward was disappointed on Christmas Day, why?

   They realized that General Westmoreland would not come and the award of Purple Hearts to the courageous combat wounded was not to happen.

6. Why couldn't the author fall asleep?

   The pain in his arms and a violent headache made it difficult for him to fall asleep.

7. What did the nurse do when he signalled to her?

   She came to his side and looked into his tearing eyes. Quietly, she sat on the side of his bed, held his arm, removed the IV, and then lightly massaged his swollen, painful arms.

8. Why did the nurse shed tears?

   Because she felt his pain.

9. What present did he receive on Christmas night?

He received a long, tender hug from the nurse.

10. Why was the Christmas of 1967 unforgettable for the author?

The nurse's kindness and sensitivity moved him, and the author would cherish her compassion forever.

Writing Practice

Put your answers to the above questions together and form a summary about the text and share with your classmates the summary you have completed.

The author spent the Christmas Day of 1967 at the Ninety-Third Hospital near Saigon, Vietnam. He was wounded because he was ambushed along a jungle path by a small group of guerillas. His right thumb was ripped from his body by a claymore mine blast. He was especially unhappy because he was placed next to a Cambodian wounded soldier. As time passed, his attitude changed and hatred disappeared. They never said a word to each other, but they glanced into each other's eyes and smiled. Communication emerged. When the American soldiers realized General Westmoreland would not come and the award of Purple Hearts to the courageous combat wounded was not to happen, everyone felt disappointed. The pain in his arms and a violent headache made it difficult for him to fall asleep. At that time, the nurse came to his side and looked into his tearing eyes. Quietly, she sat on the side of his bed, held his arm, removed the IV, and then lightly massaged his swollen, painful arms. The nurse felt the soldier's pain. He received a long, tender hug from the nurse. The nurse's kindness and sensitivity moved him, and the author would cherish her compassion forever.

Unit 7

Dreams

Unit Goals

After studying this unit, students should be able to:

☞ **understand some basic facts about dreams;**

It is hard to imagine that someone has never had dreams in sleep, but we have very limited knowledge of dreams and we sometimes tend to become superstitious about them. The two articles of this unit will just open us a window to dreams. The information will also help shed light on what attitude we should hold toward dreams.

☞ **know how to pronounce /d/, /k/ and /g/, and how to utilize the useful words and structures that contribute significantly to the texts;**

In this section, the instructor should explain to the students how to pronounce these consonants and demonstrate the correct pronunciation of each one. They should also help the students discern between right pronunciations and the wrong ones. The instructor should help the students analyze the reason for errors and to help them avoid further mistakes. It is strongly suggested that the instructor encourage the students to read aloud tongue twisters before class and follow the advice provided in the section **Before Learning**.

☞ **understand the role that dreams may play in our lives.**

Text B offers us interesting information about the potential role that dreams play. Even if the conclusions may not be so precise or reliable, as indicated by the text, they provide us with valuable insights into understanding how dreams can help us have a better life.

Before Reading

Hands-on Activities and Brainstorming

The instructor should allow 15—20 minutes for students to do presentations or share their dream experience.

A Glimpse at Words and Expressions

A. "Not see eye to eye" means "always disagree with someone." It is often used in the negative sense. For example: *His parents do not see eye to eye on anything*.

B. "Tap into" here means "use or to draw from," so "explore" is the closest in meaning to "tap into." For example: *He told me to use these reports to tap into the minds of customers*.

C. "Let go of" means "give up an idea or an attitude, or control of sth." For example: *Chinese parents should let go of the idea that they have the absolute authority over their kids*.

D. "Guard against" can be understood as "take care to prevent sth. from happening." For example: *Students are told to guard against grammatical mistakes in the writing test*.

E. "Recognize" means "know or be aware of." For example: *Please recognize the differences between the two words. The first one is very formal while the second is relatively colloquial*.

F. "Arise" refers to "appear." For example: *Tremendous difficulties arise in learning a foreign language for an adult*.

G. "Respond to" can be explained as "do sth. as a reaction." For example: *Our stomach responds to whatever food we eat. When it is unhappy, we would feel it*.

Keys

A-3 B-6 C-1 D-7 E-4 F-2 G-5

Text A

Introduction of the Text

Dreams are so commonplace in our life that most people tend to ignore. But when asked why we have dreams, what dreams can tell us or how dreams affect our sleep and health, few can give a ready and convincing answer. This text may set you thinking over your dreams. Perhaps your crazy idea in the dream today contribute significantly to amazing discoveries about your life today or in the future.

When used figuratively, dreams may refer to human ambition. What do you think of ambitious people? Are they cheerful, light and interesting to you or dull, workaholic and overwhelmed? Do you think it is wise to stick to one's dream or change one's dream to be more realistic? Do you really know your ambitions? Are you an ambitious person? These questions may kindle students' interest in their discussion about dreams.

Suggested Explanations on Text A

1. Thirty-one-year-old Lisa was 16 the night she <u>dreamed of</u> a beautiful evergreen forest where her mother was a witch.

   ▶ dream of: to experience a series of images, events and feelings in one's mind while he/she is asleep

   eg. My little daughter dreamed of a moveable fairyland last night.

   ▲ dream of: to imagine or think about sth. that one would like to happen

   eg. 1) Being tired of the tedious office work, Kate dreams of running her own business.

   2) The ambitious young man dreams of the day when he becomes the richest person in town.

2. I suppose I was <u>processing</u> that my mother was becoming <u>more of</u> a real person to me, <u>with flaws and faults</u>, and that I was going to <u>go further</u> in life than she had.

   ▶ process (*v.*): to calculate based on the information gained or what has happened

   eg. 1) I was processing that psychology had become a very important discipline for my future career.

   2) She was processing that the salesman was not the sort of Mr. Right she had been looking for.

   ▶ more of (idiom): to a greater extend or degree; more likely

   eg. 1) Although Thomas is a composer, he is more of a singer.

   2) That is not a concert, but more of a rehearsal.

   ▶ with flaws and faults: with shortcomings or weaknesses

   eg. Well, they were human with flaws and faults just like the rest of us.

   ▶ go further: to do more or better

   eg. 1) I never believe that I am more intelligent than my father though I had gone further in education.

   2) To reach our final goal, we have to go further with our current research.

3. We want to tap into those nighttime <u>fantasies</u> that have us flying, saving the world and <u>dating</u> movie stars.

▶ fantasy (*n*.): a pleasant situation that one imagines but that is unlikely to happen

eg. 1) He still remembers his childhood fantasy about becoming a pop singer.

   2) Her parents often told her to stop living in fantasies.

▶ date (*v*.): to have a romantic relationship with sb.

eg. Tom started dating the governess two months ago.

▲ date (*n*.): a meeting that one has arranged with boyfriend or girlfriend

eg. Paul cannot come because he has a date with Nancy.

▲ date (*n*.): someone that one has a date with

eg. Of course, you can bring your date to my party.

4. After a century of dream research, North American experts have recently <u>cracked a few more of the codes</u> that run through our heads as we sleep.

Meaning: After a century of dream research, North American experts have recently found out some more truths than before about dreams.

▶ crack a few codes: to find a solution or an explanation to a long existing problem

eg. 1) After years of research, doctors have cracked a few codes about bird flu.

   2) People have cracked a few more of the codes about how languages are acquired.

5. First, say dream researchers, you should let go of the idea that what you dream has a <u>universal</u> meaning.

▶ universal (*adj*): true or right at all times or at all places

eg. 1) People have been dreaming of inventing a universal language for centuries.

   2) Few have actually realized that our local culture has a universal appeal.

6. For 3,000 years people have been trying to read things into dreams as if they're fortune cookies.

Meaning: For 3,000 years people have been adding their interpretation to dreams as if dreams are like fortune cookies that predict one's fortune.

7. Indeed, recent research by Joseph De Koninck, a psychology professor at the University of Ottawa, seems to show dream symbols <u>differ</u> <u>depending on</u> the individual.

▶ differ (*v*.): to be different

eg. 1) In regard to the predicate, Chinese language differs a lot from English.

   2) The twin sisters differ very much in personality.

▶ depend on: to be affected or decided by

eg. 1) Your future depends on your dreams.

2) The success of your project design depends on the weather condition.

8. He asked ten <u>volunteers</u> to list details of their recent dreams and make a second list of what they'd been doing in waking life.

▶ volunteer (*n.*): a person who does a job without being paid for it or who is willing to offer to help someone

eg. 1) The relief work after the earthquake was mostly done by the PLA men and volunteers.

2) We need someone to mow the lawn, any volunteers?

▲ volunteer (*v.*): to offer to do sth. without expecting any reward

eg. 1) Peter volunteered to have the Spring Festival get-together at his house.

2) Bob volunteered to take care of the old man in the nursing centre.

9. When others tried to <u>figure out</u> who dreamed what by matching the two lists, they failed.

▶ figure out: to think about a problem or a situation until getting the answer or understanding what has happened

eg. 1) I couldn't figure out what they were saying when they were talking in Spanish.

2) No one can figure out why she behaves like that.

10. Often our dreams may even <u>give an alarm</u>.

▶ give an alarm: to warn sb. about sth. bad or dangerous. Similar expressions are "sound/raise the alarm."

eg. 1) He is one of the first colleagues to give an alarm to her about her risky plan.

2) The unusual silence of the enemy gave an alarm that their next attack was approaching.

11. On this point, today's dream experts agree with Freud and his colleague Carl Jung, both of whom believed that dreams were the <u>subconscious</u> way of communicating with ourselves.

▶ subconscious (*adj.*): connected with feelings that influence one's behavior even though he/she is not aware of them. It is often used before a noun.

eg. 1) My husband suffers from subconscious fears about snakes. Unfortunately I was born just in the year of snake.

2) The article shows his subconscious prejudice against women writers.

12. Similarly, if you're <u>repressing</u> something, it often <u>arises</u> in your dreams.

repress 和 suppress 同时都有"抑制感情"的意思,但又略有不同。suppress 指"成功地完成了抑制,终止对情感的流露",而 repress 仅仅指"去抑制"。

131

► repress (*v.*): to try not to show an emotion, a feeling, etc.

eg. 1) Linder tried to repress her urge to shriek at her kids.

   2) Mr. Green has been repressing his painful memories of marriage.

▲ suppress (*v.*):

eg. 1) Isaac Newton suppressed for decades his invention of calculus, laws of motion, and optics, and harbored implacable hatred for those who disputed him.

   2) He had to suppress his anger because he needed the care of the doctors.

　　arise, rise 和 raise 三个词都有"上升、上涨、由低向高移动"的意思,但在用法上有所不同。arise 和 rise 都是多作为不及物动词使用,后面不加宾语;raise 是及物动词,后面有宾语。在语用中,rise 的使用频度比较高,是一个非常通用的词,而 arise 的使用范围比较窄,在多数情况下都具有特殊的修辞色彩,具有比喻的特点。arise 的主语(主体)往往是:an argument, a problem, a doubt, a question, a disagreement 等具有负面色彩的名词。参看以下的例句:

► arise (*vi.*): to happen or appear

eg. 1) Many new problems arise when we are revising the traffic law.

   2) A serious disagreement arises between the two parties at the negotiating table.

▲ rise (*vi.*): to move from lower position to higher position

eg. 1) The sun rises in the East.

   2) The man became too weak to rise.

▲ raise (*vt.*): to move from lower position to higher position

eg. 1) Now the wounded simply can't raise the barbell.

   2) In this county, there is a strange tradition. When an elected official tries to raise his salary for any reason, he will be subject to criticism.

13. Sure enough, those students <u>were more likely to dream</u> about that friend than another group, who were not told to suppress their thoughts.

► be likely to do sth.: probably sb. is going to do sth.

eg. 1) Many local citizens fear that oil price is likely to rise next month.

   2) Russia is likely to veto the proposal at UN assembly.

▲ likely (*adj.*): probable

eg. 1) It is not likely that a person like her will accept an offer like that.

   2) We think it likely that we will get the budget for the program.

   3) Where do you think is most likely his hiding place?

▲ likely (*adv.*): probably

eg. 1) Very likely the child will cry when you send him to the kindergarten.

   2) Very likely they would be late due to the heavy snow.

14. About five dreams out of seven are <u>negative</u> and considered nightmares if they wake you up.

 ▶ negative (*adj.*): bad or harmful

 eg. 1) If you hold such a negative attitude, it is hard to learn anything.

   2) Your professor's criticism is not exactly negative.

 ▲ negative (*adv.* spoken): no, not

 eg. —Will you come to my party?

   —Negative. Don't want to be thought as an idiot.

15. But Antonio Zadra, psychology professor at the University of Montreal, says nightmares can be caused by <u>stress</u>, anxiety or depression.

 ▶ stress (*n.*): pressure or worry caused by the problems in one's life

 eg. 1) It is not true that everyone can cope with the stress of modern technology.

   2) The stresses of everyday responsibilities made him dull and uninteresting.

 ▲ be stressed /stressed out: too anxious and tired to be able to relax

 eg. 1) He was very stressed and unhappy about what had happened.

   2) My son told me on the phone he was stressed out and he wanted to come home.

 ▲ stressful (*adj.*): causing a lot of anxiety and worry

 eg. 1) Being a university faculty member seems to be very stressful nowadays.

   2) You should learn how to stay positive in a stressful situation.

 ▲ stress (*n.*): emphasis

 eg. 1) This program lays great stress on children's adaptability in a new environment.

   2) In this unit we are going to put stress on passive voice.

 ▲ stress (*v.*): to emphasize a fact, an idea, etc.

 eg. 1) The president stressed that government officials should learn to listen to the grassroots.

   2) We stressed our commitment to a constructive and determined effort to host a successful Olympic Games.

 ▲ stress (*n.*): an extra force used when pronouncing a particular word or syllable (重音)

 eg. 1) Many beginners tend to misplace the stress of this word.

   2) The stress is on the last syllable.

16. <u>Recurring</u> dreams or nightmares, however, might indicate a person has an unresolved issue or pain in the past.

 ▶ recur (*v.*): to happen again or a number of times

 eg. 1) Inflation becomes a real headache for his administration as it keeps recurring in the past four years.

   2) Take this medicine if pain recurs in 24 hours.

17. "I think maybe these dreams started because I was sent to boarding school," says Gardner, who finds the nightmares <u>frustrating</u>.

▶ frustrating (*adj.*): causing to feel annoyed and impatient

eg. 1) After ten and half hours frustrating delay, our plane finally arrived.

   2) Yesterday's drizzling was very frustrating.

▲ frustrate (*v.*): to make one feel annoyed or angry because he/she is unable to do what he/she wants

eg. 1) It frustrates him when the film does not come out the way he expects it to.

   2) The readers were frustrated by the poor translation.

18. Bars would suddenly <u>land</u> and lock her in.

▶ land (*v.*): to come down to the ground

eg. 1) In spite of the severe weather, the plane landed safe and sound.

   2) A large bag of food landed heavily on the playground.

19. "Often my dreams will <u>respond to</u> questions I have in mind before I go to sleep," says Tore Nielsen, director of the Dream and Nightmare Laboratory at Montreal's Sacré-Coeur Hospital.

▶ respond to: to do sth. as a reaction to sth.

eg. 1) Jane's negative attitude responds to her sad experience in childhood.

   2) Our body responds very quickly to what we eat.

20. "The dream made me feel more confident about <u>taking risks</u>," she says. A few months later she <u>quit</u> her job and went to Cuba for three months to study Spanish.

▶ take risks/ take a risk: to do sth. even though one knows that sth. bad could happen as a result

eg. 1) Do you think you have the right to take risks with the child's life?

   2) It's true that people are envying me. But few of them are prepared to take the risks I had taken.

▲ risk (*v.*): to put sth. valuable or important in a dangerous situation in which it could be lost or damaged

eg. 1) The young man was risking his life in trying to save the drowning child.

   2) We cannot risk missing the plane.

▶ quit (*v.*): (informal) to leave one's job, school etc.

eg. 1) The doctor advised her to quit Boston and live in a warmer town.

   2) The police did not quit their posts all night long.

Better Know More

1. What is a fortune cookie?

A fortune cookie (签语饼) is a cookie of-fered by most Chinese restaurants in western countries. It is made from a thin layer of dough folded and baked around a strip of pa-per with a prediction of fortune or a maxim

(格言). The griddle-baked (用煎锅烘烤) wafer cookie, when cooled, becomes crispy and one must break it to get the fortune slip out.

2. Freud's Psychoanalytical Viewpoint

According to Freud, the symptoms of hysteria (歇斯底里) were directly related to re-pressed psychological trauma. He started the practice of "free association" (自由联想), de-signed to reveal one's unconscious emotions, and sexual development as the basis for the psychological tension.

3. Carl Jung's Development of Psychoanalysis

Carl Jung [juŋ] refused to accept Freud's view of sex as the determinant (决定因素) of action. He also attached less importance to repression as a factor directly related to psycholog-ical symptoms. He was the first person who introduced the concept of "collective-uncon-scious" (集体无意识). According to Jung, collective-unconscious originated in the most primitive ages, when human experience was passed from generation to generation. It can be observed that the patterns of ancient life and thought called "archetypes" (原型) still survive in modern man and form a substantial element in the unconscious of each individual. One of Jung's propositions sounds familiar to most Chinese, that is "personality is destiny" (性格决定命运). Another two words "extravert" (外向) and "introvert" (内向) were also introduced by Jung.

*C*heck *Y*our *U*nderstanding

Translate the following sentences into Chinese. Please make sure that your language flows smoothly.

1. I suppose I was processing that my mother was becoming more of a real person to me, with flaws and faults, and that I was going to go further in life than she had.

   我想,(在梦境中)我把母亲想成一个更加真实的人,她有缺点,会犯错;这样我便可以在现实生活中去超越她。

2. When others tried to figure out who dreamed what by matching the two lists, they failed.

   当其他人试图将两组(信息)对应起来,以此来推测谁做了什么梦的时候,他们失败了。

3. "The dream made me feel more confident about taking risks," she says.

   她说:"这个梦让我对冒险更加有信心。"

4. For 3,000 years people have been trying to read things into dreams as if they're fortune cookies.

   三千年来,人们一直试图对梦境赋予种种解释,似乎梦就像签语饼(能够预测未来一样)。

5. Sure enough, those students were more likely to dream about that friend than another group, who were not told to suppress their thoughts.

   当然这些学生和另一组不需要压抑他们思想的学生相比,更容易梦到那个朋友。

6. At that time in her life, Lisa and her mother didn't see eye to eye, and in the dream, Lisa's mother attacked her with a huge wave of snow.

   那段时间,丽萨和母亲有些合不来,丽萨曾经梦见母亲掀起巨大的雪波击打她。

7. We want to tap into those nighttime fantasies that have us flying, saving the world and dating movie stars.

   我们希望深入了解诸如翱翔天空、拯救世界以及约会电影明星这样的梦境。

Answer the following questions based on the text you have just learned.

1. What made Lisa feel strong?

   In the dream, her mother attacked her with a huge wave of snow. Unafraid, Lisa used her mind to defend herself and discovered she had power over all things white. Lisa woke up feeling strong because her mother was becoming more of a real person to her with flaws and faults, and that she was going to go further in life than her mother.

2. What did Dr. Allan Hobson think of dreams?

Dr. Allan Hobson did not think that dreams have a universal meaning or can predict the future.

3. How did Joseph De Koninck interpret dream symbols?

Dream symbols differ depending on the individual.

4. According to Joseph De Koninck what can dreams do?

Dreams may help one better recognize the link between the details in their dreams and their daily activities and memories.

5. How did Freud and Carl Jung understand dreams?

They believed that dreams were the subconscious way of communicating with ourselves. Jung, especially, thought that getting to know our dreams was a way to learn about ourselves.

6. What might recurring dreams or nightmares mean?

Recurring dreams or nightmares might indicate a person has an unresolved issue or pain in the past.

7. How do you think Lisa changed the ending of her dream?

Probably she recalled the dream she had had, and then deliberately changed the ending of it in her waking hours.

8. What can be summarized about dreams?

While many dreams are dark, they do have a purpose—most importantly, perhaps, helping us to solve problems and develop insight.

9. What have you learned about dreams?

Dreams do not have a universal meaning. Dream symbols differ depending on the individual. Dreams may help one better recognize the link between the details in their dreams and their daily activities and memories. Recurring dreams or nightmares might indicate a person has an unresolved issue or pain in their past. While many dreams are dark, they do have a purpose—most importantly, perhaps, helping us to solve problems and develop insight.

A Sip of Phonetics

/d/, /k/, /g/ 都是英语中的爆破音,其中 /k/ 为清辅音,发音时声带不振动,送气要强;/d/, /g/ 为浊辅音,发音时声带振动。

发 /d/ 音时应将舌前缘贴住上齿龈,不让气流通过,这样口腔内压力增大,然后舌身快速离开上齿龈,气流冲出口腔,发出爆破辅音。/k/ 和 /g/ 是软腭爆破音。发音时舌后部隆起紧贴软腭,阻碍气流通过,口腔内压力增大,然后舌后部突然离开软腭,气流冲出口腔,发出爆破辅音。请注意,发这几个音时不要在后面加上 /ə/ 的音,例如,不要把 and /ənd/ 误读成 /əndə/,不要把 luck /lʌk/ 误读成 /lʌkə/。

需要特别提醒学生,如果 /k/ 音出现在 /s/ 音的后面,则送气减弱,读成浊辅音 /g/。因此,要特别注意下面这些单词的读音:sky, school, scale, scholar, score, scream, describe。

在教授这部分内容时,教师除了要做到发音正确外,还应该教会学生识别字母或字母组合的发音规律,强化学生朗读词汇的能力;同时,教师还可以利用下列绕口令,强化练习。因为发摩擦音时气流不断受阻,故朗读绕口令会有一定的难度。教师应指导学生如何换气和断句、领悟句意,帮助学生朗读时做到又快又准。绕口令中重点练习的辅音及建议停顿处如下:

1. A big black bug /bit a big black bear, made the big black bear/ bleed blood.

2. How much wood /would a woodchuck chuck, if a woodchuck could chuck wood? He would chuck, he would, as much as he could, and chuck as much wood as a woodchuck would /if a woodchuck could chuck wood.

3. A bloke's back bike brake block broke.

4. Gertie's great-grandma /grew aghast at Gertie's grammar.

You'd Like to Be

A Strong Bridge Builder

Fill in the blanks with the given words to complete the following sentences. Please note that some can be used more than once.

in	of	from	into	out	to	against	over

1. Scientists have cracked the entire genetic code of breast cancer, offering new treatment hopes to those who are suffering from this disease. The discovery sufficiently answers the urgent demand for more effective ways to diagnose cancer in its early stages. But the findings suggest that cancer is more complex than experts had believed. The mutated (变异的) genes in breast cancer were almost completely distinct, which could explain why cancers can behave very differently from person to person, the scientists said.

2. I am a perfectionist, but please do not read too much into it just because I admit it. Perfection has many advantages; meanwhile I have figured out that it has dark sides, too. Over the years, I have learned how to tap into the strengths and benefits of pursuing excellence; at the same time, I have endeavored to guard against its limiting, self-defeating, and even paralyzing facets. As such, I consider myself to be an informed perfectionist; more to the point, I am a recovering perfectionist.

A Smart Word Player

Fill in the blanks with the proper words that need to be transformed from the ones provided in the brackets.

Xiao Zhang dreamed of becoming a billionaire, but he was recently <u>frustrated</u> (frustrating) with how to fill the gaps between "here" and "there". Hired by a travel agency after graduating from university, he was pulled farther and farther from his dream and the <u>recognition</u> (recognize) he had been longing for. Planning to apply for a higher position, he registered to take evening classes to hone his foreign language skills. But the classes were so boring that he almost fell asleep. He was thinking of taking a shortcut to become rich, when the bell finally rang. "Class is over!" He headed directly to the lottery stand to grab a ticket and rushed back home to turn on the TV. Just on time! He was very <u>anxious</u> (anxiety), waiting for the result. "7788999! Wow, I won the Jackpot!" 30.5 million RMB will definitely make a <u>difference</u> (differ) in his life. "Calm," he said to himself, holding in the <u>repressed</u> (repress) <u>excitement</u> (exciting). He said, "I need to plan for my future. A BMW is a must, <u>symbolizing</u> (symbol) wealth; then a membership at a golf club, the <u>typical</u> (typically) <u>indication</u> (indicate) of a man's <u>confidence</u> (confident)." He picked up the phone, gibbering to the lady in the lottery office. Her <u>response</u> (respond) was distant and calm: "Your case is still being <u>processed</u> (process). Please get your ticket ready." Ticket, where is the ticket? He searched every of his pocket for the ticket, but it was to no avail. "I had it!" he yelled, arousing laughter from his classmates. It was a dream. On his way back home, Xiao Zhang was a little <u>depressed</u> (depression), recalling a saying: "You can't fit something in where it does not naturally belong."

A Skilled Text Weaver

Fill in the blanks with the words you have learned in this text. One word is for each blank. Here is a piece of advice: You must be really familiar with the text to accomplish the following tasks.

<u>Stress</u> is the most common cause of poor health. It emerges when we are exposed to <u>frustrating</u> situations. In order to cope with it, we need to <u>figure</u> out the indicators representing the reasons we are tense. Frequent nightmares provide an <u>alarm</u> revealing that we are <u>psychologically</u> disturbed. For example, you may <u>dream</u> of scolding a couple of your subordinates because they messed up the proposal that day. You are trying to <u>control</u> yourself at work, and as a result, the act of trying to do so <u>recurs</u> in your dream.

Since we understand what has <u>run</u> through our heads as we sleep, we need to find solutions. First, we should let <u>go</u> of the nightmare, and <u>guard</u> against the danger of being further bothered. More importantly, we should learn to do exercises to reduce the pressure.

A Sharp Interpreter

Please paraphrase the following sentences. Change the sentence structure if necessary.

1. After a century of dream research, North American experts have recently cracked a few more of the codes that run through our heads as we sleep.

   ✤ *Paraphrasing:*

   As a result of a hundred years of effort on dream research, scientists in North America have recently had some new discoveries in understanding what is happening in our minds when we sleep.

2. Indeed, recent research by Joseph De Koninck, a psychology professor at the University of Ottawa, seems to show dream symbols differ depending on the individual.

   ✤ *Paraphrasing:*

   Recent research by Joseph De Koninck, professor of psychology at the University of Ottawa, seems to tell us that dream images symbolize different things to different people.

3. Recurring dreams or nightmares, however, might indicate a person has an unresolved issue or pain in their past.

   ✤ *Paraphrasing:*

   Repeated dreams or nightmares, however, might suggest that a person has an unaccomplished task or a painful experience in the past.

4. While many dreams are dark, they do have a purpose—most importantly, perhaps, helping us to solve problems and develop insight.

   ✤ *Paraphrasing:*

   Though many dreams are not clearly known, they have an important role to play: they may help us to solve problems and achieve better understandings of them.

5. Often my dreams will respond to questions I have in mind before I go to sleep.

   ✤ *Paraphrasing:*

   Often my dreams will react to the questions I have been considering before I go to sleep.

6. After that, I enjoyed those dreams because I could make the ending whatever I wanted.

   ✤ *Paraphrasing:*

   After that, I liked those dreams because I could end the story in whatever way I wanted.

A Solid Sentence Constructer

Please make a sentence with each word or expression listed below.

1. to figure out

   ❖ *Original sentence in the text:*

   When others tried to figure out who dreamed what by matching the two lists, they failed.

   ❖ **Suggested sentence:**

   It is very difficult to figure out the exact motivation of human behavior.

2. more of

   ❖ *Original sentence in the text:*

   "I suppose I was processing that my mother was becoming more of a real person to me, with flaws and faults, and that I was going to go further in life than she had."

   ❖ **Suggested sentence:**

   He is more of a manager than a teacher in the classroom.

3. to take risk

   ❖ *Original sentence in the text:*

   "The dream made me feel more confident about taking risks," she says.

   ❖ **Suggested sentence:**

   I often wonder why he always has the courage to take risks in business.

4. to give an alarm

   ❖ *Original sentence in the text:*

   Often our dreams may even give an alarm.

   ❖ **Suggested sentence:**

   Insomnia may even give an alarm about the stress you are working under.

5. to read into

   ❖ *Original sentence in the text:*

   "For 3,000 years people have been trying to read things into dreams as if they're fortune cookies," says Dr. Allan Hobson, a professor at Harvard University. "It's nonsense."

   ❖ **Suggested sentence:**

   I am afraid that you are reading into her statement more than she intended.

6. to be more likely to do

   ❖ *Original sentence in the text:*

   Sure enough, those students were more likely to dream about that friend than another group, who were not told to suppress their thoughts.

   ❖ **Suggested sentence:**

   The DNA report shows that the suspect was 7 times more likely to be white than Asian.

7. to see eye to eye

◈ *Original sentence in the text:*

At that time in her life, Lisa and her mother didn't see eye to eye, and in the dream, Lisa's mother attacked her with a huge wave of snow.

◈ **Suggested sentence:**

He has asked for a transfer because he doesn't see eye to eye with the new manager.

8. to tap into

◈ *Original sentence in the text:*

We want to tap into those nighttime fantasies that have us flying, saving the world and dating movie stars.

◈ **Suggested sentence:**

Many people doubt the necessity to spend huge sum of money tapping into the mysteries of Loch Ness (尼斯湖).

📖 A Superb Bilingualist

Please translate the following sentences into English with the prompts provided in the brackets.

1. 他对我说的话做了那么多的曲解，我觉得十分可笑。(read into, find... ridiculous)

◈ *Suggested translation:*

I find it really ridiculous that he has read so much into what I said.

2. 下岗让他认识到不管发生什么,生活永远都不会停滞,他必须继续努力。(it take... to..., stay still, go further)

◈ *Suggested translation:*

It takes his loss of job to make him realize that he must keep going further whatever happens as life will never stay still.

3. 在沉默了一个月之后,公司终于就新款汽车的安全问题做出了反应。(respond to)

◈ *Suggested translation:*

The incorporation finally responded to the safety problem of its latest car model after it had remained silent for a month.

4. 幸福没有一个统一的定义,每个人对它的理解是不一样的。(universal, differ)

◈ *Suggested translation:*

There is not a universal definition for happiness. Its implication differs depending on the individual.

5. 过去的事情就让它过去吧。向前看,心情就会好的。(let go of)

◈ *Suggested translation:*

Just let go of the past. You will feel better if you can look ahead.

Text B

﹏Introduction of the Text

This text offers us some more information about human dreams. It mainly tells us why it is necessary to study our dreams, how we may better recall our dreams and in what way we may try to interpret our dreams. As mentioned in the text, there are many good reasons for looking into this valuable part of our experience, namely the dreams during our sleep. When we are asleep, our mind is free to wander. It is busy making sense of the experiences we have had during the day. It is making connections between events in our past and present, so that you can make better sense of them. Analyzing your dreams can help you understand your emotions, discover your feelings towards the people in your waking life, solve problems and tap into your creative side.

Comprehension Questions

After reading Text B, please answer the following questions based on what you' ve learned from Text B.

1. Why don't many people take the time to explore their dreams?

For one thing, people appear to be too busy to do that in their waking life. For another, many of them have lost their ability to recall their dreams. Moreover, our culture doesn't place much importance on the understanding of dreams.

2. What can you make out of analyzing your dreams?

Analyzing your dreams helps make sense of the experiences you have had during the day or in the past because dreams tend to make connections between events in your past and present, so that you may develop a better understanding of them. Analyzing your dreams can also help you understand your emotions, discover your feelings towards the people in your waking life, solve problems and tap into your creative side.

3. What can you do to help you recall your dreams?

You may try the following:

First, take time to prepare yourself for sleeping. Have a relaxing bedtime routine and give your body a smooth transition to sleep.

Second, prepare yourself for dreaming. Review the events of your day, since those events may have an important place in our night time dramas.

Third, as soon as you wake up, remain in bed with your eyes closed and recall what you've been dreaming.

Fourth, keep a dream journal.

4. What are Lisa Lenard's suggestions to better understand your dreams?

Lisa Lenard suggests pondering questions such as: Does the dream have any connections with something that happened the day before? Are the dream events possible or imaginary? Do I know the people in the dream? What is the dream's theme? Once you have taken notes on your dreams for several nights, review them and start looking for common patterns and recurring themes and elements.

5. What might a dream in which you are chased or attacked mean?

It can mean that we feel a threat in our waking life. When analyzing this dream, try to figure out what or who the thing or person chasing you reminds you of.

6. How would you interpret a dream in which your car brake does not work?

If you have this sort of dream, it may suggest that you are trying too hard at something and that you had better slow down a little bit.

Writing Practice

Put your answers to the above questions together and form a summary about the text and share with your classmates the summary you have completed.

Very often people seem to be preoccupied with their waking life. Yet many of them have in fact lost their ability to recall their dreams. Analyzing dreams helps make sense of the experiences you have had during the day or in the past because dreams tend to make connections between events in your past and present. It helps you understand your emotions, discover your feelings towards the people in your waking life, solve problems and tap into your creative side. Before you analyze your dreams, you need to be able to recall them. To do that, you may try taking time to prepare yourself for sleeping, having a relaxing bedtime routine, reviewing the events of your day etc. Once you have taken notes on your dreams for several nights, review them and start looking for common patterns and recurring themes and elements.

Unit

8

Great Minds

Unit Goals

After studying this unit, students should be able to:

☞ **acquire the basic knowledge of the origin of Buddhism and the essence of Buddhist religion;**

       Text A is the story of the founder of Buddhism—Siddhartha Gautama, commonly known as Buddha. The philosophy of Buddhism has a profound impact on Asian ideology, tradition, culture and so forth. The authors of this textbook hold that Chinese English majors should achieve a better understanding of their own culture, tradition and history, besides the knowledge of the western counter parts. By learning **Text A**, students will learn about the origin, major principles of Buddhism and the commonly used terms involved in the theory.

☞ **know how to pronounce /f/, /v/, /s/ and /z/, and how to utilize the words and structures that contribute significantly to the texts;**

       In this section, the instructor should draw the students' attention to the fact that the first pair of friction consonants is completely empty in Chinese phonetics. It is suggested that students should not base their pronunciation on what they think the equivalence from Chinese. The most important is to demonstrate the correct pronunciation of each consonant and make contrast the English friction consonants to the counterpart of Chinese. It is strongly suggested that the instructor encourage students to read aloud tongue twisters before class. The instructor may refer to the advice provided in the section **A Sip of Phonetics**.

       Most useful words and structures of **Text A** can be found in **You'd Like to Be**. This is where students practice what they have learned from **Text A**.

☞ **learn to appreciate the perseverance displayed in the characters of the great individuals.**

       Students should learn to appreciate the spiritual strength from these two great individuals. Both Siddhartha Gautama and Socrates can be regarded as gurus who were persistently searching for the truth of life for human beings, and passionately teaching students regardless of their social backgrounds. A close study of their contributions to mankind offers us insight into the significance of their sacrifice in defense of truth, virtue and their life principles.

Before Reading

Hands-on Activities and Brainstorming

The instructor should allow 15—20 minutes for students to do presentation either on Siddhartha Gautama or on Socrates.

A Glimpse at Words and Expressions

Please read the following sentences. Pay attention to the underlined part in each sentence in Column A, and match it with the corresponding meaning in Column B.

A. The instructor should draw the students' attention to the cohesive meaning of the idiom "to be expecting a baby/child" rather than a common verb meaning "to expect." Another point worth noticing is that the idiom always stays in progressive tense. In this sense, "to expect" that takes an object of "a baby/child" goes beyond its original meaning of "to be looking forward to." Rather, it means "to be pregnant."

B. The instructor may initiate a question like "what does the verb 'to raise' strike them when reading the sentence." The instructor can chase this question by offering a couple of nouns that "raise" is able to take to help work out the answer, such as "to raise one's voice," "to raise spirits," "to raise a cheer," and "to raise a child." The instructor should impart to the students that these expressions share a point up-going either in intensity or in vigor. Though "to raise a child" doesn't seem to follow the pattern, it means "bring up a child," which also suggests having a child grow better. For example: *I was born and raised a city boy.*

C. The instructor should get the students able to understand the word "restless" by asking the student to explain the inflection "less." To make it easy, the instructor may supply them with expressions like "color-less, value-less, count-less, wire-less, tire-less," from which, students are able to conclude the inflection "less" means "without," "that cannot be," "that does not." Returning to "restless," the instructor should come up with examples such as "After listening to the teacher for an hour, the kids became restless." "She became so restless that she could not lie in bed." "The patient has had many restless nights." These examples help the students approach the meaning of "restless," which means "anxious, unable to stay still." For example: *After five years in the job, he began to feel restless.*

D. The instructor may make up one or two sentences using the phrase "to win the hand of sb." Such examples like "A resourceful thief helps a handsome prince fight an evil wizard and win the hand of a beautiful princess" and "Gatsby felt that he needed wealth to win the hand of Daisy" are of great help for the students to understand the phrase as "make sb. fall in love with someone" or "to win sb.'s heart."

E. The problem can be easily solved if the instructor tells a story of *The Farmer and the Snake* in which the farmer took pity on the dying snake in a freezing winter, but in return he got a deathly bite rather than gratitude. The story shows that the phrase "take pity on" means "show sympathy to." For example: *Please have pity on him! He has no place to stay.*

F. The key word that hinders the students' understanding in the phrase "to prevent this great occurrence" is "occurrence." The instructor may go to the root of the noun, "to occur," which means "to happen." In this case, "occurrence" can be interpreted as "a happening without intent, volition, or plan." Then "great occurrence" is assumed to mean "an occurrence of some importance and frequently one having antecedent cause." For example: *They got involved in the great occurrence which is related to the future of human beings.*

G. It is suggested that the instructor address the students on the inflections that build up the word "enlightenment" so that the students are made aware of the root of "enlightenment," "light." With a suffix "en" added to it, a new word "lighten" comes into existence, which is defined as "to shed light on." When added another prefix "en" to "lighten," the verb "enlighten" is produced, which is interpreted as "to give spiritual insight into to," the meaning of which corresponds to the noun "enlightenment" with another suffix "ment" attached to it. In this sense, "to achieve enlightenment" is explained as "to completely understand the truth."

Keys

A-6   B-4   C-7   D-2   E-3   F-5   G-1

Text A

Introduction to the Text

Studying Text A familiarizes students with the life story of Siddhartha Gautama, commonly known as Buddha. The text provides easy access to the essence of ancient culture of Asia that enables the students to approach and touch the spirit of truth which is worth a life-time pursuit even at the expense of self sacrifice. The great spiritual character conveyed in the text inspires people to achieve their goal with perseverance in the course of life.

Dr. C. George Boeree

The author, Dr. C. George Boeree, born in 1952 in a small town near Amsterdam in the Netherlands, is now a faculty member of the Psychology Department of Shippensburg University in the United States. He specializes in personality theories and the philosophical side of psychology, and is especially interested in phenomenological, existential, and Buddhist psychology, and in epistemological and moral development. Among his other interests are languages, history, and the web.

Detailed information of Dr. C. George Boeree can be found at his personal webpage http://webspace.ship.edu/cgboer/.

Suggested Explanations on Text A

1. She had had a strange dream in which a baby elephant had blessed her with his trunk, which was understood to be a very <u>auspicious</u> sign.
   Meaning: Strangely, she had dreamed that a young elephant touched her with its trunk, as was considered as a very lucky signal that suggested bless to her.
   ▶ auspicious (*adj.*): (formal) of good omen; favorable
   eg. 1) The wedding costumes are usually embroidered with auspicious patterns such as the dragon and phoenix, mandarin ducks or flowers and plants.
      2) The torch is modeled after ancient Chinese scrolls and features an auspicious cloud design.

2. <u>As</u> was the <u>custom</u> of the day, when the time came near for Queen Mahamaya to have her child, she traveled to her father's kingdom for the birth.
   ▶ as (*pron.*): a relative pronoun that introduces a noun clause functioning as an attribute,

usually non-restrictive. "As" does not normally qualify a specific noun or a pronoun, but a whole sentence or at least part of the sentence. This sort of clause enjoys a flexibility of either being positioned at the start of and at the end of a sentence, or sometimes in the middle. To go further, "as" shares the same function as "if" when both playing the same role with an exception that only "as" can be put in front of a sentence.

eg. 1) In electrical usage the term potential, as will be pointed out later, has a definite quantitative meaning.

2) The facts of science are not as some think, dry and lifeless. They are living things, filling with sweetest poetry the ear that listens to them, and with fadeless harmony of colours the eye that looks upon them.

3) As is generally accepted, economic growth is determined by the smooth development of production.

4) She is extremely popular among students, as (which) is common knowledge.

► custom (*n.*): a practice followed by people of a particular group or region

eg. 1) It is the custom in that country for women to marry young.

2) As was the custom of the day, girls were not allowed to go to school.

▲ custom (*n.*): business patronage; regular dealings or customers

eg. 1) Thank you for your custom. Please call again.

2) We have lost a lot of custom since prices went up.

3. In a small town, she asked her handmaidens to assist her to a nearby grove of trees for delivery.

► a grove of: a group of

eg. 1) An enormous white pagoda stands out in prominence among a cluster of temples and a grove of trees. It is regarded as the signpost of Mount Wutai.

2) I remember when I was a boy, my first exploit in squirrel hunting was in a grove of tall walnut trees that covers one side of the valley.

► delivery (*n.*): the process of giving birth to a baby

eg. 1) When I entered the delivery room, Kathy was in absolute agony, crawling around on her hands and knees and screaming out in pain.

2) The family was so poor that they couldn't afford a proper delivery in hospital.

▲ delivery (*n.*): the way in which sb. speaks, sings a song, etc. in public

eg. 1) The beautiful poetry was ruined by her poor delivery.

2) His speeches were magnificently written but his delivery was hopeless.

4. He could speak, and told his mother that he had come to free all mankind from suffering.

► to free... from...: to remove sth. unpleasant from sth.

eg. 1) The United Nations are trying to free the world from the threat of war.

2) The centre aims to free young people from dependency on drugs.

3) We hope we can be freed from piles of documents and numbers of meeting as soon as possible.

▲ free from: without; having no

eg. 1) It is a day free from wind.

2) Surfing the Internet these days is a hazardous occupation, but a few simple precautions will keep your computer free from infection.

5. Asita <u>proclaimed</u> that he would be either a great king, even an emperor, or he could become a great sage and savior of humanity.

Meaning: Asita declared/told that he would become a great king, even an emperor. In other words, he could be a saint and guru to save the mankind.

▶ to proclaim (*v.*): to publicly and officially tell people about sth. important

eg. 1) The ringing bells proclaimed the news of the birth of the prince.

2) Pennsylvania becomes the ninth state to proclaim Campus Fire Safety Month.

▲ to proclaim (*v.*): to show sth. clearly

eg. 1) This building, more than any other, proclaims the character of the town.

2) His manners proclaimed him a gentleman.

6. The king, eager that his son should become a king like himself, <u>was determined to</u> keep the child from anything that might <u>result in</u> him <u>taking up</u> the religious life.

Meaning: The king had so strong a desire for his son to become a king like himself that he made up his mind to prevent his son from approaching anything that might trigger an idea of practicing religion.

▶ to be determined to do sth.: to make up one's mind to do sth.

eg. 1) Stressing her background and experience, she is determined to become the first woman elected to the White House.

2) The premier told a news conference that the government was determined to hand over the power to the newly elected president.

▲ to determine (*v.*): to discover the facts about sth.; to calculate sth. exactly

eg. 1) An inquiry was set up to determine the cause of the accident.

2) We set out to determine exactly what happened that night.

▲ to determine (*v.*): to make sth. happen in a particular way or be of a particular type

eg. 1) Before you start looking at new systems, it's important to determine your organization's needs for new computer systems.

2) Upbringing plays an important part in determining a person's character.

▶ to result in: to cause sth. happen

eg. 1) These policies resulted in many elderly and disabled people suffering hardship.

2) Three diet drugs recommended for long-term use result in minimal weight loss but carry

some serious side effects.

▶ to take up: to enter into (a profession or business)

eg. 1) He will take up his position as the head of the civil courts at the end of next month.

2) Since taking up writing romance in 1967 she has brought out over fifty books.

▲ to take up: to fill or use an amount of space or time

eg. 1) These files have been zipped up to take up less disk space.

2) Her time was fully taken up with writing.

▲ to take up: to resume after an interruption

eg. 1) The band's new album takes up where their last one left off.

2) It's my turn to take up the story where Betty stopped.

7. And so Siddhartha was kept in the palace, and was prevented from experiencing much of what ordinary people might consider quite commonplace.

▶ to experience (*v.*): to have and be aware of a particular emotion or physical feeling

eg. 1) I experienced a moment of panic as I boarded the plan.

2) Despite these efforts, human rights organizations and journalists who have experienced persecution by the government still do not trust the government.

▲ experienced (*adj.*): having knowledge or skill

eg. 1) You need to be experienced in team management, passionate with building a strong team, delegating and empowering others to succeed.

2) It is important to seek assistance and advice from a qualified and experienced car accident lawyer as soon as possible following the incident.

▶ commonplace (*adj.*): having no remarkable features

eg. 1) Some scientists believe that soon it will be commonplace for people to travel to the moon.

2) The fashionable remarks of today often become the commonplace expressions of tomorrow.

8. He was not permitted to see the elderly, the sickly, the dead, or anyone who had dedicated themselves to spiritual practices.

▶ to dedicate oneself/sth. to sth.: to commit (oneself) to a particular course of thought or action

eg. 1) She dedicates herself to the course of science.

2) The doctor dedicated much of his time and energy to finding a cure for the disease.

▲ to dedicate sth. to sb.: to write (sth.) in honour of (someone)

eg. 1) The writer dedicated his first novel to his deceased wife.

2) This movie is dedicated to Jane—a friend in memory.

▲ dedicated (*adj.*): working hard at sth. because it is very important to you; devoted eg. 1) Mrs. Johnson is a dedicated teacher as well as a fine researcher.

2) His death is of a great loss because he was such a dedicated musician who had composed more than 100 pieces in his life.

9. As he was led through the capital, Siddhartha <u>chanced</u> to see a couple of old men who had <u>accidentally</u> wandered near him.

▶ to chance (*vi.*): to come about sth. without purpose

eg. 1) At the age of sixteen he chanced to read a book of *Popular Lectures on Experimental Philosophy, Astronomy and Chemistry.*

2) It chanced that a King's son came into the wood, and went to the dwarfs' house, meaning to spend the night there.

▶ accidentally (*adv.*): unintentionally

eg. 1) As I turned around, I accidentally hit him in the face.

2) The damage couldn't have been caused accidentally.

10. Amazed and confused, he chased after them to find out what they were. Then he <u>came across</u> some people who were severely ill.

▶ to come across sb./sth.: to meet or find sb./sth. by chance

eg. 1) I came across children sleeping under bridges.

2) Our librarian has come across this site and asked for comments.

▲ to come across: to make a particular impression

eg. 1) She comes across well in interviews.

2) He comes across as a very sincere individual.

▲ to come across (with sth.): [no passive] to provide or supply sth. when needed

eg. 1) I hoped she'd come across with more information.

2) To pay over money that is demanded: came across with the check.

11. Siddhartha also saw a monk who had <u>renounced</u> all the pleasures of the flesh.

Meaning: Siddhartha also saw a monk who had given up enjoying any physical pleasure.

▶ to renounce (*v.*): to abandon, surrender, give up (a claim, right, possession)

eg. 1) The State Department does not record the annual number of Americans renouncing their citizenship.

2) The United States still considers Hamas a terrorist organization, and is refusing to back a Hamas government unless they renounce violence.

12. He had discovered suffering, and wanted <u>more than anything</u> to discover how one might overcome suffering.

▶ more than anything: very much; above all

eg. 1) Jenny likes dancing more than anything else.

    2) Memories are usually worth more than anything you can buy.

    3) I accepted the beer but what I wanted more than anything else was a cup of tea.

13. For six years, he practiced austerities and self-mortifications...

Meaning: For six years, he was living a simple and plain life, denying himself all forms of physical pleasure by experiencing pain and discomfort.

▶ to practice (*v.*): to do sth. regularly as part of your normal behavior

eg. 1) Parents need make their children practice self-restrain.

    2) Do you still practice your religion?

▲ to practice (as sth.): to work as a doctor, lawyer, etc.

eg. 1) There are over 50,000 solicitors practicing in England and Wales.

    2) He was banned from practicing medicine.

14. He redoubled his efforts, refusing food and water, until he was in a state of near death.

Meaning: He exerted far greater efforts than ever before by refusing food and water to achieve his purpose, which affected his health to the extent that he was dying.

▶ to redouble (*v.*): to make or grow greater or more intense or numerous

eg. 1) Cheney will urge political leaders to redouble their efforts to achieve reconciliation.

    2) This anniversary is a good time to redouble our commitment to legal, safe abortions and increased access to the most effective tools to prevent unintended pregnancy.

    3) Understanding the obligations that I had imposed on myself, I set to work, trying to redouble enthusiasm.

▶ in a state of: (a person or a thing) in a mental, emotional or physical condition

eg. 1) We are witnessing a gradual change in the psychology of the children—they are living in a state of constant fear.

    2) For years these refugees were kept in a state of limbo, forbidden to go to the United States by overly broad antiterrorist legislation.

15. Siddhartha then realized that these extreme practices were leading him nowhere, that in fact it might be better to find some middle way between the extremes of the life of luxury and the life of self-mortification.

Meaning: Siddhartha later came to understand that his choice to experience excessive sufferings contributed little to answering his questions and that he favoured the idea of being neither self-indulgent nor imposing severe discipline on himself to deny all forms of physical pleasure.

▶ practice (*n.*): habitual action or performance

eg. 1) The anti-Negro practice constitutes the most shameful page in the history of the United

States labor movement.

2) It is a dangerous practice to get off a bus before it stops.

3) It was a practice in the shop that if you spoil any material, you had to pay for it out of your piece-work earnings.

▶ middle way: the eightfold path of Buddhism between indulgence and asceticism

eg. 1) The way to overcome such desires and attain enlightenment (nirvana) is to follow the Eightfold Path, which is called the Middle Way between desire and self-denial.

2) The Middle Way advises us to take refuge in the Three Jewels: the Buddha or fully enlightened One, the Buddha's teaching, and the community of those seeking enlightenment.

3) The path of the Middle Way is one of moderation and balance. Balanced in our body, mind, and spirit, we are able to live in a state of health and are free of pain and illness.

16. Siddhartha <u>remained</u> completely calm. Then he sent his three beautiful daughters to <u>tempt</u> him, again to no avail.

▶ to remain (*v. intr.*): to continue to be sth.; to be still in the same state or condition

eg. 1) Train fares are likely to remain unchanged.

2) It remains true that sport is about competing well, not winning.

3) In spite of their quarrel, they remain the best of friends.

▲ to remain (*v.*): to still need to be done, said, or dealt with

eg. 1) Much remains to be done.

2) It remains to be seen whether you are right.

3) There remained one significant problem.

▶ to tempt (*v.*): to attract sb. to do a wrong or forbidden thing

eg. 1) The man claimed that he had been tempted into stealing the jewels with a promise of a good share of the profit.

2) Don't tempt thieves by leaving valuables clearly visible.

3) These school children are easily tempted into a life of crime.

▲ temptation (*n.*): the desire to do or have sth. usually bad or wrong

eg. 1) His business failure is due to the temptation of easy profits.

2) I am tempted to leave my work but I'm fighting against the temptation.

17. Finally, he tried to <u>ensnare</u> Siddhartha in his own ego with his own pride. That, too, failed.

Meaning: In the end, he tried to trap Siddhartha to bring more glory to satisfy his vanity, power and importance, but did not come to anywhere.

▶ to ensnare (*v.*): to make sb./sth. unable to escape from a difficult situation

eg. 1) The brothers fled to Germany, only to be ensnared in war.

2) The corruption scandal that has rocked Siemens, a pillar of Germany Incorporation, is gathering pace in a way that could ensnare the company's top management for the first time.

18. ...he gave his first sermon, which is called "setting the wheel of the teaching in motion."
   ▶ "setting the wheel of the teaching in motion" is not the tile of his first sermon. This is used to describe his action of giving the first sermon. "to set the wheel in motion" means "to start doing sth."

19. The king of Magadha, having heard Buddha's words, granted him a monastery near his capital, for use during the rainy season.
   ▶ to grant (*v.*): to bestow; to give formally or legally
   eg. 1) The authorities wouldn't grant us permission to fly to San Francisco.
      2) Software developers are angry that Microsoft has been granted a patent for the conversion of objects into XML files.
   ▲ to grant (*v.*): to admit that sth. is true, although one may not like or agree with it
   eg. 1) I grant the genius of your plan, but you still will not find supporters.
      2) I grant you that it looks good, but it is not very practical.
      3) I readily grant (you) that I was to blame for the mistake.
   ▲ grant (*n.*): a sum of money that is given by the government or by another organization to be used for a particular purpose
   eg. 1) I was given a student grant for four years.
      2) The research was carried out under a federal grant.
   ▲ to take sth. for granted: to assume sth. to be true or valid; cease to appreciate through familarity
   eg. 1) He seemed to take it for granted that he should speak as a representative.
      2) I just took it for granted that he'd always be around.
      3) We take having an endless supply of clean water for granted.
      4) We have to re-educate the public very quickly about something they have always taken for granted.
      5) I came into adult life clueless about a lot of things that most people take for granted.

20. This and other generous donations permitted the community of converts to continue their practice throughout the years...
   ▶ convert (*n.*): a person who has changed their religion, beliefs or opinions
   eg. I thought he was a Buddhist, but it turned out he was a convert to Islam.
   ▲ to convert (*v.*): to change or make sb. change their religious beliefs
   eg. 1) He converted from Christianity to Islam.

2) She was soon converted to the socialist cause.

▲ to convert (*v.*): to change or make sth. change from one form, purpose, system, etc. to another

eg. 1) The hotel is going to be converted into a nursing home.

2) What rate will I get if I convert my dollars into Euros?

3) We've converted from coal to gas central heating.

21. Over time, he was <u>approached</u> by members of his family, including his wife, son, aunt, and his father, Shuddodana.

▶ to approach (*v.*): to come near to sb./sth. in distance

eg. 1) I heard the sound of an approaching car.

2) As you approach the town, you will see the university on the left.

3) Be sure to ask if this is a good time to approach the professor for your specific purpose.

▲ to approach (*v.*): to come close to sth. in amount, level or quality

eg. 1) The company's profit this year is approaching 30 million dollars.

2) Few writers approach his richness of language.

▲ approach (*n.*): a way of dealing with sb./sth.; a way of doing or thinking about sth. such as a problem or a task

eg. 1) The school has decided to adopt a different approach to discipline.

2) I think you have taken the wrong approach in your dealings with them.

▲ approach (*n.*): a path, road, etc. that leads to a place

eg. 1) All the approaches to the palace were guarded by troops.

2) We found a taxi on our way out the approach to the museum.

▲ approach (*n.*): movement nearer to sb./sth. in distance or time

eg. 1) She hadn't heard his approach and jumped as the door opened.

2) The approach of winter brings cold weather.

22. His aunt and wife asked to be permitted into the Sangha, which <u>was originally composed only of</u> men.

▶ to be composed of: to be made up of

eg. 1) Her charm was composed partly of shyness, partly of warmth, but chiefly of quiet determination.

2) The unit was composed entirely of mercenary troops.

▲ to compose (*v.*): to combine together to form a whole

eg. 1) Twenty lawyers composed the committee.

2) Many ethnic groups compose our nation.

▲ to compose (*v.*): to write music, a letter, a speech, a poem, etc.

eg. 1) Mozart composed his last opera shortly before he died.

2) He composed the opening paragraph in his mind.

23. The culture of the time <u>ranked</u> women far below men in importance, and at first it seemed that permitting women to enter the community would weaken it.

Meaning: At the time, conventionally women held much lower social status than men. It seemed that women's involvement in Buddhism would go against the tradition and spoil the practice.

▶ to rank (*v.*): to give a particular position on a scale according to quality, importance, success, etc.

eg. 1) This town ranks high among beauty spots.

2) This university is ranked number one in the country for engineering.

▲ rank (*n.*): a position in a hierarchy

eg. 1) It is significant that the nations possessing the most extensive libraries maintain the foremost rank in civilization.

2) English literature holds a very high rank among the literatures of the West.

▲ rank (*adj.*): foul-smelling, offensive; loathsome, indecent, corrupt

eg. 1) He came in, rank with the sweat of his night's work.

2) I could make out the rank smell of the whisky on his breath.

3) Never use rank language.

24. <u>Impermanent</u> are all created things; <u>strive</u> on with awareness.

Meaning: No compounded things endure but change, break up or decay for the coexistence of causes and condition.   Make constant efforts until you gain enlightenment to the truth of life.

▶ Impermanent are all created things.

This sentence is inverted with the adjective "impermanent" coming ahead of the verb to achieve cohesion in a sentence.

eg. 1) Less common are the sentence patterns that begin with a part of speech other than the subject, as is the case with this sentence, in which the adverb/predicate adjective pair "Less common" comes first.

2) Masterly and dry and desolate he looked, his thin shoulder-blades lifting his coat slightly. (A series of three adjectives precedes the subject.)

3) Immoral Ovid was, but he had high standards in art.

▶ impermanent (*adj.*): transient, not lasting nor intended to last or function indefinitely

eg. 1) Politics is an impermanent factor of life.

2) Everything that exists is impermanent: with birth there is death; with arising, there is dissolving; with coming together, there is separation.

Note: "im" is an inflectional prefix which means "not" when added to the adjective "permanent."

▶ to strive (*v.*): to endeavor

eg. 1) We have striven successfully to improve conditions for the refugees.

2) We call on a campaign striving against corruption.

3) I strove in vain to control myself.

Better Know More

释迦牟尼是佛教创始人。本名悉达多·乔达摩。因父为释迦族,成道后被尊称为释迦牟尼,意为"释迦族的圣人"。释迦牟尼的父亲,名首图驮那,汉译净饭王,是迦毗罗卫的国王。母亲名摩诃摩耶,是与迦毗罗卫城隔河相对的天臂城善觉王的长女。

佛教是世界性的宗教。北以中国为中心,后传至日本、朝鲜、蒙古等国。7世纪中叶,藏语系佛教在西藏兴起。而南以锡兰为中心,后传至泰国、缅甸等国家。佛教传进中国将近两千年,思想体系发展演变成十多个派别,对中国的思想、文化、艺术都产生了巨大的影响,并延伸到中国民族文化的各个领域。

佛教与其他宗教不同之处是,佛教不承认有全知全能的造物主,而认为一切众生都有得到觉悟的可能性,即一切众生,皆有佛性。佛教的宗旨在于解脱世界及众生的痛苦。在佛教看来,世间一切苦痛即生老病死等八种苦恼。世间一切又皆虚幻不实、变化无常,不足贪恋。因此,众生必须通过修行来解脱烦恼,达到寂静快乐的境界。如果做出家信徒,出家时不经父母允许便不能出家。而且只要信仰佛教,广施善行,不一定非出家不可。同时,佛教鼓励人生的建设,要求人们修善努力,以改造现实的及至未来的命运。佛教戒律里已明确规定不杀生、不偷盗、不淫邪、不赌博、不饮酒等戒律。

佛教教义的基本内容是说世间的苦(existence is suffering)和苦的原因(the cause of suffering),说苦的消灭(the cessation of suffering)和灭苦的方法(the way to accomplish this),这苦谛、集谛、灭谛、道谛总称为四圣谛(The Four Noble Truths)。"谛"就是不颠倒,即是真理;"圣谛"是圣人所知之绝对正确的真理。佛阐释四圣谛的目的,是要告诉我们世间的因果以及出世间的因果。而想真正了解这些真理,需要通过修行八正道(The Eightfold Path)来实现,即正知(right understanding)、正见(right thought)、正语(right speech)、正业(right action)、正命(right livelihood)、正精进(right efforts)、正思维(right awareness)和正定(right meditation)。

Check Your Understanding

Translate the following sentences into Chinese. Please make sure that your language flows smoothly.

1. Because Shuddodana was saddened by the departures of his son and grandson into the monastic life, he asked Buddha to make it a rule that a man must have the permission of his parents to become a monk.

   首图驮那因为儿子和孙子出家而难过，他请求佛立下一个规矩，男人只有得到父母的许可才可以出家。

2. Impermanent are all created things; strive on with awareness.

   世间一切事物皆为幻影，要用心寻找生活的真谛。

3. As he was led through the capital, Siddhartha chanced to see a couple of old men who had accidentally wandered near him.

   当悉达多被他人带着经过首都的时候，他碰巧看到两个老人从他身边走过。

4. The king, eager that his son should become a king like himself, was determined to keep the child from anything that might result in him taking up the religious life.

   国王渴望自己的儿子能像他一样成为国王，他拿定主意让儿子远离一切可能会导致他从事宗教的事情。

5. He was not permitted to see the elderly, the sickly, the dead, or anyone who had dedicated themselves to spiritual practices.

   不允许他见到老人、病人和故去的人，也不允许他见任何全心投入宗教的人。

6. The king of Magadha, having heard Buddha's words, granted him a monastery near his capital, for use during the rainy season.

   马加达国的国王听到过佛的布道，在他的首都附近为佛祖立了一座寺庙，供雨季时使用。

Answer the following questions based on the text you have just learned.

1. What happened when Siddhartha was born?

   First, a gentle rain fell on him and his mother to cleanse them. Second, he was born fully awake. He could even speak, and told his mother that he had come to free all mankind from suffering. He could stand, and he walked a short distance in each of the four directions. Lotus blossoms rose in his footsteps.

2. What was Siddhartha's destiny according to the fortuneteller?

   The fortuneteller proclaimed that Siddhartha would be either a great king, even an emperor, or he could become a great sage and savior of humanity.

3. Was Siddhartha happy when he was living in the palace? Why?

No, he wasn't happy at all. Because he was kept in the palace, and was prevented from experiencing much of what ordinary people might consider quite commonplace. He was not permitted to see the elderly, the sickly, the dead, or anyone who had dedicated themselves to spiritual practices.

4. How did Siddhartha feel when he came across the people that he had never met before?

He felt amazed and confused.

5. How did Siddhartha start his search for the answer to the problem of sufferings with which people were confronted?

First he left his palace without saying goodbye to his family. Then for six years, he practiced austerities and self-mortifications. He even redoubled his efforts, refusing food and water, until he was in a state of near death. In spite of that, the answers to his questions were not forthcoming.

6. How did he realize the right way to find the answer?

One day, when Siddhartha was on verge of death, a peasant girl begged him to eat some of her milk-rice. He then realized that these extreme practices were leading him nowhere, that in fact it might be better to find some middle way between the extremes of the life of luxury and the life of self-mortification.

7. In what way did Mara try to prevent Siddhartha from achieving enlightenment?

He first tried to frighten Siddhartha with storms and armies of demons. Siddhartha remained completely calm. Then he sent his three beautiful daughters to tempt him. Finally, he tried to ensnare Siddhartha in his own ego with his own pride. All this suffered crushing defeat.

8. How did Buddha rank his followers?

The Buddha ranked his followers according to the time when they took vows. No matter what kind of status a person had, or what his background or wealth or nationality might be, he is welcome into the Sangha.

9. How do you interpret the last words of the Buddha?

It's an open-ended question.

A Sip of Phonetics

Know Their Faces

本课涉及的四个辅音 /f/, /v/, /s/ 和 /z/ 是摩擦音，其中 /f/ 和 /v/ 是唇齿摩擦音，/s/ 和 /z/ 是舌齿摩擦音。学生在发音的时候，容易出错的是 /v/ 和 /z/ 这两个音。

在发 /v/ 时,声带要振动。由于在汉语中没有这个音,学生很容易用 /w/ 这个音来代替。教师在讲解的时候应该提示学生,强调 /v/ 是唇齿摩擦音,上齿一定要和下唇形成对气流的阻碍,从而正确发音。练习以下的词,可以让学生体会 /v/ 和 /w/ 发音的区别,避免出现错误。

<u>v</u>ary　<u>w</u>ary　en<u>v</u>y　a<u>w</u>ay　<u>w</u>a<u>v</u>e　o<u>v</u>er<u>w</u>helm

另外一个发音错误较多的是 /z/。英语中,发 /z/ 时舌尖贴近齿龈,气流由舌端齿龈间送出形成摩擦音。而汉语中,发 /z/ 时,舌位较高,舌尖几乎贴到上齿,阻碍力强,故而气流也较强。例如,学生常常错误地把 zoo/zuː/ 这个词发成汉语的[zū](租)。教师应该特别提示这一点并做正确的发音示范。

在教授这部分内容时,教师应该训练学生的认知能力,除了做到正确的发音外,应该教会学生识别这些字母或字母组合的发音规律,强化学生学习词汇的能力。教师应在课堂上领读示范,并及时纠正学生的一些错误发音。

📖 Train Your Tongue

1. A Finnish fisher named Fisher / failed to fish any fish / one Friday afternoon / and finally / he found out a big fissure / in his fishing-net.
2. Singing Sammy / sung songs / on sinking sand.
3. A noisy noise / annoys an oyster.
4. Five fuzzy French frogs / frolicked through the fields / in France.
5. Sweet Sally Sanders said / she saw seven segregated seaplanes / sailing swiftly southward /Saturday.
6. A flea and a fly / were trapped in a flue, / and they tried to flee for their life. The flea said to the fly / "Let's flee!" / and the fly said to the flea / "Let's fly!" / Finally / both the flea and fly / managed to flee through a flaw in the flue.

You'd Like to Be

📖 A Strong Bridge Builder

Fill in the blanks with the given words to complete the following sentences. Please note that some can be used more than once.

in	of	against	about	from	into	after
to	up	beyond	across	with	for	down

1. Edith received much compliments <u>for</u> her lifelong dedication <u>to</u> writing. She is considered one of the leading American authors <u>throughout/in/of</u> the twentieth century.

2. Thus Enlightenment must be considered both as a process <u>in</u> which men participate collectively and as an act <u>of</u> courage to be accomplished personally.

3. It may indirectly result <u>in</u> the increase of the living standards. Some people have to take <u>up</u> a part-time job <u>in</u> their spare time to earn more money.

4. In southern states, such as Alabama and Mississippi, African Americans were often prevented <u>from</u> registering to vote in 1965, when Stella was only 8 years old. She was curious <u>about</u> the demonstrations <u>in</u> the streets.

5. Today's lawsuits could lead <u>to</u> action <u>against</u> Microsoft's business. But Gates said that nothing should be discussed further <u>beyond</u> Windows 98 working system.

6. Because we couldn't get the permission <u>of/from</u> the doctor to stay <u>with</u> our little baby at night, Greg and I had to sneak <u>into</u> the hospital.

7. We came <u>across</u> a shop while wandering <u>about</u> the street. A milkman rushed out of a fenced yard, <u>with</u> a dog crazily chasing <u>after</u> him, and a stout old lady was chasing <u>after</u> the dog.

A Smart Word Player

Fill in the blanks with the proper words that need to be transformed from the ones provided in the brackets.

1. The Association for Research and Enlightenment (A.R.E.) held its annual Egypt conference August 17—20, 2000. The organization studies and preserves the Edgar Cayce's <u>information</u> (inform) regarding Maya Hall of Records. During the conference, Cayce's <u>amazing</u> (amaze) story of the history and the ancient <u>origin</u> (originally) of the Mayas were reviewed. If this <u>discovery</u> (discover) could be scientifically proved and generally accepted, it would have an <u>extraordinary</u> (ordinary) impact on the research of ancient human civilizations.

2. The April 1986 disaster at the Chernobyl nuclear power plant in the Ukraine was the product of a flawed Soviet reactor design <u>coupled</u> (couple) with serious mistakes made by the plant operators in the context of a system where training was minimal. It was a direct consequence of Cold War isolation and the <u>resulting</u> (result) lack of any safety culture. The <u>accident</u> (accidentally) destroyed the Chernobyl-4 reactor and killed 30 people, including 28 from radiation exposure. Large areas of Ukraine, Russia and beyond were polluted in varying degrees.

   The Chernobyl disaster was a unique event in the history of commercial nuclear power where radiation-related fatalities <u>occurred</u> (occurrence). However, its relevance to the rest of the nuclear industry outside the Eastern Union is minimal. Reliable information about the accident and the consequential pollution was not <u>available</u> (avail) to affected people for about two years following the accident. This led to distrust and <u>confusion</u> (confused) about health effects.

Many other international programs were initiated following Chernobyl. The International Atomic Energy Agency (IAEA) safety review projects have started some funding <u>arrangement</u> (arrange) to focus on safety improvements. In 1998 an <u>agreement</u> (agree) with the US provided for the establishment of an international radioecology laboratory inside the exclusion zone.

A Skilled Text Weaver

Fill in the blanks with the words you have learned in this text. One word is for each blank. Here is a piece of advice: You must be really familiar with the text to accomplish the following tasks.

1. Buddha's life wasn't without disappointments. One of his cousins, Devadatta, was an ambitious man, who had <u>converted</u> to Buddhism already. As a <u>monk</u>, he felt that he should have greater power in the Sangha. He managed to get some <u>followers</u> with a call to a return to <u>extreme</u> asceticism. <u>Eventually/Finally</u>, he decided to have the Buddha killed and to take over the <u>Buddhist</u> community. Of course, he <u>failed</u>.

2. When Prince Siddhartha had finished his <u>meditation</u>, he opened his eyes and saw a man who was dressed like a poor beggar. "Please tell me," the Prince asked, "who are you?" The man answered, "I am someone who has become frightened by the sufferings of the world. I have grown tired of the so-called <u>pleasures</u> to be found in the company of others, so now I <u>wander</u> alone. I have given up my home and now live and sleep in caves, in the forest or wherever I find myself. My only interest is in <u>finding/discovering</u> the highest and most happiness." When he had spoken these words, the man disappeared. "At last I have found the true <u>meaning</u> for my life," Siddhartha thought. With this thinking, he went back to the palace.

A Sharp Interpreter

Please paraphrase the following sentences. Change the sentence structure if necessary.

1. She had had a strange dream in which a baby elephant had blessed her with his trunk, which was understood to be a very auspicious sign.
   ✿ *Paraphrasing:*
   Strangely, she had dreamed that a young elephant touched her with its trunk, as was considered as a very lucky signal that suggested bliss to her.

2. Asita proclaimed that he would be either a great king, even an emperor, or he could become a great sage and savior of humanity.

⊕ *Paraphrasing:*

Asita declared/told that he would become a great king, even an emperor. What is more, he could be a saint and guru to save the mankind.

3. Siddhartha also saw a monk who had renounced all the pleasure of the flesh.

⊕ *Paraphrasing:*

Siddhartha also saw a monk who had given up enjoying any physical pleasure.

4. He redoubled his efforts, refusing food and water, until he was in a state of near death.

⊕ *Paraphrasing:*

He exerted far greater efforts than ever before by refusing food and water to achieve his purpose, which affected his health to the extent that he was dying.

5. He sat there for many days in deep thinking, opening himself up to the truth.

⊕ *Paraphrasing:*

He sat there many days, thinking deeply and becoming aware of the truth and meaning of suffering.

6. The culture of the time ranked women far below men in importance, and at first it seemed that permitting women to enter the community would weaken it.

⊕ *Paraphrasing:*

At the time, conventionally women held much lower social status than men. It seemed that women's involvement in Buddhism would go against the tradition and spoil the practice.

7. The Buddha said that it didn't matter what a person's status in the world was, or what their background or wealth or nationality might be.

⊕ *Paraphrasing:*

The Buddha claimed that neither a man's background, nor wealth, nationality would make a difference in the Buddhist world.

8. Impermanent are all created things; strive on with awareness.

⊕ *Paraphrasing:*

No compounded things endure but change, break up or decay for the coexistence of causes and condition. Make constant efforts until you gain enlightenment to the truth of life.

A Solid Sentence Constructer

Please make a sentence with each word or expression listed below.

1. to be determined to

   ❖ *Original sentence in the text:*

   The king, eager that his son should become a king like himself, was determined to keep the child from anything that might result in him taking up the religious life.

   ❖ **Suggested sentence:**

   They were determined to do everything in their power to recover the fresco(壁画).

2. to take up

   ❖ *Original sentence in the text:*

   The king, eager that his son should become a king like himself, was determined to keep the child from anything that might result in him taking up the religious life.

   ❖ **Suggested sentence:**

   Chris threw up his job to take up more respectable, more rewarding employment.

3. to dedicate... to

   ❖ *Original sentence in the text:*

   *He was not permitted to see the elderly, the sickly, the dead, or anyone who had dedicated **themselves to** spiritual practices.*

   ❖ **Suggested sentence:**

   She dedicated herself whole-heartedly to the study of English poety.

4. to chance to

   ❖ *Original sentence in the text:*

   Siddhartha chanced to see a couple of old men who had accidentally wandered near him.

   ❖ **Suggested sentence:**

   It was one Saturday afternoon in September that I chanced to meet Mr. Weldon Thompson, an English-speaking native American, at a Watson's store in my neighborhood.

5. to grant

   ❖ *Original sentence in the text:*

   The king of Magadha, having heard Buddha's words, granted him a monastery near his capital, for use during the rainy season.

   ❖ **Suggested sentence:**

   The anti-virus company established an effective mechanism. If the user submitted something new for virus killing purpose, then he would be granted full access to the resources and could download an unlimited quantity of anti-virus software.

6. to make it a rule
   ✧ *Original sentence in the text:*
   ...he asked Buddha to make it a rule that a man must have the permission of his parents to become a monk.
   ✧ **Suggested sentence:**
   <u>Make it a rule that</u> your children check in with you when they arrive at or depart from a particular location and when there is a change in plans.

7. to strive
   ✧ *Original sentence in the text:*
   Strive on with awareness.
   ✧ **Suggested sentence:**
   If we desire to reap huge fruits from our limited life, we must <u>strive on</u> and on. It isn't wise to sleep on the honour of one success.

A Superb Bilingualist

Please translate the following sentences into English with the prompts provided in the brackets.

1. 我们渴望一个和平的世界，人们不再饱受战争和饥饿等各种苦难。这是我们全人类共同的心愿。(peaceful, suffering, mankind)
   ✧ *Suggested translation:*
   We are all eager for a peaceful world with people free from sufferings such as war and starvation, which is the shared wish of all mankind.

2. 在新年来临之际，请允许我代表全体工作人员说几句。虽然我们的岗位平凡，但我们肩负着这个社区的安全重任。我们会尽全力让大家生活在一个祥和的环境里。最后，祝愿大家安康、幸福！(forthcoming, permit, commonplace, community, auspicious)
   ✧ *Suggested translation:*
   At the moment of the forthcoming New Year, please permit me to say something on the behalf of our staff. Although our work is of mere commonplace, it involves our great responsibility for people's safety in this community. We are going to redouble our efforts to make the environment cozy and auspicious. Finally, I wish everyone good health and happiness.

3. 我们收到了来自祖国四面八方的慷慨捐赠，有大量的捐款、生活用品，还有很多书籍。(throughout, donation, be composed of)
   ✧ *Suggested translation:*
   We have received generous donation throughout the country, which is composed of a large sum of money, life necessities and many books.

4. 昨天他偶然遇到了一位他大学的同学小赵。聊了一会儿,他就发现才过了两年,小赵的变化非常大了。(come across, come to realize)

　　◈ *Suggested translation:*

　　Yesterday he came across Xiao Zhao, one of his former classmates in college. After a short conversation, he came to realize that Xiao Zhao had changed a lot only after two years.

5. 母亲的去世是她皈依佛教的一个重要因素。现在她每天都打坐两个小时。(convert, a couple of)

　　◈ *Suggested translation:*

　　Her mother's death was a key factor that caused her to become a convert to Buddhism. Now she practices meditation a couple of hours every day.

Text B

〰 Biography of Socrates

Socrates (469—399 BC), one of the greatest Greek philosophers, has a profound influence on Western philosophy.

At the outset, Socrates followed the craft of his father. Later Socrates believed in the superiority of argument over writing and therefore spent the greater part of his mature life in the marketplace and public places of Athens. He made dialogues and arguments with anyone who would listen or who would submit to questioning. He enjoyed life greatly and achieved social popularity because of his sense of humor. Socrates obeyed the laws of Athens, but he generally avoided politics, and therefore he served his country best by devoting himself to teaching. However, he neither wrote any books nor established any school of philosophy.

Socrates' contribution to philosophy was primarily ethical in character. He taught people to understand such concepts as justice, love, and virtue. His logic emphasized particular importance of rational argument and the pursuit of general definitions, as was evidenced in Plato's works, specifically *The Republic*. Through these works, Socrates profoundly influenced the whole course of Western thought.

〰 Ancient Greek Philosophers

Generally speaking, ancient Greek philosophy is dominated by three very famous men: Socrates, Plato, and Aristotle. Plato was Socrates' pupil and Aristotle's teacher. In the 200's B.C., after the death of Plato and Aristotle, three famous kinds of philosophy started up in the schools which Plato and Aristotle had established—Stoics, the Skeptics, and the Epicureans. Each of these continued to be vital in shaping people's way of thinking about the world all the way throughout the Roman Empire and even after that.

The instructor is suggested to learn more about Socrates, Plato and Aristotle by visiting the website http://www.historyguide.org/ancient/lecture8b.html.

Comprehension Questions

After reading Text B, please answer the following questions based on what you've learned from Text B.

1. Why was Socrates arrested and put on trial?
Because Socrates believed that there was a God greater and better than any they worshiped, hence he was charged with doing harm to young people he was teaching.

2. What was Socrates' sentence?
He was sentenced to death as a base criminal.

3. How were the criminals executed on the day they were put to death?
Criminals were forced to drink a cup of a deadly poison at sunset on the day of their condemnation.

4. What did Socrates' friends and pupils try to do for him? How did Socrates respond?
Socrates' friends and his pupils tried to save his life by arranging an escape. But Socrates refused to do so for the sake of the law that he never disobeyed, for his belief in his innocence and for a noblest death.

5. What did Socrates do before his death?
Before his death, he gave his last sermon to his disciples about life and death, and especially about the immortality of the soul.

6. What were Socrates' last words as recorded by Plato?
His last words were recorded by Plato: "Thus died the man who, of all with whom we are acquainted, was in death the noblest, and in life the wisest and best."

7. How did people feel about Socrates' death and what did they do for him?
After his death, the Athenians regretfully found out their mistake. In token of their sorrow, they set up a statue of him in the heart of their city to honor him.

Writing Practice

Put your answers to the above questions together and form a summary about the text and share with your classmates the summary you have completed.

Socrates was arrested and put on trial because believed that there was a God greater and better than any they worshiped, hence he was charged with doing harm to young people he was teaching. He was sentenced to death as a base criminal. According to the law at that time, criminals were forced to drink a cup of a deadly poison at sunset on the day of their condemnation. Socrates' friends and his pupils tried to save his life by arranging an escape. But Socrates refused to do so for the sake of the law that he never disobeyed, for his belief in his innocence and for a noblest death. Before his death, he gave his last sermon to his disciples about life and death, and especially about the immortality of the soul. His last words were recorded by Plato: "Thus died the man who, of all with whom we are acquainted, was in death the noblest, and in life the wisest and best." After his death, the Athenians regretfully found out their mistake. In token of their sorrow, they set up a statue of him in the heart of their city to honor him.

Language and Thought

Unit Goals

After studying this unit, students should be able to:

☞ **understand the Sapir-Whorf Hypothesis that involves language determinism and language relativity;**

The Sapir-Whorf Hypothesis is in its most extreme version described as linguistic determinism that our thinking is determined by language and linguistic relativity that people who speak different languages perceive and think about the world quite differently. **Text A** starts out by asking the reader if the language one speaks influences the way one thinks and continues to examine the differences between English and some languages. Then author is approaching the conclusion that language, thoughts and culture grow up together, with one affecting the other. To a great extent, language and thoughts are greatly influenced by culture.

It is suggested that the instructor take the students into a deeper discussion based on the text and also their own experiences to explore to what extent language shapes the way people think and how much the sociocultural context affects the way people interpret the world.

☞ **know how to pronounce /ʃ/, /ʒ/, /θ/, /ð/, and how to utilize the words and structures that contribute significantly to the texts;**

In this section, the instructor should explain to the students how to pronounce these consonants and demonstrate the correct pronunciation of each consonant. The instructor should remind the students of the potential problems in pronouncing these sounds. The sound /ʃ/ shares some similarity with the Chinese /sh/, but the latter is voiced and the tongue positions differently from the former. The sound /ʒ/ is the most difficult and the majority of Chinese English language learners have a hard time doing the right thing. The pair /θ/ and /ð/ can be flawed if pronounced without putting the tip of the tongue between the teeth, which does not match any sound in Chinese language.

It is suggested that the instructor encourage students to read aloud tongue twisters before class.   The instructor may refer to the advice provided in the section **Before Reading**.   Most useful words and structures of **Text A** can be found in **You'd Like to Be**.

☞ **understand the language varieties and the power of language.**

To help the students understand the language varieties,   the instructor should ask the students to list some differences between Chinese and English in terms of vocabulary, grammar or structure. Then ask the students if they have different view of the world when using the two different languages.

It is also suggested the instructor try an assumption that words get their power because they are put into particular kinds of grammatical structure,   which functions differently depending on the culture in which it is used.   However,   grammar is not about rules but choice.   The grammar of one language,   or many languages,   if one happens to be bilingual or multilingual,   consists of systems of simultaneous,   inter-locking choices.   These choices of grammatical organization provide one with the means by which he /she makes sense of his/her experience. In this sense, it is grammar that powers the language.

Before Reading

Hands-on Activities and Brainstorming

The instructor should allow 15—20 minutes for students to do presentations or share their understanding of language diversity with each other.

A Glimpse on Expressions

A. It is suggested that the instructor should first go to the noun of "shape" with such an example as "He has some difficulty in giving shape to his idea;" "The idea took shape in the minds of the promoters." The two sentences may offer some clues that "shape" can be interpreted as "form," with which the students are familiar. In such case "to form an idea" shares with "to shape one's thought" in some way. In this sense, the meaning of "a language shapes one's thoughts" becomes explicit, that is "to have direct influence on sb. in terms of one's interpretation of the world." For example: Our families shape our lives and make us what we are.

B. Before defining the expression "chick-and-egg," the instructor should ask the students such a question as "What came first, the chicken or the egg?" The question deserves no definite answer but suggests the difficulty in identifying the first case of circular cause and consequence. To be exact, the expression means that it is "impossible to decide which of two things causes the other one." For example: "New graduates often complain about this chicken and egg problem. Employers want experience, but to have a work record they need an opportunity from one of them."

C. The sentence "Reform and the open policy involve risks" might bring light to the expression "to involve," which finds no satisfactory English equivalent in that the sentence suggests the potential relationship between reform and the open policy and risk. The instructor should chase this with another point: it is challenging to implement both reform and open polity. To follow the logic, we come to the point that to take challenge is to take risk. For example: Forecasts and assumptions involve uncertainties.

D. Rather going directly to the definition of "interact with," the instructor should first touch "inter," the inflection prefix that tells the meaning of "mutually, reciprocally," then "to act," which means "to do." In this sense, "to interact" can be understood as "have an effect on each other." For example: A lesson plan should encourage ESL/EFL students to interact with the teacher.

E. The phrase "to grow up" itself is not new to the students. What is important is the implication with the three things—the culture, the thought and habits, and the language growing up together. On the one hand, it is natural that they start to exist at the same time, and on the other, they are dependent on one another in that thoughts and habits are closely related to culture, without which, language dies. So to speak, "together" is the key word in the interpretation of the phrase "to grow up," which means "to start to exist and become more important and larger." For example: IT industry has grown up and developed enormously in China.

F. The instructor should draw the students' attention to the original "broken up into chunks." Ask the students: "If you can break time into chunks," do you think "chunk" is no longer anything considered a whole? To enable the students to answer the question, the instructor is obliged to give examples such as: "a chunk of good time"; "a chunk of bread"; "I slipped off on a chunk of ice." In this way, the students can be motivated to work out the meaning of "chunk," which means "a piece of sth. broken." For example: It wants to capture a big chunk of the fast-growing market for ads. A huge chunk of the audience got up and left before the end of the show. Paris Hilton and the rest of her family have lost a huge chunk of potential inheritance.

G. To make it easier for the students to understand "fall under" is to change "fall" into "be" since "fall" falls under the category of link verb. To "fall under a single label" is explained as to be categorized into one group. For example: Do these asthma symptoms fall under mild, moderate, or severe? Any sexual assault may now fall under rape. Blood does not fall under the same standards as other healthcare products.

Keys

A-3   B-4   C-6   D-5   E-7   F-1   G-2

Text A

Suggested Explanations on Text A

1. ...Whorf <u>claimed</u> that speakers of Hopi and speakers of English see the world differently because of the differences in their languages.

   ▶ claim (*v.*): to say that sth. is true although it has not been proved and other people may not believe it

   eg. 1) Scientists have claimed that they have achieved a major breakthrough in the fight against AIDS.

   2) It was claimed that some workers in that factory were working 60 hours a week.

2. <u>To some extent</u>, it's a chicken-and-egg question.

   Meaning: In certain sense, it is an unresolved question as to which of two things causes the other.

   ▶ to ... extent: used to show how far sth. is true or how great an effect it has

   eg. 1) Can someone that speaks French to some extent please translate this for me?

   2) To some extent, it is this determination, not the tragedy itself, that is being commemorated today.

   3) Is it reasonable to some extent that a man expects his wife not to gain a lot of weight?

3. Part of the problem is that there is more involved than just language and thought.

   Meaning: One problem with the hypothesis is its narrowness that comprises only language and thought, not other factors beyond.

4. Or has a difference in cultural habits <u>affected</u> both our thoughts and our language?

   ▶ affect (*v.*): to produce a change in sb./sth.

   eg. 1) It is said that political bias affects judicial choices.

   2) Experts say global warming is likely to affect people living in Africa more than on any other continent.

5. ...with Hopi speakers <u>focusing more on</u> the source of the information and English speakers on the time of the event.

   Meaning: ...with Hopi speakers paying more attention on the cause of the event, whereas the English speakers on the time.

   ▶ to focus on/upon: to give attention, effort, etc. to one particular subject, situation or person rather than another

   eg. 1) Many web professionals know about certain ways to focus on users.

       2) The Chancellor is giving a lecture that focuses on challenges of education.

   ▲ focus (*n*.): centre of interest/attention

   eg. 1) He was the main focus of attention at the press conference.

       2) The focus has now shifted towards the problem of long-term unemployment.

6. Objects are treated differently by the <u>syntax</u> of different languages as well.

   Meaning: The differences in grammatical structure of languages bring forth people's disagreement from one another in dealing with objects.

   ▶ syntax (*n*.): grammatical arrangement of words, showing their connection and relation and a set of rule attached

   eg. 1) Sentence structure is an invisible but essential part of the mental processing, which is called syntax.

       2) Syntax is the grammar, structure, or order of the elements in a language statement.

       3) This document will eventually outline the full specification for the syntax and grammatical structure of the language.

7. Other languages, like Japanese, don't make this <u>distinction</u>.

   Meaning: Other languages, such as Japanese, have no such clear difference.

   ▶ distinction (*n*.): a clear difference between people or things similar or related

   eg. 1) This hospital is an equal opportunity employer and does not discriminate on basis of race, color, national origin, gender, sexual orientation, age, religion, disability or veteran status (服兵役情况).

       2) Jupiter has the distinction of being the largest planet.

   ▲ distinctive (*adj*.): having a quality or characteristic that makes sth. different and easily noticed

   eg. 1) She is charmed by the clothes with a distinctive style shown in that shop.

       2) She had a distinctive appearance.

8. Whorf said that because English treats time as <u>being broken up</u> into chunks that can be counted...

   ▶ to break up: to separate into smaller pieces

eg. 1) The ship was broken up into pieces when it hit the rock.

   2) He broke the bread up into chunks to share with the others.

   3) This is a time where students break up into small groups and work on tasks independently.

▲ to break up: to come/put to an end

eg. 1) Their marriage has broken up.

   2) They decided to break up their partnership when the business dropped sharply.

   3) The police fired tear gas and water cannon to break up an illegal rally Saturday by ethnic Indians demanding racial equality.

9. ... English speakers <u>tend</u> to treat time as a group of objects...

▶ to tend (to): to be likely to do sth. or to happen in a particular way because this is what often or usually happens

eg. 1) However, economists tend to oppose gun control laws, since such laws generally have nothing to do with economic increase.

   2) A liberal essay shows that people with higher IQ tend to be less superstitious.

▲ tendency (*n.*): a particular way that people are likely to behave or act

eg. 1) He has a tendency to lie when he doesn't want to go to school.

   2) He has the tendency to break up the bonds with the people he protects.

10. ...it could also be that our view of time is <u>reflected</u> in our language.

▶ reflect (*v.*): to show or be a sign of the nature of sth. or of someone's attitude or feeling

eg. 1) Now we are approaching the end of the year, and it's the perfect time to reflect what we have done in the past year.

   2) The organization hopes the change will more accurately reflect their long-term goals.

▲ reflection (*n.*): careful thought about sth., sometimes over a long period of time

eg. 1) Internet is a reflection of society.

   2) Currencies are nothing but the reflection of the value of national capitals.

11. It seems likely that language, thought, and culture form three parts of a braid, with each one affecting the others.

Meaning: It is probable that language, thought, and culture are so tightly bound like the three strands that make a rope that it loses its intensity without anyone of the three with each working on the others.

▶ to be/seem likely that: to be probable that

eg. 1) It seems likely that medical marijuana may be sold at a dispensary (规模较大的药房) in Claremont in the near future.

   2) It is not likely that I should accept such an offer.

3) It's certainly a lot more likely that Microsoft violates patents than Linux does.

12. The Dani of New Guinea have only two basic color <u>terms</u> in their language...
   ▶ term (*n.*): word or phrase used as the name of sth., especially one connected with a particular type of language
   eg. 1) "Register" is the term commonly used to describe different levels of formality in language.
   2) Many of the terms in the technical vocabulary of computing, the kind that reach user manuals, are drawn from other disciplines.
   3) One should acquire essential literary terms for understanding Renaissance dramas.

13. So our language doesn't force us to see only what it gives us words for, but it can affect how we put things into groups.
   Meaning: So our language doesn't aim to restrict people to understanding only things that can be expressed in words, but it plays a vital role in grouping things.

14. One of the jobs of a child learning language is to <u>figure out</u> which things are called by the same word.
   ▶ to figure out: to think about sb./sth. until you understand them/it
   eg. 1) I've never been able to figure her out.
   2) Scientists have long struggled to figure out how the brain guides the complex movement of our limbs.

15. ...the child may see a cow and say *dog*, thinking that the two things <u>count as</u> the same.
   ▶ to count as: to be considered in a particularly way
   eg. 1) The place is eminent for its natural scenery and counts as deserving a visit.
   2) The ancients counted courage as the main part of virtue.

16. ...but what counts as being similar enough to fall under a single label may <u>vary</u> from language to language.
   Meaning: ...but what is believed to share with the features of the former to be granted the same single name may differ from language to language.
   ▶ vary (*v.*): to make changes to sth. to make it slightly different
   eg. 1) Opinions in the committee vary from approval to complete opposition.
   2) Prices of vegetables vary from season to season.

17. ...the people we <u>refer to</u> as 'Eskimos' speak <u>a variety of</u> languages in the Inuit and Yupik language families.

▶ to refer to: to mention or speak about sb./sth.

eg. 1) The minister referred to the importance to the nation of the increased exports.

2) If you don't like what happened, that's fine, but why must you refer to her?

▲ to refer to: to describe or be connected to sth./sb.

eg. 1) APA citation style refers to the rules and conventions established by the American Psychological Association for documenting sources used in a research paper.

2) Genocide refers to the mass murder of a tribe or an entire people.

▲ a variety of: several different sorts of the same thing

eg. 1) There is a wide variety of pictures for you to choose from.

2) The campus has a variety of ways of disseminating information to the student.

18. ...it may give you some <u>insight</u> into another culture and another way of life.

▶ insight (n.): the ability to see and understand the truth about people or situations

eg. 1) He's a writer of great insight and honesty, but what makes him different today is that he has a more developed sense of humility in his fiction.

2) Achieving environmental sustainability requires the insight and participation of business leaders, for many reasons.

Notes

The following information can be helpful in assisting the students to better understand the concept of Sapir-Whorf hypothesis:

"Human beings do not live in the objective world alone, nor alone in the world of social activity as ordinarily understood, but are very much at the mercy of the particular language which has become the medium of expression for their society. It is quite an illusion to imagine that one adjusts to reality essentially without the use of language and that language is merely an incidental means of solving specific problems of communication or reflection. The fact of the matter is that the 'real world' is to a large extent unconsciously built upon the language habits of the group. No two languages are ever sufficiently similar to be considered as representing the same social reality. The worlds in which different societies live are distinct worlds, not merely the same world with different labels attached... We see and hear and otherwise experience very largely as we do because the language habits of our community predispose certain choices of interpretation." (Sapir, 1958)

"We dissect nature along lines laid down by our native languages. The categories and types that we isolate from the world of phenomena we do not find there because they stare every observer in the face; on the contrary, the world is presented in a kaleidoscopic flux of impressions which has to be organized by our minds—and this means largely by the linguistic systems in our minds. We cut nature up, organize it into concepts, and ascribe significances as we do, largely because we are parties to an agreement to organize it in this way—an agreement that holds throughout our speech community and is codified in the patterns of our language. The agreement is, of course, an implicit and unstated one, but its terms are absolutely obligatory; we cannot talk at all except by subscribing to the organization and classification of data which the agreement decrees." (Whorf, 1940)

References:

Sapir, E. (1958). *Culture, language and personality*. Berkeley, CA: University of California Press.

Whorf, B. L. (1940). Science and linguistics. *Technology Review* 42(6), 229—231, 247—248.

Check Your Understanding

Translate the following sentences into Chinese. Please make sure that your language flows smoothly.

1. After learning that the family's St. Bernard is a dog, the child may see a cow and say *dog*, thinking that the two things count as the same.

   在孩子懂得家里的圣伯纳德是一条狗以后，他可能把奶牛也称为"狗"，以为这两样东西是一样的。

2. One of the jobs of a child learning language is to figure out which things are called by the same word.

   一个牙牙学语的孩子必须弄清楚哪些事物是用同一个词命名的。

3. In other words, the influence of language isn't so much on what we can think about, or even what we do think about, but rather on how we break up reality into classes and label them.

   换句话说，语言对于我们想什么或者想到什么的影响并不那么大；而影响大的是对我们如何对事物进行分类以及如何命名这些事物。

4. Your culture—the traditions, lifestyle, habits, and so on that you pick up from the people you live and interact with—shapes the way you think, and also shapes the way you talk.

   (是)你所处的文化，也就是你从和你一起生活、接触的人那里学到的传统思想、生活方式、习惯等在影响着你的思维方式和说话的方式。

5. Has our language affected our way of thinking? Or has a difference in cultural habits affect-ed both our thoughts and our language?

我们的语言是否影响我们的思维方式？或许文化习惯的不同对我们的思想和语言同时产生影响？

6. English speakers tend to treat time as a group of objects—seconds, minutes, hours—instead of as a smooth unbroken stream.

说英语的人往往把时间当成一组事物，即秒、分、小时，而不是把它看作顺滑而不可分割的静流。

Answer the following questions based on the text you have just learned.

1. Why did Benjamin Lee Whorf study the Hopi language and what did he find out?

Because Whorf tried to prove if the language we speak shape our thoughts. He found out that the speakers of Hopi and English see the world differently due to the differences in their languages.

2. What else contributes to the development of the discussion that language has a direct im-pact on thought?

One's culture, which involves traditions, lifestyle, habits, contributes significantly to the way he thinks and talks.

3. What does the author infer from the example of the Australian aboriginal tribal language without location words?

The author infers from the example of one of the Australian aboriginal tribal language that the culture, the thought habits and the language have all grown up together with one affecting another.

4. In what way did Whorf think that language had affected both the Hopi and English speak-ers, with the former focusing more on the source of the information and the latter on the time of the event?

The English speakers use a past or present tense of a verb to describe events, while the Hopi speakers don't do that, but use the forms of verbs to tell how the speaker came to know the information. Whorf believed that because of this difference, Hopi speakers and English speakers think about events differently, with Hopi speakers focusing more on the source of the information and English speakers on the time of the event.

5. What is the quality of the English language that has made its speakers more conscious of the difference between substances and individual objects?

It is the dual quality of nouns in the English language, sometimes being countable and some other times uncountable that makes the English speakers more aware of the dis-tinction between substances and individual objects.

6. Why do the English speakers differ from Hopi in their explanation of time?

Because English treats time as being broken up into chunks that can be counted while it is a continuous cycle in Hopi. The English speakers treat time as a group of objects, such as seconds, minutes, hours rather than a smooth unbroken stream in Hopi.

7. Why does the author offer the examples of a can of red paint, the two basic color terms in the language of New Guinea and the Russian blue?

Because the author tries to claim that people can think or see and do things beyond the words they use in their languages.

8. Why does the author tell us the story of the St. Bernard and the child who considers the cow a dog?

Because she uses this as an example to show that our language affects us in grouping things.

9. Do the Eskimo languages have more words for snow compared with the English language? Why or why not?

No. On the one hand, Eskimos speak a variety of languages, and if we pick a single dialect of a single language, we won't find more words for snow than in English. On the other hand, the Eskimo languages have far more word-forming activities than English, with a single "root" word leading up to hundreds of related words.

A Sip of Phonetics

📖 Know Their Faces

/ʃ/ 和 /ʒ/ 是硬腭齿龈擦音。发音时,学生容易将这两个音发成汉语拼音中的[sh]和[r]。汉语中[sh]和[r]是舌尖后擦音,或舌尖—硬腭擦音,又称为"卷舌音"。发这两个音时,舌位要比发 /ʃ/ 和 /ʒ/ 靠后。教师在讲解的时候应该特别提示学生,并做出正确示范。

另外一组 /θ/ 和 /ð/,很容易被错误发成 /s/ 和 /z/ 这两个音。教师应该特别提示,发这两个音时,气流应该从舌齿间通过。教师可以让学生练习下列词汇,体会这四个辅音的发音异同,同时应做正确发音的示范。

1. thing   sing   thank   sank   thin   sin
2. this   zip   that   Zack

在教授这部分内容时,教师应该训练学生的认知能力,除了做到正确的发音外,应该教会学生识别这些字母或字母组合的发音规律,强化学生学习词汇的能力。教师应在课堂上领读示范,并及时纠正学生的一些错误发音。同时,教师还可以利用绕口令,强化这四个辅音的练习。

Train Your Tongue

1. Thirty thousand thoughtless boys / thought they'd make a thundering noise; / so with thirty thousand thumbs/ they thumbed / on thirty thousand drums.
2. I thought a thought,/ but the thought I thought / was not the thought / I thought I thought.
3. I wish to wish the wish / you wish to wish, /but if you wish the wish / the witch wishes,/ I won't wish the wish / you wish to wish.
4. The thirty-three thieves thought/ that they thrilled the throne/throughout Thursday.
5. Susan shined shoes and socks; / socks and shoes shine Susan. / She ceased shining shoes and socks, / for shoes and socks shocked Susan.
6. Thank the other three brothers / of their father's mother's brother's side.
7. Casual clothes / are provisional / for leisurely trips across Asia.
8. Dr. Johnson and Mr. Johnson, / after great consideration, / came to the conclusion / that the Indian nation / beyond the Indian Ocean / is back in education / because the chief occupation is cultivation.

You'd Like to Be

A Strong Bridge Builder

under	to	into	as	in
between	from	up	for	of

1. Special articles called review articles discuss all the literature on a topic, and these often refer to conflicting or contradictory studies.   You could begin by looking for review articles on a potentially controversial topic.   Some databases allow you to limit your search to review articles.
2. The rescue workers picked up as many people from the burning ship as they could, for which, they broke up the rescue work into several activities, which guaranteed the safety of people on board.
3. I had no word for such a terrible behavior, which counts as what is unacceptable by convention.
4. He was under the influence of extreme emotion to the extent that he was unaware of the fact that he had been driven by passion for the woman who stayed indifferent to him.
5. Increase awareness of language teaching is reflected in the distinction between teaching English as a foreign language (TEFL) and teaching English as a second language (TESL)

📖 A Smart Word Player

Fill in the blanks with the proper words that need to be transformed from the ones provided in the brackets.

People, like other animals, are in continual <u>interaction</u> (interact) with their environment, which <u>involves</u> (involve) an assimilation of information from and about that environment. Information is thus defined as a kind of knowledge. How, then, are the two to be <u>distinguished</u> (distinguish)? Knowledge is what people know, or think they know. It resides initially in an individual mind, but in <u>various</u> (vary) forms. Some of it exists in <u>linguistic</u> (linguistically) form. Other personal knowledge may be in tacit form—we know something, or how to do something, even though we cannot verbalize and communicate it.

📖 A Skilled Text Weaver

Fill in the blanks with the words you have learned in this text. One word is for each blank. Here is a piece of advice: You must be really familiar with the text to accomplish the following tasks.

1. Researchers observed that when babies were provided with diverse plastic toys, 2-year-olds attended more to color, whereas 3-year-old and above would focus on <u>shape</u>. And they further proved that babies would not make distinction between substances and individual <u>objects</u> until 5 years old.
2. In Chinese, word usage, pronunciation, and <u>syntax</u> and grammar vary depending on the speaker's <u>dialect</u>.
3. For many of us our first observation of a light <u>spectrum</u> has been a rainbow. Later you may have noticed similar effects when light passes through or <u>reflects</u> from a glass object.
4. He <u>claims</u> to have been <u>involved</u> in close encounter with an alien, and interacting with "him."

📖 A Sharp Interpreter

Please paraphrase the following sentences. Change the sentence structure if necessary.

1. Researchers are studying whether this quality of the language makes English speakers more aware of the distinction between substances and individual objects.

⊕ *Paraphrasing:*

Researchers are working on the plural form of nouns in English, trying to work out if English speakers pay more attention to the difference between the materials of which the items are made and the objects themselves.

2. It seems likely that language, thought, and culture form three parts of a braid, with each one affecting the others.

⊕ *Paraphrasing:*

It is probable that language, thought, and culture are so tightly bound like the three strands that make a rope, being indispensable to each other.

3. Hopi speakers and English speakers think about events differently, with Hopi speakers focusing more on the source of the information and English speakers on the time of the event.

⊕ *Paraphrasing:*

Hopi speakers do not share with English speakers in interpreting what happens, because the former focus more on the cause of the event, whereas the latter on the time.

4. The color spectrum is continuous. Our language, however, isn't continuous. Our language makes us break the color spectrum up into "red," "purple," and so on.

⊕ *Paraphrasing:*

Our language, which is not continuous like the color spectrum, enables us to break the color up into individual segments as "red," "purple" and so on.

5. So our language doesn't force us to see only what it gives us words for, but it can affect how we put things into groups.

⊕ *Paraphrasing:*

So our language doesn't aim to restrict people to understanding only things that can be expressed in words, but it plays a vital role in grouping things.

6. For one thing, there's the question of what counts as a word.

⊕ *Paraphrasing:*

At first, it is still not defined what is taken as a word.

A Solid Sentence Constructer

Please make a sentence with each word or expression listed below.

1. to interact with

⊕ *Original sentence in the text:*

Your culture—the traditions, lifestyle, habits, and so on that you pick up from the people you live and interact with—shapes the way you think, and also shapes the way you talk.

⊕ **Suggested sentence:**

These two chemicals interact with each other at a certain temperature to produce a substance which could cause an explosion.

2. to affect

⊕ *Original sentence in the text:*

Or has a difference in cultural habits affected both our thoughts and our language?

⊕ **Suggested sentence:**

The economic crisis has seriously affected the country's exports.

3. to break up

⊕ *Original sentence in the text:*

Whorf said that because English treats time as being broken up into chunks that can be counted...

⊕ **Suggested sentence:**

To understand this novel, we need to break it up into smaller, more readable segments.

4. to tend to

⊕ *Original sentence in the text:*

... English speakers tend to treat time as a group of objects...

⊕ **Suggested sentence:**

She tends to lose her temper when she is tired.

5. to figure out

⊕ *Original sentence in the text:*

One of the jobs of a child learning language is to figure out which things are called by the same word.

⊕ **Suggested sentence:**

No one could figure out how the fire started.

6. to count as

⊕ *Original sentence in the text:*

After learning that the family's St. Bernard is a dog, the child may see a cow and say dog, thinking that the two things count as the same.

⊕ **Suggested sentence:**

Shelly counted this experience as part of his education. He counted himself fortunate to have such an opportunity.

A Superb Bilingualist

Please translate the following sentences into English with the prompts provided in the brackets.

1. 正如季节的交替不会影响城里人一样,同情和偏见也绝不会影响这位法官做出自己的决断。(influence, affect)
   ✧ *Suggested translation:*
   Just as the changes of season affect the townsman very little, sympathy and prejudice will never influence the judge in his decision.

2. 据这家公司的有关雇员说,工作中只要犯一个错误,就会陷入数不清的麻烦之中。(claim, involve)
   ✧ *Suggested translation:*
   It is claimed by some employees in this company that one error in work can involve you in a good deal of trouble.

3. 索赔分为两项,首先是物质损害索赔,其次是精神损害索赔。(claim, fall under)
   ✧ *Suggested translation:*
   The claim falls under two categories, the first being material damages, and the second, spiritual.

4. 价格随户型变化,所以你得先弄清楚要买什么样的。(vary, figure out)
   ✧ *Suggested translation:*
   Prices vary according to the flat type you require. So you'd better figure out the type you are going to buy.

5. 虽然是冬天,但是花店里的鲜花一应俱全。(a variety of)
   ✧ *Suggested translation:*
   Although it is in winter, there is a variety of flowers available in the florist's shop.

Text B

William Wordsworth

William Wordsworth (1770—1850), British poet, credited with ushering in the English Romantic Movement with the publication of *Lyrical Ballads* (1798), was born on 7 April 1770 in Cumberland in the Lake District, and published his debut poem in *The European Magazine* in 1787. He earned his bachelor's degree at St. John's College, Cambridge in 1791.

Wordsworth focused on the nature, children and the common people, and used ordinary words to express his personal feelings. Seeing in nature an emblem of God, he celebrated in his poetry the beauty and spiritual values of the natural world. He and his best friend Coleridge revolutionized English poetry with the publication of *Lyrical Ballads* (1798). In this book Wordsworth sought to break the pattern of artificial situations of eighteenth-century poetry written for the upper classes, and wrote in simple, straightforward language for the common man.

Most of Wordsworth's major works were produced and published between 1797 and 1808. In a letter to Lady Beaumont he said: "Every great and original writer, in proportion as he is great and original, must himself create the taste by which he is to be relished."

A Brief Introduction of Tu Fu (Du Fu)

Du Fu (712—770) lived in the Tang Dynasty (618—907), which produced the greatest literary achievements in ancient China, in the work of such poets as Wang Wei, Li Po, Tu Fu, Han Yu, Po Chu-i, etc.

Du Fu held a minor post at Chang'an in the most culturally refined courts of the Dynasty, during which, the An Lu-shan rebellion broke out, which shook the Dynasty to its foundations. For the remaining 15 years of his life, Du Fu and his wife and children wandered from town to town, trying to avoid warfare, but many of his 14 hundred poems that have come down to us can be sequenced according to places along his way. Like Dante, who was exiled from Florence and wandered around Italy for twenty years while writing the *Divine Comedy*, Du Fu's work is synonymous with the beloved topography of his country, as well as the suffering of its people. Even while living in a place short-term, Du Fu treated it as if it were his final place of residence, sensitive to its local details.

Comprehension Questions

1. What is the major difference between western lyrics and Chinese lyrics?

   Western lyrics tend to identify the lyric impulse with spontaneity and personal need, while Chinese lyrics have had much to do with society and the life of the poet.

2. What is the function of poetry composing in traditional Chinese society?

   In traditional Chinese society, poetry has been placed higher above diplomatic skill, which was considered a social grace, at least among the elite.

3. What is the main focus of Chinese literature? Why is it the main focus?

   The main focus of Chinese literature has been on daily life and has served as a vehicle for greeting friends, showing intellect and sending political concerns. And in ancient China, literature is not separate from culture.

4. How does Chinese poetry present simile and metaphor? Please state the reasons from the perspectives of language and culture respectively.

Chinese poetry presents simile and metaphor more subtly through implicit connections. Because natural images may imply much about the speaker's general situation that would not be spoken openly. And since the Chinese share the same and unbroken intellectual tradition and therefore understand the same references, it becomes possible to say something that will be generally understood by not saying it.

5. How did Tu Fu associate the expression of personal emotion with the description of political chaos in his poem "Spring Prospect"?

Tu Fu in his poem "Spring Prospect" united his personal situation of imprisonment with his sorrow at the political chaos all around him and his desire for the return of peace. Tu Fu expressed his subtle but strong emotion with the description of the "shattered" country and the "flowers" that "draw tears," which signified his sadness and sorrow resulted from the disaster the rebel armies brought to the country. He went further by personifying the crying of birds that "alarm(s) the heart" to imply his heart-broken grief over the current prospect.

Writing Practice

Put your answers to the above questions together and form a summary about the text and share with your classmates the summary you have completed.

Western lyrics tend to identify the lyric impulse with spontaneity and personal need, while Chinese lyrics have had much to do with society and the life of the poet. In traditional Chinese society, poetry has been placed higher above diplomatic skill, which was considered a social grace, at least among the elite. The main focus of Chinese literature has been on daily life and has served as a vehicle for greeting friends showing intellect and sending political concerns. In terms of rhetoric, Chinese poetry presents simile and metaphor more subtly through implicit connections. Because natural images may imply much about the speaker's general situation that would not be spoken openly and since the Chinese share the same and unbroken intellectual tradition and therefore understand the same references, it becomes possible to say something that will be generally understood by not saying it. In his masterpiece "Spring Prospect," Tu Fu united his personal situation of imprisonment with his sorrow at the political chaos all around him and his desire for the return of peace. Tu Fu expressed his subtle but strong emotion with the description of the "shattered" country and the "flowers" that "draw tears," which signified his sadness and sorrow resulted from the disaster the rebel armies brought to the country. He went further by personifying the crying of birds that "alarm (s) the heart" to imply his heart-broken grief over the current prospect.

Unit 10

Reflection on Wars

Unit Goals

After studying this unit, students should be able to:

☞ **be aware of the social reality—the existence of terrorism, and learn how to face up to it;**

      Text A provides a thorough discussion on terrorism. The author's step-by-step exposure of the American government's policies will help the students gain a deep insight into the cause and effect of terrorism and the different stances between the American government and the author. The instructor can organize discussions at different phases of teaching to help students understand the author's view and the way that he recommended to deal constructively with the threat of terror. Before moving into **Text A**, the instructor should walk the students through **A Glimpse at Words and Expressions**, which will help warm up the students. Students' preview of both **Text A** and **Text B** should be strongly encouraged.

☞ **know how to pronounce /h/, /tʃ/ and /dʒ/, and how to utilize the words and structures that contribute significantly to the texts;**

      In this section, the instructor should explain to the students how to pronounce /h/, /tʃ/ and /dʒ/ and demonstrate the correct pronunciation of each one. They should also contrast wrong pronunciations to the right ones, and help them avoid further mistakes. It is strongly suggested that the instructor encourage students to read aloud tongue twisters before class. The instructor may refer to the advice provided in the section **A Sip of Phonetics**. Most useful words and structures of **Text A** can be found in **You'd Like to Be**, where students practice what they have learned from **Text A**.

☞ **learn lessons from history.**

      Text B is a speech delivered by the former German chancellor Schröder, in which he expresses his shame to the Jewish people, a race that survived the Holocaust during the World War II. More importantly, students should learn that man needs to face up to history with dignity.

Before Reading

Hands-on Activities and Brainstorming

The instructor should allow 15—20 minutes for students to do presentation on opinions of the author and others concerning the September 11th attack.

A Glimpse at Words and Expressions

A. Another example may be more helpful for students to understand the word "alleviate": The drug did nothing to alleviate her pain/suffering. Here the instructor should remind students of the collocation of "alleviate" with words like threat, pain, suffering and so on. It means "to make sth. bad such as pain or problems less severe."

B. The instructor should first reach an agreement with students that "point" means purpose or usefulness. For example: What's the point of all the violence? By adding the suffix "less," we make the word "point" negative in meaning. Something that is pointless has no purpose and it is a waste of time doing it. For example: This is a pointless meeting.

C. "Ongoing" is an adjective, which reminds us of the phrase "going on." It means "continuing to exist or develop, or happening at the present moment." For example: No agreement has yet been reached and the negotiations are still ongoing.

D. The instructor should let students know that the word "enlighten" means "to give light to." "Enlightening" is an adjective, which is "providing sb. with information and understanding; or explaining the true facts about sth. to sb." For example: It is an enlightening experience to talk with him.

E. "Charge" is originally a formal police term representing that sb. is accused of a crime. Here it refers to "a formal criticism, when you accuse sb. of sth. bad." For example: The president responded angrily to the charge that he had lost touch with his country's people.

F. "Wage" here is a verb meaning "to fight a war or organize a series of activities in order to achieve sth." For example: They've been waging a long campaign to change the law.

G. "Sweeping" means "too general and failing to think about or understand particular examples." For example: It is just a sweeping generalization about Chinese people's characteristics.

Keys

A-3	B-5	C-6	D-2	E-1	F-7	G-4

Text A

〰 Introduction of the Author

Noam Avram Chomsky was born in Philadelphia, Pennsylvania on December 7, 1928. He received higher education at the University of Pennsylvania where he studied linguistics, mathematics, and philosophy. In 1955, he received his Ph. D. from the University of Pennsylvania; however, most of the research leading to this degree was done at Harvard University between 1951 and 1955. Since receiving his Ph. D., Noam Chomsky has taught at Massachusetts Institute of Technology, where he now holds the Chair of Modern Language and Linguistics. He is considered the Einstein of linguistics.

Noam has always been interested in politics, and it is said that politics has brought him into the linguistics field. Since 1965, he has been one of the leading critics of U.S. foreign policy. Chomsky is highly respected and has been honored numerous times in the academic arena. He has been awarded an Honorary Doctorate by the University of London and the University of Chicago, as well as having been invited to lecture all over the world. More detailed information of Noam Chomsky can be found at his personal website: http://www.chomsky.info/.

〰 Suggested Explanations on Text A

1. The primary <u>concern should naturally be</u> to take measures to alleviate the threat, which has
   　　　　　　主语＋系词　　　　　　　　　　　表语　　　　　　　目的状语
   　　　　　　　　　　　　　　　　　　主　句

been severe in the past, and will be even more so in the future.
　　　　　　定语从句

▶ alleviate (*v.*): to make sth. bad such as pain or problems less severe
eg.1) The government has taken measures to alleviate the problem of unemployment.
　　2) Schools should alleviate students' burden.
▲ alleviation (*n.*): sth. that alleviates
eg. 1) China has achieved remarkable progress in poverty alleviation since the start of the
　　　reforms.
　　2) Too many efforts have been put in pain alleviation and the cause of the disease has
　　　therefore been neglected.

2. Facts <u>matter</u>, even if we do not like them.

Meaning: Facts are important, even if we do not like them.

▶ matter (*v.*): to be important or have an important effect on sb./sth.

eg. 1) The children matter more to her than anything else in the world.

2) After his death, nothing seemed to matter any more.

3. Relative clarity matters.

Meaning: It is important to make things clear.

4. It is <u>pointless</u> to seek a truly <u>precise</u> definition of "terror," or of any other concept outside of the <u>hard sciences</u> and mathematics, often even there.

Meaning: It is useless trying to find an exact definition of "terror" or of any other concept outside of the experimental and scientific studies such as physics, chemistry, biology and mathematics. Sometimes, it is even unnecessary trying to define certain concepts within those scientific studies.

▶ pointless (*adj.*): sth. that is pointless has no purpose and it is a waste of time doing it

eg. 1) It seemed pointless to continue.

2) It's pointless arguing with him.

▲ point (*n.*): purpose or usefulness

eg. 1) I was lost in his lecture, wandering where the point was.

2) I'd like to write to him, but what's the point? He never writes back.

▶ precise (*adj.*): exact and accurate

eg. 1) I can be reasonably precise about the time of the accident.

2) The victim gave a precise account of the suspect.

▲ precisely (*adv.*): exactly

eg. 1) The fireworks begin at eight o'clock precisely.

2) What do you think the problem is, precisely?

▶ hard sciences:

Studies of physics, computer science, chemistry, biology and geology are sometimes called "hard sciences." The hard sciences are usually to rely on experimental, quantifiable data or scientific methods, focusing on accuracy and objectivity. Stereotyped view often contrasts hard sciences with the derogatory term "soft sciences," indicating social sciences. The word "soft" implies lower reliability.

5. But we should seek enough clarity at least to <u>distinguish</u> terror from two notions that lie uneasily at its <u>borders</u>: <u>aggression</u> and <u>legitimate</u> resistance.

Meaning: But at least we should tell difference between "terror" from two concepts "aggression" and "legitimate resistance," which are both closely related to "terror," but quite different in nature.

▶ distinguish (*v.*): to recognize the difference between two people or things

eg. 1) He's color-blind and can't distinguish between red and green.

　　2) I sometimes have difficulty distinguishing Spanish from Portuguese.

▲ distinguishable (*adj.*): different in nature or quality

eg. There are at least twenty distinguishable dialects of the language just on the south island.

▶ border (*n.*): a part that forms the outer edge of sth.

eg. I lost a white handkerchief with a blue border.

▶ aggression　(*n.*):　spoken or physical behavior which is threatening or involves harm to sb. or sth.

eg. 1) Television violence can encourage aggression in children.

　　2) This is an act of aggression on a peaceful nation.

▲ aggressive (*adj.*): behaving in a very determined and forceful way in order to succeed

eg. 1) Aggressive students present a significant challenge for teachers.

　　2) If he is criticized, he will get aggressive and immediately start yelling.

▶ legitimate (*adj.*): for which there is a fair and acceptable reason

eg. 1) For those with the legitimate complaints, here is a list of phone numbers and offices that might be able to help you.

　　2) Most people will have real and legitimate anger in response to the events on Tuesday.

▲ legitimately (*adv.*): in a legitimate manner; lawfully

eg. 1) Most foreign visitors to Britain enter the country legitimately.

　　2) The policy allows educational organizations to use the software legitimately for free.

▲ legitimacy (*n.*): the quality or fact of being legitimate

eg. 1) The government expressed serious doubts about the legitimacy of the military action.

　　2) I intend to challenge the legitimacy of his claim.

6. It's commonly <u>claimed</u> that critics of ongoing policies do not present solutions.

Meaning: People usually say that those who judge and comment on current policies do not offer effective ways to solve current problems.

▶ claim (*v.*): to say that sth. is true or is a fact, although you cannot prove it and other people might not believe it

eg. 1) The company claims that it is not responsible for the pollution in the river.

　　2) He claims to have met the President, but I don't believe him.

7. Check the record, and I think you will find that there is an accurate translation for that <u>charge</u>: "They present solutions, but I don't like them."

Meaning: If you check the record in history and I think you will find an accurate interpretation for the accusation against critics (that they do not offer effective ways to solve current problems). That is: those critics do offer solutions but the government does not like them. Here "they" refers to "critics" and "I" refers to "the American government."

▶ charge (*n.*): a claim of wrongdoing; an accusation

eg. 1) She rejected the charge that the story was untrue.

2) Be careful you don't leave yourself open to charges of political bias.

8. The campaign was directed to a particularly dangerous form of the plague: state-directed international terrorism.

Meaning: The war on terror launched by the Reagan administration twenty years ago was first targeted at a very dangerous form of terrorism, that is, the international terrorism managed by the government of a country.

▶ be directed to: to aim sth. in a particular direction; be targeted at

eg. 1) Initially, the policy was directed to controlling food prices in the interests of the consumer, but shifted in mid 1990s to favoring the producer.

2) The questionnaire was directed to department heads of 122 U.S. medical schools.

▶ state-directed (state-directed = noun + "-" +verb +ed): managed by state (government)

eg. 1) This model of state-directed economy seemed to combine the dynamic aspects of a market-oriented economy with the advantages of centralized government planning and direction.

2) He has in his long career actively supported state-directed industrialization in various Latin American countries.

9. The military component of the re-declared war was led by Donald Rumsfeld.

▶ component (*n.*): a part which combines with other parts to form sth. bigger

eg. 1) The factory supplies electrical components for cars.

2) Fresh fruit and vegetables are an essential component of a healthy diet.

10. There, his main task was to establish close relations with Saddam Hussein so that the US could provide him with large-scale aid, including means to develop WMD (Weapons of Mass Destruction), continuing long after the violence against the Kurds and the end of the war with Iran.

...his main task was to... so that the US could provide...aid, including..., continuing long after...
　　　主句　　　　　　　　目的状语从句　　　　插入语　现在分词（作定语）

Meaning: There, Rumsfeld's mission was to represent the United States to develop a close relationship with Saddam Hussein so that the US could provide him with large-scale aid, including means to develop Weapons of Mass Destruction. The aid had lasted for a pretty long time after Saddam Hussein committed the crime of violence against the Kurds and the end of the war with Iran.

11. The official purpose, not <u>concealed</u>, was Washington's responsibility to aid American exporters and "the markedly <u>unanimous</u> view" of Washington and its <u>allies</u> Britain and Saudi Arabia that "whatever the sins of the Iraqi leader, he offered the West and the region a better hope for his country's stability than did those who have suffered his <u>repression</u>."

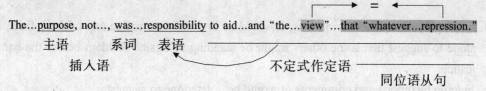

The...<u>purpose</u>, not..., <u>was</u>...<u>responsibility</u> to aid...and "the...view"...that "whatever...repression."
　　主语　　　系词　　表语
　　　　插入语　　　　　　　　不定式作定语
　　　　　　　　　　　　　　　　　同位语从句

Meaning: It was clear that the official purpose was to help American exporters make money and to support the view as agreed by America and its allies Britain and Saudi Arabia that between Saddam Hussein and his enemies that were under his oppression, the former was more capable of offering the West and the region his country's stability. And this was why America decided to provide Saddam Hussein with military aid, such as the means to develop WMD.

▶ conceal (*v.*): to hide sb. or sth.

eg. 1) I tried to conceal my surprise when she told me her age.

　　2) The robbery had been recorded on a concealed security camera.

▶ unanimous (*adj.*): if a decision or an opinion is unanimous, it is agreed or shared by everyone in a group; un (not, no) + animus (opposition, hatred, anger)→animous = unanimous (agreed)

eg. 1) After a lengthy discussion we reached a unanimous decision on the proposal.

　　2) The new format has unanimous support and could be introduced next season.

▶ ally (*n.*): a country that has agreed officially to give help and support to another one, especially during a war

eg. 1) During World War I, Turkey and Germany were allies.

　　2) He is generally considered to be the Prime Minister's closest political ally.

▲ alliance (*n.*): an association, especially of nations for a common cause

eg. 1) The three smaller parties have formed an alliance against the government.

　　2) Some of us feel that the union is in alliance with the management against us.

▶ repression (*n.*): the act of using force to control a group of people and restrict their freedom

eg. 1) The political repression in this country is enforced by terror.

2) The repression of emotions is bad for health.

▲ repress (*v.*): not allow sth., especially feelings, to be expressed

eg. 1) He repressed a sudden desire to cry.

   2) She repressed the agonizing memory until the trial was over.

12. It was in 1982 that Reagan removed Iraq from the list of states supporting terror so that aid could flow to his friend in Baghdad.

Meaning: It was in 1982 that Reagan removed Iraq from the list of states supporting terror so that he would be able to provide Saddam Hussein with aid. Here "his friend" refers to "Saddam Hussein."

13. Judging by reports and comments, it would be impolite to mention any of these facts, <u>let alone</u> to suggest that some others might be standing alongside Saddam before the bar of justice.

<u>Judging by reports and comments</u>, it would be..., let alone to suggest...

       现在分词作状语   主句

Meaning: Since most reports and comments never mentioned anything concerning the aid that American government once provided Saddam Hussein with, it would be impolite for us to tell these facts openly, not to mention to indicate that there supposed to be some others to be tried together with Saddam Hussein. Here, "some others" refers to Reagan and Rumsfeld.

► let alone (used as conjunction): not to mention

eg. 1) He hasn't enough money for food, let alone amusements.

   2) In 1970s, people were living in a very rigid and closed society. Few had the chance to meet foreigners, let alone to socialize with them.

14. Removing Saddam from the list of states supporting terrorism left a <u>gap</u>.

Meaning: By taking Iraq off the list of states supporting terrorism, the Reagan administration gave a break in the continuity of American government's anti-terrorism policy and attitude.

► gap (*n.*): an interruption of continuity

eg. 1) The president tonight will address the gap in policy.

   2) The introduction of this mechanism brought a gap in the organization's mission.

15. Since the first War on Terror was <u>waged</u> by those now carrying out the re-declared war, or their immediate <u>mentors</u>, it follows that anyone seriously interested in the re-declared War on Terror should ask at once how it was carried out in the 1980s.

► wage (*v.*): to begin and continue a war

eg. 1) The President needs Congress permission to wage war on another country.

2) They've waged a long campaign to change the law.

▶ mentor (*n.*): a person who gives another person help and advice over a period of time and often also teaches them how to do their job

16. The topic, however, is under a practical <u>ban</u>.

Meaning: But actually the topic is forbidden.

▶ ban (*n.*): an official rule that says that sth. is not allowed

eg. 1) There is a ban on smoking.

2) There should be a ban on talking loudly in cinemas.

▲ban (*v.*) to forbid, especially officially

eg. 1) She was banned from driving for two years.

2) Due to the recent charge against him, he was banned from the conference.

17. That becomes understandable as soon as we <u>investigate</u> the facts...

▶ investigate (*v.*): to carefully examine the facts of a situation, an event, a crime, etc. to find out the truth about sth. or how it happened

eg. 1) The police are investigating the robbery.

2) To investigate a problem is, indeed, to solve it.

▲ investigation (*n.*): the act or process of investigating

eg. 1) An investigation has been under way for several days into the disappearance of a thirteen-year-old boy.

2) Currently, the individuals who might have caused the accident are under investigation.

18. What happened is hardly <u>obscure</u>, but unacceptable, therefore protected from inspection.

Meaning: What happened is very clear, but unacceptable, so it is protected from being known.

▶ obscure (*adj.*): unclear and difficult to understand or see

eg. 1) Official policy has changed, for reasons that remain obscure.

2) His answers were obscure and confusing.

19. Bringing up the record is an <u>enlightening</u> exercise, with <u>enormous</u> <u>implications</u> for the future.

Meaning: Mentioning this record can provide more instructive information that may greatly help us predict the future.

▶ enlightening (*adj.*): giving sb. more information and understanding of sth.

eg. 1) That was a very enlightening program.

2) The instruction manual that came with my new computer wasn't very enlightening about how to operate it.

► enormous (*adj.*): very great in size, extent, number; or degree

eg. 1) The problems facing the President are enormous.

2) The enormous birthday cake dwarfed everything else on the table.

► implication (*n.*): a possible effect or result of an action or a decision

eg. 1) The development of the site will have implications for the surrounding countryside.

2) They failed to consider the wider implications of their actions.

20. Decent people apply to themselves the same standards that they apply to others, if not more severe ones.

Meaning: If honest and respectable people do not judge and restrict themselves by more severe standards, at least they do it by the same standards that they use to judge and restrict others.

► decent (*adj.*): morally upright; respectable

eg. 1) People around him thought that he was quite a decent young man, until he was arrested for hacking bank website.

2) Everybody said that he was a decent guy.

► apply to: to use sth. or make sth. work in a particular situation

eg. 1) These policies do not apply to non-permanent residents.

2) The new technology was applied to farming.

21. Adherence to this principle of universality would have many useful consequences.

► adherence (*n.*): the fact of behaving according to a particular rule, etc., or of following a particular set of beliefs, or a fixed way of doing

eg. 1) He was noted for his strict adherence to the rules.

2) We were amazed at their adherence to the traditional values.

▲ adhere to: to continue to obey a rule or maintain a belief

eg. 1) She adhered to her principles throughout her life.

2) They failed to adhere to the terms of the agreement.

3) The translator adheres very strictly to the original text.

22. For one thing, it would save a lot of trees. The principle would radically reduce published reporting and explanation on social and political affairs.

Meaning: Here the author is mocking the American government by saying if it adhered to the principle of applying to themselves the same standards that they apply to others, it would save a lot of efforts in publishing reports and explaining in documents to its people on social and political affairs, which has consumed a huge amount of paper, and paper is made out of trees.

23. It would almost <u>eliminate</u> the newly fashionable discipline of Just War theory.

Meaning: Adherence to the principle of universality would almost wipe out the special knowledge of Just War theory that has recently been developed and instilled into the people. "Discipline" means branch of knowledge or subject of instruction and here it is used to emphasize the so-called scientific study of Just War theory, with an ironic effect.

▶ eliminate (*v.*): to remove or take away

eg. 1) A move towards healthy eating could help eliminate heart disease.

2) The police eliminated the possibility that it could have been an accident.

▲ elimination (*n.*): the act or process of eliminating

eg. The team is now on the verge of elimination in spite of the high expectations from fans.

24. And it would wipe the record almost clean with regard to the War on Terror.

Meaning: If they had been adhering to the principle of universality, there would not have been any War on Terror in history.

25. ... the principle of universality is rejected, for the most part <u>tacitly</u>, though sometimes clearly.

Meaning: Sometimes the principle of universality is rejected clearly, but most of the time rejection of this principle is suggested indirectly.

▶ tacitly (*adv.*): indirectly, implicitly

eg. 1) The agent tacitly implied that it had contacts with Al-Jazeera (半岛电视台).

2) Salesmen do tough jobs. They are tacitly expected to work 10 hours a day.

▲ tacit (*adj.*): that is suggested indirectly or understood, rather than said in words

eg. 1) The management has given its tacit approval to the plan.

2) By tacit agreement, the subject was never mentioned again.

26. Those are very <u>sweeping</u> statements.

▶ sweeping (*adj.*): too general and failing to think about or understand

eg. 1) This report is full of sweeping statements, which does not deserve reading.

2) You shouldn't make sweeping generalizations about women drivers.

27. ...that although the statements are somewhat <u>overdrawn</u>—purposely—they nevertheless are uncomfortably close to accurate, and in fact very fully documented.

Meaning: ...that although the statements I made on purpose are a little exaggerated, they are close to the unpleasant truth and in fact they are fully supported by documents.

▶ overdraw (*v.*): to spoil the effect by exaggeration

eg. 1) I cannot overdraw the importance of this book.

2) The impact of the new legislation has been overdrawn.

28. ... terrorism is "the <u>calculated</u> use of violence or threat of violence to <u>attain</u> goals that are political, religious, or ideological in nature... through <u>intimidation</u>, <u>coercion</u> or <u>instilling</u> fear."

<u>Meaning</u>: ...terrorism is the well-planned use of violence or threat of violence to realize goals that are political, religious or conceptual in nature through threatening, using force or creating fear in people.

► calculated (*adj.*): made or planned to accomplish a certain purpose; deliberate

eg. 1) He exploded at such a calculated insult.

2) He took a calculated risk.

► attain (*v.*): to reach or succeed in getting sth.; to achieve

eg. 1) He has attained the highest grade in his music exams.

2) India attained independence in 1947, after decades of struggle.

▲ attainable (*adj.*): possible to achieve

eg. We must ensure that we do not set goals that are not attainable.

► intimidation (*n.*): the act of making sb. timid or frightened by threats

eg. 1) The campaign of violence and intimidation against them intensifies daily.

2) For sure, their intimidations won't help them win the lawsuit.

▲ intimidate (*v.*): to frighten or threaten someone, usually in order to persuade them to do sth. that one wants them to do

eg. 1) They were intimidated into accepting a pay cut by the threat of losing their jobs.

2) She refused to be intimidated by their threats.

► coercion (*n.*): the action of making sb. do sth. that they do not want to do; the act of using force or of threatening to use force

eg. 1) The superpowers got what they wanted by coercion.

2) He claimed that he had only copied the confidential document under gangsters' coercion.

▲ coercive (*adj.*): serving or intended to coerce

eg. 1) Don't underestimate coercive powers.

2) The president relied on the coercive powers of the military.

► instill (*v.*): to put a feeling, idea or principle gradually into someone's mind, so that it has a strong influence on the way they think or behave

eg. 1) It is part of a teacher's job to instill confidence into the students.

2) Courtesy must be instilled in childhood.

29. There are ways to deal <u>constructively</u> with the threat of terror, though not those preferred by "bin Laden's <u>indispensable</u> ally"...

▶ constructively (*adv.*): helpfully

eg. 1) Students should be taught how to manage conflicts constructively.

2) Sue and Dick, like many other people, have never learned to constructively handle their anger.

▲ constructive (*adj.*): If advice, criticism or actions are constructive, they are useful and intended to help or improve sth.

eg. 1) She criticized my writing, but in a way that was very constructive—I learned a lot from her.

2) If you don't have anything constructive to say, I'd rather you kept quiet.

▶ indispensable (*adj.*): essential; too important to be without

eg. 1) This full text database is an indispensable resource for researchers.

2) His long experience at the United Nations makes him indispensable to the talks.

Better Know More

Notes

1. Text A was an excerpt

Text A was an excerpt from the Amnesty International Annual Lecture hosted by TCD, delivered by Noam Chomsky at Shelbourne Hall, the Royal Dublin Society, January 18, 2006. The original lecture can be found at http://www.youmaysayimadreamer.com/code/ articles/article-terror.htm.

2. The Crime that Saddam Hussein Committed in 1982

Dujail was the site of a failed assassination attempt against Saddam Hussein. The town was a stronghold of the Shiite Dawa Party, a party strongly opposed to Saddam Hussein and his war with Iran. On July 8, 1982, Saddam Hussein was visiting the town to make a speech praising those who had served Iraq in the fight against Iran. While driving through the village centre, his motorcade was attacked by one or more members of the Dawa Party. Saddam was not harmed, but he ordered the military forces to carry out a retaliation attack against the town, killing a total of 148 of the town's men, some as young as 13 years old. 1,500 people were also arrested and tortured, while other residents, many of them women and children, were sent to desert camps. Saddam's regime destroyed the town and then rebuilt it shortly after. In addition to these punishments, 1,000 square kilometres of farmland was destroyed;

replanting was only permitted 10 years later.

Check Your Understanding

Translate the following sentences into Chinese. Please make sure that your language flows smoothly.

1. The reason is the same in all cases: the principle of universality is rejected, for the most part tacitly, though sometimes clearly.

   不论在什么情况下，原因都只有一个：（对人对己理应）一致的原则遭到拒绝，多数情况下是暗地里拒绝，可有些时候则做得明目张胆。

2. But we should seek enough clarity at least to distinguish terror from two notions that lie uneasily at its borders: aggression and legitimate resistance.

   但是我们至少应该将恐怖行径和另外两个与之相近的概念区别开来，即侵略和合理抵抗，它们虽都和恐怖相关，可性质不同。

3. Judging by reports and comments, it would be impolite to mention any of these facts, let alone to suggest that some others might be standing alongside Saddam before the bar of justice.

   按照（当今）报告和评论的标准，提及这其中的任何一项事实都是不礼貌的，更不用说点出某些人或许要与萨达姆一起接受法庭的审判。

4. That becomes understandable as soon as we investigate the facts.

   只要我们调查一下这些事实，就会立刻明白这一点。

5. Decent people apply to themselves the same standards that they apply to others, if not more severe ones.

   正派的人如果不是对自己使用更加严格的标准，至少也会用要求他人的标准同样要求自己。

6. Terrorism is the calculated use of violence or threat of violence to attain goals that are political, religious, or ideological in nature...through intimidation, coercion, or instilling fear.

   恐怖主义指的是通过恐吓、强迫或制造恐惧等方法，精心策划的暴力或威胁使用暴力，来实现政治、宗教或意识形态目的（的行径）。

Answer the following questions based on the text you have just learned.

1. Do you think terrorist attacks around the world share common themes? If the answer is yes, what are they?

   This question focuses on common features of terrorist attacks such as using violence, causing damage, public panic or blood shedding, suffering of the innocent people, hatred toward the government, etc. The instructor can ask students to discuss the question in small groups.

2. Who is the terrorist in the mirror?

If you see a terrorist in the mirror, you are the terrorist.

3. What is state-directed international terrorism?

State-directed international terrorism refers to attacks managed by the government of a country targeting civilians in other countries.

4. What was the purpose for the U.S. to establish close relations with Saddam Hussein and provide him with large-scale aid during the first stage of the War on Terror?

The purpose was on the one hand to aid American exporters and on the other hand support the belief agreed by Washington and its allies that "whatever the sins of the Iraqi leader, he offered the West and the region a better hope for his country's stability than did those who have suffered his repression."

5. What is the most elementary moral principle?

The most elementary moral principle is that decent people apply to themselves the same standards that they apply to others, if not more severe ones.

6. Why would the principle of universality almost eliminate the discipline of the "Just War" theory?

If they had been adhering to the principle of universality, in other words, if they had been using the same principle to judge and restrict themselves as well as others, they would not have come up with a Just War theory to treat others differently.

7. Please define terrorism in your own words.

Terrorism refers to planned use of violence or threat of violence to achieve goals that are political, religious, or ideological in nature...through intimidation, coercion, or instilling fear.

8. What is your understanding of the last sentence in the text?

It is no easy task, but quite necessary for a government to be honest first and restrict itself by the same standard that it uses in restricting others. This is the only constructive way to deal with terrorism.

A Sip of Phonetics

Know Their Faces

本课学习一个声门摩擦音 /h/ 和两个破擦音 /tʃ/ 和 /dʒ/。

发 /h/ 音时,嘴巴自然张开,舌头放松,气流在声门处发生轻微摩擦,随后送出口腔,口形随其后的元音而变化。声门摩擦音 /h/ 是清辅音,发音时声带不振动。指导教师需要特别留意学生不可将 /h/ 进行发音而读作汉语中的"喝"。汉语中的"喝"实际上是舌后部靠近软腭,气流通过时产生摩擦,发音部位靠前,且伴随元音 /ə/;而英语中的 /h/ 气流通过声门摩擦,发音部位靠后,但小舌不振颤,不伴随 /ə/。教师教学中要注意带领学生进行比较,并做正确发音的示范。

/tʃ/ 和 /dʒ/ 是舌端齿龈破擦音。注意破擦音要求先从爆破音 /t/,/d/ 开始,口腔各部分做到位后迅速过渡到摩擦音 /ʃ/ 和 /ʒ/。指导教师应提醒学生注意这个过渡。

教师还可以利用绕口令,让学生练习这三个音。教师应指导学生如何换气和断句、领悟句意,以便达到预期的效果。

📖 Train Your Tongue

1. The <u>h</u>unter / and <u>h</u>is <u>h</u>uge <u>h</u>orse / <u>h</u>id be<u>h</u>ind /the <u>h</u>ouse.
2. Whi<u>ch</u> wristwat<u>ch</u>es / are Swiss wristwat<u>ch</u>es?
3. The <u>ch</u>ubby <u>ch</u>ild / draws a <u>ch</u>ick / on the board / with <u>ch</u>alk.
4. A <u>ch</u>ild / on an old <u>ch</u>air / over there / holds a pea<u>ch</u> / and <u>ch</u>eers.

You'd Like to Be

📖 A Strong Bridge Builder

Fill in the blanks with the given words to complete the following sentences.　Please note that some can be used more than once.

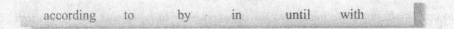

| according | to | by | in | until | with |

Knowledge began to increase as soon as the thoughts of one individual could be communicated to another <u>by</u> means of speech. <u>With</u> the invention of writing, a great advance was made, for knowledge could then be not only communicated but also stored. Libraries made education possible, and education <u>in</u> turn added <u>to</u> libraries: the growth of knowledge followed a kind of compound-interest law, which was greatly enhanced <u>by</u> the invention of printing. All this was comparatively slow <u>until</u>, with the coming of science, the tempo (节奏)was suddenly raised. Then knowledge began to be accumulated <u>according</u> to a systematic plan.

A Smart Word Player

Fill in the blanks with the proper words that need to be transformed from the ones provided in the brackets.

Mr. Pursey said, among other things, that there was a close relationship between the success of national and international efforts to tackle <u>unemployment</u> (employ), poverty, and <u>inequality</u> (equality), and <u>attaining</u> (attain) worldwide respect for core labour standards—that such standards put a kind of "floor of <u>decency</u> (decent)" under the operations of world economic markets. Ms. Katseli said there was a need to reinstate the <u>legitimacy</u> (legitimate) of policy making at the national and international levels. Participating in the discussion were <u>representatives</u> (represent) of Spain, Iran, Syria, United States, China, etc.

*Note: The "core labor standards" are four principles that all countries should support no matter what their level of development: (1) freedom of association and the right to organize and bargain collectively, (2) abolition of forced labor, (3) elimination of child labor, and (4) nondiscrimination in employment.

A Skilled Text Weaver

Fill in the blanks with the words you have learned in this text. One word is for each blank. Here is a piece of advice: You must be really familiar with the text to accomplish the following tasks.

There is a <u>ban</u> on students smoking at school. Doctors say cigarettes contain nicotine, which is harmful to adults, <u>let</u> <u>alone</u> kids. People say our kids are still too young and they cannot <u>distinguish</u> right <u>from</u> wrong. Adults smoke because they believe cigarettes can help them <u>alleviate</u> pressure from daily work. There is no reason for kids to smoke except that they are curious and just want to try something new and to look cool apparently. At present, the whole society is <u>waging</u> a war against cigarette smoking. Parents <u>unanimously</u> believe that schools should <u>instill</u> basic knowledge of health to students and make sure students <u>adhere</u> <u>to</u> the principles of behavior.

〜〜 A Sharp Interpreter

Please paraphrase the following sentences. Change the sentence structure if necessary.

1. Facts matter, even if we do not like them.

   ✧ *Paraphrasing:*

   Facts are significant, even if we do not like them.

2. The topic, however, is under a practical ban.

   ✧ *Paraphrasing:*

   But actually this topic is forbidden.

3. What happened is hardly obscure, but unacceptable, therefore protected from inspection.

   ✧ *Paraphrasing:*

   What happened can be easily observed and found out, yet, as it is acceptable, it is protected from being inuestigated.

4. Decent people apply to themselves the same standards that they apply to others, if not more severe ones.

   ✧ *Paraphrasing:*

   Honest and respectable people use the same standards or even more severe ones to judge and restrict themselves as well as others.

5. It would wipe the record almost clean with regard to the War on Terror.

   ✧ *Paraphrasing:*

   If they had been adhering to the principle of universality, there would not have been any War on Terror in history.

6. The principle of universality is rejected, for the most part tacitly, though sometimes clearly.

   ✧ *Paraphrasing:*

   In most cases, the principle of universality is rejected secretly, but sometimes it is rejected openly.

7. I purposely put them in a stark form to invite you to challenge them, and I hope you do.

   ✧ *Paraphrasing:*

   I deliberately (on purpose) put them in an obvious form to ask you to question them and I hope you can do so.

8. Although the statements are somewhat overdrawn—purposely—they nevertheless are uncomfortably close to accurate and in fact very fully documented.

   ✧ *Paraphrasing:*

   Although the statements I made on purpose are a little exaggerated, they are very close to the unpleasant truth and in fact they are fully supported by documents.

A Solid Sentence Constructer

Please make a sentence with each word or expression listed below.

1. for the most part

   ✤ *Original sentence in the text:*

   The reason is the same in all cases: the principle of universality is rejected, for the most part tacitly, though sometimes clearly.

   ✤ **Suggested sentence:**

   The contributors are, for the most part, professional scientists.

2. to distinguish ... from ...

   ✤ *Original sentence in the text:*

   Now, let's turn to the third background issue: defining "terror" and distinguishing it from aggression and legitimate resistance.

   ✤ **Suggested sentence:**

   I sometimes have difficulty distinguishing Spanish from Portuguese.

3. to let alone

   ✤ *Original sentence in the text:*

   Judging by reports and comments, it would be impolite to mention any of these facts, let alone to suggest that some others might be standing alongside Saddam before the bar of justice.

   ✤ **Suggested sentence:**

   He hasn't enough money for food, let alone amusements.

4. to investigate

   ✤ *Original sentence in the text:*

   That becomes understandable as soon as we investigate the facts...

   ✤ **Suggested sentence:**

   The police are investigating the robbery.

5. to apply to

   ✤ *Original sentence in the text:*

   Decent people apply to themselves the same standards that they apply to others, if not more severe ones.

   ✤ **Suggested sentence:**

   They applied a very detailed questionnaire to 22 private schools and 10 public ones with similar characteristics.

6. to instill

   ✤ *Original sentence in the text:*

   Terrorism is "the calculated use of violence or threat of violence to attain goals that are political, religious, or ideological in nature...through intimidation, coercion, or instilling fear," typically targeting civilians.

◈ **Suggested sentence:**

It is part of a teacher's job to instill confidence in/into his or her students.

A Superb Bilingualist

Please translate the following sentences into English with the prompts provided in the brackets.

1. 他的话并非针对我,可我还是忍不住对他发了火。(direct to, repress)

◈ *Suggested translation:*

His words were not directed to me, but I still could not repress my anger.

2. 虽然他坚持说公司的经营一切正常,但我们都觉得事实并非如此。(claim, conceal)

◈ *Suggested translation:*

Although he claimed that everything was all right in his company, we all believed that he was trying to conceal the truth.

3. 没有人欣赏他的方案,更不用说全体通过了。(let alone, unanimous)

◈ *Suggested translation:*

Nobody appreciated/liked his plan, let alone a unanimous approval.

4. 因局势尚不明朗,官方并未取消这一计划。(obscure, eliminate)

◈ *Suggested translation:*

The authority has not eliminated this plan since the situation still remains obscure.

5. 政府通过取消农业税来减轻农民负担。(alleviate, ban)

◈ *Suggested translation:*

The government tries to alleviate burden of farmers by putting a ban on their taxes.

6. 新技术正在被应用到现代生活的方方面面。(apply to)

◈ *Suggested translation:*

New technology is being applied to almost every aspect of our modern life.

7. 沉溺于网络像瘟疫一样在青少年中蔓延。有报道说有些年轻人甚至在网上犯罪。
(cyber addiction, plague, commit)

◈ *Suggested translation:*

Cyber addiction spreads among adolescents like a plague. It is reported that some youngsters even commit crimes on the Internet.

Text B

Introduction of the Text

Upon the 60th anniversary of the liberation of the Nazi death camp at Auschwitz by Russian soldiers, a commemoration was held in a Berlin theater. The commemoration attendees included Holocaust survivors and various political functionaries including German Chancellor Gerhard Schröder. Standing before a film screen depicting a photo of Auschwitz, Schröder gave this remarkable speech containing some of the most forthright sentiments regarding the Holocaust yet expressed by a leader of postwar Germany.

Introduction of the Author

Gerhard Fritz Kurt Schröder (1944—), German politician, was Chancellor of Germany from 1998 to 2005. Before becoming a full time politician, he was a successful lawyer.

Comprehension Questions

After reading Text B,   please answer the following questions based on what you have learned from Text B.

1. Who delivered this speech?

   Former German Chancellor Schröder.

2. Does he believe that words are enough when confronted with the murder of millions?

   He believes that words by government leaders are inadequate when confronted with the murder of millions.

3. Former Chancellor Schröder mentions a manifestation of absolute evil, but what should we do about it?

   He points out that there is evil in the hate-driven genocide but it does not permit Germany to circumvent its responsibilities.

4. What does the Chancellor say to the dead and the survivors?

   He expresses his shame to the dead and the survivors.   He says although nothing can make up for the horror, the torment and the agony, the government is willing to provide a certain amount of compensation to the victims.

5. What is the current state of the Jewish Community in Germany?

   Today the Jewish Community in Germany is the third largest in Europe and an irreplaceable part of the German society and culture.

6. At the end of his speech, what does Schröder call on the whole society to do?

   He calls on the whole society to protect the Jewish community against the anti-Semites and to work together to fight former Nazis and neo-Nazis. He emphasizes the need to preserve the history and the need for all to bear the historical responsibility and to protect and respect life and human dignity.

Writing Practice

Put your answers to the above questions together and form a summary about the text and share with your classmates the summary you have completed.

Former German Chancellor Gerhard Schröder delivers a speech at the invitation of the International Auschwitz Committee, for which he believes that words by government leaders are inadequate when confronted with the murder of millions. First he points out that there is evil in the hate-driven genocide but it doesn't permit Germany to circumvent its responsibilities. Then he expresses his shame to the dead and the survivors. He says although nothing can make up for the horror, the torment and the agony, the government is responsible to provide a certain amount of compensation to the victims. Today the Jewish Community in Germany is the third largest in Europe and an irreplaceable part of the German society and culture. He calls on the whole society to protect them against the anti-Semites and to work together to fight former Nazis and neo-Nazis. Finally he emphasizes the need to preserve the history and the need for all to bear the historical responsibility and to protect and respect life and human dignity.

Unit 11

Menaces Around

Unit Goals

After studying this unit, students should be able to:

☞ **understand the reality of AIDS;**

      Text A is an emotional speech. In delivering this speech targeting at alerting people to the fact that AIDS is a disease that might affect anyone in the world, to the whole nation, Mary Fisher issues a plea for awareness, and calls for people's change of attitude toward those who are HIV positive. Before moving into **Text A**, the instructor should walk the students through **A Glimpse at Words and Expressions**, which will help warm up the students. Students' preview of both **Text A** and **Text B** should be strongly encouraged.

☞ **know the phonetics /m/, /n/ and /ŋ/, and how to utilize the words and structures that contribute significantly to the texts;**

      In this section, the instructor should explain to the students how to pronounce these consonants and demonstrate the correct pronunciation of each one. The instructor may refer to the advice provided in the section **A Sip of Phonetics**. With a unique stylistic feature, which is emotional, speech sets itself apart from most other writing formats. It is strongly suggested that the instructor encourage the students read aloud **Text A** in class. Most useful words and structures of **Text A** can be found in **You'd like to Be**. This is where students practice what they have learned from **Text A**.

☞ **understand the sports injuries suffered by young school athletes.**

      Text B exposes the fact that many young athletes today suffer from sports injuries. With menaces staying around, it is now exceedingly important for young athletes, their coaches and even parents to learn how to balance between success and risk.

Before Reading

Hands-on Activities and Brainstorming

The instructor should allow 15—20 minutes for students to do presentation on AIDS prevention.

A Glimpse at Words and Expressions

A. It is easy for students to see that "brutally" here is just for emphasis. The adjective "brutal" describes a situation that is unpleasant and cruel. The instructor should remind students of the occasion when it can be used. For example: To be brutally honest/frank, you look fat in that dress.

B. "Travel" is not new to students of course. But here it refers to the spreading of a disease among people.

C. "Straight" means "sexually oriented to people of the opposite sex."

D. "Unheralded" is formal. The instructor should let students know that "herald" is a sign that shows that sth. else is going to happen soon. The instructor may resort to the analysis of word formation to help students guess the meaning of "unheralded":

un (no, not) + herald (sign) + ed = no sign → happening without warning

E. In sentence E, "else" and "no" serve as very significant clues. "Else" means "otherwise," indicating that the part after "else" should be opposite to what goes before it. If people talk in one way and act in a different way, they are dishonest.

F. The instructor should help students understand the word formation of "embrace":

em (in) + brace (two arms) = put one's arms around sb./sth. to show liking "To embrace a message" is to accept an idea or a proposal esp. when it is done with enthusiasm. For example: This was an opportunity that he would embrace.

G. Another example may help students get a rough idea of "issue": The company issued a statement about its plans to the press. So "issue" means "to make sth. known formally."

Keys

A-4   B-3   C-1   D-6   E-7   F-2   G-5

Text A

Introduction to Major Features of Speech

1. Speech is for current, local audience; it is bound to context or participants. Please refer to the following examples.

1) In speech, terms of address or pronouns used are usually "you," "we," "let's," etc.

"I have a message for you: it is not you who should feel shame; it is we—we who tolerate ignorance and practice prejudice, we who have taught you to fear." (Line 61—62, Text A, Unit 11)

2) Common deixis of speech are "this country," "our society," "here," "in front of me," "right now," etc.

"In the context of an election year, I ask you to hear, in this great hall, or to listen in the quiet of your home—to recognize that the AIDS epidemic is not a political creature."(Line 8—9, Text A, Unit 11)

3) Speech usually adopts a certain attitude, such as "really," "surely," "kind of," "maybe," "I guess," etc.

"We may take refuge in our stereotype but we cannot hide there long because HIV asks only one thing of those it attacks: Are you human?" (Line 29—32, Text A, Unit 11)

2. Speech is produced in real time, which justifies the following occurrences.

1) Hesitations, false starts, repetitions and clarifications are common in speech.

"I want my children to know that their mother was not a victim. She was a messenger. I do not want them to think, as I once did, that courage is the absence of fear; I want them to know that courage is the strength to act wisely when most are afraid. I want them to have the courage to step forward when called by their nation, or their Party, and give leadership—no matter what the personal cost." (Line 65—69, Text A, Unit 11)

2) Elisions, omissions, reduced forms and shorthands are common in speech.

"Each of them is exactly what God made: a person, not evil deserving of our judgment, not victim longing for our pity. People, ready for support and worthy of compassion." (Line 39—43, Text A, Unit 11)

3) Stress, pitch, intonation and tempo guarantee an effective communication.

"Peter bought a book." is different from *"Peter bought a book."* or *"Peter bought a book."*

3. Other features particular to speech.

1) Discourse markers such as "ok," "well," etc. are particular to speech.

"Well, the next step is ..."
"Ok, since we've been quite clear about this point, then..."

2) Utterance launchers such as "the point is ...," "what I mean is...," "What I am saying is...," "as far as I know," etc. are very common in speech.

"What I am talking about is the deliberate leaking of highly sensitive operational intelligence, often classified, and the unauthorized release of which can be a criminal ..."

3) Tag questions are not uncommon in speech.

"It's very interesting, isn't it?"
"We have done the right thing, haven't we?"
"It's a challenging job, right?"

4) Terms of address such as "Sir," "Your Excellency," "comrade," etc. are also one of the unique features of speech.

"Ladies and gentlemen,..."
"Whatever happens to you, my comrade, I promise..."

Suggested Explanations on Text A

1. The reality of AIDS is <u>brutally</u> clear.

Meaning: The reality of AIDS is clear but cruel.

▶ brutally (*adv.*): in a brutal manner, not caring about one's feelings

eg. 1) To be brutally honest/ frank, you look fat in that dress.

2) The old man had been brutally attacked/ murdered.

▲ brutal (*adj.*): cruel, completely without feelings

eg. 1) She spoke with brutal honesty—I was too old for the job.

2) The mother could not face the brutal truth that her child died in a car accident.

2. But despite science and research, White House meetings and congressional hearings, despite good intentions and bold initiatives, campaign slogans and hopeful promises— despite it all, it's the epidemic which is winning tonight.

   Parallelism(排比)is one of the most useful and flexible rhetorical techniques. It refers to any structure which brings together parallel elements. Done well, parallelism imparts grace and power to passage. In this speech, Mary Fisher uses three "despite's" to lay emphasis on the disappointing fact that "it's the epidemic which is winning tonight."

   ▶ bold (*adj.*): brave, not fearing danger

   eg. 1) He was a bold and fearless climber.

   　2) The newspaper made the bold move/took the bold step of publishing the names of the men involved.

   ▶ initiative (*n.*): the ability to decide and act on one's own without waiting for sb. to tell what to do

   eg. 1) The peace initiative was welcomed by both sides.

   　2) You should take the initiative to solve the problem.

   ▶ epidemic (*n.*): the appearance of a particular disease in a large number of people at the same time

   ▲ epidemic (*adj.*): spreading rapidly and extensively by infection and affecting many individuals in an area or a population at the same time

   eg. 1) Last winter there was an epidemic outbreak of influenza.

   　2) Violence is reaching epidemic levels in some of the films and TV plays.

3. It does not ask whether you are black or white, male or female, gay or straight, young or old.

   Again, the author uses parallelism in this sentence. Pay attention to the "or's." Many other similar cases can be found in the speech. See if students are able to find them.

4. ...I am one with a black infant struggling with tubes in a Philadelphia hospital.

   Meaning: I view myself the same as a black little baby who is struggling between life and death with the help of medical devices in a Philadelphia hospital. There is no difference between us because we are AIDS patients and we both belong to the same group.

   ▶ tube (*n.*): a long hollow pipe made of metal, plastic, rubber, etc. through which liquids or gases move from one place to another

   eg. Blood flowed along the tube into the bottle.

5. I am one with the lonely gay man sheltering a flickering candle from the cold wind of his family's rejection.

Meaning: I view myself the same as a lonely gay man who cannot get love and support from his family and is still struggling with life which is as weak as the flickering of the candle. There is no difference between us because we are AIDS patients and we both belong to the same group of people.

► shelter (*v.*): to provide cover or protection for

eg. 1) Local people risked their own lives to shelter resistance fighters from the army.

2) Plant flowers next to a wall to shelter them from the wind.

▲ shelter (*n.*): (a building designed to give) protection from bad weather, danger or attack

eg. 1) They opened a shelter to provide temporary housing for the city's homeless.

2) The trees gave/ provided some shelter from the rain.

► flicker (*v.*): (of a light or a flame) to keep going on and off as it shines or burns

eg. 1) The candle flickered in the wind.

2) The flame is flickering in the stove.

6. ...but it won't be third for long because, unlike other diseases, this one travels.

Meaning: AIDS will not remain the third killer for a long time and it could possibly become the second or even the first leading killer in the world because it is different from other diseases as it spreads among people.

7. And we have helped it along.

Meaning: We have helped AIDS spread to other people.

8. We have killed each other—with our ignorance, our prejudice and our silence.

► ignorance (*n.*): a lack of knowledge or information

eg. 1) Ignorance of the law is no excuse.

2) The patients were left in ignorance of what was wrong with them.

▲ ignore (*v.*): to intentionally not listen or give attention to

eg. 1) Safety regulations are being ignored by company managers in the drive to increase profits.

2) I tried to tell her but she ignored me.

▲ ignorant (*adj.*): not having enough knowledge, understanding or information about sth.

eg. 1) Many teenagers are surprisingly ignorant about current politics.

2) We remained blissfully ignorant of the troubles that lay ahead.

► prejudice (*n.*): an unfair and unreasonable opinion or feeling, especially when formed without enough thought or knowledge

eg. 1) Laws against racial prejudice must be strictly enforced.

2) A judge must be free from prejudice.

▲ prejudiced (*adj.*): showing an unreasonable dislike for sb./sth.

eg. 1) The campaign is designed to make people less prejudiced about AIDS.

   2) Some companies are prejudiced against taking on employees who are over the age
   of 40.

9. We may take <u>refuge</u> in our <u>stereotype</u> but we cannot hide there long...

   Meaning: We may seek protection from our fixed traditional thinking, attitude and ideas
   towards things like the cause of disease or poverty, etc., but we will soon find it
   not helpful...

   ► refuge (n.): (a place which gives) protection or shelter from danger, trouble, unhappi-
   ness, etc.

   eg. 1) The climbers slept in a mountain refuge.

   2) The woman had fled from her violent husband to a women's refuge.

   ▲ refugee (n.): a person who has escaped from their own country for political, religious
   or economic reasons or because of a war

   eg. 1) Thousands of refugees fled across the border.

   2) There is a refugee camp in the north of this country.

   ► stereotype (n.): a fixed idea that people have about what sb. or sth. is like, especially an
   idea resulted from the conventionality

   eg. 1) He doesn't conform to/ fit/ fill the national stereotype of a Frenchman.

   2) The characters in the book are just stereotypes.

   3) Sometimes we hold a cultural stereotype toward Japanese.

10. Because people with HIV have not entered some <u>alien</u> state of being, they are human.

   Meaning: Because people with HIV have not turned themselves into a different kind of
   being other than us, they are still human.

   ► alien (adj.): belonging to, characteristic of, or constituting another and very different
   place, society, or person; strange

   eg. 1) In this novel he imagined an alien spaceship was discovered by his family.

   2) Entire groups were driven from their homes to alien regions.

11. They have not earned cruelty and they do not deserve <u>meanness</u>.

   Meaning: They have their own right and should not be regarded as evil so we should not
   be cruel and unkind to them.

   ► meanness (n.): unkindness

   ▲ mean (adj.): unkind, or nasty

   eg. 1) That was a mean thing to do.

   2) Don't be so mean to her.

12. People, ready for support and worthy of compassion.

Meaning: They are people who need our support and they deserve our sympathy.

13. ...much of the good has gone unheralded...

Meaning: Much of the good has been done without being noticed or known by many people.

▶ unheralded (*adj.*): (formal) sth. or someone that is unheralded is not known about by many people and is sometimes not considered very good or important when it really is.

eg. 1) Although it is largely unheralded, the changes in currency rate are quite significant.

2) People cannot explain their unheralded achievement.

▲ herald (*v.*): to be a sign that sth. important, and often good, is starting to happen, or to make sth. publicly known, especially by celebrating or praising it

eg. 1) The president's speech heralds a new era in foreign policy.

2) This drug has been heralded as a major breakthrough in the fight against breast cancer.

14. We must be consistent if we are to be believed.

Meaning: We must always behave in the same way or have the same opinions, if we are to be believed.

▶ consistent (*adj.*): always behaving in the same way, or having the same opinions, standards, etc.

eg. 1) There has been a consistent improvement in her attitude.

2) This statement is not consistent with what you said at yesterday's meeting.

15. ...we must act as well as we speak—else we have no integrity.

Meaning: We must act as well as we speak, otherwise we are dishonest.

▶ integrity (*n.*): the quality of being honest and having strong moral principles

eg. 1) No one doubted that the president was a man of the highest integrity.

2) Academic integrity is essential to this school.

16. My call to the nation is a plea for awareness.

Meaning: I sincerely ask the nation to be aware of it.

▶ plea (*n.*): an urgent and emotional request

eg. 1) He made a plea for help/mercy.

2) The speaker spoke out in a plea for greater tolerance.

17. If you do not see this killer <u>stalking</u> your children, look again.

Meaning: If you do not see this killer moving slowly and quietly towards your children, look again.

▶ stalk (*v.*): to move slowly and quietly towards an animal or a person in order to kill, catch or harm it or them

eg. 1) The police had been stalking the thief for a week before they arrested her.

2) It might take ten minutes or more for a cat.

18. Until we sincerely <u>embrace</u> this message, we are a nation at risk.

Meaning: We are living in a dangerous country, as long as we refuse to admit that there is no family or community, no race or religon, no place left in America that is safe.

▶ embrace (*v.*): to accept an idea or a proposal especially when it is done with enthusiasm

eg. 1) This was an opportunity that he would embrace.

2) He is always ready to embrace new ideas.

19. You <u>weep</u> silently; you <u>grieve</u> alone.

▶ weep (*v.*): to shed tears as an expression of emotion

eg. 1) People in the street wept with joy when peace was announced.

2) She wept when she heard the bad news.

▶ grieve (*v.*): to feel very sad

eg. 1) She is still grieving for her dead husband.

2) People need time to grieve after the death of a loved one.

▲ grief (*n.*): very great sadness, especially at the death of someone

eg. 1) She did not show her grief when her son died.

2) Her grief at her son's death was terrible.

20. We must lift our covering of silence, making it safe for you to reach out for compassion.

Meaning: We must remove our veil of silence so as to have the AIDS victims heard and we must ensure that they will not be victimized twice when they speak out their sufferings and ask for help and sympathy from the society.

21. I do not want them to think, as I once did, that courage is the absence of fear;

Meaning: I once thought that I had courage only because I was not afraid of this disease. Now I do not want them to think in the way I did.

22. I ask no more of you than I ask of myself, or of my children.

Meaning: What I ask you to do, I also ask myself or my children to do or even to do more than that.

23. To the millions who are strong, I <u>issue</u> this plea: <u>set aside</u> prejudice and politics to make room for compassion and sound policy.

    Meaning: I want to ask the millions, who are strong, to abandon prejudice and politics so that we can have the opportunity to show our sympathy and make the right policy.

    ▶ issue (*v*.): to make sth. known formally

    eg. 1) The company will be issuing stocks next month.

    　　2) The government issued a statement to the public.

    ▶ to set aside: to decide that one will not be influenced by a particular feeling, belief, or principle, because sth. else is more important

    eg. 1) I had to set aside my social life, to free up the time to complete the book.

    　　2) Setting aside all health considerations, do you believe this law is fair to smokers?

24. Your silly <u>giggle</u> gives me hope.

    ▶ giggle (*n*.): a nervous or silly laugh

    eg. 1) There were a few nervous giggles from people in the audience.

    　　2) He was especially afraid of the giggles produced by those girls.

    ▲ giggle (*v*.): to laugh repeatedly in a quiet but uncontrolled and childish way, often at sth. silly or rude or when one is nervous

    eg. 1) The girls were giggling in class.

    　　2) Stop giggling behind the door.

25. I will seek a place where <u>intimacy</u> will not lead to suffering.

    Meaning: I will seek a place where having a close relationship will not lead to suffering.

    ▶ intimacy (*n*.): the state of having a close friendship or a sexual relationship with sb.

    ▲ intimate (*adj*.): having, or being likely to cause, a very close friendship or personal or sexual relationship

    eg. 1) No intimate relationships can be tolerated in this special military camp.

    　　2) He's become very intimate with an actress.

26. To all within sound of my voice, I <u>appeal</u>: learn with me the lesson of history and of grace...

    ▶ appeal (*v*.): to make a serious or formal request, especially to the public, for money or help

    eg. 1) The police are appealing to the public for any information about the missing girl.

    　　2) Church leaders have appealed to the government to stop the war.

    ▲ appealing (*adj*.): attractive, inviting

    eg. 1) The idea of not having to get up early every morning is rather appealing to me.

    　　2) He had a nice smile and an appealing personality.

▶ grace (*n.*): a quality of behavior that is polite and pleasant and deserves respect

eg. 1) The speaker answered their questions with grace.

2) He didn't even have the grace to apologize.

Better Know More

Philadelphia

Philadelphia is the largest city of Pennsylvania, in the southeast part of the state on the Delaware River. It was founded as a Quaker colony by William Penn in 1681 on the site of an earlier Swedish settlement. The First and Second Continental Congresses (1774 and 1775—1776) and the Constitutional Convention (1787) met in the city, which served as the capital of the United States from 1790 to 1800. The population of Philadelphia is 1,470,000.

Check Your Understanding

Translate the following sentences into Chinese. Please make sure that your language flows smoothly.

1. To the millions who are strong, I issue this plea: set aside prejudice and politics to make room for compassion and sound policy.

   我向千百万身体健康的人郑重请求:恳请你们抛弃偏见和政治,给同情和可行的政策留一席之地。

2. They don't benefit from being isolated or treated as those who have been excluded from our society.

   将他们孤立起来或是排斥在社会之外,对他们毫无益处。

3. Each of them is exactly what God made: a person, not evil deserving of our judgment, not victim longing for our pity.

   他们每一个人都由上帝创造,他们是人,不是需要由我们来评判的邪恶化身,更不是渴望着我们同情的牺牲品(或可怜虫)。

4. To my children, I make this promise: I will not give in, because I draw my courage from you.

   我向我的孩子们承诺:我从你们身上得到了勇气,因此我决不屈服。

5. If you do not see this killer stalking your children, look again.

   如果现在你还没有看到这个杀手正悄悄逼近你的孩子们,那么再仔细瞧瞧。

Answer the following questions based on the text you have just learned.

1. What is the reality of AIDS that is threatening American society?

   The reality of AIDS is brutally clear.   Two hundred thousand Americans are dead or dying; a million more are infected.   Worldwide forty million or sixty million or a hundred million infections will be counted in the coming few years.

2. What does the author mean by claiming that the AIDS epidemic is not a political creature?

   It does not care which party you belong to.   It does not ask whether you are black or white, male or female, gay or straight, young or old.

3. What does the author attempt to voice by contrasting her situation with that of a gay man?

   The author implies that she is very lucky to have the warm support of her family but there are still many people who cannot get the understanding and support from families and society.

4. In what sense is AIDS different from other diseases?

   AIDS is different from other diseases as it is epidemic. People may give each other AIDS only because they are in love and have intimate relationship.

5. According to the author, how did people help AIDS travel?

   According to the author,   people were ignorant of AIDS,   had prejudiced ideas about it and they remained silent in face of it, which helped the disease spread among people.

6. Why does the author say HIV positives are not victims?

   Because the author believes that HIV positives are the same human as others. They have not earned cruelty and they do not deserve meanness. They are worthy of sympathy and capable of helping others as she (Mary Fisher) did.

7. According to the author, when will the nation be safe from AIDS?

   This nation will be safe from AIDS if we can acknowledge the reality that there is no family or community, no race or religion, no place left in America that is safe.

8. In what way does the author interpret courage?

   The author says that courage is more than the absence of fear,   but the strength to act wisely when most are afraid.   She wants people to have the courage to step forward when called by their nation or their Party to give leadership, no matter what the personal cost is.

A Sip of Phonetics

Know Their Faces

本课介绍三个鼻辅音 /m/, /n/ 和 /ŋ/。

发音提示：

/m/ 是双唇鼻音,发音时双唇闭拢,软腭下垂,气流从鼻腔送出,震动声带发声。这里请注意中国学生容易将它读作"摸"而与汉语拼音"m"相混。教学中注意提醒并纠正,去掉"摸"后面的那个 /ə/ 音。

/n/ 是齿龈舌尖鼻辅音,发音时舌尖紧贴上齿龈,形成阻碍,双唇微张,软腭下垂,气流从鼻腔泄出,同时声带振动,产生鼻音。这里请注意中国学生容易将它读作"呢"而与汉语拼音"n"相混。教学中注意提醒并纠正,去掉"呢"后面的那个 /ə/ 音。

/ŋ/ 是软腭舌后鼻辅音,发音时,舌后部上抬,舌位和 /k/, /g/ 相同,但软腭下垂,堵住口腔通道,气流只能从鼻腔泄出,发音时声带震动。/ŋ/ 与汉语"ng"的音素相似,但值得注意的是 /ŋ/ 音的舌后软腭接触点与汉语"ng"的位置不同,英语的发音靠后,汉语的靠前。

教师教学中可将这三个鼻音放在一起,带领学生对比发音差异。

Train Your Tongue

1. Mike/ likes to write/ by the nice bright light/ at night.
2. Mother/ met a monkey/ in the middle of the market/ and made a mailbox of money.
3. The next number/ is neither nine/ nor nineteen.
4. No need/ to light/ a night light/ on a light night/ like tonight.
5. The owner/ of the inside inn/ was inside/ his inside inn/ with his inside/ outside his inside inn.
6. Don't spring/ on the inner-spring/ this spring/ or there will be an offspring/ next spring.
7. Singing Sammy/ sung songs/ on sinking sand.
8. Just think, / that sphinx/ has a sphincter/ that stinks!

You'd Like to Be

A Strong Bridge Builder

Fill in the blanks with the given words to complete the following sentences. Please note that some can be used more than once.

| to | for | in | from | out | along | at | of |

In 1843, Aja was born a slave in Mannor Plantation. Rebellious and disobedient, the young slave grew up under the whips and lashes of the plantation master. This was also the case for his father and brothers, and they all accepted this upbringing <u>in</u> the quiet of plantation society. <u>In</u> the context of plantation culture, obedience was considered an indicator of good slave, and Aja's father was just such an example, whose tameness helped cruelty <u>along</u>. But Aja simply wouldn't give <u>in</u>. He was so much longing <u>for</u> a life in which the efforts <u>of</u> farmers were worthy of respect, where his hard work would not lead <u>to</u> scold and despise.

Aja sheltered a flickering candle <u>from</u> the darkness <u>of</u> Mannor Plantation. He wanted to be sold <u>to</u> a neighboring plantation. It was said that the master of Libey Plantation, Mr. Linton, purchased slaves only to free them. Soon Aja's only light went <u>out</u> as he learned that Mr. Linton had left <u>for</u> New York to join the Union's Army to fight for the anti-slavery cause, and therefore, had stopped purchasing slaves. Aja then decided to reach <u>out</u> for freedom on his own, knowing that his life would be put at risk if this action could not succeed. On a rainy night, in the absence <u>of</u> moonlight, Aja escaped.

A Smart Word Player

Fill in the blanks with the proper words that need to be transformed from the ones provided in the brackets.

Zhong was one of a limited number of doctors informed of the disease from the moment the first few SARS cases were reported. He was very surprised at how fast this epidemic had <u>traveled</u> (traveling) from a single patient to almost everyone who once had close contact with him. But worst surprises were soon to follow as doctors and nurses who had treated the patient fell ill with the same disease. Zhong and his colleagues were aware that they were facing a highly <u>infectious</u> (infection), unknown disease, and their <u>ignorance</u> (ignorant) was putting their lives at risk. However, none of the doctors or nurses withdrew, because they all believed that any patient was <u>worth</u> (worthy) a treatment. Dozens of medical workers were <u>infected</u> (infection), but the rest continued to do their jobs without any <u>reluctance</u> (reluctantly). During the interview, Zhong could not hold back his <u>grief</u> (grieve) concerning the lost doctors and nurses and burst into tears. "They were my colleagues and friends," said Zhong. "They did their job knowing how <u>risky</u> (risk) it was. " Zhong issued an <u>appeal</u> (appeal) to all medical researchers for the determination of the disease's pathogen (病原体) and he worked crazily in the lab until he succeeded in <u>isolating</u> (isolate) the corona (冠状)virus.

A Skilled Text Weaver

Fill in the blanks with the words you have learned in this text. One word is for each blank. Here is a piece of advice: You must be really familiar with the text to accomplish the following tasks.

It was in Cape Town in 2001 that Harald Schmied, editor of the Austrian street paper, and Mel Young, co-founder of *The Big Issue*, came up with the <u>initiative</u> of the Homeless World Cup. According to Schmied and Young, the society's attitude toward the homeless can never be <u>consistent</u> with the concept of equality advocated for decades until we <u>embrace</u> the view that the homeless, too, are <u>worthy</u> of encouragement and recognition, something more than merely a <u>shelter</u>. Schmied and Young soon set <u>aside</u> all their routine work to start a <u>campaign</u> appealing to media for funding and encourage the homeless to join the program. Eight months later, they held the first 2003 Homeless World Cup, which involved 18 nations. They adopted the <u>slogan</u>: "18 nations, one goal!"

By 2006, 5400 homeless people from 48 nations had been involved in the program. The impact results turned out to be impressive. 94% of the players have a new motivation for life, and 58% have regular employment. Here is a good example: Since childhood, Michael had <u>suffered</u> from mental illness. A dysfunctional family life led him to alcoholism and drug addiction and he spent four years living on the street, <u>grieving</u> over his pains. Then he discovered the Homeless World Cup... Now he runs a boys' football team consisting of 37 teenagers in Glasgow. Michael told the reporter: "I no longer feel ashamed of my <u>account</u>, but if you do want to write a story about me, please write a complete one."

📖 A Sharp Interpreter

Please paraphrase the following sentences. Change the sentence structure if necessary.

1. ...despite good intentions and bold initiatives, campaign slogans and hopeful promises—despite it all, it's the epidemic which is winning tonight.

   ✪ *Paraphrasing:*

   Although people have good intention, take brave actions, wave slogans in the movement against AIDS and have made hopeful promises, they fail to put the AIDS epidemic under control.

2. I am one with the lonely gay man sheltering a flickering candle from the cold wind of his family's rejection.

   ✪ *Paraphrasing:*

   I see myself together with a gay man who cannot get love and support from his family and is still struggling with life. There is no difference between us because we are AIDS patients and we both belong to the same group of people.

3. We must lift our covering of silence, making it safe for you to reach out for compassion.

   ✪ *Paraphrasing:*

   We must remove our veil of silence so as to have the AIDS victims heard and we must ensure that they will not be victimized twice when they speak out their sufferings and ask for help and sympathy from the society.

4. I do not want them to think, as I once did, that courage is the absence of fear.

   ✪ *Paraphrasing:*

   I once thought that I had courage because I was not afraid of this disease. Now I want them to think in a different way (or now I want them to think more than that).

5. To the millions who are strong, I issue this plea: set aside prejudice and politics to make room for compassion and sound policy.

   ✪ *Paraphrasing:*

   I want to ask the millions of healthy people to abandon prejudice and politics so that it's possible for us to show our sympathy and make effective policy.

6. I will seek a place where intimacy will not lead to suffering.

   ✪ *Paraphrasing:*

   I will seek a place where having a close relationship will not push people to disasters.

7. I want them to have the courage to step forward when called by their nation, or their Party, and give leadership—no matter what the personal cost.

   ✪ *Paraphrasing:*

   I want them to have the courage to do something when they are called by their nation, or their Party, and give direction to other people as a leader regardless of their personal cost.

8. But when I go, I pray that you will not suffer shame on my account.

⊕ *Paraphrasing:*

But when I die, I pray that you will not feel ashamed of yourselves because of me.

A Solid Sentence-Constructer

Please make a sentence with each word or expression listed below.

1. to set aside

⊕ *Original sentence in the text:*

To the millions who are strong, I issue this plea: set aside prejudice and politics to make room for compassion and sound policy.

⊕ **Suggested sentence:**

Through college and into his twenties, he set aside his creative ambitions to pursue a career as a banker.

2. to benefit from

⊕ *Original sentence in the text:*

They don't benefit from being isolated or treated as those who have been excluded from our society.

⊕ **Suggested sentence:**

Most of the people can benefit from the new policy.

3. to deserve

⊕ *Original sentence in the text:*

They have not earned cruelty and they do not deserve meanness.

⊕ **Suggested sentence:**

After all that hard work, you deserve a holiday.

4. to long for

⊕ *Original sentence in the text:*

Each of them is exactly what God made: a person, not evil deserving of our judgment, not victim longing for our pity.

⊕ **Suggested sentence:**

I'm longing for news of him.

5. to stalk

⊕ *Original sentence in the text:*

If you do not see this killer stalking your children, look again.

⊕ **Suggested sentence:**

The police had been stalking the woman for a week before they arrested her.

6. to draw...from...

♦ *Original sentence in the text:*

  To my children, I make this promise: I will not give in, because I draw my courage from you.

♦ *Suggested sentence:*

  The old lady drew strength from her religious faith.

A Superb Bilingualist

Please translate the following sentences into English with the prompts provided in the brackets.

1. 警方向公众发出协助调查的请求。(issue, plea)

♦ *Suggested translation:*

The police issued a plea to the public for assistance in investigation.

2. 面对水资源的匮乏,政府呼吁人人要节约用水。(appeal)

♦ *Suggested translation:*

The government is appealing to everyone to save water in face of the lack of water resource.

3. 只有我们全然接受文化的多样性，对有色人种的偏见才可能被消除。(embrace, prejudice)

♦ *Suggested translation:*

The prejudice against the colored people will not be eliminated until we embrace cultural diversities completely.

4. 政府应该主动为那些无家可归的人提供庇护,使他们免于沦落街头。(take initiatives, shelter... from..., grieve)

♦ *Suggested translation:*

The government should take initiatives to shelter the homeless from grieving alone in the street.

5. 这篇报道描述了 HIV 阳性患者所经历的一切。该报道有助于公众消除偏见、给予患者同情。(set aside, make room for)

♦ *Suggested translation:*

The report describes what the HIV-positives have gone through. It helps the public to set aside prejudice and make room for compassion.

Text B

Introduction to the Author

Michael J. Weiss is an award-winning journalist, author, and marketing consultant. A contributing editor to the *Washingtonian* and *Ladies' Home Journal*, he has also written for the *Atlantic Monthly*, the *Newport Times*, *Redbook*, *Reader's Digest* and *People*. His first book, *The Clustering of America*, was named one of the best business books of 1988.

Writing Practice

You are now working toward writing a summary for Text B. You may follow the guidelines to write the summary:

I. Read through the entire text to get an understanding of the whole piece, and annotate by underlining the sentences containing the major points as you read.

II. Locate the thesis statement. While it may appear early in the essay—the first paragraph or two, it may not, in fact, be stated until the end of the piece, almost as if it were a conclusion.

Sports injuries among young athletes are common and serious especially for those who practice and compete at school.

(Please write down the thesis statement on the above line.)

III. Dissect the article. Re-read the underlined parts and divide it into sections based on the topics addressed. Each section may be one paragraph, but, more likely, it includes several paragraphs. Now you need to decide how many sections Text B contains.

Text B includes 2 3 4 5 ... sections. (Please circle the number as you wish.)

IV. Write a summary. First, write a sentence or two to summarize each section; then synthesize them into a coherent and cohesive passage. You may need a careful proofreading and revision before the final completion.

1. *(Paragraph 1) Many young athletes today follow a 12 month cycle of practice and competition. They are at risk for injuries.*

2. *(Paragraph 2—3) Mark, age 16, is a figure skater from suburban Philadelphia. He started training at the age of 9, working six days a week. When he was repeatedly practicing triple loops in March 2004, he tore his right groin muscle.*

3. *(Paragraph 4) It is impossible to protect kids from all injuries, especially in contact sports. A brain injury can easily cause concussion, which cannot be seen by parents and coaches and is often ignored, leading to a higher risk of death.*

4. *(Paragraph 5—6) Cheerleaders and drill teams and many participants suffer just as much as the ball players. Ashlee is an example, who fractured her skull in a cheerleading accident and has never fully recovered.*

Summary:

Sports injuries among young athletes are common and serious especially for those who practice and compete at school. They have no off-season which means they have to practice 12 months a year. Their muscles are overused and they are at risk for injury. Mark, a figure skater, age 16, who felt a spasm in his right groin muscle while practicing triple loops, had to stop for 6 months for micro tears caused by overuse of the muscle. It's impossible to protect kids from all injuries, especially in contact sports. New Jersey high school senior Kurt died from a head injury in a football game. Even today's well-designed helmets and body equipment cannot protect them from brain injuries—mostly concussions causing memory loss, headaches, blurred vision, dizziness and nausea, symptoms often underestimated or even ignored by parents and coaches. More concussions lead to a higher risk of a disastrous injury or death. In addition to ball-players, cheerleaders, drill teams and many participants are also victims of sports injury. Ashlee, 14, fractured her skull in a cheerleading accident and permanently lost her sense of smell and partially lost her hearing and now still struggles with reading comprehension.

Unit 12

Poverty

Unit Goals

After studying this unit, students should be able to:

☞ **understand the urgency of combating child trafficking and child labour in Africa;**

      When learning **Text A**, students should be alerted to the surprising 80 million child workers across Africa and able to identify the graveness of the problem of child trafficking resulted from poverty, the root of child labour that has brought about disaster. With the estimated rise of child labourers to 100 million by 2015, more and more children will be exposed to severe danger. Factors such as inadequate educational opportunities, a higher demand of cheap labour not only deprived the children of the rights to receive education but also led to ignorance of the risk of child trafficking, which keeps the vicious circle continuing. Students should also note even though it is difficult to end child labour, education plays an indispensable role in getting the governments and societies mobilized to fight against child labour.

☞ **know how to pronounce /r/, /j/, /w/ and /l/, and how to utilize the words and structures that contribute significantly to the texts;**

      In this section, the students should not only acquire the rules of pronunciation, that is, the corresponding letters "r," "wr," "y," "w," "wh," and "l" pronounced as /r/, /j/, /w/ and /l/ respectively, but also the related terms in English for these phonetic symbols, /r/ being frictionless continuant, /j/ and /w/, glides, and /l/ lateral. This section in the text book is lectured in Chinese to facilitate the students to study on their own. It is important for the instructor to familiarize the students with the terms when teaching this section. It is also suggested that the instructor make some comparison with the corresponding Chinese Pinyin as detailed in **A Sip of Phonetics** section after the explanation of the text.

☞ **understand the roots of poverty and what can be done to reduce poverty.**

      If the root of child labor is poverty, which, according to the author, is a major and ever-present causal factor, it is well-reasoned to point out that ignorance is the origin of poverty. To alleviate poverty is to grant the children access to education and improve the school system to promote literacy. Measures should be taken to draw the public attention to the danger of the most exploitative and abusive forms of child labour and appeal to society to combat the tragic trend.

Before Reading

Hands-on Activities and Brainstorming

The instructor should allow 15 to 20 minutes for the students to do presentation either on the root of child labor—poverty, or on the origin of poverty—ignorance.

A Glimpse at Words and Expressions

Please read the following sentences. Pay attention to the underlined part in each sentence in Column A, and match it with the corresponding meaning in Column B.

A. It is suggested that the instructor should approach the word "link" initially as a noun with such examples that the students are familiar with: a) "A link is a connection from one Web resource to another." b) "A link has two ends—called anchors—and a direction." c) "In basic link terminology, back links are also called incoming links, inbound links, and inward links." After working out the meaning of the noun form, the instructor should follow up with a well-acquainted example in its use of verb: "The two factors are directly linked," which can be used to locate the interpretation of the expression in the text. Thus, "be closely linked to" means "be closely related to," as in the example: *Do you think that the increase in violent crimes is closely linked to the declining economy?*

B. The instructor should clear away the barrier that hinders the students' understanding of the expression, "to get on the policy agenda." The key word that affects comprehension is the meaning of "agenda." Some examples are required to contribute to locating the exact meaning of the expression in the text: "Safety at work is on the agenda for the next month's meeting." The opposite of the expression on the agenda is suggested by another expression in the following sentence: "An expensive holiday is definitely off the agenda." With these examples the students are able to figure out the meaning of the expression by contrasting the interpretation of the two sentences: "To get on the policy agenda" here means "to be listed as a major issue to make policy on," as is presented in the example: *How to deal with poverty should be placed on the policy agenda.*

C. The instructor should focus on the usage of the prepositional phrase because it is not difficult for the students to work out its meaning. However the preposition "on" still plays a key role in this phrase, which suggests that an action is in motion even though there is no verb available in this expression. For example: "Crime is on the rise;" "Their influence is rapidly on the rise." These examples throw light on the interpretation of "on the rise," defined as "increasing," as in the example: *The number of female smokers is on the rise in recent years.*

D. The instructor should help the students work out the object of the verb "present" takes. "To present a paper" is the collocation. To approach the meaning, the instructor should offer more examples: "The committee will present its final report to the Parliament in June;" "Why is Sir Francis presenting the note?" With these examples, the students will find it easier to understand the expression—presented to, which can be understood as "delivered in public at." For example: *In an article presented to the seminar, she developed a new model for consumer behaviour research.*

E. The first thing to make clear for the students is that "counter" can be used as a prefix, added to nouns, verbs and adjectives, meaning "against" or "opposite." The instructor may initially offer examples for the students to interpret the meaning. There are some suggested examples for the instructor: attack→counterattack; revolution→counterrevolution; current→countercurrent; clockwise→counterclockwise. Through these examples, students are able to grasp the meaning of "to counter," which means "to act in opposition against." For example: *My boss countered my request for a salary raise by threatening to fire me.*

F. The instructor should make best use of context in this sentence that contributes to the understanding of the phrase. The instructor may start by asking a question like "What are the important elements that contextualize the situation that contributes to your understanding of the expression?" If the students are able to locate the meaning of contribute to in this question, they have no difficulty in defining the phrase in the sentence. "To contribute to" can be explained "to become one of the causes of sth." For example: *Some exercise and plenty of clean and fresh air contribute to good health.*
This expression may also mean "to increase, improve or add to sth." For example: *She did not contribute an idea to this discussion.*

G. Students might associate the meaning of the adjective "easy" with that of the noun "ease." The instructor may start right here to motivate the students to offer expressions with "easy" based on what they have learned in high school. It is also important for the instructor to get involved in this activity and offer his/her own examples, such as "I'll agree to everything for an easy life;" "I don't feel easy about letting the kids go out alone." "Easy" in the two sentences can be explained by "comfortable," "relaxed" and "not worried." Right after this, the instructor can avail the students with an example: "The whole machine is designed for ease of use." In this case "ease" in the sentence is explained as "freedom and easiness." More examples: *Cars make it possible for people to move with ease. The car brings ease of access to the country.*

Keys

A-6; B-1; C-5; D-2; E-4; F-7; G-3

Text A

Introduction of the Text

Africa's poverty resulted in child labour. What shocks the world is not only the alarming number of child labourers, but its "worst forms" that involve slavery, prostitution, employment in the drug trade and occupations that threaten children's health and security because of the child trafficking that has illegally legalized the maltreatment of child labourers. The inhuman nature of child trafficking that forces children to work 10 to 20 hours a day without adequate food and drink has claimed children's lives. If poverty contributes to child labour trafficking, such issues as inadequate educational opportunities, ignorance among families and children about the risks of trafficking, higher demand among employers for cheap and submissive child labour and inadequate political commitment have made the ever-present causal factor all the more tougher.

Africa has the largest number of child labour compared with Asia and Latin America because of the deterioration of the school system that results in a higher drop-out rate. What is worse is that deeply-rooted poverty hinders people from escaping the suffering and misery even tough some African countries have been moving more systematically to counter this trend. Therefore, the urgent challenge for many African nations is to educate the public about the severity of child labour emanated from poverty.

Suggested Explanations on Text A

1. Across Africa, there are an <u>estimated</u> 80 million child workers, a number that could rise to 100 million by 2015.

   ► estimated (*adj.*): (formal) a rough idea about the size, cost, value etc. of sth.; supposed, approximated

   eg. 1) The database will cost the university an estimated a quarter million.

   2) There are an estimated 2, 800 TB patients in the city, a number that could hit 6000

by 2015.

▲ It is estimated that...: It is likely that... In this sentence pattern, "estimate" functions as a verb but in its passive form, followed by a noun clause serving as a subject.

eg. 1) It is estimated that 80 million people are learning English in this country.

　2) It is estimated that 30 thousand new private cars are put to the city streets every month.

▲ to be estimated to: "Estimate" serves as a predicate verb in its passive form followed by an infinitive as a compound predicate.

eg. The deal is estimated to be worth around $ 1.5 million.

2. Since the problem is closely linked to the continent's poverty, and can only <u>be eliminated</u> with increases in family incomes and children's educational opportunities, UNICEF, the ILO and other groups are <u>focusing initially on</u> the "worst forms" of child labour.

Meaning: Africa's poverty directly gives rise to the problem of child labour. The only way to deal with the problem is to do away with poverty by raising family incomes and the rate of education. UNICEF, the ILO and other organizations are beginning to draw their attention to child labour as the first-rate matter, whose severity leads to fatal consequences.

▶ to be eliminated: (in passive form) to be removed

eg. 1) Disappointment turned to violence in downtown Madrid after Spain lost 3 to 1 to France and was eliminated from the World Cup, news reports said Wednesday.

　2) The need to carry cash was practically eliminated when credit card came into existence.

▲ eliminate (v.): to remove or get rid of sth./sb.

eg. If tax cut is successful, it would eliminate more than half the state's tax revenue, forcing deep cuts or even elimination of programs such as education, health care, and public safety.

▶ to focus on: to give attention, effort, etc. to one particular subject, situation rather than another

eg. 1) Students can focus their attention on the meaning of each sentence.

　2) These meetings also focused on strategies for the future.

▶ initial (adj.): happening at the beginning; first. Note that it is usually used before a noun.

eg. 1) To get the position, your initial move must be to obtain the committee's approval.

　2) Franklin's initial efforts in election were not successful.

▲ initiate (v.): to make sth. begin

eg. 1) The museum initiated fund-raising drive with a special exhibition.

　2) He initiated the reforms, but the government agency instituted them.

▲ initiation (*n.*): (uncountable noun) the act of starting sth.

eg. 1) Who is responsible for the initiation of hospitalities?

2) During her initiation to marriage she followed the same pattern of life.

3. Mr. Alec Fyfe, a senior adviser on child labour for UNICEF told *Africa Recovery*, "Trafficking is beginning to get on the policy agenda."

Meaning: Mr. Alec Fyfe, an experienced advisor on child labour for UNICEF, spoke to the renowned magazine *Africa Recovery*, now called *Africa Renewal*, that the illegal trading for child labour can no longer be hidden away but has been listed as a top political issue that demands a world wide discussion.

▶ trafficking (*n.*): (The trafficking of human beings is) the recruitment, transportation, transfer, harbouring or receipt of people for the purpose of exploitation

eg. 1) Provide information to combat human trafficking through prevention, prosecution, and victim protection.

2) Trafficking is the fastest growing means by which people are forced into slavery.

▲ traffick (*v.*): also spelled "traffic," meaning "to buy or sell sth. illegally"

eg. The US government estimates that between 800,000 and 900,000 people are trafficked each year across international borders, with between 18,000 and 20,000 trafficked annually into the United States.

4. Because trafficking tears children away from the protection of their families and communities, it is especially dangerous to their well-being.

Meaning: The illegal trade of children for child labour deprives them of parents' protection and forces them to leave their families and communities, which consequently, causes them to sacrifice family happiness and puts their lives at risk.

▶ well being: general health and happiness

eg. 1) She was filled with a sense of well-being.

2) A better water supply would contribute dramatically to the villagers' well-being.

5. The trafficking of children for commercial sexual exploitation was also reported.

Meaning: It was also reported that the illegal trading for child labour is profit-orientated by taking advantage of child labourers and trap them into prostitution.

▶ exploitation (*n.*): the act to utilize and take advantage of (esp. a person) for one's own ends

eg. 1) The family amassed these possessions through a century of ruthless exploitation.

2) Migrant workers are vulnerable to exploitation.

▲ exploit (*v.*): to utilize and take advantage of a person

eg. 1) The company exploited its workers through long hours and low pay.

2) He pursued his interests, cynically exploiting his privileged position as trustee.

6. They often lack adequate food and drink.

▶ adequate (*adj.*): enough in quantity or good enough in quality, for a particular purpose or need

eg. 1) The residents in the apartment building are frustrated because there is never an adequate supply of hot water.

2) He failed to give adequate treatment to the immediate issues.

▲ inadequate (*adj.*): not enough in quantity or good enough in quality, for a particular purpose or need

eg. 1) Although other countries announced some positive steps at the conference, the response of the United States remained insufficient and inadequate.

2) In Iraq, hospitals and clinics lacked properly trained workers and had inadequate screening for mental health problems.

▶ synonyms: "adequate," "enough" and "abundant"

adequate (*adj.*): 表示"足够的,充分的"。强调"达到要求"、"符合标准"、"适宜某一场合"。既可以指数量,也可以指质量。

eg. 1) The wages are adequate to support three people.

2) His knowledge of French was adequate for the job, although he was not fluent in the language.

3) The government has taken adequate measures to stop the air pollution. (政府已采取适当的措施制止空气污染。)

enough (*adj.*): 表示"充足的,足够的"。侧重"总的量或程度"刚好满足需要,不强调质量。既可用于一般场合,也可用于正式场合。

eg. 1) He had enough intelligence to see that what he did was wrong.

2) One mad action is not enough to prove a man mad.

abundant (*adj.*): 指某物"极为丰富"或有"大量供应"。有时暗指由于过量而导致挥霍浪费。

eg. 1) There were streams with abundant fish in them.

2) We have lived on a broad and abundant land, and we have made it flourish.

7. Others contracted sexually transmitted diseases, including HIV/AIDS.

Meaning: Others caught diseases, such as HIV/AIDS passed onto them by unprotected sexual activities.

▶ contract (*v.*): (formal) to get an illness or disease

eg. 1) Three doctors contracted SARS while trying to help the patients.

2) She contracted yellow fever when she was working in the tropical region.

▲ contract (*v.*): to make a legal agreement to work for sb. or provide them with a service

eg. 1) The engineer has contracted to work 12 hours a day for the firm.

2) Four super stars in the team have contracted to come to Hong Kong for the charity match.

▶ transmit (*v.*): to pass sth. from one person to another

eg. 1) Parents may easily transmit their own characteristics to their children.

2) The terrible disease is transmitted to human beings by mosquitoes.

▲ transmission (*n.*): the act of passing sth. from one person to another

eg. 1) The FBI arrived in time to prevent the transmission of the secret documents.

2) Mass public transport is playing the primary role in the transmission of tuberculosis.

8. Although parents were sometimes persuaded by recruiters to send their children away to earn some extra income, often neither the children nor the parents were paid.

Meaning: People entrusted with hiring child labourers occasionally succeeded in talking the parents into allowing their children to leave the family for extra income, but they cheated both children and parents by not paying them anything.

▶ to recruit (*v.*): to find new people to join a company, an organization, the armed forces etc.

eg. 1) The government had to recruit some women into the navy during the war.

2) We need to recruit a few native speakers for our foreign language program.

▲ recruit (*n.*): someone who has recently joined an organization, team or a group of people

eg. It is a rule in the bank that young recruits should work as tellers at grass-roots level for at least 6 months.

9. In a paper presented to a conference on "human trafficking" held in Nigeria in February 2001, Dr. Salah, a UNICEF regional director for West and Central Africa, agreed with the ILO assessment that child labour trafficking has become a "substantial problem" in the region.

▶ assessment (*n.*): an opinion or judgement about sb./sth., that has been thought about very carefully

eg: 1) The critic's assessment of the book is that it is beautifully written.

2) The new manager carried out an assessment of the sales department.

▲ to assess (*v.*): to make a judgment about a person or situation after thinking carefully about it.

eg. 1) It is difficult to assess the building's value properly without seeing it.

2) It is hard to assess how much time and energy they have spent on the project.

► substantial (*adj.*): considerable in importance, value, degree, amount, or extent

eg. 1) These victims may have a substantial threat of harm if they are sent home.

2) It used to be a very substantial family in the salt trade.

▲ substantial (*adj.*): large enough in amount, number or degree to be noticeable or have an important effect

eg. 1) In the process of urbanization, a substantial number of old houses had been pulled down.

2) The survey indicates that a substantial number of consumers are not satisfied with the new product.

10. Poverty, a major and ever-present <u>causal</u> factor, which greatly limits <u>vocational</u> and economic opportunities in rural areas in particular and pushes families to use all <u>available</u> means to increase their <u>meagre</u> incomes.

Meaning: Poverty always remains the chief cause that triggers the problem of child labour and surprisingly robs the children of many on-the-job training opportunities and reduces job accesses, specifically in rural areas, and drives families to take whatever job within reach to make their small income grow.

► causal (*adj.*): (formal) connected with the relationship between two things, where one causes the other to happen

eg. 1) Do you believe in the causal relationship between laziness and poverty?

2) We can easily see the causal relationship between advancement of technology and improvement of life.

3) Of course, none of these statements express a causal connection between the antecedent and consequent.

► vocational (*adj.*): connected with the skills, knowledge, etc. that people need to have in order to do a particular job

eg. 1) One striking feature with German educational system is its vocational education.

2) New recruits, who are all vocational school graduates, lack special training in how to detect flaws with the equipment.

► available (*adj.*): that you can get, buy and find

eg. 1) There were no available statistical tables to present this growth accurately.

2) Concert tickets are available free of charge at the reception desk.

▲ available (*adj.*): (of a person) free to see or talk to

eg. 1) Sorry I won't be available tomorrow afternoon. How about Friday?

2) Tutors are easily available in the office every afternoon.

▲ to avail of: to give oneself the use or advantage of (sth.)

eg. 1) We should avail ourselves of every chance to improve our spoken English.

2) Many students avail themselves of government loan programs to help pay for college.

▶ meagre (*adj.*): small in quantity and poor in quality

eg. 1) Many people just don't understand why the billionaire has a meagre dinner every day.

    2) There was a meagre attendance to the yard sale last Sunday.

11. In order to help their children search for the opportunity for education, parents willingly move them from the protective envelope of the family.

Meaning: Parents allow their children to leave the sheltered family life for the purpose of getting their children access to education.

12. <u>Migration</u> of adults from villages to urban slums, which <u>exposes their children to</u> greater risks.

▶ migration (*n.*): the movement of large numbers of people, birds or animals from one place to another

eg. 1) Scientists have studied the migration of fish from one part of the ocean to another over long distances.

    2) Wars always cause massive migration of people.

▲ migrate (*v.*): to move from one town, country etc. to go and live/ work in another

eg. 1) Thousands were forced to migrate to neighboring states because of the hurricane.

    2) His family migrated from the east coast to the west in search of better job opportunities.

▶ to expose... to: put sb. or sth. in a vulnerable position where they are not protected from sth. harmful or unpleasant

eg. 1) The child has never been exposed to measles.

    2) The metal was exposed to corrosives and extreme temperature.

    3) Hundreds of thousands of people, mostly in the U.S., have been exposed to the risk of file ransom after the Web site of the world's largest online recruiter was hacked.

▲ to expose sb. to sth.: to let sb. find out about sth. by giving them experience of it or showing them what it is like

eg. 1) As far as possible, the teacher should expose the students to real life situation.

    2) I had been exposed to music when I was three years old.

▲ to expose oneself to: to put sb./sth. in a place or situation where they are not protected from sth. harmful or unpleasant

eg. 1) The man exposed himself too much to the sun.

    2) What politician dare expose himself to public opinion?

    3) She exposed herself to criticism when she stubbornly decided to close down the firm.

▲ exposure (*n.*): noun form of "expose"

eg. 1) Brief exposures to secondhand smoke may have adverse effects on the heart and respiratory systems and increase the severity of asthma attacks, especially in children.

2) Early exposure to literature is facilitative to students' overall progress in language learning.

13. <u>Ease</u> of travel across regional borders.

▶ ease (*n.*): freedom from difficulty. Note that its adjective form is "easy."

eg. 1) The car brings ease of access to the countryside.

2) The back of the garment is split for ease in walking.

3) The whole machine is designed for ease of use.

▲ ease (*v.*): to become or make sth. less unpleasant, painful, severe etc.

eg. 1) My doctor told me to take the pills to ease the pain.

2) This highway is about to be widened to ease the traffic congestion.

14. Inadequate political <u>commitment</u>, legislation and judicial <u>mechanisms</u> to deal with child traffickers.

Meaning: The inability and irresponsibility of the government with little effort made to strengthen law and law-reinforcement departments to hunt down illegal trading for child labour.

▶ commitment (*n.*): a promise to do sth. or behave in a particular way; a promise to support sb./sth.

eg. 1) Next month my father will not be available because of his filming commitments.

2) What did the government do regarding its commitment to combat corruption?

▲ commit (*v.*): (often used in passive structure) to promise sincerely that you will definitely do sth., or keep to an agreement or arrangement etc.

eg. 1) The new prime minister is committed to create one million jobs.

2) The six parties are committed to settle the issue before June.

▶ mechanism (*n.*): a method or a system for achieving sth.

eg. 1) The problem lies in the ineffective mechanism of price control.

2) There is not an effective mechanism to evaluate the actual performance of a university professor.

15. Child trafficking is only one of the more harmful aspects of a much broader problem. Africa has the highest <u>incidence</u> of child labour in the world.

Meaning: The illegal trading for child labour only characterizes one of the more severe features in a broad sense of the whole issue. Africa makes up the highest percentage of frequency of child labour.

▶ incidence (*n.*): (usually in written form) the extent to which sth. happens or has an effect

eg. 1) The country has the lowest incidence of Aids cases proportional to its population.

2) The study noted an increased incidence of heart disease in women.

16. According to the ILO, 41 percent of all African children between the ages of 5 and 14 are involved in some <u>form</u> of economic activity, <u>compared with</u> 21 percent in Asia and 17 percent in Latin America. Among girls, the participation rate also is the highest: 37 percent in Africa, 20 percent in Asia and 11 percent in Latin America.

▶ form (*n.*): the particular way sth. is, seems or looks or is presented

eg. 1) To them, help in the form of money is both superficial and transient.

2) Our training program took the form of dozens of seminars.

3) Before we leave, we need to reach some form of agreement.

▶ compared with (sometimes "compared to"): in comparison with, a past participial phrase, either put in the beginning or at the end of a sentence, which functions as an adverbial

eg. 1) I've had some difficulties but they were nothing compared to yours.

2) It's just nothing compared with the hardships my parents had experienced.

3) In 2005, the retail revenue of Shanghai social consuming goods summed up RMB 297.297 billion at a growth rate of 11.9%, compared with the previous year.

17. It is no <u>coincidence</u> that Africa also is the poorest region, with the weakest school systems.

Meaning: It is by no means incidental that Africa, in addition to child labour and child trafficking, is also the poorest region and has the worst education systems.

▶ coincidence (*n.*): the fact of two things happening at the same time by chance, in a surprising way

eg. 1) What a happy coincidence to meet you at the airport just when I wanted to see you.

2) It was pure coincidence that they were both in Paris on the same day.

▲ coincide (*v.*): to take place at the same time

eg. 1) The strike coincided with the opening of G-7 meeting this year.

2) The singer's arrival was timed to coincide with the opening of the festival.

▶ synonyms: "to coincide" and "to agree"

在表示"对某一意见政策看法一致"时:

to coincide 表示"一致"、"相吻合"。强调不同情况相遇时即相互吻合,一致。主语常常是看法、愿望、判断、利益等。

eg. 1) His tastes and habits amazingly coincide with those of his wife.

2) It is fortunate when a young man's career goals and the wishes of his parents for him coincide.

3) Does the witness's story coincide with that of the defendant?

to agree 表示"一致"、"相合"。强调思想的一致,即使发生过争执,此时的看法是一致的。

eg. 1) This is a point upon which all persons agree.

2) When the details are agreed upon, the results would be proclaimed.

3) He has sometimes agreed with things I have said to him.

18. A 1999 Child Labour Survey in Zimbabwe, <u>conducted</u> by the ILO, found that about 88 percent of economically <u>active</u> children aged 5—17 came from households with incomes below 36 US dollars per month.

Meaning: A 1999 Child Labour Survey done by the ILO in Zimbabwe indicated that those children employed between the ages of 5 to 17 were from families with incomes below 36 US dollars per month.

► conduct (*v.*): to organize and/or do a particular activity. Please notice some useful collocations: to conduct an experiment; to conduct a survey; to conduct an interview; to conduct business etc.

eg. 1) Researchers in the university are going to conduct an experiment about how learning outcome would be affected by the types of questions teachers ask in the classroom.

2) Whether right or wrong, he has ideas about how the lesson should be conducted.

3) Modern technology makes it possible to conduct business at home.

▲ conduct (*v.*): to direct a group of people who are singing or playing music

eg. Sir Colin Davis will conduct a choir for the first time this Friday evening.

▲ conduct (*n.*): a person's behaviour in a particular place or in a particular situation

eg. 1) Our organization sets high standards for professional conduct.

2) The committee concluded that the senators had been engaged in improper conduct.

19. According to an ILO study on Tanzania, the <u>incidence of</u> child labour in the country has risen partly because of the <u>deterioration</u> of the school system, itself a result of economic decline.

Meaning: The study on Tanzania made by ILO shows that the rate of child labour has gone up partly because of the worsening of the school system resulted from economic collapse.

► incidence of: the extent to which sth. happens or has an effect

eg. 1) This article focuses on the last of these factors, the incidence of both legal and illegal abortions in each country or area.

2) For old people, higher level of chronic psychological distress is associated with increased incidence of mild cognitive impairment.

▲ incident (*n.*): sth. happens, especially sth. unusual or unpleasant; a serious or violent event, such as a crime, an accident or an attack

eg. 1) In a recent incident two bombs exploded.

    2) There has been a most painful incident in his family history.

▶ synonyms: 表示"事件、故事"时，"incident," "event," "occurrence" and "episode" 近义。

incident 专指偶然发生或附随某事件发生的小事，也指在性质或意义上不同一般的情节。

eg. 1) Her tone implies that bedroom fires were a quite ordinary incident of daily life in a place like Bursley.

    2) The book narrates a series of thriving incidents.

event 常指由某种情况引起的重大或值得注意的大事件

eg. 1) Today's programme looks back at the main events of the year.

    2) Today is the hospital's fiftieth anniversary, and there will be a party to mark the event.

occurrence 是大小事件的通用语，偏重于事件的发生及出现。

eg. 1) It was the strangest occurrence I can remember.

    2) A storm is an unusual occurrence at this time of year.

episode 比 incident 更加强调事件或情节的不同寻常。

eg. 1) These facts illustrated episodes in its earlier history.

    2) The completion of the transcontinental railroad was an important episode in our own history.

▶ deterioration: noun form of "deteriorate," which means "make or become bad or worse"

eg. 1) Deterioration in the relations between the two countries began in 1985 when trade dispute broke out.

    2) Each fall has caused further deterioration in Tim's health.

▲ deteriorate (*v.*): to grow or become worse

eg. 1) Her health deteriorated rapidly and she died shortly afterwards.

    2) Contrary to expectations, the unrest rapidly deteriorated into civil war.

    3) Economic situation deteriorated after the Taliban assumed power in the country.

20. Poor infrastructure, low teacher spirits and the introduction of school fees under the country's structural adjustment program have contributed to higher drop-out and absence rates.

Meaning: The increase in the number of students who skip class and even quit school was brought about by poor school facilities, unenthusiastic teachers and initiation of the tuition policy enforced by the country's fundamental reform campaign.

▶ spirits (*n.*): (plural form) a person's feelings or state of mind.

eg. 1) The team's spirits to fight to win the game is not dampened though there has been a string of defeats so far.

    2) He was deeply depressed and no one could lift his spirits.

▶ introduction (*n.*): the act of bringing sth. into use or existence for the first time or bringing sth. into a place for the first time

eg. 1) The introduction of compulsory education in the county began in late 1990s.

    2) The dramatic increase in sales is largely due to the introduction of that set of sophisticated equipment.

▶ drop-out (*n.*): (also "dropout") a person who leaves school or college before they have finished their studies

eg. 1) A large proportion of primary school drop-outs complain that learning is so dull that they can't tolerate it any more.

    2) Increase in school costs is partly responsible for the increase of drop-outs.

21. Thirty percent of all children between 10 and 14 are not attending school, and many <u>end up</u> working.

▶ end up: to find yourself in a place or situation that you did not expect or intend to be in

eg. 1) Every time she tried to argue with her husband, she ended up crying her eyes out.

    2) You would end up in disaster if you keep driving in a reckless way.

22. Recognizing that the roots of child labour <u>lie in</u> family poverty—and that it cannot simply be legislated <u>out of existence</u>—the ILO <u>draws a distinction</u> between normal family obligations and work which <u>gives rise to</u> exploitation and <u>abuse</u>.

Meaning: The ILO has realized that it is family poverty that has resulted in child labour, and family poverty cannot simply be eradicated by law or dies out by itself. The ILO works on distinguishing children duties for family from profit-oriented child employment that causes them to suffer maltreatment.

▶ to lie in: to exist or be found in

eg. 1) The charm of travel lies in its new experiences.

    2) All our hope lay in him, but he disappointed us.

▶ out of existence: the state of no longer being present

eg. 1) It was the entrance of a new competitor into the market that has driven the company out of existence.

    2) If you jump into the hole you will get torn apart and crushed out of existence.

▲ to come/spring into existence: to come into being

eg. 1) The organization came into existence ten years ago.

    2) What are the chances of these molecules springing simultaneously into existence?

▲ to bring sth. into existence: to cause to come into being

eg. 1) The space has brought into existence a whole new body of scientific and technical words.

2) A new army was brought into existence as a result of moving divisions from another front.

► to draw/make a distinction: to make a clear difference or contrast between people or things that appear similar or related

eg. 1) It is difficult to make exact distinctions between all the meanings of a word.

2) She draws an important distinction between the different kinds of illness.

► to give rise to: (formal) to cause sth. to happen or exist

eg. 1) The depression gave rise to widespread unemployment.

2) The circumstances of his death gave rise to a suspicion of murder.

► abuse (*n*.): unfair, cruel or violent treatment of sb. or non-appropriate use of sth.

eg. 1) She suffered years of physical abuse.

2) They talked about the uses and abuses of figures to prove things in politics.

▲ abuse (*v*.): to treat a person or an animal in a cruel and violent way; to use power or knowledge unfairly or wrongly

eg. 1) All the children had been physically and emotionally abused.

2) She abuses her position as principal by giving jobs to her friends.

3) The privilege has been much abused.

23. The UNICEF study on Eastern and Southern Africa similarly admits that African culture allows children to work within the family and community, but economic hardships, HIV/AIDS and other disasters have <u>distorted</u> traditional forms of child work into <u>exploitative practices</u>.

► distort (*v*.): to twist or change facts, ideas, etc. so that they are no longer correct or true

eg. 1) He was accused of deliberately distorting the facts.

2) Newspaper accounts of political and international affairs are often distorted.

► exploitative (*adj*.) ("exploitive" in American English): treating sb. unfairly in order to gain an advantage or make money

eg. 1) Migrants may be confronted with exploitation like trafficking, smuggling or exploitative labour in a country of which he or she is not a national.

2) Exploitative migration is often used as synonymous to forced migration and irregular migration.

► practice (*n*.): a way of doing sth. that is the usual or expected way in a particular organization or situation

eg. 1) It is a bad practice to allow a boy much pocket money.

2) Lanny followed his usual practice of not giving his own address.

3) It was the practice in the shop that if you spoilt any material, you had to pay for it out of your piece-work earnings.

24. Since the conditions do not yet exist to end all types of child labour, the immediate challenge is to educate <u>the public</u> about the dangers to children of the most exploitative and <u>abusive</u> forms of child labour and to mobilize governments and societies to <u>combat</u> them.

▶ the public: ordinary people in society in general

eg. 1) The royal palace is open to the public on weekends.

2) The public have a right to know how a new government policy comes into being.

▶ abusive (*adj.*): rude or offensive; criticizing rudely and unfairly

eg. 1) The little boy became abusive towards his father.

2) Her abusive husband often appears in her nightmares.

▶ combat (*v.*): to fight against sb. or sth.; to stop sth. unpleasant or a happening from getting worse

eg. 1) We should not take simplistic measures to combat inflation.

2) The governor is committed to combat unemployment in his term of office.

▶ synonyms: "combat," "fight," "resist," "oppose"

在表示"作斗争或竞争"时：

fight 和 combat 都指"激烈斗争的行为"，前者暗示斗争是由主语所指的一方发起的，强调轻率和好斗。后者强调斗争的力量、影响或迫切，但不暗指由哪一方发动或后果是否成功。

eg. 1) The steel companies fought the strike with every weapon at their disposal.

2) Russell combats the philosophers who denied the possibility of a three-dimensional non-Euclidean space (三维非欧几里得空间)。

resist 指用积极行动抵抗某人或阻止某事发生，暗示公开承认对方是有敌意或有威胁的势力。

eg. He made an attempt to resist his attackers.

oppose 的含义较广，指对某种看法怀有不满但不争辩的态度或行动。

eg. 1) Several of the speakers opposed the project.

2) I'm very much opposed to your going abroad.

Better Know More

1. Bonded Child Labour

Bonded children are delivered in repayment of a loan. They work as slaves in agriculture, domestic work, brick kilns, glass industries, tanneries, gem polishing and many other manufacturing and marketing industries. They are forced to work for little or no wages, being denied their freedom to change employment, pursue their lives and their own development with dignity. Bondage is the term for bonded child labour, which is understood as forced labour. Those who are bonded work for their employer under some form of promise, contract or agreement to which they are consented. For some, the consent is a matter of custom or history in the communities in which they live. This consent is entail to an obligation of the workers to labour under whatever conditions the employer chooses to impose.

2. Commercial Sexual Exploitation

Exploitation of children in commercial sex trade remains the worst form of child labour in Asia. In a system known as *chucri*, girls arriving in brothels are indebted through taking an advance to cover the cost of makeup, clothes and the bribe to the police. Girls are then to work without being paid, sometimes for more than a year, in order to pay the debts off. UNICEF estimates that 1 million children are lured into sex trade in Asia every year, wherein 40% were sold by parents, 15% by their relatives.

Check Your Understanding

Translate the following sentences into Chinese. Please make sure that your language flows smoothly.

1. Because trafficking tears children away from the protection of their families and communities, it is especially dangerous to their well being.
   非法儿童交易迫使儿童脱离家庭和社区的保护，对他们的生存状况构成特别的危险。

2. Poor infrastructure, low teacher spirits and the introduction of school fees under the country's structural adjustment program have contributed to higher drop-out and absence rates.
   基础设施落后、教师工作热情低落、因国家结构调整政策而开始的学校收费，都对高辍学率和高旷课率造成直接影响。

3. According to the ILO, 41 percent of all African children between the ages of 5 and 14 are involved in some form of economic activity, compared with 21 percent in Asia and 17 percent in Latin America.
   据国际劳工组织统计，在所有 5 岁至 14 岁的非洲儿童中，41%在从事获取报酬性劳动；与此相比，亚洲是 21%；拉美是 17%。

4. Since the problem is closely linked to the continent's poverty, and can only be eliminated with increases in family incomes and children's educational opportunities, UNICEF, the ILO and other groups are focusing initially on the "worst forms" of child labour.

童工问题与非洲大陆的贫困密切相关,只有增加家庭收入,增加儿童受教育机会,才可能根除这一顽疾,因此,联合国儿童基金会、国际劳工组织和其他一些国际机构目前先集中精力解决"最严重"的童工问题。

5. Mr. Alec Fyfe, a senior adviser on child labour for UNICEF told *Africa Recovery*, "Trafficking is beginning to get on the policy agenda."

联合国儿童基金会童工问题高级顾问阿莱克·菲弗先生对《非洲复兴》杂志说,"非法儿童交易问题开始被提到政策问题议事日程。"

6. Over the past year, however, African countries have been moving more systematically to counter this trend.

过去一年里,非洲国家一直在寻求更加系统的办法遏制非法买卖童工趋势。

7. They often lack adequate food and drink. Nigeria reported that one out of five children trafficked in that country died of illness or accidents.

这些儿童经常得不到足够的食品及饮料。来自尼日利亚的报告说,这个国家五分之一被非法买卖的儿童死于疾病和意外事故。

Answer the following questions based on the text you have just learned.

1. How many child workers are there across Africa?

   Across Africa, there are an estimated 80 million child workers.

2. What are the "worst forms" of child labour?

   The "worst forms" of child labour include forced labour and slavery, prostitution, employment in the drug trade and other criminal activities, and occupations that are especially dangerous to children's health and security.

3. Why are international organizations focusing on the "worst forms" of child labour?

   They are doing so because the "worst forms" of child labour that involves child trafficking tears children away from the protection of their families and communities and threatens their well-being.

4. What are the possible causes of child labour?

   The possible causes for child labour are as follows:

   1) Poverty that greatly limits vocational and economic opportunities in rural areas in particular and pushes families to use all available means to increase their meagre incomes.

   2) Inadequate educational opportunities.

   3) Ignorance among families and children about the risks of trafficking.

   4) Migration of adults from villages to urban slums, which exposes their children to greater risks.

   5) High demand among employers for cheap and submissive child labour, especially in the informal sector.

6) Ease of travel across regional borders.

7) Inadequate political commitment, legislation and judicial mechanisms to deal with child traffickers.

5. What would happen to those trafficked children?

Trafficked children would be working between 10 to 20 hours a day, carrying heavy loads and operating dangerous tools without adequate food and drink. They would have accident and get killed. They would contract sexually transmitted disease, including HIV/AIDS.

6. What caused child labour trafficking to become a substantial problem in West and Central Africa?

Poverty, inadequate educational opportanities, ignorance about the risks of trafficking, migration of adults from villages to urban slams, high demand for cheap and submissive child labour, ease of travel across regional borders, the desire of young people to travel and explore, and inadequate political commitment, legislation and judicial mechanism form the roots of child labour trafficking.

7. How is child labour related to educational problems in Tanzania?

According to an ILO study on Tanzania, the incidence of child labour in the country has risen partly because of the deterioration of the school system. Poor infrastructure, low teacher spirits and the introduction of school fees under the country's structural adjustment programme have contributed to higher drop-out and absence rates.

8. What is the immediate challenge to combat child labour?

The immediate challenge is to educate the public about the dangers to children of the most exploitative and abusive forms of child labour and to mobilize governments and societies to combat them.

A Sip of Phonetics

In this section, the instructor should draw the students' attention to the fact that these four phonetic symbols share exactly the same features as the four initials in Chinese Pinyin. The difference lies in that though all /r/, /j/, /w /and /l/ are voiced, they are not pronounced as distinctively as the counterparts of Chinese Pinyin because in Pinyin each initial is sounded as if it goes with a final. When teaching these four phonetic symbols, the instructor should contrast /r/, /j/, /w/and /l/ with those in Pinyin.

The English phonetic symbol /r/ is pronounced differently from "r" in Pinyin. The pronunciation of /r/ in English is called a frictionless continuant while "r" in Pinyin is sounded with a final "i."

/j/ is sounded similar to /i/ in English, but "j" in Pinyin finds no equivalent in English.

The similarities between /w/ and /l/ and those in Pinyin lie in that: /w/ in English is pronounced with a quick glide from the vowel /u/ to whatever vowel follows. The letter "w" in Pinyin may be considered as an initial or a final, and may be pronounced as /wu / or /u/.

However, the letter "l" in Pinyin is pronounced somewhere between /l/ and /r/, always clear rather than dark because it is an initial that goes with proper finals, as is in the combinations of "li," "lao," "lei" and "lai."

Train Your Tongue

1. Which witch/ wished /which wicked wish?
2. Twelve twins/ twirled twelve twigs.
3. While we were walking,/ we were watching/ window washers/
   wash Washington's windows/ with warm washing water./
4. Very well,/ very well, /very well./
5. Roberta ran rings/ around the Roman ruins./
6. Round and round/ the rugged rock/ the ragged rascal ran./
7. Real rock wall,/ real rock wall, /real rock wall./
8. Luke's duck/ likes lakes./ Luke Luck/ licks lakes./ Luke's duck/ licks lakes/
9. She sells sea shells/ on the sea shore;/
   The shells that she sells/ are sea shells/ I'm sure./
   So if she sells sea shells/ on the sea shore,/
   I'm sure/ that the shells/ are sea shore shells./

You'd Like to Be

A Strong Bridge Builder

Fill in the blanks with the given words to complete the following sentences. Please note that some can be used more than once.

in	with	of	to	on	from	at	about
by	over	as	among	rather	than	into	out of

1. Across China, there are an estimated 800 thousand online shoppers, a number that could rise <u>to</u> 10 million <u>by</u> 2010. Since e-shopping is different <u>from</u> conventional shopping <u>in</u> many aspects, new rules and regulations are needed to exercise control <u>over</u> the new trend.

2. It is said that counter smoking campaign is <u>on</u> the policy agenda. Although it seems <u>to</u> be common sense that smoking is harmful to health, the number <u>of</u> smokers is <u>on</u> the rise. This is particularly the case <u>among</u> young women partly because many of them view smoking <u>as</u> something that is <u>in</u>. While smokers claim that it is a human right to smoke, they must be aware <u>of</u> the existence of non-smokers who are innocently exposed <u>to</u> possible dangers created by smokers.

3. In a paper presented <u>to</u> last year's conference <u>on</u> preschool English teaching, Dr. Loving agreed <u>with</u> the principle that we must take kids' interests <u>into</u> consideration and that preschool English teaching should not be made compulsory. The general picture is that <u>on</u> the one hand some people are committed <u>to</u> an early beginning for English teaching; <u>on</u> the other hand we do suffer <u>from</u> a lack of competent teachers. A 2003 survey conducted <u>by</u> English Teaching Association showed that two <u>out of</u> five preschool English teachers were just high school graduates. Perhaps the real problem lies <u>in</u> inadequacy of competent teachers rather than whether it is too early to do it.

A Smart Word Player

Fill in the blanks with the proper words that need to be transformed from the ones provided in the brackets.

1. Trust is hard to create, but <u>easy</u> (ease) to destroy, and trust-destroying events are the ones that most of us remember. When someone was told that his or her heartfelt concerns are <u>ignorant</u> (ignorance) and ill-informed, trust understandably shrinks after that.

2. After the fire, the insurance company conducted a damage <u>assessment</u> (assess). But the amount of compensation was so low that the family was almost <u>exposed</u> (exposure) to the danger of living on street. The most unacceptable thing was, when challenged how such a low amount had been reached, the insurance company claimed that they were not allowed to reveal business <u>secrecy</u> (secret).

3. Such an electronic payment service must have a <u>secure</u> (security), reliable and efficient system design. Dan Schutzer of Citibank noted that the key needs of electronic <u>commerce</u> (commercial) include security, privacy, and intellectual property protection.

A Skilled Text Weaver

Fill in the blanks with the words you have learned in this text. One word is for each blank. Here is a piece of advice: You must be really familiar with the text to accomplish the following tasks.

1. Heart disease has become one of the most serious threats to the Nation's health and economic well-being. Today, an estimated 4.5 million Americans—1 in 10 persons over age 50 have heart trouble.

2. Equality in health care still remains a challenge in this country. It needs to get on the government's policy agenda.

3. Disappointingly, the number of HIV/AIDS cases in Jamaica and other Caribbean islands are still on the rise. According to the annual health report of this area, the factors contributing to such a situation include inadequate health care, lack of education about the disease, the use of illegal drugs and the notorious (臭名昭著的) sex industry.

4. With the introduction of red light camera (交通监视摄像机), the incidence of red light running (闯红灯) has been reversed.

5. To me, the roots of jealousy lie in the lack of self-confidence, not the introduction of competition, and can hardly be wiped out of existence.

A Sharp Interpreter

Please paraphrase the following sentences. Change the sentence structure if necessary.

1. ...UNICEF, the ILO and other groups are focusing initially on the "worst forms" of child labour.

   ✤ *Paraphrasing:*

   UNICEF, the ILO and other organizations are beginning to draw their attention to the most severe and fatal cases in the illegal trading for child labour.

2. ...Dr. Salah, a UNICEF regional director for West and Central Africa, agreed with the ILO assessment that child labour trafficking has become a "substantial problem" in the region.

   ✤ *Paraphrasing:*

   Dr. Salah, a UNICEF regional director for West and Central Africa, agreed with the ILO appraisal that the illegal trade for child labour has become a very serious problem in the region.

3. In order to help their children search for the opportunity for education, parents willingly move them from the protective envelope of the family.

✤ *Paraphrasing:*

Parents allow their children to leave the secure family life in the expectation of getting their children access to opportunities for education.

4. According to an ILO study on Tanzania, the incidence of child labour in the country has risen partly because of the deterioration of the school system, itself a result of economic decline.

✤ *Paraphrasing:*

The study on Tanzania made by ILO shows that the rate of child labour has gone up because of the worsening of the school system resulted from economic collapse.

5. Recognizing that the roots of child labour lie in family poverty, and that it cannot simply be legislated out of existence, the ILO draws a distinction between normal family obligations and work which gives rise to exploitation and abuse.

✤ *Paraphrasing:*

The ILO has realized that it is family poverty that has resulted in child labour, and family poverty cannot simply be eradicated by law or dies out by itself. The ILO works on distinguishing children duties for family from profit-oriented child employment that causes them to suffer maltreatment.

6. Since the conditions do not yet exist to end all types of child labour, the immediate challenge is to educate the public about the dangers to children of the most exploitative and abusive forms of child labour and to mobilize governments and societies to combat them.

✤ *Paraphrasing:*

Given the current conditions, it is practically impossible to end all types of child labour, the demanding task that follows is to enlighten people about the inhuman treatment that endangers children by the profit-driven employers. The task also requires that all governments and communities work hand in hand to tackle the problem.

A Solid Sentence Constructer

Please write sentences by using the following words or phrases

1. to focus on

   ✤ *Original sentence in the text:*

   Since the problem is closely linked to the continent's poverty, and can only be eliminated with increases in family incomes and children's educational opportunities, UNICEF, the ILO and other groups are **focusing** initially **on** the "worst forms" of child labour.

   ✤ **Suggested sentence:**

   He inevitably focuses on his own concerns, with only a passing query about Jeff.

2. to tear... away from

◈ *Original sentence in the text:*

Because trafficking tears children away from the protection of their families and communities, it is especially dangerous to their well-being.

◈ **Suggested sentence:**

If you could tear Patrick away from his game, perhaps we could all go out for a drive.

3. on the agenda

◈ *Original sentence in the text:*

*Mr. Alec Fyfe, a senior adviser on child labour for UNICEF told Africa Recovery, "Trafficking is beginning to get **on the** policy **agenda**."*

◈ **Suggested sentence:**

In our company, quality is firmly on the agenda.

4. to counter

◈ *Original sentence in the text:*

*Over the past year, however, African countries have been moving more systematically **to counter** this trend.*

◈ **Suggested sentence:**

The secretary countered my proposal with one of her own.

5. to lack

◈ *Original sentence in the text:*

*They often **lack** adequate food and drink. Nigeria reported that one out of five children trafficked in that country died of illness or accidents.*

◈ **Suggested sentence:**

Perhaps you simply lack the intelligence to realize just how serious this is.

6. compared with

◈ *Original sentence in the text:*

*According to the ILO, 41 percent of all African children between the ages of 5 and 14 are involved in some form of economic activity, **compared with** 21 percent in Asia and 17 percent in Latin America.*

◈ **Suggested sentence:**

Compared with what he had already, the new stamps were not very interesting.

7. to contribute to

◈ *Original sentence in the text:*

*Poor infrastructure, low teacher spirits and the introduction of school fees under the country's structural adjustment program have **contributed to** higher drop-out and absence rates.*

◈ **Suggested sentence:**

Parental involvement contributes significantly to children's learning.

A Superb Bilingualist

Please translate the following sentences into English with the prompts provided in the brackets.

1. 这个女孩子从厌学、辍学到走上犯罪的道路绝非偶然。(coincidence, end up)

✡ **Suggested translation:**

It is no coincidence that the girl was initially tired of school, later a drop-out and ended up in prison.

2. 与去年相比，今年教师人数下降了 10%，而学生人数增加了 30%。(compared with)

✡ **Suggested translation:**

Compared with last year, the number of teachers falls by 10% while that of students rises by 30%.

3. 我们清醒地认识到与贫困的斗争将会漫长而艰难。(combat, be likely to)

✡ **Suggested translation:**

We are sober-minded and aware that the campaign launched to combat poverty is likely to be difficult and long-lasting.

4. 贫困的根源在于教育的缺失。要消除贫困，我们应该调动一切资源办好教育。(root, the lack of, mobilize)

✡ **Suggested translation:**

The public should be aware that poverty is rooted in the disadvantage of a meagre education. To eradicate poverty, we should mobilize all resources to further facilitate education.

5. 彩票能引发不劳而获的错误想法和对人生的扭曲观点，甚至会导致道德水准的下降。(give rise to, misconception, distorted, contribute to)

✡ **Suggested translation:**

(Deep addiction to)Lottery is liable to give rise to the misconception of gaining without efforts, lead to a distorted viewpoint on life, and even contribute to deterioration of moral standards.

Text B

Introduction of the Text

Poverty deprives people of their dignity and freedom. However, it propels people to take action to drive it out of existence. The text focuses on the discussion of the nature of poverty. Its multi-dimensional nature involves not only income-based but also non-income based measurement. It is believed that "poverty line" is measured in relation to income or consumption levels. However, the non-income based dimensions of poverty complicate the matter in that poverty does not stand alone like an island. These dimensions include all comparable and high-quality social indicators. The expanding range of indicators of poverty with the integration of data from sample surveys using participatory technique offer an insight into poverty. To understand the nature of poverty and its multi-dimensional conception is to discover the uneven progress of world economic development to eradicate extreme poverty; achieve universal primary education; promote gender equality and empower women; reduce child mortality; improve maternal health; combat HIV/AIDS, and other diseases; ensure environmental sustainability; and develop a global partnership or development.

Writing Practice

You are now working toward writing a summary for Text B. You may follow the guidelines to write the summary.

I. Read through the entire text to get an understanding of the whole piece, and annotate by underling the sentences containing major points as you read.

II. Locate the thesis statement. While it may appear early in the essay—the first paragraph or two, it may not, in fact, be stated until the end of the piece, almost as if it were a conclusion.

As poverty has many dimensions, it has to be looked at through a variety of indicators-levels of income and consumption, social indicators, and indicators of vulnerability to risks and of social/political access.

(Please write down the thesis statement on the above line.)

III. Dissect the article. Re-read the underlined parts and divide it into sections based on the topics addressed. Each section may be one paragraph, but, more likely, it includes several paragraphs. Now you need to decide how many sections Text B contains.

Text B includes 2 3 4 5... sections.

IV. Write a summary. First, write a sentence or two to summarize each section; then synthesize them into a coherent and cohesive passage. You may need a careful proofreading and revision before the final completion.

1. *(Paragraph 1) Poverty is the powerlessness, lack of representation and freedom.*
2. *(Paragraph 2—3) As poverty has many dimensions, it has to be looked at through a*

variety of indicators—levels of income and consumption, social indicators, and indicators of vulnerability to risks and of social/political access.

3. *(Paragraph 4—7) A common method to measure poverty is based on income or consumption levels.*

4. *(Paragraph 8—9) Non-income dimensions of poverty may include comparable and high-quality social indicators for education, health, access to services and infrastructure.*

5. *(Paragraph 10—11) The uneven progress of development is worrying in that the flow of trade and capital that integrate the global economy may bring benefits to millions, but poverty and suffering persist.*

Summary:

Poverty is the powerlessness, lack of representation and freedom. As poverty has many dimensions, it has to be looked at through a variety of indicators-levels of income and consumption, social indicators, and indicators of vulnerability to risks and of social/ political access. A common method to measure poverty is based on income or consumption levels. Non-income dimensions of poverty may include comparable and high-quality social indicators for education, health, access to services and infrastructure. The uneven progress of development is worrying in that the flow of trade and capital that integrate the global economy may bring benefits to millions, but poverty and suffering persist.

Unit 13

Renaissance Art

Unit Goals

After studying this unit, students should be able to:

☞ **achieve a basic understanding of the art and architecture in the Renaissance;**

In learning **Text A**, students should not only know about Michelangelo's life story and his masterpieces, but also understand from what perspective the Renaissance profoundly influenced European culture and thought. Introductory information on the Renaissance is especially important in helping the students achieve a basic understanding of art in the Renaissance.

☞ **know how to pronounce /tr/, /dr/, /ts/ and /dz/, and how to utilize the words and structures that contribute significantly to the texts;**

In this section, the instructor should explain to the students the different opinions on /tr/, /dr/, /ts/ and /dz/, and more importantly teach the students how to pronounce right. Words in both **Text A** and **Text B** involving /tr/, /dr/, /ts/ and /dz/ have been listed in **A Sip of Phonetics**.

Text A is excerpted from *Michelangelo: The Complete Sculpture, Painting, Architecture*. Its author William Wallace has excellent credentials as a writer and his style of writing is warm, thoughtful, insightful, and informative. Therefore, students should pay special attention to the language subtlety of the text.

☞ **understand how to appreciate the works by Michelangelo, for example, the statue *David*, the Rome *Pietà*, the great paintings left on the altar wall of the Sistine Chapel, and the wonderful design of St. Peter's Cathedral.**

To teach the students how to appreciate the Renaissance sculptures and paintings, the instructor should

A Medieval representation of Jesus Chris

"Christ at the Column" by Antonello da Messina

help them discover one of the characteristics of Renaissance art—a rebirth of the value of the individual. It is especially important for students to observe that many life-size statues were created with different facial expressions, a feature that differed strongly from the art products in the Middle Ages.

Before Reading

Hands-on Activities and Brainstorming

The instructor should allow 15—20 minutes for students to do presentation either on Michelangelo or on the Medicis.

A Glimpse at Words and Expressions

A. To help the students understand the meaning of "genius," the instructor should remind them of the verb "admire" that appears before "genius," which indicates that "genius" must be something good or valuable. And it would be interesting to observe if the students are able to guess the meaning of "genius" after the instructor refers to the link between "gene" and "genius" in class.

B. "Obscure" is usually used as an adjective, for example, *Jude, the Obscure*, however, it is used as a verb in the present context, meaning "to make (it) difficult to see, hear or understand." The instructor may resort to the analysis of word formation to help students guess the meaning of "obscure":

ob (over)+scure (covered)=fully covered→to make (it) difficult to see, hear or understand

C. "Unforgiving" literally means "unwilling to forgive other people when they have done sth. wrong," while the extended meaning of it is "requiring extreme carefulness," allowing no chance to correct the wrong doing. It would be helpful for the instructor to contrast "unforgiving" with "unforgivable."

D. "Lowly" means unimportant or being low in status. Here is another example of "lowly": He was not ashamed of his lowly origins.

E. To help the students guess the meaning of "imprisoned," the instructor should indicate the root of "imprisoned"—"prison," and then prompt the students to track the logic suggested by "figure" and "release" in the sentence. One needs to release something that is "imprisoned."

F. "Incapacitated" stems from the root "capacity," which means ability, with "in-" carrying a negative meaning. The word formation goes like:

in (not)+capacitated (able)=not able→being unable to live or work normally

He was incapacitated by old age and sickness.

G. "Remission" is originated from the verb "remit." The word formation goes like:

re (back)+mit (send)→to cancel or free sb. from a debt, duty or punishment

For those in remission from cancer, exercise can help them return to their normal health state.

Keys

A-2   B-4   C-5   D-6   E-1   F-3   G-7

Text A

Hands-on Activities and Brainstorming

William E. Wallace is a professor of art history at Washington University in St. Louis. He is an internationally recognized authority on Michelangelo and his contemporaries. In addition to more than forty articles, he is the author and editor of four books on Michelangelo: *Michelangelo at San Lorenzo: The Genius as Entrepreneur* (Cambridge, 1994), *Michelangelo: Selected Scholarship in English* (Garland, 1996), *Michelangelo: The Complete Sculpture, Painting, and Architecture* (Hugh Lauter Levin, 1998), and most recently, *Michelangelo: Selected Scholarship in English* (Garland, 1999). He is currently writing a new biography of Michelangelo.

Suggested Explanations on Text A

1. The R*ome Pietà* and the *David*, for example, are amazing works that <u>obscure</u> the facts of their creation.

    Meaning: The two masterpieces, the *Rome Pietà* and the *David*, are so enchanting that they have the admirers overlook the hardships in creating them.

    ▶ obscure (*v.*): to make it difficult to see, hear or understand

    eg. 1) The clouds obscured the sun.

      2) Betty Benson is a woman writer whose status as a philosopher has been obscured by the fact that she wrote novels.

    ▲ ...so...that it obscures...:

    eg. 1) The friendship between them was so intense that it obscured the fact that they represented groups of different interest (利益群体).

      2) The music was so loud that it obscured what he was saying.

2. We tend to overlook that they <u>were shaped from</u> raw and resistant stone, by hands that were strong and skillful but also were tired from time to time or easily bruised.

Meaning: We usually neglect the fact that they (the sculptures) were made from raw and hard stone by human hands that, though strong and skillful, easily get tired and bruised.

▶ to be shaped from: to be made from

eg. 1) Analyze the reasons for your interests and how they were shaped from your upbringing.

2) A lot of his views were shaped from his life experience in China.

3. Every blow of hammer to chisel is a collision of metal against metal striking stone.

该句的修饰关系如下图所示：

Every **blow** of hammer to chisel **is a collision** of metal against metal striking stone.

每一次锤凿相击都是铁器敲击铁器后与石头的碰撞。

4. Modern stone workers wear goggles; Michelangelo did not.

这句话由两个并列分句组成，中间用分号隔开，第二分句采用了与第一分句同样的句式，省略了前面出现过的动词和宾语。这句话看似简单，但却蕴藏着一种韵味，给人戛然而止、意味深长的感觉，用以强调米开朗琪罗制作雕塑时的艰苦。建议教师就这句话的韵味向学生作讲解。

5. He could not <u>afford to</u> slip.

▶ to afford to: (usually with can or could, especially in negative sentences) one should not do...because it will cause problems if he does it

eg. 1) The company gave up the ownership, because it could not afford to do anything else.

2) I knew that I couldn't afford to lose confidence in myself.

▲ to afford to: to have enough money to do...

eg. 1) Wilber did not bother to apply to MIT, because his family could not afford to send him there.

2) He couldn't afford to live in Beijing, so he commuted from Langfang—an hour and a half each way by train and bus.

6. Here, and in the surrounding hills, Michelangelo grew up and <u>was first exposed to</u> stone carving.

▶ to be exposed to: to find out about sth. by experiencing it

eg. 1) He became addicted to heroin when he was first exposed to drugs.

2) From a very early age, she was exposed to music and expected to learn and participate.

▲ to be exposed to: to be put in a place or situation which is harmful or unpleasant

eg. 1) Babies should not be exposed to strong sunlight.

    2) During different historical stages, the city was exposed to many invasions.

▲ exposure to: an instance of being subjected to an action or an influence

eg. 1) Henry decided to live in a very rural setting, reducing his exposure to "big city" life as much as he could.

    2) He was born and raised in Georgia, the son of a minister, and his first exposure to performing came via singing in church.

7. Michelangelo was drawn to art rather than to the world of the banker and merchant.

  ▶ to be drawn to: to be attracted by

eg. 1) He was drawn to the newspaper business even as a child. He would write up neighborhood news on a single sheet of paper, take photographs and then take the page door to door and have neighbors read it.

    2) Decades ago, I was drawn to music that seemed full of emotional honesty.

8. In the large Medici household, Michelangelo came in contact with the most learned men of the century, and the patron of them all, Lorenzo de' Medici.

  ▶ to come in contact with: to be meeting with

eg. 1) Alice was a lovely baby and a joy to everyone that she came in contact with.

    2) Working for Oxford University Students' Union gave him the opportunity to come in contact with international students.

▲ contact (*v.*): to get in touch with; communicate with

eg. 1) You can contact me by sending mail to 123@123.com .

    2) Don't contact me until I contact you.

9. He had access to the works of classical authors that were considered "musts" for a good education: Plato, Aristotle, Ovid, and Virgil.

Meaning: He was able to read the works by classical authors such as Plato, Aristotle, Ovid, and Virgil, the masterpieces one had to read to become a well-educated person.

    Plato (428/427 BC—348/347 BC) was an ancient Greek philosopher, the second of the great trio of ancient Greeks—succeeding Socrates and preceding Aristotle—who between them laid the philosophical foundations of Western culture.

    Ovid (43 BC—17 AD) was a Roman poet who wrote on topics of love, abandoned women and mythological transformations.

    Virgil was a classical Roman poet, the author of *the Eclogues* (牧歌), the *Georgics* (农事诗) and the substantially completed *Aeneid* (埃涅阿斯纪), the last being an epic poem of twelve books that became the Roman Empire's national epic.

▶ access (*n.*): (always used with "to") the ability to approach, or make use of

eg. 1) Whereas in 1998, only 26% of American households had access to the Internet, by the end of 2001 that group had grown to 50%.

　　2) There are over 100 computers in the library, all having access to the Internet.

▲ access (*v.*): to reach, enter or use sth.

eg. 1) It is ridiculous that he accessed FBI files only to satisfy his own curiosity about FBI investigations.

　　2) The computer log recorded all the details of what files they accessed and how long. (Please make sure that the students accept the fact there is no such a structure of "sb. access to.")

▶ must (*n.*): sth. that is absolutely required or indispensable

eg. 1) During my first period in China in 1970s, the "Three Musts" for many people were still a watch, a bicycle and a sewing machine. But now the "Three Musts" are more like a car, an apartment and a DVD player with a giant screen.

　　2) Remember the two musts when touring Italy: you must sit at a sidewalk cafe, and you must try a pizza!

10. Michelangelo moved to Rome and lived in the household of Cardinal Raffaele Riario, the richest and most powerful man in Rome, <u>second only to</u> the pope.

▶ second only to: next in order of importance, size or quality

eg. 1) Cancer ranks second only to heart disease as a leading cause of death in this country, making it a tremendous burden in years of life lost, patient suffering, and economic costs.

　　2) The traditional Chinese Moon Festival is one of the most important festivals in China, second only to Chinese New Year of lunar calendar.

11. ...Michelangelo <u>rose to</u> the opportunity and created the *Bacchus*.

Meaning: When given the opportunity to carve the *Bacchus*, Michelangelo demonstrated his ability in accomplishing the task.

▶ to rise to: to show the ability to deal with an unexpected situation or problem

eg. In the difficult situation, more than a thousand donors rose to the challenge, contributing more than $3.8 million to the College Fund.

12. ...it was even said that he could see the figure <u>imprisoned</u> in it, and all he would do was to release it.

Explanation: Michelangelo was asked once how he carved and created such magnificence and beauty from a slab of cold marble. He then replied, "I didn't do anything. God put *Pietà* and *David* in the marble, they were already there. I only had to carve away the parts that kept you from seeing them." And he went on saying, "I saw an angel in the marble and carved until I set him free."

▶ imprison (*v.*): to put sb. in a prison or another place from which they cannot escape

eg. 1) We have to admit that far too little attention has been paid to children of imprisoned mothers and their welfare, let alone their rights.

2) The ex-police officer had been wrongly imprisoned for 6 years until evidence showed that he was not involved in murdering.

13. The success of *Bacchus* brought Michelangelo the commission for a *Pietà* from a powerful French cardinal, a new task that Michelangelo gave his best effort to.

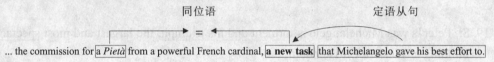

14. <u>Thanks to</u> the head of government, Michelangelo was entrusted with the old and partially worked block.

▶ thanks to: sth. good happened because of...

eg. 1) Thanks to the tech person, the audio system was back in 15 mins.

2) Thanks to modern technology, we generally live longer, healthier, cleaner, and physically easier lives than did most of our ancestors.

3) Thanks to the Internet, the age of the door-to-door encyclopedia salesperson is essentially over.

15. <u>There appears to have been</u> trust and mutual respect between the two men.

这句话使用 appear 表示不确定性,再使用不定式的完成式"to have been"表示事情发生在过去。二者连用表达对过去发生事情的推测口吻。

16. Paul <u>lost no time in making</u> the use of Michelangelo's talents, commissioning him to paint the altar wall of the Sistine Chapel.

▶ to lose no time in doing sth.: start to do sth. at once

eg. 1) The doctor lost no time in giving the patient first aid.

2) He lost no time in getting to London.

17. ...Michelangelo said that he <u>was still under obligation to complete</u> another project...

▶ to be under obligation to do sth.: the state of being forced to do sth. because it is one's duty

eg. 1) Doctors are under obligation to report when they received evidence of abuse.

2) We have reached the consensus that we are under the obligation to help the poor.

▲ **oblige** (*v.*): (usually passive) be forced to do sth. by law, or because it is a duty

eg. 1) Parents are obliged to send their kids to school.

　　2) At one time he was obliged to leave his wife and family, and for a considerable period remained hidden.

18. I have <u>nursed</u> this ambition for thirty years, and now that I'm pope, am I not to have it satisfied?

▶ **nurse** (*v.*): (formal) to have a strong feeling or idea in your mind for a long time

eg. 1) For two years I have nursed the plan of going to Paris.

　　2) For a long time he has nursed the dream of building and running a "boxing academy."

19. St. Peter's was Michelangelo's <u>torment and his triumph</u>, the largest and most <u>spectacular</u> building in Western Christendom.

Meaning: St. Peter's was a difficult task for Michelangelo to accomplish, but he had it done beautifully. It was the largest and the most outstanding building in western Christian world.

▶ **torment and triumph**: In the first part of the sentence, the author uses "and" to link "torment" and "triumph," two words with contrasting meanings, to convey the contrasting transition of meaning.

▶ **spectacular** (*adj.*): very impressive

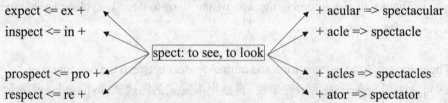

eg. 1) A total solar eclipse is the most spectacular sight that can be seen.

　　2) While this image is nice looking here on the net, it is quite spectacular in a print and magnificent in prints of 16×20 inches and larger.

20. The artist died on February 18, 1564, just two weeks <u>shy of</u> his eighty-ninth birthday.

▶ **shy** (*adj.*) **of**: (not before noun) lacking the amount that is needed

eg. 1) Just two years shy of 60, he remains fit and trim by swimming, skiing and bicycling.

　　2) Herbert will leave office one month shy of serving twenty years as university president.

21. This afternoon that most excellent and true miracle of nature, Michelangelo Buonarroti passed from this to a better life.

Meaning: The most excellent and real genius of the world, Michelangelo Buonarroti, left this world for Heaven this afternoon.

Better Know More

Notes

1. The Essence of Renaissance Art

The Italian Renaissance was one of the most productive periods in the history of art that marked the close of the Middle Ages and the beginning of the modern Western world. And it produced an extraordinary amount of art that differed from that in the Middle Ages.

The ancient world of Rome and Greece, greatly influenced Renaissance painting, sculpture, and architecture. Renaissance artists and humanists studied the surviving buildings and monuments, and absorbed the humanist emphasis on man and his actions and perceptions. Humanism is the idea that mankind has a high degree of autonomy in the world. It contrasts sharply with the Medieval religious idea that the present world is a transitory place in which man makes preparations for the afterlife. Man, in the humanistic view, is regarded as rational, beautiful and heroic—worthy of happiness and capable of great achievement. This well explains why Byzantine and Medieval craftsmen portrayed people as stiff and expressionless, while with the renewed emphasis on the individual, Renaissance artists portrayed the individual characters with real expressions on their faces.

2. Understanding Michelangelo's *David*

Michelangelo's *David*, sculpted from 1500 to 1504, is a masterpiece of Renaissance sculpture and one of Michelangelo's two greatest works of sculpture, along with the *Pietà*. The statue *David* was inspired by the story of young David who chose to fight a far stronger enemy in order to save his people from invasion. Wearing no armor, David defeated Goliath (哥利亚, 被大卫杀死的巨人) using superior skill and courage. Interestingly, Michelangelo shows David not as a triumphant victor, but as a thinking, resolute being—the preconditions for victory. As someone looks upon the statue, all of the qualities praised by humanists are definitively illustrated by David's expression, posture, and the great details. David's face is represented like the calm before a storm. He puts forth an image of confident intelligence and calmness.

Check Your Understanding

Translate the following sentences into Chinese.   Please make sure that your language flows smoothly.

1. There he learned to speak and write well, and was exposed to a world of learning.

   在那里,他学习如何自如地表达与写作,置身于知识的世界。

2. In the large Medici household, Michelangelo came in contact with the most learned men of the century, and the patron of them all, Lorenzo de' Medici.

   身居梅第奇家族的豪宅,米开朗琪罗有机会接触到那个世纪最博学的人,以及他们的恩主——罗兰佐·梅第奇。

3. Challenged by high expectations, and given the opportunity to carve a larger than life-size marble, Michelangelo rose to the opportunity and created the *Bacchus*.

   面对着(公众的)极高期待,米开朗琪罗抓住机遇,在一块比真人还高大的大理石料上创造出《巴克斯》,充分展示了他的实力。

4. With the twin achievements of the *Pietà* in Rome and the *David* in Florence, Michelangelo's reputation was now firmly established; he would never again lack for commissions.

   靠着罗马《圣母怜子图》和佛罗伦萨《大卫》这两项成就,现在米开朗琪罗的声望已经稳稳地建立起来了;(从此)他再也不缺订单了。

5. Paul lost no time in making the use of Michelangelo's talents, commissioning him to paint the altar wall of the Sistine Chapel.

   保罗抓紧一切时间充分利用米开朗琪罗的(艺术)才华,立刻委托他绘画西斯廷教堂的圣坛壁。

6. Nonetheless, Michelangelo remained devoted to the project even when his great admirer, Duke Cosimo de' Medici, tried repeatedly to persuade him to return to Florence. Michelangelo gave all his energy, and the last twenty years of his life, to completing St. Peter's, which was his best hope for a remission from sins in the afterlife.

   然而,米开朗琪罗对工程恪尽职守,他的敬慕者科西莫·梅第奇曾多次试图说服他返回佛罗伦萨,他也不为所动。他将生命中的最后 20 年时间全部献给了圣彼得教堂工程,企盼着以此在来生获得救赎。

7. And he succeeded; Paul kept Michelangelo busy throughout much of his fifteen-year ruling.

   而且他成功了;保罗在其统治的 15 年大部分时间里,令米开朗琪罗始终保持在忙碌的状态中。

8. The *David* testifies to Michelangelo's ambition, as well as his recent experience and successes in Rome.

   《大卫》展示了米开朗琪罗的远大理想,同时也(向世人)反映了他在罗马的生活经历和取得的成功。

Answer the following questions based on the text you have just learned.

1. Who is Michelangelo?

   Michelangelo was the greatest sculptor of the sixteenth century in Italy.

2. Where did Michelangelo learn to speak and write well?

   Michelangelo learned to speak and write well in the large Medici household, the successful bankers and the most influential family in Florence.

3. Can you name three major sculptures by Michelangelo?

   The David, the Pietà and the Bacchus.

4. Besides marble carving, what else could Michelangelo do?

   Michelangelo was also a great architect, who directed the construction of St. Peter, the largest and most spectacular building in Western Christendom.

5. When the Sistine Chapel is mentioned, people tend to think of Michelangelo. Why is that?

   Michelangelo gained much fame by painting the altar wall of the Sistine Chapel.

6. What is the link between Michelangelo and Pope Paul III?

   Pope Paul III was the greatest and wisest of Michelangelo's numerous patrons. There appears to have been trust and mutual respect between the two men. It was Paul who commissioned him to paint the altar wall of the Sistine Chapel, and patronized him as an architect, having him direct the construction of St. Peter's.

7. Which part of Michelangelo's life story impresses you most? Can you state why?

   This is an open question.

8. Toward the end of Text A, the author wrote, "That same year Galileo and William Shakespeare were born." Can you figure out what the author's intention is by doing so?

   This is an open question.

A Sip of Phonetics

When teaching this section, the instructor should be aware that /tr/, /dr/, /ts/ and /dz/ are rather different from the rest of phonemes. While most language experts agree that there are 48 international phonetic alphabets in English, naming /tr/, /dr/, /ts/ and /dz/ as compound consonants or affricates, some tend to hold that spoken English consists of 44 phonemes only, with /tr/, /dr/, /ts/ and /dz/ counted as consonant clusters (辅音连缀), not phonemes. Frankly speaking, the authors of this textbook will not take side with either opinion, but hold that /tr/, /dr/, /ts/ and /dz/ must be learned and practiced by students of English major.

To pronounce right /tr/, /dr/, /ts/ and /dz/, the students are suggested to take each one of the four as a double-phoneme compound, for example: /dr/ = /d/ + /r/, and /tr/ = /t/ + /r/. It seems that when pronouncing these compounds, one should get ready to pronounce the first part, but to hold the sound, and then quickly turn to pronounce the second part, which really sounds like: /dr/ = /d/→/r/, /tr/= /t/→/r/, /dz/= /d/→/z/, /ts/= /t/→/s/. Since two of the compounds involve the phoneme /r/, it is necessary for the instructor to help students review how to pronounce /r/ correctly.

It is also necessary to indicate that /tr/ tends to be special when placed after phoneme /s/. In that case, /tr/ will be pronounced as /dr/, for example: street should actually be read as /sdri:t/, though the written form remains as /stri:t/. Similar examples are: strange, struggle, straight, strategy, straw, stream, stress, strike, structure...

You'd Like to Be

A Strong Bridge Builder

Fill in the blanks with the given words to complete the following sentences. Please note that some can be used more than once.

| against | aside | for | on | of | within |
| away | by | to | into | from | without |

Clownfish Nemo has been really unhappy and that has been lasting <u>for</u> a while, because his father Marlin is <u>against</u> his desire to venture <u>into</u> the open sea. A predator attack that happened outside the Great Barrier Reef three months ago left Marlin <u>without</u> a wife and Nemo <u>without</u> a mother. Therefore, the father is unwilling to expose Nemo <u>to</u> any possible danger in the sea. Marlin gives his best effort <u>to</u> keeping his son <u>within</u> sight, placing Nemo's safety <u>on</u> the top of the list, second only <u>to</u> searching for food.

But Nemo is drawn <u>to</u> the world beyond the Great Barrier Reef. He once swam to its edge and heard the beautiful clanging produced <u>by</u> the collision of metal <u>against</u> metal. According to the teacher, it was <u>from</u> the deck of a huge ship; unfortunately ships tend to stay <u>away</u> <u>from</u> the Great Barrier Reef.

—A ship! What is a ship like?

Denied several times access <u>to</u> the open sea, Nemo feels imprisoned in the Great Barrier Reef. He decides to leave secretly <u>for</u> the outer world, setting <u>aside</u> his father's warnings and forgetting the fact that he is a week shy <u>of</u> six months old, and therefore lacking <u>for</u> long distance travel experience...

A Smart Word Player

Fill in the blanks with the proper words that need to be transformed from the ones provided in the brackets.

His <u>miraculous</u> (miracle) talents were swiftly recognized in the circle of architecture. The <u>commissioned</u> (commission) design of the City Hall entrusted by the Mayor, who was <u>amazed</u> (amazing) at his genius, brought him the greatest success in life. He was soon <u>immersed</u> (immersion) in flowers and applauses, never again lacking for <u>commissions</u> (commission). Following the Mayor, there came a whole bunch of demanding customers <u>commissioning</u> (commission) him for important projects. These people actually pushed his <u>triumphant</u> (triumph) experience to an end, because it was the same group of customers who later rejected his works for the reason that most of them were effortless imitations of the <u>classics</u> (classical) and that was <u>unforgivable</u> (unforgiving).

A Skilled Text Weaver

Fill in the blanks with the words you have learned in this text. One word is for each blank. Here is a piece of advice: You must be really familiar with the text to accomplish the following tasks.

1. The artist was deeply absorbed in the beauty of this amazing <u>creation</u>, and eventually had to be dragged away from observing the <u>sculpture</u> of the *David*.
2. According to Aristotle, drama should be the <u>condensation</u> of events, people, actions and ideas, all confined into a no more than 24-hour flow that the audience can follow.
3. A <u>patron</u> is a noble or wealthy person in ancient Europe who granted favor and protection to someone with talents in exchange for certain services.
4. Critics are now wondering where his <u>legendary</u> creativity has gone, as during the past ten years audience had only been <u>exposed</u> to his <u>imitations</u> of <u>classical</u> works.
5. Should any humane (人性化的) <u>adjustment</u> be made to that safety system, considering that drivers are mere humans, instead of machines, who may get tired from time to time, the tragic <u>collision</u> with other vehicles would be easily avoided.

A Sharp Interpreter

Please paraphrase the following sentences. Change the sentence structure if necessary.

1. We tend to overlook that they were shaped from raw and resistant stone, by hands that were strong and skillful but also were tired from time to time or easily bruised.

   ◈ *Paraphrasing:*

   We usually neglect the fact that they (the sculptures) were made from raw and hard stone by human hands that, though strong and skillful, can easily get tired and bruised.

2. Marble carving is difficult and unforgiving.

   ◈ *Paraphrasing:*

   Marble carving is difficult, which does not allow even the smallest mistake.

3. Michelangelo was drawn to art rather than to the world of the banker and merchant.

   ◈ *Paraphrasing:*

   Michelangelo was more attracted to art than to learning to become a banker or businessman.

4. He had access to the works of classical authors that were considered "musts" for a good education: Plato, Aristotle, Ovid, and Virgil.

   ◈ *Paraphrasing:*

   He had the opportunity to read the works by classical authors such as Plato, Aristotle, Ovid, and Virgil, whom one had to read to become a well-educated person.

5. When Michelangelo said that he was still under obligation to complete another project, the Pope is said to have burst out: "I have nursed this ambition for thirty years, and now that I'm Pope, am I not to have it satisfied? I shall tear the contract up. I'm determined to have you in my service, no matter what."

   ◈ *Paraphrasing:*

   When Michelangelo told the Pope that he was engaged in carving another sculpture, the Pope is said to have exploded, because he had had a strong desire for this ambition for thirty years, and when he became Pope, he felt the first thing he would do was to satisfy the desire. He threatened that he would terminate Michelangelo's other contract as he had made up his mind to have him do this project, regardless whatever happened.

6. This afternoon that most excellent and true miracle of nature, Michelangelo Buonarroti passed from this to a better life.

   ◈ *Paraphrasing:*

   This afternoon that most excellent and real genius of the world, Michelangelo Buonarroti left this world for Heaven.

A Solid Sentence Constructer

Please write sentences by using the following words or phrases.

1. to tend to
   ✥ *Original sentence in the text:*

   We tend to overlook that they were shaped from raw and resistant stone, by hands that were strong and skillful but also were tired from time to time or easily bruised.

   ✥ **Suggested sentence:**

   I wonder why intelligent people tend to be unhappy.

2. to be exposed to
   ✥ *Original sentence in the text:*

   Here, and in the surrounding hills, Michelangelo grew up and was first exposed to stone carving.

   ✥ **Suggested sentence:**

   During his Harvard years, Henry David Thoreau was exposed to the writings of Ralph Waldo Emerson, who later became his chief mentor and friend.

3. in contact with
   ✥ *Original sentence in the text:*

   In the large Medici household, Michelangelo came in contact with the most learned men of the century, and the patron of them all, Lorenzo de' Medici.

   ✥ **Suggested sentence:**

   Government officials say that they have been in contact with an armed group that kidnapped the five embassy staff in Kenya.

4. to have access to
   ✥ *Original sentence in the text:*

   He had access to the works of classical authors that were considered "musts" for a good education: Plato, Aristotle, Ovid, and Virgil.

   ✥ **Suggested sentence:**

   Should the government have access to personal e-mails?

5. to rise to the opportunity
   ✥ *Original sentence in the text:*

   Challenged by high expectations, and given the opportunity to carve a larger than life-size marble, Michelangelo rose to the opportunity and created the Bacchus.

   ✥ **Suggested sentence:**

   After the successful spacewalk by the astronauts on "Shenzhou Ⅶ," China will surely rise to the challenge of building its own space station.

6. to lack for

⨁ ***Original sentence in the text:***

   ...*he would never again lack for commissions.*

⨁ **Suggested sentence:**

   The White House does not lack for people willing to give advice on policy, if not too many.

7. to lose no time in

⨁ ***Original sentence in the text:***

   Paul lost no time in making the use of Michelangelo's talents, commissioning him to paint the altar wall of the Sistine Chapel.

⨁ **Suggested sentence:**

   The police lost no time in sending the clothing to the FBI for fiber analysis.

8. to be devoted to

⨁ ***Original sentence in the text:***

   Nonetheless, Michelangelo remained devoted to the project even when his great admirer, Duke Cosimo de' Medici, tried repeatedly to persuade him to return to Florence.

⨁ **Suggested sentence:**

   The family remained devoted to their land and continued to farm it, but on a rather small scale.

9. to keep...busy

⨁ ***Original sentence in the text:***

   Paul kept Michelangelo busy throughout much of his fifteen-year ruling.

⨁ **Suggested sentence:**

   It was stressful trying to keep my son busy while I did my homework.

10. to testify to

⨁ ***Original sentence in the text:***

   The David testifies to Michelangelo's ambition, as well as his recent experience and successes in Rome.

⨁ **Suggested sentence:**

   The role he played in those stormy years testifies to his personal courage as well as to his deep devotion to the ideal of fair education.

📖 A Superb Bilingualist

Please translate the following sentences into English with the prompts provided in the brackets.

1. 数学运算在航天计划中是最苛刻的部分,容不得半点失误。(aerospace, unforgiving, afford)

   ✧ *Suggested translation:*

   Mathematical computation in aerospace is unforgiving, which cannot afford even the smallest error.

2. 尤金第一次接触油画的时候,就被深深地吸引住了。他的老师对此很高兴,因为兴趣是一个成功的画家必不可少的条件。(be exposed to, be drawn to, must)

   ✧ *Suggested translation:*

   Eugene was deeply drawn to painting when he was first exposed to it. His teacher was quite delighted to see this, as interest is a must for a painter in achieving success.

3. 她把手边所有的工作都放在一边,将准备博士生入学考试置于仅次于照顾女儿的位置。(set aside, second only to, nurture)

   ✧ *Suggested translation:*

   She set aside all the work that she needed to do, placing the preparation for doctoral student entrance examination on the top list, second only to nurturing her daughter.

4. 小镇缺乏训练有素的建筑师,出于两人间的相互信任,镇长将市政厅的设计和施工全都委托给他一个人。(lack for, mutual respect, entrust)

   ✧ *Suggested translation:*

   The town lacks for well-trained architect. Out of the mutual respect between them, the mayor entrusted both design and construction of the City Hall to him.

5. 他虽然年事已高、体力不支,但他并没有选择放弃,而是毅然决然地开始了一项新工程的筹划。(incapacitated, rather than, project)

   ✧ *Suggested translation:*

   Although getting old and therefore incapacitated, rather than gave up, he started the planning of a new project.

6. 他画技神奇,仅用寥寥数笔便能使一只小猫或是小狗跃然纸上。(legendary, stroke, come alive)

   ✧ *Suggested translation:*

   He has a legendary painting ability, and he can have a cat/kitten or a dog/puppy come alive on paper with merely a few strokes.

7. 父亲爱子心切,却忽视了对孩子的管教。(obscure)

   ✧ *Suggested translation:*

   The love from father was so strong that it obscured the necessity of disciplining the child.

Text B

📖 Introduction to Carolingian Architecture

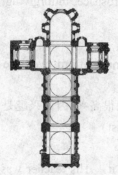

The Plan of St.Pierre

The new architecture (8th century—9th century), inspired by the forms of antiquity, abandoned the small boxlike shapes of the Merovingian period (梅罗文加时期)and used instead spacious basilicas (长方形基督教堂) often intersected by vast transepts (教堂的十字形翼部). An innovation of Carolingian builders, which was to be of incalculable importance for the later Middle Ages, was the emphasis given to the western extremity of the church. The facade (正面), flanked symmetrically by towers, or simply the exterior of a massive complex(联合体), became the focal point of the structure.

📖 Introduction to Gothic Architecture

In the 12th—13th centuries, feats of engineering permitted increasingly gigantic buildings. The rib vault (拱肋), flying buttress(飞扶壁), and pointed (Gothic) arch (尖拱)were included into the design while preserving as much natural light as possible. Stained-glass(彩色玻璃)window panels were used to produce sun-dappled interior effects. One of the earliest buildings to combine these elements into a coherent style was the abbey of Saint-Denis, Paris and Chartres Cathedral (see the picture on the right), Germany. Britain and Spain produced variations of this style, while Italian Gothic stood apart in its use of brick and marble rather than stone. Other late Gothic styles include the British Perpendicular style (垂直哥特式)and the French and Spanish Flamboyant style(火焰式风格).

Writing Practice

You are now working toward writing a summary for Text B. You may follow the guidelines to write the summary:

I. Read through the entire text to get an understanding of the whole piece, and annotate by underlining the sentences containing the major points as you read.

II. Locate the thesis statement. While it may appear early in the essay—the first paragraph or two, it may not, in fact, be stated until the end of the piece, almost as if it were a conclusion.

<u>The era in which the Romanesque structures arose was a time of great significance for European culture, and architecture is a central component of that story.</u>

(Please write down the thesis statement on the above line.)

III. Dissect the article. Re-read the underlined parts and divide it into sections based on the topics addressed. Each section may be one paragraph, but, more likely, it includes several paragraphs. Now you need to decide how many sections Text B contains.

Text B includes 2 3 4 5 ... sections. (Please circle the number as you need.)

IV. Write a summary. First, write a sentence or two to summarize each section; then synthesize them into a coherent and cohesive passage.   You may need a careful proofreading and revision before the final completion.

1. *(Paragraph 1) After the Carolingian period, the Romanesque architecture emerged between the eleventh and twelfth century in Europe, a style that was later succeeded by the Gothic architecture style.*

2. *(Paragraph 2—4) Typical Romanesque architecture features in its massiveness, the vault, and the Norman facade.*

3. *(Paragraph 5—6) Much of the great developments of the Romanesque period are overshadowed by later works, especially the Gothic architecture.*

4. *(Paragraph 7—9) Actually, both Romanesque and Gothic architecture benefited greatly within Carolingian period, in which master builders were given a deserving respect.*

5. *(Paragraph 10—11) The era in which the Romanesque structures arose was a time of great significance for European culture, and architecture is a central component of that story.*

Summary:

After the Carolingian period, the Romanesque architecture emerged between the eleventh and twelfth century in Europe, a style that was later succeeded by the Gothic architecture style. Typical Romanesque architecture features in its massiveness, the vault, and the Norman facade. Much of the great developments of the Romanesque period are overshadowed by later works, especially the Gothic architecture. Actually, both Romanesque and Gothic architecture benefited greatly within Carolingian period, in which master builders were given a deserving respect. The era in which the Romanesque structures arose was a time of great significance for European culture, and architecture is a central component of that story.

14

Student Life

Unit Goals

After studying this unit, students should be able to:

☞ **know what to learn from examples of straight-A students;**

    Text A gives us some good examples of straight-A students and tells us secrets in their study and everyday life. Before moving into **Text A**, the instructor should walk the students through **A Glimpse at Words and Expressions**, which will warm up the students. When students are confronted with difficulties doing matching, the instructor should encourage them to guess the answers based on the language context. Students' preview of both **Text A** and **Text B** should be strongly encouraged.

☞ **understand how to link consonants with vowels and with other consonants, and how to utilize the words and structures that contribute significantly to the texts;**

    In this section, the instructor should explain to the students the basic pronunciation rules of sound-linking and incomplete plosion. It is strongly suggested that the instructor encourage students to read aloud the given paragraph before class. The instructor may refer to the advice provided in the section **A Sip of Phonetics**. Most useful words and structures of **Text A** can be found in **You'd Like to Be**. This is where students practice what they have learned from **Text A**.

☞ **think critically about the consequence of academic cheating and how to solve this problem.**

    Text B is about the problem of academic cheating in American high schools and universities. It tells us the reasons behind dishonesty and the attempts from students to solve this problem.

Before Reading

Hands-on Activities and Brainstorming

The instructor should allow 15—20 minutes for students to do presentation on secrets of academic success.

A Glimpse at Words and Expressions

A. Another example may help students get the idea of "account for": The heat wave accounts for the food spoilage. So the phrase means "to explain or to give reasons for sth."

B. "Count" originally means "to say numbers in the correct order or to calculate the total number of sth." The instructor should remind students that "count" in this sentence does not refer to numbers but to sth. that has value or importance. For example: Happiness counts more than money.

C. "Ready" is not new to students. However not many can produce a sentence like the following one—"Don't be so ready to believe the worst about people." Here "ready" means "willing and quick to do or give sth." Another example: "He is always ready to help others." The instructor should help students understand the adjective first and then students may readily learn the adverb in the following sentence—"Truth comes out of error more readily than out of confusion.—Francis Bacon" So the adverb "readily" means "quickly, effortlessly, without difficulty."

D. Another example: This is not strictly true. So "strictly" means "in all details, exactly."

E. The instructor should remind students that it is a cross-country runner who "worked out." Another example is: He works out with weights every other day. So "work out" means "to do physical exercise."

F. "Fresh" usually goes with "air," "flowers," "vegetables," "fruits"... However, it also describes "memory." For example: The old memory was still fresh. So here it means "recent enough to be remembered clearly."

G. The instructor should let students know that the root "over" often indicates "too much," for example, "overdo," "overeat," "overflow" or "overestimate." "Overwhelming" means "too great to resist or overcome, too difficult to handle." For another example: She felt an overwhelming urge/desire/need to tell someone about what had happened.

Keys

A-6　　B-4　　C-2　　D-1　　E-3　　F-7　　G-5

Text A

〰️ Suggested Explanations on Text A

1. We see them frequently in TV sitcoms and in movies like *Revenge of the Nerds*.

   ▶ revenge (*n.*): action taken in return for an injury or offense

   eg. 1) She took revenge on him for leaving her by smashing up his car.

      2) He is believed to have been shot by a rival gang in revenge for the shootings last week.

   ▲ revenge (*v.*): to harm sb. as a punishment for harm that they have done to someone else

   eg. 1) to revenge oneself on sb.: The red team revenged themselves on the blue team by winning the semi-final.

      2) be revenged on sb.: She vowed to be revenged on them all.

2. They get high grades, all right, but only by becoming dull grinds, their noses always stuck in a book.

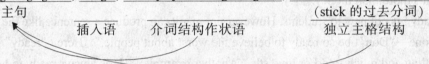

   Meaning: OK, it is true that they get high grades, but they get them only by reading books all the time and they become dull.

   ▶ grind (*n.*): (informal) a student who works or studies excessively

   ▶ stuck (*adj.*): unable to move or to be moved

   eg. 1) The wheels were stuck in the mud.

      2) She got the key stuck in the lock.

3. How, then, do we account for Domenica or Paul?

   ▶ to account for: to explain or to give reasons for

   eg. 1) The heat wave accounts for the food spoilage.

      2) Icy roads account for the increase in accidents.

4. For two years she has maintained a 4.0 grade-point average (GPA), meaning A's in every subject.

   ▶ maintain (*v.*): to continue to have

   eg. 1) The army has been brought in to maintain order in the region.

      2) Despite living in different countries, the two families have maintained close links.

3) The film has maintained its position as the critics' favorite for another year.

5. Paul, now a freshman at the University of New Mexico, was <u>student-body</u> president at Valley High School.

     英语中的复合名词出现频率较高，多数情况下，朗读复合名词时应该是重音在先。在这里，编者特别提醒指导教师留心学生对复合名词的重音处理。比如，student-body 应该读成 'student ˌbody，而不是 student 'body。课文中还有一些类似的例子，虽不都属于复合名词，但也是由名词和名词叠加在一起使用，如：tennis team, student council, mathematics society, television station, bonus points, college athletes, biology terms, medicine cabinet, exam time, text assignment。

6. He played varsity soccer and junior-varsity basketball... and did student <u>commentaries</u> on a local television station.

    ► commentary (*n.*): critical explanation or analysis

    eg. 1) The commentary on the Olympic Games was much better on the other channel.

        2) There's a good arts coverage in the newspaper, but not much political commentary.

7. <u>Valedictorian</u> of his class, he achieved a GPA of 4.4...

    ► valedictorian (*n.*): the student with the best grades who delivers the valedictory at graduation

    ▲ valediction (*n.*): a speech or statement made as a farewell

8. Top grades don't always go to the brightest students...

Meaning: The brightest students don't always get the highest grades.

9. Knowing how to make the most of your <u>innate</u> abilities <u>counts</u> for more.

Meaning: Knowing how to make full use of the abilities that you are born with is more important.

    ► innate (*adj.*): possessed at birth

    eg. 1) Her most impressive quality was her innate goodness.

        2) It relies on the innate knowledge of right and wrong.

    ► count (*v.*): to have value or importance, to matter

    eg. 1) Their opinions count for little.

        2) First impressions always count.

10. Hard work isn't the whole story, either.

Meaning: Hard work is not the only secret of straigh-A students. There are other reasons for their success.

11. The kids at the top of the class get there by mastering a few basic techniques that others can readily learn.

▶ readily (*adv.*): quickly, effortlessly, without difficulty

eg. 1) I can readily believe that she is lazy at home—she is very lazy at school.

　　2) Wherever he goes, he readily accommodates to changed conditions.

12. Set priorities.

Meaning: Choose the most important thing to do first.

▶ priority (*n.*): status established in order of importance or urgency

eg. 1) The management did not seem to consider office safety to be a priority.

　　2) My top priority is to find somewhere to live.

13. Once the books are open or the computer is booted up, phone calls go unanswered, TV shows unwatched, snacks ignored.

Meaning: Once they open their books or they turn on the computer, they will not answer telephone calls or watch TV programs or eat light meals.

▶ boot (up) (*v.*): When a computer boots (up), it becomes ready for use by getting the necessary information into its memory; and when someone boots (up) a computer, he causes it to do this.

14. Claude Olney, ... assigned to tutor failing college athletes, recalls a cross-country runner who worked out every day.

▶ assign (*v.*): to give a particular job or piece of work to sb.

eg. 1) UN troops were assigned the task of rebuilding the hospital.

　　2) The case has been assigned to the senior officer.

▲ assignment (*n.*): a piece of work given to sb., typically as part of their studies or job

eg. 1) I have a lot of reading assignments to complete before the end of this term.

　　2) She is in Paris on an assignment for one of the Sunday newspapers.

▶ tutor (*v.*): to instruct or teach privately

eg. 1) Children are routinely tutored for hours after school.

　　2) He tutors students in mathematics.

▲ tutor (*n.*): a teacher who works with one student or a small group, either at a college or university or in the home of a child

eg. 1) His tutor encouraged him to read widely in philosophy.

　　2) At that time, I was taught by a series of home tutors.

▶ recall (*v.*): to bring the memory of a past event into one's mind, and often to give a description of what he remembers

eg. 1) I seem to recall that Barry was with us at the time.

2) She recalled seeing him outside the shop on the night of the robbery.

▶ work out: to do physical exercise

eg. 1) How often do you work out every week?

2) Tom works out in the gym two or three times a week.

15. Olney persuaded him to use the time to <u>memorize</u> biology terms.

A reminder: Chinese students tend to use "recite" to imply the meaning of "背下来" or "牢记", in fact, they are supposed to use the verb "memorize." "Recite" means "背诵, 朗诵等". Look at the following examples:

▶ memorize (*v.*): to learn sth. so that you will remember it exactly

eg. 1) When I was at school, we were required to memorize a poem every week.

2) He memorized the list of dates, but neglected the main facts corresponding to them.

16. Among the students we interviewed, study times were <u>strictly</u> a matter of personal preference.

Meaning: Among the students we interviewed, study times were exactly their personal things that they would like to arrange by themselves.

▶ strictly (*adv.*): in all details, exactly

eg. 1) They remained strictly loyal to the king.

2) This is not strictly true.

17. All agreed, however, on the need for <u>consistency</u>.

Meaning: However, all the students agreed that they should stick to their own way of learning all the time and should not change it often.

▶ consistency (*n.*): the quality of always being the same or always being good

eg. 1) They've won a few matches this season but they lack consistency.

2) It's important to show some consistency in your work.

▲ consistent (*adj.*): always behaving or happening in a similar, especially positive, way

eg. 1) There has been a consistent improvement in her attitude.

2) Her work is sometimes good, but the problem is she's not consistent.

18. Whatever I was doing, I maintained a <u>slot</u> every day for studying...

Meaning: Whatever I was doing, I always had a period of time set every day for studying.

▶ slot (*n.*): a time assigned on a schedule or agenda

eg. 1) The program will occupy that half-hour slot before the nine o'clock news.

2) He has a regular slot on the late-night program.

19. In high school, Ian ran track, played rugby and was in the <u>band and orchestra</u>.

 ▶ the difference between band and orchestra:

An orchestra（管弦乐队）is comprised of string instruments (violin, viola, cello, bass), woodwinds (flute, clarinet, etc.), brass (trumpets, trombone, etc.), and percussion (timpani, chimes, bells, etc). It may also include piano and harp. A band（乐队）is made up of woodwinds, brass, and percussion only.

20. I like to get it down on paper early, so I have time to <u>polish</u> and review.

 Meaning: I like to write it down on paper early so I have time to improve on it and go over it again.

 ▶ polish (v.): to bring to a highly developed, finished, or refined state

 eg. 1) In general, the revised text retains the ideas of the original version, but the style has been polished.

 2) You still need some time to polish your piano technique.

21. Still, if you want A's, you make sure to hit the deadline.

 Meaning: Again, I stress, if you want A's grade, you make sure to complete your work within the time limit.

22. Anderson uses those few minutes to write a two- or three-sentence summary of the lesson's principal points, which she <u>scans</u> before the next day's class.

 ▶ scan (v.): to look quickly

 eg. 1) He scanned the newspaper while eating breakfast.

 2) I scanned through the booklet but couldn't find the address.

23. In short, the parents <u>impressed</u> the lessons of responsibility on their kids, and the kids <u>delivered</u>.

 Meaning: In short, the parents taught their kids to be responsible for themselves and the kids just did what their parents had expected.

 ▶ impress (v.): to produce or attempt to produce a vivid impression or image of sth.

 eg. 1) Parents should impress the value of money on their children.

 2) The president was impressed by her sincerity.

 3) But she was impressed that the young king had come so far to find her.

 ▶ deliver (v.): to produce or achieve what is desired or expected

 eg. 1) He has promised to finish the job by June and I am sure he will deliver.

 2) I think we can count on her, because she always delivers on her promises.

Better Know More

〰 Writing Style of Text A

　　文章是写给读者的,作家针对不同的读者使用不同的语言。本单元的两篇文章主要针对在校学生,因此采用学生们日常交谈的口气娓娓道来,语言活泼生动,使人感到亲切,易于学生理解和接受。教师在讲授文章时要有意识地提醒学生注意这种非正式的语言风格。非正式文体的语言标记反映在语音、词汇、语法和语篇四个方面,教学中要注意寻找。

Check Your Understanding

Translate the following sentences into Chinese.   Please make sure that your language flows smoothly.

1. They're bad at sports and their face turns red when it comes to the opposite sex.
   他们不善于运动,而且一谈到异性就脸红。

2. How, then, do we account for Domenica or Paul?
   那么我们又如何解释多明尼卡和保罗呢?

3. Knowing how to make the most of your innate abilities counts for more.
   知道如何尽可能利用好与生俱来的才能更重要。

4. Indeed, some of these students actually put in fewer hours of homework time than their lower-scoring classmates.
   事实上,这些学生中有一些人做作业所花费的时间确实要比成绩较低的同学少。

5. Claude Olney, an Arizona State University business professor assigned to tutor failing college athletes, recalls a cross-country runner who worked out every day.
   亚利桑那州立大学商务专业教授克劳德·奥尼曾经被指派辅导一些成绩不及格的运动员学生,他回忆起一名每日进行户外训练的越野长跑运动员。

6. But when that happens, they face up to it.
   但是一旦那样的事情发生,他们会勇于面对。

Answer the following questions based on the text you have just learned.

1. What is the people's common impression of straight-A students?
   They get high grades but they are bookworms and become very dull.

2. What extra-curricula activities is Domenica engaged in?

Domenica is on the tennis team at Fairmont Senior High School.   She also sings in the chorus, serves on the student council and is a member of the mathematics society.

3. What are the secrets of straight-A students?

The first secret is to set priorities.   The second one is to study anywhere or everywhere.   The third one is to get organized.   Another one is to be an active reader when reading.   What's more, other secrets are to schedule your time and to take good notes and use them.

4. What is important for people with different preferences regarding study time?

It is important for people with different preferences to stick to their own way of study.

5. Why should students get organized?

It can help them save a lot of time.

6. What has Christy learned in speed-reading class? And what benefit did she receive?

Christy has learned to look at a book's table of contents, graphs and pictures first. By doing so,   Christ could have a sense of the material and store more information in the memory.

7. What does Gordon W. Green Jr. tell us in his book about the secret of good reading?

Gordon W. Green Jr. tells us the secret of good reading is to be an active reader. That is to continually ask questions that lead to a full understanding of the author's message.

8. What contributions have parents made to today's super-achievers?

They have helped their kids develop a love for learning at an early age and they set high standards and encouraged their kids to work hard by themselves to reach the standards.

9. Of all the secrets elaborated in this article, which one impresses you the most?

This is an open question.

A Sip of Phonetics

Know Their Faces

一、连音

连音现象在英语发音中非常普遍且十分重要。平时朗读或讲英语时很多学生抱怨自己读不快或说不快，或者读得和说得都不够味儿，其中一个重要原因是学生没有掌握连音规则。本课建议教师充分利用课上时间为学生讲解连音知识并指导学生进行练习。

二、失去爆破和不完全爆破

英语发音失去爆破和不完全爆破现象也十分普遍。在平时朗读课文或口语会话中，尤其应该注意。教师应提醒学生当爆破音与其后面的某些音相邻时,爆破音往往失去爆破或不完全爆破。请教师指导学生练习朗读下面的段落,并注意划线部分爆破音的发音。

We got off the train at the same station, she said goodbye and disappeared. I was kicking myself for not getting her telephone number. But then, thank goodness, she came back and said she had to wait on the same platform for her next train. We carried on talking, but when her train arrived, I realized I still didn't have her number. This was my last chance. I pushed a pen at her and she scribbled her number on a piece of paper just as the train pulled out. A year later we got married. It's the only thing in my life I've ever felt absolutely certain about. I've never wanted to marry anyone else.

Train Your Tongue

During the school holidays my teenage son spends most of (h)is mornings asleep in bed. I think (h)e is unbelievably lazy, but (h)e says it's based on an American theory that people should wake up when their own body clock tells them to and should not be woken up by alarm clocks or people shouting at them. He reacts angrily if anyone goes near (h)is bedroom. What can I do?

You'd Like to Be

A Strong Bridge Builder

Fill in the blanks with the given words to complete the following sentences. Please note that some can be used more than once.

between	by	up	out	in	about
down	for	to	of	on	

1. I found out the phone number by looking it up in the directory. In case I forget it soon, I put it down on paper.

2. When it comes to poverty, it is still a big problem in the 21st century. Just think about the hungry children who are in need of food. The world governments should take responsible actions to narrow down the gap between the rich and the poor and provide opportunities for all children to receive good education.

3. Modern technologies contribute to the improvement of productivity but they also account for the increase of today's unemployment rate. Mass production is the result of the

industrial revolution, when machines were invented to do the production processes originally completed <u>by</u> hand. Due <u>to</u> mass production, companies have cut <u>down</u> their unit cost. The main disadvantage of mass production is the lack <u>of</u> product uniqueness.

A Smart Word Player

Fill in the blanks with the proper words that need to be transformed from the ones provided in the brackets.

It is recommended that the <u>assignment</u> (assign) handed in should be <u>accompanied</u> (accompany) by a signed <u>declaration</u> (declare). It must be <u>organized</u> (organize) in a way which should include information of <u>tutorial</u> (tutor) guidance, <u>frequency</u> (frequent) of your <u>athletic</u> (athlete) training and records of your <u>prior</u> (priority) sports injures.

A Skilled Text Weaver

Fill in the blanks with the words you have learned in this text. One word is for each blank. Here is a piece of advice: You must be really familiar with the text to accomplish the following tasks.

There is a common assumption towards those who get the highest grades in school. People say they get high grades but they become dull <u>grinds</u>. They are boring and not fashionable. Sometimes people even call them <u>nerds</u>. They are not good at sports because they seldom <u>work</u> <u>out</u>. They are not popular among other students. They always feel shy and embarrassed, <u>when</u> <u>it</u> <u>comes</u> to the opposite sex.

However, the assumption is not always true. This text introduces to us many straight-A students who are active members of their school. How can we <u>account</u> <u>for</u> their success? Brains aren't the only answer. Top grades don't always <u>go</u> <u>to</u> the brightest students. To further develop one's <u>innate</u> potentials <u>counts</u> for more.

According to the straight-A students, secrets of their study include <u>setting</u> <u>priorities</u>, <u>studying</u> <u>anywhere</u> or everywhere, getting <u>organized</u> and so on. For these super-achievers, their own efforts are not the whole story. All of them also owe their success <u>to</u> the contribution of their <u>parents</u>.

A Sharp Interpreter

Please paraphrase the following sentences. Change the sentence structure if necessary.

1. They get high grades, all right, but only by becoming dull grinds.

   ✤ *Paraphrasing:*

   OK, it is true that they get high grades, but they get them only by studying all the time and becoming dull.

2. Top grades don't always go to the brightest students.

   ✤ *Paraphrasing:*

   The brightest students don't always get the highest grades.

3. Hard work isn't the whole story, either.

   ✤ *Paraphrasing:*

   Hard work is not the only secret of straight-A students. There are other reasons for their success.

4. Once the books are open or the computer is booted up, phone calls go unanswered, TV shows unwatched, snacks ignored.

   ✤ *Paraphrasing:*

   Once they open their books or they turn on the computer, they will not answer telephone calls or watch TV programs or eat light meals.

5. All agreed, however, on the need for consistency.

   ✤ *Paraphrasing:*

   However, all the students agreed that they should stick to their own way of learning all the time and should not change it often.

6. Whatever I was doing, I maintained a slot every day for studying.

   ✤ *Paraphrasing:*

   Whatever I was doing, I always had a period of time set every day for studying.

7. In short, the parents impressed the lessons of responsibility on their kids, and the kids delivered.

   ✤ *Paraphrasing:*

   In short, the parents taught their kids to be responsible for themselves and the kids just did what their parents had expected.

A Solid Sentence Constructer

Please make a sentence with each word or expression listed below.

1. when it comes to ...
   ⊕ *Original sentence in the text:*
   > *They're bad at sports and their face turns red when it comes to the opposite sex.*

   ⊕ **Suggested sentence:**
   > My grandpa is crazy about gardening. When it comes to it, I am all ears.

2. to account for
   ⊕ *Original sentence in the text:*
   > *How, then, do we account for Domenica or Paul?*

   ⊕ **Suggested sentence:**
   > Icy roads account for the increase in accidents.

3. to make the most of
   ⊕ *Original sentence in the text:*
   > *Knowing how to make the most of your innate abilities counts for more.*

   ⊕ **Suggested sentence:**
   > They should make the most of the library resource to study.

4. to put in
   ⊕ *Original sentence in the text:*
   > *Indeed, some of these students actually put in fewer hours of homework time than their lower-scoring classmates.*

   ⊕ **Suggested sentence:**
   > I should put in all my efforts to achieve this goal.

5. to work out
   ⊕ *Original sentence in the text:*
   > *Claude Olney, an Arizona State University business professor assigned to tutor failing college athletes, recalls a cross-country runner who worked out every day.*

   ⊕ **Suggested sentence:**
   > How often do you work out every week?

6. to face up to
   ⊕ *Original sentence in the text:*
   > *But when that happens, they face up to it.*

   ⊕ **Suggested sentence:**
   > Some people say we should face up to the economic crisis.

A Superb Bilingualist

Please translate the following sentences into English with the prompts provided in the brackets.

1. 你应该学会充分利用好你的时间，因为每一秒钟都很重要。(make the most of, count)

   ✧ *Suggested translation:*

   You should learn to make the most of your time, because every second counts.

2. 如果你想保持健康，你就应该每周花一些时间做运动。(put in, work out)

   ✧ *Suggested translation:*

   If you want to stay healthy, you should put in some time every week to work out.

3. 你怎么解释这接二连三的事故呢？(account for)

   ✧ *Suggested translation:*

   How do you account for the accidents one after another?

4. 只要一谈到烹饪，他就一无所知了，因为他天生对做饭没兴趣。(when it comes to, in-nate)

   ✧ *Suggested translation:*

   When it comes to cooking, he is quite ignorant because he doesn't have the innate interest in it.

5. 在互联网上，信息能在数秒钟内轻而易举地传遍全世界，真是势不可挡。(readily, overwhelming)

   ✧ *Suggested translation:*

   Within seconds, information spreads readily on the Internet to every corner of the world, which is overwhelming.

Text B

Introduction to "Twisted Sister"

Twisted Sister is an American heavy metal band from New York City. Many of the band's songs explore themes of parent vs. child conflicts and criticisms of the educational system. Twisted Sister created brash, simple songs that buzzed with subversive energy, giving the band the appeal of bad-boy cartoon characters.

"We're Not Gonna Take It" is a 1984 hit song by the band Twisted Sister from their album *Stay Hungry*. The song was written by vocalist Dee Snider. The song was first released as a single on April 27, 1984. The *Stay Hungry* album was released 2 weeks later, on May 10, 1984. The single made No. 21 on the Billboard Hot 100 singles chart, and the song ranked

No. 47 on VH1's (Video Hits One, an American cable television channel) 100 Greatest 80's Songs.

Lyrics—"We're Not Gonna Take It" in Text B

Oh We're Not Gonna Take It
no, We Ain't Gonna Take It
oh We're Not Gonna Take It Anymore

we've Got The Right To Choose And
there Ain't No Way We'll Lose It
this Is Our Life, This Is Our Song
we'll Fight The Powers That Be Just
don't Pick Our Destiny 'cause
you Don't Know Us, You Don't Belong

oh You're So Condescending
your Gall Is Never Ending
we Don't Want Nothin', Not A Thing From You
your Life Is Trite And Jaded
boring And Confiscated
if That's Your Best, Your Best Won't Do

oh...
oh...
we're Right/yeah
we're Free/yeah
we'll Fight/yeah
you'll See/yeah

oh We're Not Gonna Take It
no, We Ain't Gonna Take It
oh We're Not Gonna Take It Anymore
no Way!

just You Try And Make Us
we're Not Gonna Take It
come On

no, We Ain't Gonna Take It

you're All Worthless And Weak

we're Not Gonna Take It Anymore

now Drop And Give Me Twenty

we're Not Gonna Take It

oh Crinch Pin

no, We Ain't Gonna Take It

oh You And Your Uniform

we're Not Gonna Take It Anymore

Writing Practice

You are now working toward writing a summary for Text B. You may follow the guidelines to write the summary:

I. Read through the entire text to get an understanding of the whole piece, and annotate by underlining the sentences containing the major points as you read.

II. Locate the thesis statement. While it may appear early in the essay—the first paragraph or two, it may not, in fact, be stated until the end of the piece, almost as if it were a conclusion.

Academic cheating is epidemic in the country's high schools and colleges.

(Please write down the thesis statement on the above line.)

III. Discuss the article. Re-read the underlined parts, dividing it into sections based on the topics addressed. Each section may be one paragraph, but, more likely, it includes several paragraphs. Now you need to decide how many sections Text B contains.

Text B includes 2 3 4 5 ... sections. (Please circle the number as you need.)

IV. Write a summary. First, write a sentence or two to summarize each section; then synthesize them into a coherent and cohesive passage. You may need a careful proofreading and revision before the final completion.

1. *(Paragraph 1—6)Academic cheating is epidemic in the country's high schools and colleges.*

2. *(Paragraph 7) Cheating nowadays has become widespread and obvious. People who once cheated were in the minority and they kept it a secret. Now they are the majority and they are bold about it.*

3. *(Paragraph 8—10)First, advances in technology have made cheating easier. Second, bad behaviors across society make things worse. Third, the pressure to succeed that drives some to cheat starts early.*

4. *(Paragraph 11—14) Schools now have taken measures to prevent students from cheating. It is encouraging that some kids are acting against cheaters.*

Summary:

A Kansas State University Junior was caught and suspended for using online technology to give himself passing scores for the tests he had not taken. Similar examples show that academic cheating is epidemic in the country's high schools and colleges. A report by Rutgers University professor Donald McCabe showed 70 percent of students at 60 colleges admitted to some cheating within the previous year; one in four admitted to engaging in serious cheating. McCabe's high school findings were similarly severe. A recent Gallup survey reinforced those findings. Cheating isn't new, but what is alarming is that today the majority rather than the minority cheat and people are not ashamed of it. As to the reasons of their cheating, on the one hand advances in technology have made cheating easier, and on the other hand bad examples across society influence the students. Their goal is to succeed and the pressure to succeed drives them to cheat or do whatever they can at all costs. This pressure drives them to cheat even earlier today. As a response, some schools have banned cell phones, cameras or other gadgets during school hours. Honor codes have been reinvigorated. Teachers are now using technology to fight against cheating and even some kids are taking a series of actions against cheaters such as establishing an honor council and using video clips to discuss the importance of honor.

15

Oxford University

Unit Goals

After studying this unit, students should be able to:

☞ **understand the history and the development of Oxford University;**

Text A reveals to us the origin, early development and the glory acclaimed of the gorgeous University of Oxford. Other than that, students will also learn about the two outstanding educational systems that set the university apart from others, namely the collegiate system and the tutorial system. Students' hand-on activities such as visiting the official web sites for further information on the University of Oxford, or the University of Cambridge, are strongly encouraged.

☞ **know about the stress in English pronunciation, and how to use the words and structures that contribute significantly to the texts;**

In teaching **A Sip of Phonetics** the instructor should explain to the students the importance of the stress in English pronunciation. It is especially important to have the students informed that many pronunciation mistakes are actually errors on stress. Upon locating a student's incorrect pronunciation, the instructor should not correct these mistakes, rather, model the correct pronunciation. It is strongly suggested that the instructor encourage students to read aloud the text before and after class.

Most useful words and structures of **Text A** can be found in **You'd like to Be**. This is where students practice what they have learned from **Text A**.

☞ **understand about the university ideas and the concept of the Wisconsin idea.**

University students should know about the concept of the university idea. And this is why **Text B** has been integrated into this textbook. Background information can be found in the notes to **Text B** in this teacher's book.

Before Reading

Hands-on Activities and Brainstorming

The instructor should allow 15—20 minutes for students to do presentation on the University of Oxford or its alumni.

A Glimpse at Words and Expressions

A. "Spires" are pointed structures on top of a building. A picture of spires might also be helpful. Of course, that requires better teaching facilities.

B. Another example of "boost" is: The war against Iraq in early 1990s gave a boost to the weakening economy, but did not secure the re-election of the president.

C. It might be helpful to tell the students that in old days, scholars and students wore gowns, the attire that distinguished them from the local townsmen.

D. Here is another example of "hastened": The poor treatment she received may, in fact, hastened her death.

E. The instructor may want to try setting another example of "fosters a sense of community": The new living style of apartment does not foster any sense of community. People living in the same building do not even know each other.

F. To help the students better understand the meaning of "be comprised of," the instructor may want to try the following sentences and even make a comparison between them.
The committee is comprised of two lawyers, two journalists and a teacher.
The committee consists of two lawyers, two journalists and a teacher.

G. "Consistently": continuously. Here is an example: Her work has been of a consistently high standard.

Keys

A-4   B-2   C-7   D-6   E-1   F-3   G-5

Text A

Suggested Explanations on Text A

1. The students who attended either Oxford or Cambridge universities set an intellectual standard that <u>contrasted</u> strongly <u>with</u> the norm of Medieval England.

   <u>Meaning</u>: Both two universities have much different intellectual standards from what they were in Medieval England. The sentence implies that those two universities have become much more developed since they were founded in the Medieval period.

   Schools in the Medieval period were very small. Many had just one room for all the boys and one teacher who invariably had a religious background. The teacher would teach the older boys who were then responsible for teaching the younger ones. Lessons frequently started at sunrise and finished at sunset. This meant that in the spring/summer months, school could last for many hours. The opposite was true for the winter. Discipline was very strict. Mistakes in lessons were punished with the birch. In theory pupils would never make the same mistake again after being birched, as the memory of the pain inflicted was too strong. The sons of the peasants could only be educated if the lord of the manor had given his permission. Any family caught having a son educated without permission was heavily fined. Very few girls went to school. Girls from noble families were taught at home or went abroad to be educated. Regardless of where they went, the basis of their education was the same—how to keep a household going so that their husband was well kept.

   ▶ to contrast with: to show a clear difference when compared

   eg. 1) Her actions contrasted sharply with her words.

   　　2) Henry's research results contrasted greatly with those of his forefathers.

2. Today both universities are internationally <u>renowned</u> centers for teaching and research, attracting students and scholars from all over the world.

   ▶ renowned (*adj.*): famous and respected

   eg. 1) Professor Thompson's research is renowned across the globe and he and his team have emerged among the leading scholars studying global climate change.

   　　2) The photographer is renowned for capturing Alaska's rich landscapes in his work.

3. Oxford is situated about 57 miles <u>north-west</u> of London in its own county of Oxfordshire.

   ▶ north-west (西北)

   　　Although this may not be the first time for students to come across the expression of direction and location, it would be necessary for the instructor to reiterate that in English.

Unlike Chinese, western people determine direction in a reversed order. They say "north-west," "south-east," "north-east" and "south-west." Also, students should learn how to express locations.

eg. 1) The plant is situated 100 miles south-east of Detroit.

2) The resort is on the Orange County coast, about 14 miles southeast of Disneyland, and 50 miles southeast of Los Angeles.

4. The story of Oxford is <u>one of</u> war, plague, religious persecution, heroes and the emergence of one of the greatest universities in the world.

Meaning: The history of Oxford is the history filled with war, plague, religious persecution, heroes, but it also witnessed the rise of one of the greatest universities in the world.

▶ one of (formal): "one" is used here to avoid repetition. In this sentence, it indicates "the story." Students should learn to use this sentence structure in formal English.

eg. 1) The history of this bank is one of helping the poor and those who are badly in need.

2) The mission of this university is one of teaching, research and community service.

5. Known as the city of "Dreaming Spires," Oxford <u>is dominated by</u> the university's Medieval architecture and <u>exquisite</u> gardens.

▶ to be dominated by: to be the most important or noticeable feature of sth.

eg. 1) His hometown is more of a small town than a village, which is dominated by a ruined castle, recently taken over by the National Heritage Committee.

2) The garden is dominated by the landscape, especially by the view of Loch Ness.

▲ to be dominated by: to be controlled or strongly influenced

eg. 1) The early years of Australian press were dominated by censorship laws and controlled by British government agencies.

2) Technology is dominated by two types of people: those who understand what they do not manage, and those who manage what they do not understand.

▶ exquisite (*adj.*): extremely beautiful and carefully designed

eg. 1) Dora was impressed by the exquisite art of wood-carving.

2) In this city you can admire the exquisite architecture—if you want—spend a night there.

6. According to legend, Oxford University was founded by <u>King Alfred</u> the Great in 872 when he happened to meet some monks there and had a scholarly debate that lasted several days.

King Alfred (849—899) was king of the southern Anglo-Saxon kingdom of Wessex from 871 to 899. Alfred is noted for his defense of the kingdom against the Danish Vikings (维京人——丹麦·海盗), becoming the only English King to be awarded the epithet (称号)

"the Great." A learned man, Alfred encouraged education and improved the kingdom's law system.

7. Long after Alfred, during the late 11th or early 12th century, it is known that Oxford became a centre of learning for clerics, <u>from</u> which a school or university could have <u>sprung</u>.

Meaning: Many years later, during the late 11th or early 12th century, Oxford first became a centre of learning for churchmen, and then developed into an academic institution.

▶ to spring from: to start from

eg. 1) Did life originally spring from clay?

2) Many educational innovations spring from action research.

8. Instead, the university <u>consists of</u> a large number of colleges and associated buildings, scattered throughout the city.

▶ to consist of: to be composed of or made up of

eg. 1) The Family Health Service consists of Maternal, Child Health Service and Woman Health Service.

2) The School consists of three departments: Economics, Accounting & Finance, and Management.

The instructor should make sure that students be able to discern the difference in form between "consist of," "be composed of" and "be comprised of." The three phrases actually express the similar idea, but "consist of " is in active voice, while both "be composed of" and "be comprised of" are in passive voice.

▲ to be composed of : to be formed by

eg. 1) Forever is composed of nows.

2) The editorial board is composed of seven professors from renowned universities.

▲ to be comprised of : to be made up of

eg. 1) The Student Union is comprised of 30 full-time undergraduate students.

2) This collection is comprised of 500 photographs taken during World War II by an American serviceman, Mr. Hensley.

9. However it was a strain on the resources of the community to have to <u>provide for</u> the large number of people from elsewhere.

Meaning: It was very hard for the local people to provide for the large number of students with the already limited resources.

▶ to provide for: to accommodate or to give sb. the things that they need to live by, such as food, money and clothing eg. 1) The objective of the organization is to provide for the aged that are in need.

   2) We need to ensure that they have the same opportunities to pursue their dreams', provide for their families, and live lives of dignity and self-reliance.

10. ...three students were at once executed by the citizens, in revenge for the woman's death.

   ▶ in revenge for: in return for

   eg. 1) Saddam was executed in revenge for the Shiites he killed.

   2) Some scientists warn that elephants might be attacking humans in revenge for years of abuse.

11. It is now widely agreed that these scholars from Oxford started Cambridge's life as a university in 1209.

   Meaning: People now tend to agree that Cambridge was not a university until those scholars from Oxford moved there in 1209.

12. Rioting in the 13th century between students and local people hastened the establishment of primary halls of residence.

   Meaning: It was the conflict between students and local people in the 13th century that accelerated the building of the earliest student halls.

   ▶ hasten (*v.*): to urge or accelerate

   eg. 1) Corruption hastened Rome's downfall.

   2) Malnutrition hastened the death of the baby panda.

   ▲ hastened death: the process by which a person speeds up the dying willfully

   eg. 1) In most cultures, hastened death remains illegal.

   2) Researchers find that desire for hastened death is not significantly associated with pain intensity.

13. What set Oxford (and Cambridge) apart from most other universities is the collegiate system and the tutorial system.

   Meaning: The collegiate system and the tutorial system are two unique features that make Oxford and Cambridge outstanding among the universities.

   ▶ to set... apart from: to make noticeable or outstanding

   eg. 1) By providing the students with more individualized attention, Brown High School sets itself apart from his competitors in student retention.

   2) What sets his novel apart from the others is the language style.

   ▲ to set...apart: to reserve to a particular use

   eg. 1) The government set apart 10,000 acres of land for military purpose.

   2) These rooms were set apart for use as libraries.

14. The collegiate system <u>fosters</u> a sense of community between tutors and students, and among students themselves.

► foster (*v.*): to promote the growth or development of

eg. 1) Educational technology fosters professor-student dialogue.

    2) For 10 years, Debbie and her family fostered 15 children of all ages.

15. Most students find their tutors understanding and approachable, and the ones who will encourage them to work hard and achieve their best by stimulating their interest rather than by coercion.

Meaning: Most tutors are understanding and easy-going, who will positively encourage the students to learn as much as possible by fostering their interests instead of forcing them to learn.

16. Oxford's teaching and research is <u>consistently</u> in the top rank nationally and internationally, and is at the <u>forefront</u> of medical, scientific and technological achievement.

Meaning: Oxford's teaching and research has been continuously on top of the field home and abroad, holding the leading position in medicine, science and technology.

► consistently (*adv.*): with a steady continuity, continuously

eg. 1) China has consistently opposed the weaponization of outer space.

    2) He has been consistently inconsistent.

► forefront (*n.*): in the position at the front

eg. 1) Black women particularly stood out in the forefront as social workers, nurses, doctors, and volunteers.

    2) This hospital has been at the forefront of AIDS research.

Better Know More

The History of the University of Oxford

There is no clear date of the foundation of the University of Oxford, but teaching existed at Oxford in some form in 1096 and developed rapidly from 1167, when Henry II banned English students from attending the University of Paris.

In 1188, the historian, Gerald of Wales, gave a public reading to the assembled Oxford dons (牛津或剑桥的讲师) and in 1190 the arrival of Emo of Friesland (荷兰弗里斯兰省), the first known overseas student, started the university's tradition of international scholarly links. In 1201, the university was headed by a magister scolarum Oxonie (牛津学长), on whom the title of Chancellor was conferred in 1214, and in 1231 the group of masters (老师宿儒) were recognized as a universitas (拉丁文中的大学).

In the 13th century, rioting between town and gown hastened the establishment of primitive halls of residence. These were succeeded by the first of Oxford's colleges. Less than a century later, Oxford had achieved eminence in learning, and won the praises of popes, kings and sages by virtue of its antiquity, curriculum, doctrine and privileges. In 1355, Edward III paid tribute to the university for its invaluable contribution to learning; he also commented on the services rendered to the state by distinguished Oxford graduates.

The university assumed a leading role in the Victorian era, especially in religious controversy. From 1833 onwards The Oxford Movement sought to revitalize the Catholic aspects of the Anglican Church. One of its leaders, John Henry Newman, became a Roman Catholic in 1845 and was later made a Cardinal.

From 1878, academic halls were established for women, who became members of the university in 1920. Since 1974, all but one of Oxford's 39 colleges have changed their statutes to admit both men and women. St Hilda's remains the only women's college.

During the 20th century, Oxford added to its humanistic core a major new research capacity in the natural and applied sciences, including medicine. In so doing, it has enhanced and strengthened its traditional role as an international focus for learning and a forum for intellectual debate.

Check Your Understanding

Translate the following sentences into Chinese. Please make sure that your language flows smoothly.

1. Instead, the university consists of a large number of colleges and associated buildings, scattered throughout the city.

   相反,(牛津)大学是由散布在市内的很多个学院和学院的楼宇组成的。

2. It is now widely agreed that these scholars from Oxford started Cambridge's life as a university in 1209.

   人们现在公认正是这些来自牛津的学者在 1209 年开创了剑桥大学的历史。

3. In 1209, a woman was accidentally killed by one of the gownsmen; three students were at once executed by the citizens, in revenge for the woman's death.

   1209 年,一位妇女被学生意外致死,市民立即处死三名学生,以此进行报复。

4. In protest at the hanging, the University of Oxford went into voluntary suspension, and scholars moved to a number of other locations, including the pre-existing school at Cam-

bridge, which is situated about 50 miles north of London.

为抗议绞死学生，牛津大学自行关闭校园，学者们纷纷迁移到其他地方，其中包括一个在伦敦以北 50 英里处早先成立的学部，那便是剑桥。

5. Most students took lodgings with local people, who soon realized that they could charge them higher than average rent.

（开始的时候）大多数学生在居民家中食宿，这些居民很快就认识到（原来）他们可以向学生收取比常价更高的房费。

6. The students who attended either Oxford or Cambridge universities set an intellectual standard that contrasted strongly with the norm of Medieval England.

牛津及剑桥学子创立了与中世纪的准则大相径庭的学术标准。

7. Today Oxford University is comprised of thirty-nine colleges and six permanent private halls, founded between 1249 and 1996, whose architectural grandeur, together with that of the university's libraries and museums, gives the city its unique character.

牛津大学在 1249 年至 1996 年间，共设立了 39 个学院和 6 个永久私立书院。这些学院以及大学图书馆和博物馆的庄严建筑赋予这座城市一种独特的风格。

Answer the following questions based on the text you have just learned.

1. Where is the University of Oxford located?

The University of Oxford is located in the city of Oxford, which is situated about 57 miles north-west of London in its own county of Oxfordshire.

2. According to legend, who was the founder of the University of Oxford?

According to legend, Oxford University was founded by King Alfred the Great in 872 when he happened to meet some monks there and had a scholarly debate that lasted several days. A more realistic version is that it grew out of efforts begun by Alfred to encourage education and establish schools throughout his territory.

3. In what situation in the 12th century was the University of Oxford given a boost?

The university was given a boost in 1167 when, for political reasons, Henry II of England ordered all English students at Paris to return to England.

4. What are the ties between the University of Oxford and the University of Cambridge?

Because of the friction between "town and gown," scholars moved to a number of other locations, including the pre-existing school at Cambridge, which is situated about 50 miles north of London. It is now widely agreed that these scholars from Oxford started Cambridge's life as a university in 1209.

5. What makes the University of Oxford stand out from other universities? Can you define more clearly what they are?

What set Oxford (and Cambridge) apart from most other universities is the collegiate system and the tutorial system. According to the collegiate system, each college is an organized corporation under its own head,　and enjoying the fullest powers of managing its own property and governing its own members.　All colleges and halls have the same privileges as to receiving undergraduate members,　and no one can be admitted into Oxford University by the central authority, until he has been accepted by one of the colleges.

The collegiate system fosters a sense of community between tutors and students, and among students themselves. The colleges provide a certain number of rooms within their own walls for students,　the remainder living in the city.　Meals are served either in the college halls or in the students' rooms; and attached to every college is a chapel where daily service is held during the term according to the forms of the Church of England.

6. Toward the end of this article, the author provides a long list of elites who once studied at the University of Oxford. Can you figure out who's who?

John Locke:	*British philosopher of the 17th century.*
Adam Smith:	*Scottish political economist and philosopher of the 18th century.*
Percy Bysshe Shelley:	*British poet of the 18th century.*
Lewis Carroll:	*Pseudonym of Charles Lutwidge Dodgson English, the author of Alice's Adventures in Wonderland.*
Oscar Wilde:	*Irish writer of the 19th century.*
Indira Gandhi:	*Prime minister of India from 1966–77 and 1980–84.*
Baroness Margaret Thatcher:	*Prime minister of the United Kingdom from 1979 to 1990.*
Rupert Murdoch:	*CEO of news corporation—Media & Entertainment Company.*
Rowan Atkinson (Mr. Bean):	*Contemporary British comedian.*
Hugh Grant:	*Contemporary British actor.*

7. Which part of the University of Oxford impresses you most? Can you state why?

This is an open question.

8. With which of the following views do you agree more strongly? And why?

A) Quality universities make quality students.

B) Quality students make quality universities.

This is an open question.

A Sip of Phonetics

在学习英语的过程中,我们注意到人们常说某人的音调很准确,或是某人发音不准确;而当人们鉴定学习者英语发音准与不准的时候,常把精力集中在音素朗读以及连读的准确性上,却往往忽略了重音。其实,在英语学习者所犯的朗读错误中有相当一部分是重音错误,英语学习者必须了解、熟悉英语语音中的重音规律,才能做到准确发音。

下面列举一些学习者在朗读过程中常犯的重音错误,供教师参考:

ˌuniˈversity	⟶	univerˈsity
ˈhospital	⟶	hosˈpital
ˈpermanent	⟶	perˈmanent
comˈmunity	⟶	commuˈnity
ˈChrist Church	⟶	ChristˈChurch
ˈPowerPoint	⟶	PowerˈPoint
ˈe-ˈmail	⟶	e-ˈmail
ˈreadingˌroom	⟶	reading-ˈroom
ˈshoppingˌcenter	⟶	ˈshopping-ˈcenter
ˈbookstore	⟶	bookˈstore
ˈblackboard	⟶	blackˈboard

You'd Like to Be

A Strong Bridge Builder

Fill in the blanks with the given words to complete the following sentences.   Please note that some can be used more than once.

against	under	for	on	in	of	between
throughout	without	over	by	to	into	from

Pierre was born <u>into</u> a poor family north-west <u>of</u> Leon in 1920,   and grew up there until he was 16. In his memory, his childhood was one <u>of</u> poverty and hardships. He had to work really hard in a sawmill helping his parents to provide <u>for</u> his four siblings (弟妹).   He was yearning to go to school; however, there was not one <u>in/throughout</u> Paris that was affordable. He ended up having to teach himself.

By the time his family was able to save a little money,   he begged his father to send him <u>to</u> school, but his father was strongly <u>against</u> the idea, as he was planning to buy a small farm, which he thought would lead the family <u>to</u> a much better life.   It was quite a strain <u>on</u> the limited amount of money for the poor family to do both things.

Then the friction <u>between</u> father and son developed.   To force Pierre to give up the hope of going to school, the father threw all his books into a fire. <u>In</u> revenge <u>for</u> his father's brutality, Pierre left home <u>without</u> a word and swore that he would never go back home again. He went to Paris, which differed <u>from</u> Leon <u>in</u> many respects, especially education. Students <u>from</u> all <u>over</u> the world were doing "work study" in schools and universities, which was exactly what Pierre was <u>in</u> need <u>of</u>.   He was soon admitted <u>into/to</u> the University of Paris and studied Creative Writing. Being away <u>from</u> home <u>for</u> months, his hate for his father began to dissolve (消解), and he even thought <u>of</u> taking a short break <u>for</u> a family visit. Unfortunately, his excitement for a family reunion was soon succeeded <u>by</u> the deep sorrow <u>for</u> the death of his father, who died the next day after he left <u>for</u> Paris.

A Smart Word Player

Fill in the blanks with the proper words that need to be transformed from the ones provided in the brackets.

In the 14th century, Confucianism became the <u>dominant</u> (dominate) influence on Korean thought, morals, and aesthetic (审美的, 美学的)standards. Unlike Buddhism, Confucianism is not attached with a <u>legendary</u> (legend) savior, and therefore is more accepted as a life philosophy than a religion. Korean culture is also strongly influenced by Taoism, developing a close <u>association</u> (associate) with Chinese culture. In many people's eyes, the three <u>contrasting</u> (contrast) ideologies produce different faces: Confucius is described as a <u>scholastic</u> (scholar) sour-faced man, Buddha as one with a bitter expression, but Lao-Tse being the smiling one. And that might explain why people sometimes have a feel that all the three types of expressions may <u>emerge</u> (emergence) from a Korean face at the same time.

A Skilled Text Weaver

Fill in the blanks with the words you have learned in this text.   One word is for each blank. Here is a piece of advice: You must be really familiar with the text to accomplish the following tasks.

1. This conference attracts a large number of <u>renowned</u> scholars, who are closely <u>associated</u> with highly <u>respected</u> research institutions.
2. The resort is known for its unique architectural <u>grandeur</u> with <u>exquisite</u> woodcarvings, and provides high-class accommodation, dining, business and recreational facilities.
3. The <u>collegiate/tutorial</u> system fosters an atmosphere where <u>scholars</u> and students talk across academic boundaries, and helps support small group teaching by academics who are

leaders in their fields, so that students are educated "up to and beyond the frontiers of knowledge."

4. At the end of <u>seminar</u>, students will be required to share their experience in conducting research and submit a research <u>paper</u> for final grade.

5. In <u>contrast</u> to the past, she argued, such <u>persecution</u> is now against the law.

A Sharp Interpreter

Please paraphrase the following sentences. Change the sentence structure if necessary.

1. The story of Oxford is one of war, plague, religious persecution, heroes and the emergence of one of the greatest universities in the world.
   ✧ *Paraphrasing:*
   The history of Oxford is the history filled with war, plague, religious persecution, heroes, but it also witnesses the rise of one of the greatest universities in the world.

2. However, it was a strain on the resources of the community to have to provide for the large number of people from elsewhere.
   ✧ *Paraphrasing:*
   It was very hard for the local people to accommodate the large number of students with the already limited resources.

3. From the start there was friction between "town and gown."
   ✧ *Paraphrasing:*
   From the beginning of the history of Oxford, there were a lot of conflicts between the students or scholars and the local people.

4. What set Oxford (and Cambridge) apart from most other universities is the collegiate system and the tutorial system.
   ✧ *Paraphrasing:*
   The collegiate system and the tutorial system are two unique features that make Oxford and Cambridge outstanding among the universities.

5. Most students find their tutors understanding and approachable, and the ones who will encourage them to work hard and achieve their best by stimulating their interest rather than by coercion.
   ✧ *Paraphrasing:*
   Most tutors are understanding and easy-going, who will positively encourage the students to learn as much as possible by fostering their interests instead of forcing them to learn.

6. Oxford's teaching and research is consistently in the top rank nationally and internationally, and is at the forefront of medical, scientific and technological achievement.

⊕ *Paraphrasing:*

Oxford's teaching and research has been continuously on top of the field home and abroad, and is in the top rank nationally and internationally, and is holding the leading position in medicine, science and technology.

7. The colleges provide a certain number of rooms within their own walls for students, with the remainder living in the city.

⊕ *Paraphrasing:*

Only part of the students live in college buildings, with the rest living in the city.

A Solid Sentence Constructer

Please make a sentence with each word or expression listed below.

1. to contrast with

   ⊕ *Original sentence in the text:*

   The students who attended either Oxford or Cambridge universities set an intellectual standard that contrasted strongly with the norm of Medieval England.

   ⊕ **Suggested sentence:**

   Weddings in the North China contrasted with those in the South.

2. to consist of

   ⊕ *Original sentence in the text:*

   Instead, the university consists of a large number of colleges and associated buildings, scattered throughout the city.

   ⊕ **Suggested sentence:**

   The whole server (服务器)system consists of four servers, web server, mail server, file server and streaming server.

3. to take lodgings with

   ⊕ *Original sentence in the text:*

   Most students took lodgings with local people, who soon realized that they could charge higher than average rent.

   ⊕ **Suggested sentence:**

   He took lodgings with an old couple. This is all we know about his life in Paris.

4. in revenge for

   ⊕ *Original sentence in the text:*

   In 1209, a woman was accidentally killed by one of the gownsmen; three students were at once executed by the citizens, in revenge for the woman's death.

❖ **Suggested sentence:**

No one would believe that the man was murdered in revenge for the crime that he committed twenty years ago.

5. in protest at

❖ *Original sentence in the text:*

In protest at the hanging, the University of Oxford went into voluntary suspension, and scholars moved to a number of other locations, including the pre-existing school at Cambridge, which is situated about 50 miles north of London.

❖ **Suggested sentence:**

Elsewhere in Europe on Saturday, thousands took to the streets of Rome and Madrid in protest at the war.

6. to be widely agreed that

❖ *Original sentence in the text:*

It is now widely agreed that these scholars from Oxford started Cambridge's life as a university in 1209.

❖ **Suggested sentence:**

It is widely agreed that they are among the most prestigious and selective universities.

7. to set apart from

❖ *Original sentence in the text:*

What set Oxford (and Cambridge) apart from most other universities is the collegiate system and the tutorial system.

❖ **Suggested sentence:**

The South's cozy climate has always set it apart from the rest of the nation.

8. to be comprised of

❖ *Original sentence in the text:*

Today Oxford University is comprised of thirty-nine colleges and six permanent private halls...

❖ **Suggested sentence:**

Changshu is comprised of 12 towns, 2 provincial economy and technology development districts, and as a famous city of history and culture, it is known for its long history of humanity, beautiful scenery and prosperity.

9. to give... the unique character

❖ *Original sentence in the text:*

... founded between 1249 and 1996, whose architectural grandeur, together with that of the university's libraries and museums, gives the city its unique character.

❖ **Suggested sentence:**

Buddha worshipping gives the neighborhood its unique character in this Catholic country.

10. to be at the forefront of

⚙ *Original sentence in the text:*

Oxford's teaching and research is consistently in the top rank nationally and internationally, and is at the forefront of medical, scientific and technological achievement.

⚙ **Suggested sentence:**

For decades, Sweden has been at the forefront of electric power technologies.

〰 A Superb Bilingualist

Please translate the following sentences into English with the prompts provided in the brackets.

1. 天津位于北京东南 120 公里处。（be situated）

⚙ *Suggested translation:*

Tianjin is situated about 120 kilometers south-east of Beijing.

2. 这个国家的历史充斥着战争、杀戮、阴谋和报复。（be one of）

⚙ *Suggested translation:*

The history of this country is one of war, killing, conspiracy and revenge.

3. 大卫收费低廉，而且平易近人，是村民公认的"穷人的律师"。（known as, approachable）

⚙ *Suggested translation:*

Charging low and being approachable, David was known as "the lawyer of the poor" among the villagers.

4. 新政策对这个地区的经济发展起到了强有力的推动作用。（boost）

⚙ *Suggested translation:*

The economic development of this area was given a boost by the new policy.

5. 地震刚过，紧接着就发生了一场瘟疫，又有数万人丧生。（succeed, plague）

⚙ *Suggested translation:*

The earthquake was soon succeeded by a plague, in which tens of thousands of people lost their lives.

6. 在图书馆里，学院里的普通教师和卓有名气的学者享有同样的权利。（tutor, renowned, privilege）

⚙ *Suggested translation:*

In the library, ordinary tutors and renowned scholars of college enjoyed the same privileges.

Text B

Development of Modern University and the University Idea

The birth of "the university" is a very complex historical process in which its structure, identity and mission have been appropriated and re-appropriated to different needs and aspirations of different times and settings. It is the outcome of a long historical process in which knowledge/research and teaching became combined within one institution. Two inspirational models were influential in creating the modern version of the university. On one hand we have the liberal arts based model of Cardinal Newman, the chancellor of the University of Oxford and author of *The Idea of a University*; on the other hand we have the science based model of von Humboldt. In both models "liberal-arts" as well as "science" play a major role. Newman did not oppose scientific research, but he did put education at the heart of the university. Von Humboldt also combined both functions, but he placed research at the heart of the university. Von Humboldt's model has probably been the most influential in shaping the modern university. It did not eliminate the liberal arts tradition but anchored it in the research mission of the university.

The Wisconsin Idea is a philosophy embraced by the University of Wisconsin System, which holds that the boundaries of the university should be the boundaries of the state, and that research conducted at the University of Wisconsin System should be applied to solve problems and improve health, quality of life, the environment and agriculture for all citizens of the state.

For more than a century, the university system has been guided by the Wisconsin Idea, a tradition first stated by UW President Charles Van Hise in 1904. Van Hise declared that he would "never be content until the beneficent influence of the university reaches every family in the state." Today that belief permeates (渗透) the UW System's work, fostering close working relationships within the state, throughout the country and around the world.

Writing Practice

We are now working toward writing a summary for Text B. You may follow the guidelines to write the summary:

I. Read through the entire text to get an understanding of the whole piece, and annotate by underlining the sentences containing the major points as you read.

II. Locate the thesis statement. While it may appear early in the essay—the first paragraph or two, it may not, in fact, be stated until the end of the piece, almost as if it were a conclusion.

<u>The Wisconsin Idea means that the university should not be an ivory tower institution but should serve all the people of the state in relevant ways.</u>

(Please write down the thesis statement on the above line.)

III. Dissect the article. Re-read the underlined parts and divide it into sections based on the topics addressed. Each section may be one paragraph, but, more likely, it includes several paragraphs. Now you need to decide how many sections Text B contains.

Text B includes 2 3 4 5 ... sections. (Please circle the number as you need.)

IV. Write a summary. First, write a sentence or two to summarize each section; then synthesize them into a coherent and cohesive passage. You may need a careful proofreading and revision before the final completion.

1. *(Paragraph 1—4) The Wisconsin Idea means that the university should not be an ivory tower institution but should serve all the people of the state in relevant ways.*

2. *(Paragraph 5—6) To fulfill the mission, the university made the pioneering steps by introducing continuing education for professionals by offering a short-term course for teachers, admitting its first full-time women students and establishing an experimental farm, all in the 19th century.*

3. *(Paragraph 7—8) The Wisconsin Idea also fostered a long partnership between the university and government.*

4. *(Paragraph 9) The university's research efforts have led to applications that have improved the quality of life for the people.*

5. *(Paragraph 10) The university has a leading position in the environmental movement.*

6. *(Paragraph 11—12) Three professors of U.W.—Madison have been awarded Nobel Prize and the University of Wisconsin is now reorganizing and increasing co-ordination of the outreach efforts already under way by many schools and departments of the university.*

Summary:

The Wisconsin Idea means that the university should not be an ivory tower institution but should serve all the people of the state in relevant ways. To fulfill the mission, the university made the pioneering steps by introducing continuing education for professionals through offering a short-term course for teachers, admitting its first full-time women students and establishing an experimental farm, all in the 19th century. The Wisconsin Idea fostered a long partnership between the university and government. Its research efforts have led to applications that have improved the quality of life for the people, and the university has a leading position in the environmental movement. Three professors of U.W.—Madison have been awarded Nobel Prize and the University of Wisconsin is now reorganizing and increasing co-ordination of the outreach efforts already under way by many schools and departments of the university.

北大英语辞书

《热门话题汉英口译词典》	杨大亮 王运祥 主编	25.00 元
《常见英语错误例解词典》	Harry Blamires 著	26.00 元
《最新通俗美语词典》	高克毅 高克永 主编	42.00 元
《英语写作技巧》	James Aitchison 著	26.00 元
《英语常用词组用法词典》	Rosalind Fergusson 著	45.00 元
《电力科技英汉词典》	涂和平 主编	19.80 元
《当代英汉美英报刊词典》	周学艺 主编	52.00 元

北京大学 出版社

外语编辑部电话：010-62767347　　　　市场营销部电话：010-62750672

　　　　　　　010-62755217　　　　　　邮 购 部 电 话：010-62752015

Email：zbing@pup.pku.edu.cn